The

Song of Dawn

Distant Lands: Book I

Colleen Ferguson

ISBN-13: 978-1-7390893-0-6

Cover design by: Michelle Diprose
www.diprose-art.co.uk

To my husband for giving me the time and space
&
Cameron, Natasha and Ellie for believing in me.

Chapter I

Camis, run! Do not use mindspeak—just run!

And he does instinctively. Plunging into the darkness, leaving the cart and fleeing. The long grass and shrubs soak him more than the light rain. His hair whips out behind him, and his hood is thrown back, useless.

Unseen branches claw, grasp, grab. Feeling his cloak snag and hearing fibres rip, he races on. Ruts and holes try to snare him; tufts and mounds catch his feet, causing him to stumble and trip, but he staggers on, fear nipping at his heels. With his breath rasping and his heart pounding, he runs.

Trees loom on either side of him, black pillars in the night, causing him to slow and then to stop. Clutching his side, he listens between great gulps of air.

Nothing.

Sinking down, he crouches warily in the deep leaf litter, waiting for her to call him back.

His pulse races. So much to fear. She'd made sure of that. She'd made certain that from an early age Camis had understood the importance of avoiding strangers, especially those not attached to a homestead, village, or farm.

He remembers the pains she took to hide him and their cart— if she had enough time—and the way she pulled up her hood to hide her face and hair. Or the way she'd made him sit up on the cart if people approached, telling him not to speak under any circumstance.

When he was a toddler, she had grabbed his arm, pulling him back as two men walked into their camp. They were hunters and had only wanted some help as one of their group had been in an accident.

He rubs at his arm unconsciously where she had grasped it all those years ago. An owl, hunting over the grass plains hoots and brings him back to the present. Apart from the soft sound of rain, the night is silent.

Camis awakes with a sharp intake of breath and casts about, trying to make sense of where he is. It is still night, and he can see nothing, only the pallid shapes of silver birch blending with the darker trunks. He has no idea how long he has waited because the trees and clouds hide the moon. It may only have been moments, or it could have been hours.

Gradually, his heartbeat slows, but his shoulders remain rigid. He tunes his senses to the night. Hearing the breeze sighing through the treetops, the dull plash of rain hitting the woodland floor and the leaves rustling beneath him. Beyond in the distance is the snuffling scuttle and scrape of the nocturnal world carrying on its natural rhythm. He listens hard, harder than he has ever listened before.

Why hasn't she called to him?

An owl screeches as it hunts, and a pair of foxes jabber to each other. Nothing to alarm him. The air is full of the musty mould of bark and leaf litter, all comforting and normal. Breathing it in, tasting the decay, his stomach rumbles.

Who or what have they been running from all this time? He vows to make her tell him, once they are safely back together. Yes, this time, he'll make her tell him.

Wriggling, he settles more comfortably against a tree, finding a spot where the ridges stab his back a little less.

He practises the long slow breaths of relaxation that he has been taught. Picturing a flame burning atop a candle, waiting for the breathing exercises to work their magic—to smooth the worry from his brow; to still the tiny teeth gnawing at his gut. But the flame flutters and wavers, and he can't relax.

It has been too long. She will call him. She will.

Fear helps him to fight sleep for a while, but soon he drops back into a fitful doze.

The birds wake him, and the damp of dawn seeps through his britches. Rising, Camis stretches, then rolls his shoulders back, trying to work the knots out, feeling the bruises beneath his clothes and the scrapes on his hands.

He breathes in deeply, then swallows, his mouth dry, wishing he had some water. Blinking the night from his eyes, he strains to see into the predawn dark. Carefully retracing his path, he feels his way from tree to tree, walking quietly and stopping often to check for any sound that will warn him that the danger is still there.

He doesn't know what they are running from, this makes the knot in his stomach tighten. Irritated, he hugs his damp cloak tighter. He is old enough now, and he will refuse to run anymore unless she gives him answers.

The walk to the edge of the woodland seems to take forever, and it is fully light when he at last looks out over the plains. Rubbing his hands, he wonders again why she hasn't sent word? Where is she?

He stares at the distant shape of their old horse cropping the grass, unconcerned.

What did you see, old girl? Do you know what happened to her?

He looks at the wider landscape and sees a cluster of trees in full leaf on a distant hill, surrounded by green bushes. The yellow-grass plains stretch in all directions. Birds twitter and sing in the wood behind him. Others fly, swooping low across the abundant vegetation, catching insects as they rise, warmed by the sun. He can even see rabbits feeding, their white tails bobbing, and he thinks of his snares in the cart. Everything is normal, full of late-summer life and the smell of the ripening fruits of autumn. Normal—except that she is not here.

Every instinct screams at him to use mindspeak, but he resists. 'Beware of using mindspeak, Camis,' she had always said. 'You never know who is listening.' So, he waits.

3

Tension returns in his shoulders. His stomach growls, and he feels a little lightheaded, but he remains in the shadows of the trees until the sun is high in the sky. Still nothing.

It is the sight of two thief birds alighting on the side of the cart that galvanises him into action. One of them hops over to sit on top of a sack, flicking its long, black tail and eyeing it in that sideways intensity that birds have.

Pig's feet!

Stiffly, he leaves his hiding place, waving his fists and shouting. The movement alarms the birds, and they rise up in a flurry of black and white to curve around him, flying back to the woodland.

Warily, he approaches the cart. Something tickles his nose—a vague, distant smell. It reminds him of a blacksmith's forge, full of heat and steam. He breathes in slowly and deeply, trying to place the smell, but it slides away like a fish in water.

The horse wickers softly in recognition as he approaches. She comes to him, gently muzzling in his pockets. He pushes the soft, whiskery lips away, feeling angry.

'Not now, Misty. I'll feed you soon.'

Maybe he should have waited for her longer. But what if she were hurt? What if she were just waiting for the right time to contact him? How is he supposed to know? Why couldn't she just have explained things to him before now?

Everything at the site is how they left it. Nothing wrong, nothing broken, nothing missing—except her.

Their bedding tumbles out from under the cart, abandoned in the urgency of the night. Checking the ground around the camp, he finds nothing. No footprints other than his own. No scuff marks, not a blade of grass out of place. Where has she gone? How had she known someone was approaching?

For a long time, he stands transfixed, biting down again on his lower lip until the skin feels tender under his teeth. He feels small, useless. What if . . . what if she doesn't return? But she even had that eventuality covered.

'Go to the farm. Go on without me,' she had said.

He shakes his head. Unthinkable.

He rummages in a half open sack, feeling the flat, flowery scales of oat, and scoops out three big handfuls.

'There you go, Misty. Better late than never.' He combs his fingers through the coarse fringe between the horse's ears. When she has finished eating, she flicks the bucket playfully up and out of his hands.

'So, I'm forgiven, eh?' He smiles, forgetting his situation for a moment.

Sitting on the back of the cart, he breaks apart a small brown loaf, and eats, washing the dry bread down with gulps of water from his flask. Still waiting for her to call to him, waiting for her signal. Waiting.

He bites down hard on his lower lip again, a habit she has tried to get him to break.

'Camis!' he can hear her remonstrate. 'Don't do that. You are leaving a mark.' She had brushed her fingers gently along his lip. He had felt the familiar tingle of her healing.

He remembers their last stop, two days ago: his mother, bending over the baby with croup. A strand of her hair falling forward, vivid in its autumn glow, her touch tender and loving as she laid her palm gently on the baby's chest.

He had watched while she dripped a weak herbal remedy on the child's lips, while the family held their breath. The baby's tongue had flicked in and out, and the crying had abruptly stopped. The family had hugged her, thanking her over and over. The baby fed lustily while Camis' mother relaxed with the villagers, catching up with their gossip.

Camis had stood awkwardly alongside the adults, looking at a group near his age who sat in the long grass on the outskirts of the village, laughing and joking. For fifteen summers, he had never had anyone his own age to be with.

A buzzard mewls overhead and then hovers high in the blue sky. A yellow light flickers a little way above the horizon, catching his eye. It pulses, then vanishes. He waits. Is it a message from her? He watches for it again, but it does not reappear.

Jumping down from the cart, he scours the ground in more detail. He finds his own footprints smudged and blurred from the rain, but they lead away as he expected. There are no others.

He looks up across the grass plains to the shrubland and towards the stand of trees in which he'd sheltered for the night. He checks the area again for signs of a scuffle. But there is nothing. He forces down his rising panic.

Just wait, he tells himself. She trained you enough times for this. Wait and stay calm.

The next morning, it is hard to rouse himself. He doesn't know what to do. His clothes have dried on him, and now the sweat and dirt are irritating his skin, making him scratch. He should get up and wash - and feed Misty, but he doesn't want to move. His arms feel heavy. Even thinking is an effort.

It suddenly comes to him like a sharp slap - move. Keep to the plan. Head for their winter home. Anna and Luk will be waiting. Stock up on herbs and supplies on the way. She will know to look for him there. She will find him at Homefarm.

'Pigs feet!' he says out loud and sits up.

Misty stops eating, shakes her head free of the flies, and looks at him. He shivers and, sighing, looks back the way they had come, squinting into the rising sun. Then he peers, for the hundredth time, towards the distant shimmer of silver. The river. Head that way.

'Come on, Misty. Time to go.'

He packs up his bedding, ignoring the hollow in his stomach, and hitches Misty to the cart, then climbs up and clicks her into a walk. In the late afternoon, Camis stops on the riverbank by a copse of willow trees whose branches trail low into the slow-moving water and makes camp. First, a wash.

In the river, he lathers up his hair, rubbing in some soaproot and dunking his head into the clear water. The flow around him runs briefly with bubbles and dirt. His hair sticks to his face and neck, the sandy colour darkening to gold. He sweeps his hair back, squeezing it tight. Better let it dry first before tying it back in a tail.

Misty watches him as he swims and splashes. A frown wrinkles her old head as she trots up and down the riverbank, keeping pace with him as he floats on his back. He lets the slow current bob him along, recalling the reason why the old horse is so agitated.

His mother had told him of how he had nearly drowned before he was even born. Heavily pregnant, she had been crossing a river when the current suddenly caught her, whisking her off her feet. It was Misty who had rescued her. Pushing out to swim alongside her, the mare had waited until his mother had tangled her hands into the horse's rough mane, then she had hauled them both safely to the shore.

His mother had paused then, and he had glimpsed a dark shadow cross her face.

'Once we had landed, that's when you decided to show your face.' Then she had laughed, her eyes lighting up and crinkling at the corners.

Later—years later—he'd asked her why she had tried to cross the river.

'I was being chased. Luckily, the river dragged us far downstream.' But that was all she would ever say. Why had she been fleeing? Who was she running from? He wondered if her past had finally caught up with her.

Misty doesn't rest until Camis is back on dry land. Then she trots away, tail flicking, snorting, as if tutting, puts her head down to the grass, and ignores him.

Once dry and dressed, he locates a large wooden chest on the cart. He pulls a leather thong from around his neck and fits the key that hangs from it into the lock.

Carefully, he rifles through the pottery phials and removes the stopper from one. He gives it a cautionary sniff. The bitter blast of thunderdog vine shoots up his nose. Gagging, he rapidly replaces the top. He holds the small bottle up and shakes it. He can't use all of it as he doesn't know when there will be more. He will have to make do with willow bark for now.

He selects a slightly larger container and pours out a thumbnail drop of aromatic oil and massages it into his hands. His hands still ache from his first healing a few days before.

Collecting wood on his way back to camp He scouts the area, looking for good places for snares, and finds evidence of rabbits further along the bank, amongst an old thicket of bramble.

After another cold meal, he retires early, lying awake under the cart for a long time, feeling the familiar irritation that has plagued him all his life. Who or what are they running from? Why does she never explain further than "run, Camis, run"? And where in Maa Erda's name *is* she? The questions swirl and repeat. He clamps his teeth shut, stopping the tingle in his nose and the threat of tears. Nearly fifteen! he tells himself. You're too old for that!

Perhaps he'd better stick to the plan. He sighs and snuggles under his blanket, resolving to definitely leave in the morning for Homefarm.

In the morning, he squats over his snare, loosening the wire from around the rabbit's neck. As he picks the limp body up, his mind flashes back to a few days ago when his gift had first made an appearance.

He'd been checking his snares and had found a freshly caught rabbit. But it had been caught by its foot and was still alive. The creature had frozen in fear as he'd handled it, but instead of a quick twist and pull on its neck to dispatch it, something had made him hesitate.

He'd looked at the broken skin around its leg and felt pity. Then he had laid his fingers over the injury, feeling the broken bones beneath grate and grind. An intense heat had flared through his hand down to the creature. In his mind's eye he can see the bones knit and heal and although it had only been an instant, when he removed his hand, the wound on the rabbit had closed. In surprise, he had dropped the rabbit, and it had zigzagged away into the undergrowth, leaving him gaping after the white flash of its tail.

'About time!' his mother had said when he returned to their camp to tell her. The smile she'd given him had lit up the day—her green eyes had sparkled. 'Been waiting a long time for this, Camis. I was hoping you would have The Gift too. Now your training starts in earnest!'

And she had laughed at his face, saying, 'Be careful, the wind might change.'

The next day, he checks their herb supply. He opens all the bags on the cart and checks their contents. Carefully, he reseals them. He will have to restock quite a few of them on his way to their winter home.

Scanning the grassland, he walks away from the river, out into the rich green pasture. Absorbed in carefully cutting stems from wild dwarf rosemary, useful for its disinfectant qualities, he nearly misses the first warning. He feels a faint thrumming vibration beneath his feet.

Standing up, he looks around, and then he sees them—riders, racing across the wide plains. Riders coming fast and coming towards him!

He sprints towards the river, legs pumping, gripping his herb bag, racing towards camp.

As he hurtles towards Misty, the thumping of his heart grows louder, mingling with the beat of hooves. He runs with eyes wide, muscles straining. Running again in fear for his life.

In mid-leap, he hears a crack.

Blackness.

Chapter 2

Any movement makes the restraints cut into wrists and ankles, causing a biting pain—an encouragement to remain still. The bed, hard and cold as steel, vibrates, sending a barely audible hum through it. A blinding white glare makes it impossible to see anything, and it leaves a bleached bloom behind closed eyelids. For a moment, all is confusion.

Hello, Serin. Nice to see you again.

His voice needles into her mind, chilling and quiet. She gives an involuntary cry and squeezes her eyes tighter. No, no, no! This cannot be happening. She cannot be here with him.

Camis!

Her breath is stuck, jammed tight in her throat, choking her. Relax. Close him out like before. Block him. He cannot know.

You won't avoid me so easily, Serin. I must not know what? And who is Camis?

One—breathe. Two—breathe. Calm, calm.

The counting steadies her breathing; the numbers loud and reassuring inside her head. She continues until the presence in her mind recedes. The brilliance behind her eyes decreases, and cautiously, she opens them. There is not much to see—just the sparse white room of a shuttle cabin. It is as she expected; it is as she feared.

There, is that better?

His upside-down face swims into focus. Her uncle has more frown lines than before, but otherwise, he is much the same. His blue eyes crinkle at the corners, but the inverted smile echoes the grey coldness in them—always judging.

She tries to turn her head away, but he prevents it.

I am so very, very pleased to have you back, Serin. I have missed you.

He leans down towards her, and for one, heart-stilling moment, she thinks he is going to kiss her.

She squirms against his mindspeak but he merely reaches out and gently strokes her hair. Repulsed, she tries to draw backwards down into the bed. She tugs helplessly against the bindings, and he stops stroking but keeps his hand resting on her hair.

Shrinking inwards, she shudders, then lies still, trying to resume the measured count and her breathing exercise, but tension and confusion swirl in increasing undercurrents.

I took the liberty of having you washed, he says into her mind. *You were a little . . . ripe. But I don't suppose you had many luxuries where you were.*

A wild panic overwhelms her, and she whimpers, thrashing against her bonds. No. No. NO!

Shhh, he says, stroking her hair, but it is a while before she is able to calm herself enough to stop struggling.

Her anger overpowers her fear. It flares at his nearness, at her helplessness, at her realisation that she is naked and helps her to gasp in a whisper. 'Cover me up, you shrivelled phallus!'

A searing pain flashes through her mind.

She awakes with a headache. The restraints are gone, but a band of pain wraps around her head, causing her to squint in the white light of the cabin. A light fleece covers her, but the temperature is controlled, and the bed is more comfortable than the medi-table. She recognises the small bed cabin, usually allocated to one of the crew in the main ship. The main ship! That means they have left the hov—left the planet.

Her mouth is dry. She has no idea how long she has been here. This is the stuff of nightmares. Back under his control, back where he can . . . She shudders, pressing the heels of her hands into her eyes.

'Shit! Sh-sh-shit,' she finishes lamely, the effort of finding another expletive defeating her and making the throbbing worse.

Gently, she massages her temples and gradually, the pain recedes. Swinging her legs over the side of the small cot, she clutches tightly at the fleece and looks around at the tiny, sterile space. No smell, no colour, and apart from her, no life.

There is a pitcher of water on the small bedside unit. She pours herself a drink, watching the water splash and swirl in the crystal glass. She pauses as she brings the clear liquid up to her mouth and wrinkles her nose at the chemical smell of regularly recycled water. It is as bad as she remembers, but she manages to drink the whole glass. It is nothing like the pure streams and rivers she has become accustomed to.

She squeezes the white fleece in her fist, scrunching it tight against herself and bites her bottom lip. Immediately, she thinks of Camis, and tears fill her eyes.

Is he safe? Is he still waiting for her? The only light in this whole dark affair is that they hadn't seen him. That they do not even know of his existence. *He* doesn't know of his existence, and she intends to keep it that way. She hopes Camis remembers the plan.

Please, please let him be all right.

Using the fleece, she scrubs roughly at her face. Crying isn't going to help her or Camis. She must find some clothes.

She presses her fingers against the blank back wall, and a panel pops open at her touch. In a small recess on a shelf, there is some neatly folded material. She pulls out the top garment. It unfurls in an avalanche of white, draping its silky touch against her, dropping to her toes and releasing its familiar, magnolia perfume.

She pulls the garment over her head, and as the fabric envelopes her in its soft embrace, she is briefly drawn into the past. Her first white robe. The time-faded features of a woman with outstretched arms, smiling, holding the delicate vestment.

So, it seems there were some things she had missed.

The cloth falls in folds down to the floor, the deep *V* of the neckline ending obscenely low—much, much lower than any she remembers. The garment is embroidered around the neck and hem in gold thread.

On the shelf there is also a hairbrush, a gold chain belt, and some delicate gold sandals. She fastens the belt around her waist and sits on the bed and brushes her hair. The motion is soothing, hypnotic.

She thinks again of Camis, alone and bewildered, waiting for her to call to him. Her eyes and nose sting.

Please let him make his way to the safety of Anna and Luk, she prays and all at once stops herself. It is annoying how easy she had found herself slipping back into her previous life, using the empty appeals of Temple doctrine. Anna and Luk had saved them both once before. They would take care of him.

The door hisses open. *He* stands on the threshold, tall and straight, his dark hair oiled and slicked back, his beard neatly trimmed., An old, familiar fragrance wafts towards her—sandalwood and musk. Royal in every sense of the word. His eyes take in every aspect of her, making her feel naked again, vulnerable. Her knees threaten to give way. In the background, she can hear the gentle hum of the engines.

We are on our way home and have already docked with the mothership, so you may exit your cabin now, he says directly into her mind, and the door starts to slide shut.

'Wait!' She must know.

The door stops moving. He raises an eyebrow.

'Why?' She asks.

Why what?

Twenty years her senior, popular in court always surrounded by women— she hates and despises every cell of this man.

'Why do you want to take me back? I was doing you no harm. I was out of your way. One less thing for you to worry about,' she says in a rush, returning his stare, amazed at how calm her voice sounds.

A light smile touches his lips. The smile that she remembers so well and hoped never to see again. The smile that says he knows things about her that she wishes to keep hidden.

The door hisses shut. Guard your thoughts, she tells herself.

Crossing back to the bench that forms the bed, she sits, her legs shaking. He makes her feel like a child again, when he would sneak into her mind undetected, listen to her innermost thoughts, and then use the information against her. Eroding her confidence, pitting her against her brother. Always undermining, always controlling. That was why she and Myriad had developed a system for closing him out.

A lump blocks her throat at the sudden memory of her brother, her twin. She instinctively puts a hand up to her neck and tries to swallow. Together, they had fought him, kept things from him, made plans, believed in dreams.

He must never find out about Camis. The mere thought that there was a child would send him into . . .

She cuts across her internal dialogue, placing a small, lit candle firmly in her mind's eye. She concentrates on the wavering flame. Its shape tapers, its tip flickers, as though touched by the internal breeze of her thoughts.

In the centre of the light, around the wick, is a smaller, darker flame. Focusing hard on this, she concentrates on slowing her breathing and deepening it. Slowly, her mind relaxes, and she starts to block out all incriminating past experiences as though the last lifetime has never been.

She visualises Camis, the cart and horse, the land and life she has been wrenched from. Slowly, she withdraws her mind, as though walking backward, away from the image. It shrinks until the images are just a speck of colour. Then in her mind, she shuts a door and firmly locks it and pockets the key. For now, she must behave as though those years have never existed. He must never be able to enter that part of her mind and work out who Camis is. Never be able to find and use him the way he had used her brother, used her.

Camis, above all else, must be free, free to lead his own life and not be a pawn in her uncle's games.

She concentrates, bringing her focus back repeatedly to the flame, keeping that door shut, keeping Camis firmly locked behind it. A single tear tracks down her cheek.

A timid tapping brings her back to the cabin.

'Enter.' She tilts her head, wiping the side of her face on the top of her shoulder. The door slides open to reveal a young woman. She is slim and boyish, and the ship's uniform is tight and figure-hugging—typical of the way he would dress his female staff.

'His Imperial Highness D'Ruja A'Riman, may The Crystal preserve him, demands your presence, your excel—your High—'

'Tell my uncle'—to go boil his head—'tell him I have a headache.'

Serin! His voice sears into her mind. *This is not a request. You will do as you are told. I* will not *be kept waiting.*

The door slides shut behind Serin, and she follows the young girl through the spotless white corridors of the ship, passing the countless metal doors recessed into the walls. The only distinguishing feature in this endlessly monotonous environment is the black uniform of her escort. Everything is lit by a flat white light from the crystals set flush at regular intervals in the ceiling and in the walls. She wants to scream.

They ride up several floors in a shiny silver lift and walk down another identical corridor. But this one is longer, wider, and curves slightly, sloping gently upward. The mothership is immense. Much larger than she remembers. But she had only looked around it once. She must have been fourteen or fifteen. It was before . . . No, don't think of that!

The corridor stops abruptly in front of them, ending in a smooth, white wall. The young woman presses her hand against a screen to their right, and a panel in the wall slides away to reveal another lift, only this one has a black, non-slip floor and a silver guard rail.

Serin steps into this space and holds the handrail as the guard nods at her, backs away, and presses the screen on the wall again. The door closes, leaving her escort behind. The floor rises swiftly up, slowing as it reaches its destination, the walls dropping away, leaving her on the exposed platform, deposited directly into the back of the command centre.

The command centre is a vast, circular room, alive with activity. People sit at consoles with screens showing numbers or letters or graphs. They tap on the black tabletop in front of them. Others hurry across the room, holding incomprehensible pieces of equipment. Some wear headphones and talk to themselves. They are all dressed in the stark black uniform of the royal fleet command with a small *V* of red cloth around their necks, a nod to the neckerchief that protects his soldiers from the desert dust.

Her eye is drawn to the large viewing windows that extend around the whole room. The windows are angled and form a near-perfect circle, but they are shuttered now and show nothing.

He is there, standing in the centre of the room on a raised dais, surveying everything. He looks across at her and clicks his fingers. A flash of annoyance crosses Serin's mind, and she hesitates, calling the flame on the candle, giving herself time to compose herself.

She straightens before crossing the room, then climbs the steps to join him, guarding her tongue as well as her thoughts. He beckons her closer impatiently, standing tall on the raised dais. He towers over everything; his arrogance hasn't diminished one drop.

'Open viewing deck windows one, two, and three,' he commands. 'Yes, all of them!' he barks at a question from a crew member.

The windows on Serin's left appear to melt, changing from dull to shiny, revealing the scene outside the ship. The deep, unfathomable ebony of space replaces the flat black metal. Distant stars shine bright and unwinking, scattered across the view. A few cluster together, forming long strings, like necklaces; others bunch in out-of-focus clumps, as if she were looking at them through mist. But right in the centre, dominating the view, is a large green-and-blue orb.

Well, that's it, he says using mindspeak. *That is Planet V713. Your playground for the last fifteen years. You've had your time 'playing', helping those simple primitives.*

She feels disoriented. The floor seems to tilt, making her feel nauseous. She reaches out to steady herself on a metal bar that passes at waist height around part of the dais, but he intercedes and takes hold of her elbow.

I have to say, you were pretty good at evading my searchers. Although you did have a winter's head start on us. Clever of you to take the last shuttle back to the mothership. I had to wait for winter to pass before I could search for you.

He managed to make it sound as though she were a young child who had stayed out all night, worrying her parents to death—as though her time away had been short and just a bit of an inconvenience to him.

And who is this Camis? he asks. *A friend? A lover, maybe?*

Her stomach roils, but she stares back at him, keeping her features bland.

No matter, he says. *They are of no consequence. You are back with me now.*

A young man with a long thin face and a large nose approaches them. He reaches a small black tablet towards her uncle, apologising for the interruption, and asks him to verify some figures.

The young man glances at her while her uncle is occupied, his eyes raking over her and it makes her feel unclean, but she refuses to let her hands twitch towards the neckline of the gown. She hopes her uncle will look up and catch him. He won't live to do it again.

Her uncle finishes and hands the tablet back, pointing out an alteration. The young man's expression snaps back to full attention.

She studies the view and lets the moment pass. There will be plenty of time to remind people of who she is. Plenty of time to resume the role of princess. Her uncle is hardly likely to let her forget it. She sighs, staring out, barely registering the voices around her.

Maa Erda is smaller now. Her home—her beautiful home sliding out of reach. It glows blue and green with patches of white. Unbelievably brilliant, suspended in the ebony of space. Splendid, bright and vibrant. She drinks it in. Even though she has never seen it from space before, she would recognise it in a heartbeat.

The first time she had crept on board the mothership, she had hidden herself in the back of one of the shuttles, squeezing herself into the cupboard that held the emergency supplies and prayed no one needed them. She'd come out only when the shuttle docked with the mothership and the crew had left the hanger, but she hadn't dared explore further than the darkened hold.

As the planet slowly recedes, there is prickling sensation in her nose. She closes her eyes to stop the flow of threatening tears.

No. No. Not that. Do not give him the satisfaction.

She takes slow, deep breaths and concentrates on the vibration of the engines through her thin-soled sandals. She remembers that sensation, that hum that had resonated through her body, remembering the last time she had been on a shuttle taking off. Only then she had no way of knowing or seeing exactly what was happening.

She had practised meditation back then. She'd had nothing else to do but meditate. To focus on the flame flickering in her mind and the life quickening in her belly. But not even the flame could protect her from the fear of what lay ahead or what he would do if he found her. She remembers peeking out and watching the crew, wishing she could come out of hiding.

Oh, Princess, pray, do continue. I was enjoying your little excursion down memory lane. I always wondered how you'd done it. You know, I had those hov guards executed. Pity. I never believed their story of innocence. Seems you were more resourceful than I gave you credit for.

She freezes, locking all her muscles and forcing herself to stay upright. Block. Block him out.

The candle flame wavers, but it is replaced by lazily waving wheat, a warm day, filled with the sweat of horse and the buzz of flies. Cool water. The smell of flowers and trees in bloom. An elderly couple in the distance wave to her. Smoke rises lazily into the sky from a farmhouse chimney. She feels lightheaded.

Looks very primitive.

She doesn't know if he means what he can see out of the ship's window or if he is reading the pictures in her head. She clears her mind and steels herself to watch the only place she has ever felt truly happy fade. The long-forgotten fear of his power washes over her, drowning her spark of rebellion.

A primitive place with a primitive people who aren't even aware of the worlds above their heads, he sneers.

A part of her fades along with the gradually receding planet.

You know, you were more than lucky. Normally, the hovs and crews come back here for the winter cycle, but I had sent a small force to explore the mountain caverns on V713 to see if it held any crystal deposits. I had thought that a planet so close to the crystal moon would share a similar structure. But all we found was dirt and some nasty little black creatures dwelling within the honeycomb caves. Vicious beasts. I lost a lot of men to their bite until we learned to fire the caves and tunnels before entering.

He paused and looked lost in thought.

You asked me why, he says, moving his hand from her arm to lay it gently on her shoulder. *I think you know the answer to that, but I will spell it out to you. I want what is mine.* He stops, and she waits for him to continue, only he doesn't.

'What do you—' she starts to say, but he cuts across her question.

Princess, mind what you say aloud.

She stops and faces him, moving away enough to dislodge his hand. Her face screws up in distaste but she moves into mindspeak.

Please let me go home, she pleads.

You are going home, he says flatly.

You know what I mean, she says.

But he just stares straight ahead, stone-faced. She glances back to the world she wants and is genuinely puzzled. He already has it all—the throne, the land, the people.

Please, she whispers. Her eyes slide to the planet then back to him. His gaze is piercing and direct, his eyes a deep, vibrant blue, seeming to reflect the light from the slowly receding planet.

'Sir, you asked me to report to you when processing was about to start.' The young man is back.

All thoughts of finding out what her uncle wants with her are forgotten.

You are still taking these people? she cries.

There is fury in his eyes, which narrow, and his jaw tightens. She can physically feel the pressure of his anger, though he does not move a muscle. But she can't help herself. The floodgates are open. Somehow, naively, she had thought the practice had ended. That all these years later he would have enough of his damned crystal.

Her hands clench. *How can you—*

I will not replay old arguments with you, he cuts into her mind. *This is my business. You relinquished your responsibilities when you ran away.*

But—

Go!

A familiar pain builds in her head, and she flees.

Chapter 3

Lights flicker out of focus. Voices mumble, but the words are lost to Camis. All is just noise. Jolting. Then pain.

A sudden jostling of his body brings more agony followed by feather softness.

Comfort, darkness, sleep. Sleep. Silence.

His eyes open and shut. Sluggishly, he realises that he is looking at vivid saffron embroidery. A neat picture of precise stitches on brown cloth. He stares fixedly. Something—what was it?—fades to an itch in the back of his mind. His head pounds. Where is he? What happened?

'Ah! There you are.'

He chokes back a cry and pulls his knees up. Covers tangle his legs, adding to his panic.

He is in a shadowy room, lying on a raised bed. His head throbs as an old woman he does not know looms over him. His heart thuds in his chest, and the pain in his head pulses.

'I thought you'd never wake. I don't have the skill of your mother.' The crow's feet around her brown eyes crinkle as she smiles. 'Didn't think I'd be nursing the healer's son.'

'Where am I?' he croaks. Moving causes a wave of nausea and dizziness. His hand darts forward, clutching at the bed. He retches. Swiftly, the woman lifts a bowl under his chin.

'Aye, lad, that will pass. You took quite a blow to the head.' She pulls the bolster from behind him and plumps it up. 'It will take time, but you're young and strong.' She holds a wooden beaker to his lips, and he tastes cool, clean water. He tries to drain the cup, but she pulls it away.

'Just a little at a time or you'll be sick again. Let me fetch you some food, that will help.' He watches as she limps away, a small, round figure, grey hair neatly twisted into a bun.

Confused, he lies back. The room spins, and he closes his eyes briefly. Questions swirl in his mind, questions he has no answers for. Where is he? Who is this woman? What does she want with him?

He raises his hand to the pain above his left ear. Touching the tender area, he concentrates hard. It is a bigger task to heal than the simple cuts he has tried before. The swoosh of blood is loud in his ears. A pulsating pain flares as his hand heats up. Dried flakes of skin, matted hair, and debris slough away. The hairs beneath his hand lift and separate. He winces as a sharp pang stabs behind his ear, followed by a rapid cooling and the return of the ache that permeates deep into his palm.

His fingers curl, claw-like. Will healing become easier with time? He doubts it. His eyes close.

'Here, my dear, eat this.' And the woman is back, holding a clay bowl.

He shuffles himself forward. He's not sure if he has the strength to hold the spoon she is offering, but the smell wafts into his senses—meaty, honeyed, earthy. He takes the bowl and shovels in the thick, amber liquid. Watching him eat, she smiles and nods. Then she crosses the room and pins back an animal skin that covers the door, and the late afternoon sun washes the wooden floor.

'That's it. You'll be out and about in no time.' As she comes towards him, he notices again the yellow starburst stitched on her dress just above her heart. He frowns and puts his hand up to his head. Something snags his mind but remains just out of reach.

The woman wrings out a cloth from a basin of water at her feet. 'Now be a brave, lad. Put your hand down and let me bathe that wound again.' She holds his chin and turns his head gently, the cloth poised ready in her other hand.

Her mouth hangs open, gaping, like a baby bird. 'What . . . what did you do?' Her tone is sharp and accusing, and she stares at the spot on his head where the wound had been, snatching her hand off him as though scalded.

'I . . . ' and he feels his face heat. He has broken their rule. His mother would be disappointed. Defiantly, he meets her stare. 'I didn't do anything.'

'Trickery!' she hisses, backing away, pausing on the threshold. 'What are you?' But she doesn't wait and flees out through the opening. The hide curtain drops into place behind her.

Frowning, he shouts after her. 'Wait! Let me explain.' But she doesn't return.

His legs shake as he swings them over the side of the bed to stand, so he sits instead. There is a well-scrubbed kitchen table, a pot resting on the stone hearth, glowing embers of logs in the log burner, a kettle, a comfortable chair covered in colourful blankets and cushions, both with beautiful sunbursts embroidered on them.

'Never disclose your gift,' his mother had told him. 'Be knowledgeable about the herbs and use them. What is not understood is often feared.'

A waft of cold fresh air enters the room, followed by a bear of a man. He stops in front of Camis and gives a little nod of his head by way of greeting. His thick, grey hair, wavy and short, is swept back from his face, leaving his eyes free. They are brown, like the woman's, but one squints at him suspiciously, while the other fixes him with wide-open scrutiny.

'So, laddie, we have met before. Your mother called in now and again if her travels brought her this way.' He sits down beside him and the wood of the bed creaks. 'I am Tor, village elder.'

'I'm Camis, son of Serin. I would like to know where I am. Do you have my mother?'

The words tumble out, and as he draws breath, Tor holds up his hand. 'We owe you an explanation, but let's slow down, shall we?' He pauses, then continues. 'I am told that you were camped about a two days' hard ride from here. I'm sorry, but we don't have your mother- and I don't know where she is.'

He looks at the old woman who has returned, hovering in the doorway. 'Martha'—he holds out his hand to the woman—'tells me that you have fixed that bump on your head.'

Camis' stomach lurches. 'I . . . ' He doesn't know what to say. Martha twists at a leather thong around her neck.

'I had a feeling there was more to your mother's herbs and medicines than she let on,' Tor says quietly in the silence. He glances at Martha. 'Now Martha, Camis' mother came here and saved many a life. Remember Etta's labour, when we expected to lose both mother and child? And Sam's broken arm with the infection? And before that, when six of the village children were sick and wasting? Cured. All of them.'

'A witch and her spawn!' Martha spits and wrenches her arm free, backing away. She makes the old sign to ward off evil, the thumb and first finger of her left-hand meeting to form an eye shape.

A flood of anger flushes Camis' face, and he locks eyes with her. Standing up Tor shoos Martha away.

'Enough of this nonsense! I will not have it.' He turns back in the entrance. 'Rest, young Camis. There is nothing you can do this late in the day.'

'Where is my horse?' Camis asks.

'I had her fed and looked after. We have your cart and things. We will talk more tomorrow.'

Camis sits on the bed, all his muscles locked in indecision. Surely a short nap wouldn't hurt. He yawns and leans back on the bed. Just a quick one to get his strength back. And then he'll find a way to leave.

The dull interior fades into darkness.

Opening his eyes with a snap, Camis is shocked to discover that he has slept without waking or dreaming for a whole night. His bladder is full and it is this need that has woken him. The new day casts soft light across the room. Camis can smell freshly baked bread and looks across to find Martha staring directly at

24

him. She stirs something on the stove, but flinches when she realises that he is awake, one hand rushing up to clutch at her throat.

'Hello, Martha,' Camis says and swings his legs out of bed. She doesn't reply. 'I need to, ah . . . to . . . '

She gestures towards the open door, her expression hard. But he notices her arm shaking as she points the way. She is afraid, he thinks, frowning.

The dark brown cowhide is tied back across the only opening in the hut, allowing in the morning light and cool crisp air. Stepping through, he briefly wonders where Martha slept as he looks around for the small outhouse latrine.

There are three wooden homes in front of him, sitting a respectful yet comfortable distance from each other. The roofs are low with a deep overhang, under which are neatly stacked logs. Camis can hear children playing and, in the distance, a horse neighs.

Past the three houses, the rock shelf drops away gently, revealing more huts sprawled below. People are busy, both men and women, carrying wood and water, sweeping, weaving, and a myriad of other everyday tasks. They talk and laugh and shout. The regular clang of metal-on-metal rings, telling him the village has its own forge.

Back inside, Martha has laid a place at the table. There are chunks of warm bread on a wooden board and a steaming meat-and-vegetable stew in a bowl. She gestures for him to sit, and when he does, she leaves.

Tor arrives almost instantly. 'How do you feel today?' he asks.

'Well. Really well. I can't thank you enough for your kindness, but I really need to get back.'

'Back? Back where?'

'I was . . . we were travelling towards the great forest for the winter to a steading where my mother has planned for food and lodging in exchange for some work. I need to get back to the path so she can find me.' His voice fades to a whisper.

'I need to hear your whole story, Camis, and I will see if we can help. It is because of one of mine that you ended up here. But first, eat.' He waits patiently until Camis is finished, then pushes himself up from the table.

'I would like you to meet someone.' He leaves, only to return a moment later with a young girl not much older than Camis. She is slight, with dark, almost black, wild hair, which is tied back loosely. She keeps her focus firmly on the floor in front of her. There is a sunburst embroidered on her tunic, just like the one Martha wears.

'Nenna, here, has something to say to you.' They both look at the girl.

'Well?' Tor prompts.

She looks up. Her lightly tanned face flushes. 'I'm sorry for what happened, but you were running, and I thought . . . thought that you might be heading back to your camp to warn others and that they might escape.' She says it all in one defiant rush.

'I don't understand.' Camis looks from the girl to Tor.

'You see, Camis,' says Tor, sitting down again, 'we've lost someone as well. My—Nenna's brother, Hadders, also vanished, and she was out searching for him when she found you.'

'Why didn't you call out to me?' Camis asks the girl—Nenna. 'Or head me off and ask me, instead of cracking me over the head?' He picks up a beaker of water from the table and drains it. His knuckles are white, his shoulders tense.

The flush on her face deepens. She rolls her eyes up and draws her lips tight.

'Huh! Was that going to stop you? I don't think so.'

'But you didn't even try.'

'What and give you time to shout a warning?'

'A warning to who? I was on my own.'

'I didn't know that. There might have been hundreds of others and you—'

'But there wasn't. It was just me.' His voice rises in pitch and intensity.

'So you said.' Her fists clench and unclench at her sides.

'Enough! This is not what we discussed Nenna. You owe him an explanation.'

'I told you, I thought there were others, and that he was going to warn them. I thought Hadders was there.' She stalks to the door.

'Wait!' Tor commands her. 'You will not go until I say. You attacked a defenceless boy.' Camis' face glows scarlet, and he opens his mouth to speak. Tor holds up a hand. 'This is not the first time I have had to warn you against your temper, Nenna. You will stay within the confines of the village today.' She spins to face them, the force sending her hair out, like the tail of a horse in full gallop, and takes a deep breath.

'Do not argue with me! And when I say you can leave, it will be to help Camis.'

Nenna and Camis look at each other. Her eyes are hard with open animosity. He feels injured again, this time by the ice in her eyes.

Tor gets up, filling the space, and the moment is broken.

'Right, young Camis. We'll put another search party together. We do not like our people to travel alone.' He pauses and looks straight at Camis. 'There have been other mysterious disappearances over the years, but only of people travelling alone. Nenna,' he says, looking at the girl, 'go and ask Ash to meet me outside shortly.' He turns back to Camis. 'Do you feel up to a little fresh air?' He gestures to the door and waits for Camis to walk through first.

'I have already made arrangements for you to move somewhere with a bit more space,' Tor continues. 'Now that Martha does not have to tend to you, she can have her own bed back.'

'I . . . oh, I didn't think.' Camis' face reddens. 'I should . . . '

'No, young Camis, that is her way, and she wouldn't have let me change it until she was sure you were recovered. Mistress Gen has agreed to take you in.'

'Thank you for your hospitality, Tor, but I am anxious to get on my way. My mother will expect me to go to the farm. She could even be there now, worrying about me.'

'Can you tell me in detail exactly what happened?' Tor asks, settling himself down onto a bench just outside Martha's hut.

Camis looks around at the nearest huts. His hands itch, and he rubs them together absently. Maybe something new might make itself clear if he tells the whole story to someone.

'I see,' Tor says getting up as Camis finishes. 'I will arrange for one of our hunters, Ash, to go with you. I would like him to accompany you safely to this farm.'

'Oh, that won't be necessary, Tor. I can look after myself,' Camis says hurriedly, squaring his shoulders.

'I know you can look after yourself, lad,' Tor replies with a hint of a smile, 'but there could be something dangerous out there. Someone or something is keeping your mother and our Hadders from getting back to us. I, for one, would like answers. I have search parties already out. Can you wait for a day for them to return with news?' Tor meets his gaze and waits patiently for Camis to make his decision. Camis feels like he has no choice at all.

'Mistress Gen is expecting you,' Tor says as they walk through the village. 'She has space since her mother went to the spark last winter. She is looking forward to having someone to care for again.'

Camis nods and says nothing. He has no intention of delaying any longer.

Chapter 4

Shit, shit, shit!

Why had that boy run? It had made him look guilty. Anyone would have reacted like she had.

Hadders, where are you? You can't just have vanished!

Nenna scrubs a hand furiously across her nose, hoping the force will keep the threatening tears at bay. The anger she'd first felt at her Da's punishment has abated, but her face still heats up at the embarrassment of it all. It was not her fault.

'I will not cry,' Nenna states to the sky and launches herself off the rocky outcrop where she had been sitting. Her dog, Quarrel, follows closely behind her, his tail down, ears back, picking up her mood.

It is a short drop to the scrubland below and on to the grass plains that spread out in all directions, like a green-and-gold sea.

A shrill whistle brings Nettle, trotting, his tail swishing, head erect and ears forward, eager to be away. Hadders' horse, Blade, a heavy chestnut with a wide, white flash down his nose, looks up, but seeing that his master is not there, puts his broad head back down and continues cropping the grass. Wilted white-and-yellow flowers of mayweed and feverfew are still tangled in the chestnut's tail, and a stab of pain shoots through her chest.

'Oh, Nettle,' she says, tugging a burr from her horse's dark grey mane and scratching his ears. 'We should be out there searching for Hadders, but I'm stuck here in the village, all because of that stupid boy.'

She rests her chin on the horse's neck, breathing in the late-summer smell of meadow grass, and gazes out across the plains. There is a brown tinge to the grass that hadn't been there a few days ago when she and Hadders had set out to bring in the herd for winter. She remembers her laughter as she raced ahead of her brother with Quarrel lolloping alongside, his long tongue lolling out of his mouth, his ears flat. He had kept up with her and Nettle easily—a brown-and-black streak that seamlessly blended into the landscape.

Hadders had been so mad when he'd found the meadow flowers woven into Blade's mane and tail, but there hadn't been time for him to get rid of them all. She'd laughed at his face as he tried to untangle them before he'd given up.

'I'll get you back!' he'd shouted after her as she rode away and she knew he would. She really could not imagine life now without him. Life without her big-hearted, hard-working brother. The one person who understood how she felt and looked out for her.

She remembers how it had all started.

It had been a difficult archery class, and she had been wondering what she could do to bring this latest batch of youngsters up to a reasonable level before she was asked to join the hunters. She had paused to enjoy the late-summer flowers that she had planted in the small garden patch. Their hut was larger than most of the others because of her father's position as chief elder. Situated on the outskirts of the village, it had a commanding view over the vastness of the plains. She could even glimpse the great forest on the horizon to the south-east and the mountains in the west.

She had picked a few flowers to put on the table and thought of sitting on the porch to unwind a little before supper, but as she'd approached the door, she'd heard a heated discussion coming from inside.

'But you can't, Da. You just can't,' her brother was saying. He'd sounded both angry and distressed. To be this upset must mean that the argument has been going on for some time, because it took a lot to rouse her brother.

She'd paused, waiting outside.

'I've said my piece. She needs to settle down now,' her father had said.

'But she is too young, Da. You'll break her heart.'

'She is young, yes, but in another year or two, she will be accepted into the Hunter Family, and you know that I can't let that happen. Not after what happened to her mother. Not knowing where she is or if she is safe. Knowing that she is out there somewhere and maybe on her own. The hunters have delayed in asking her this year out of for respect me, but I can't stall them forever.'

Nenna crushes the stalks of the flowers in her fist. He was blocking her becoming a hunter. How dare he! But her father's next words extinguished the anger building in her as quickly as a candle being snuffed out.

'I would rather see her safely married and settled here as a goodwife, but I wouldn't force her into that against her wishes. So, I have discussed her future with Martha, and she has agreed to apprentice her.' The flowers slide silently out of her grasp to the floor. A student sage!

'But her skill as an archer will—'

'Will continue. She can keep training youngsters here between her chores.'

'But—'

'You said yourself that she is the best trainer that the village has ever had,' her father says. 'Would you risk that skill being lost to a hunting accident?' There are a few moments silence.

'I cannot bear to lose her too,' her father's voice continues softly.

Nenna's head screams at her to barge in, to say something, to run, to hide, to do something.

When her brother speaks again, his voice low and quiet. 'I only meant to praise her to you, to make you proud of her, not condemn her to a prison.'

'Hadders! You exaggerate. I am proud of her.'

31

'Then you have a very strange way of showing it. You never tell her.' And the skin curtain over the door is swept to one side as Hadders stalks out. He sees her waiting, and a pained expression passes over his face.

Then he'd taken off down the path towards the corral. She'd followed behind slowly, stopping beside him to lean on the rails to watch their horses cropping the grass. Nettle looks up expectantly, but seeing that they haven't come with food, goes back to ripping up the grass shoots.

'I'm sorry you had to hear that,' her brother said after a while, but he doesn't look at her.

'I'm not marrying,' she had stated, staring straight ahead. 'I am not marrying, and I'm not working for *Martha*, stuck inside all day with her potions and powders.' She'd clenched her teeth tight and leaned her chin on her hands, resting on the top rail. They'd stood together for a long while before she suddenly turned to him.

'Oh, Hadders, what shall I do?' She'd gripped the wooden rail, making her knuckles white. A pain had bloomed in her chest, making it difficult for her to breathe.

'I don't know,' he'd said quietly. 'But I'm going to think of something. 'And he had put his arm around her shoulders as large, hot tears streamed down her face, and she remembered leaning against him and crying, probably one of the last times he had held her close. The last time she had felt safe.

Hadders is the only person in the world she has ever allowed to see her upset. The only person she trusts. True to his word, he had persuaded their father to let her have one more trek out with him, to round up the stragglers before winter and look how that had ended up.

Her horse huffs into her hand, nudging her back to the present. It's not a pleasant place, the here and now. Hadders is gone. Her father won't search for him. And to top it all, now, he won't let her go either.

It is all her fault. She turns away from Nettle and trudges back up the long path to their village, thinking about Hadders.

***

Banging the wooden board with fresh bread down onto the table, Nena makes the bowls bounce. Her father ignores her outburst, calmly spooning the meaty soup into his mouth. He reaches for the bread and breaks off a hunk. He wipes a hand across his mouth and down through his greying beard.

'That's a good loaf, Nenna, thank you,' he says, buttering a second chunk.

'Well?' she asks.

He gestures to the empty chair at the table and continues to eat, waiting for her to sit. Eventually, with a sigh, she does.

'I will send Ash out to search for Hadders again. He can bring back any small game that he can catch at the same time, but all searches will stop after the winter festival.' He holds up a hand, stalling her reply. 'The winter is hard enough without losing any more people.'

She looks down at her untouched bowl, and he reaches across to touch her hand. 'I miss him as much as you.' Standing up and scraping her chair back so fast that it falls to the floor, she bursts out,

'How can you say that? If you really missed him, you would be out there searching. We would both be out there, and we would not return until we'd searched every blade of grass and turned over every stone looking for him. Instead, you confine me to the village and you stay here playing the dutiful elder.' Her hand angrily swipes back strands of her unruly hair from her face.

'Nenna! That's enough.' Her father's voice is firm. Standing up, he crosses to her. 'The hunters will find him. They are skilled at tracking. You know as well as I do that your brother is quite capable of looking after himself and of getting back home. You caused the situation with the healer's son and you must face the consequences.'

They stare at each other, and she sees how tired he is—the dark circles under his eyes, the increased worry lines etched onto his forehead. As usual under his intense gaze, she is the first to back down. She turns her head away, biting down hard on the inside of her mouth.

He says softly, 'I can't lose you as well.'

The moment stretches, and she wonders if he will choose to tell her of his plans for her, but he says nothing, going to the front door and lifting his cloak from a hook. Before he leaves, he turns back.

'We have each other,' he says.

Chapter 5

As Serin takes the lift down from the control deck, her face burns. That cruel bastard is still taking prisoners to work as slaves in his mines, just so he can have his precious crystal. The slow agonising death that they suffer. The skin lesions and the fits they endure. Why? He must have a huge stockpile of crystal by now.

She only went with him to the mines once and that was enough.

The doors slide open, and Serin walks quickly past the young guard without acknowledging her. Footsteps follow behind her, and she turns to confront the woman. What does she want?

'I . . . I have to accompany you everywhere, your highness,' the slim young woman says, one of her hands fluttering forward, her brown eyes holding an appeal.

Serin bites back a retort. It isn't this woman's fault; she is only following orders. *His* orders.

'What's your name?' she asks none too gently, gesturing for the young guard to walk along with her.

The poor girl looks petrified, shrinking back, her eyes wide. But she straightens up and catches up with Serin. 'My name is Marianna, your Highness,' the girl replies, running her fingers through her short, tight curls. Beads of sweat shine on her forehead.

'Please, call me Serin.' When Marianna's eyes look as though they will pop out of her head at the impossible suggestion, she continues. 'In front of my uncle I suppose 'Your Highness' would be more proper.'

They stand in silence in the lift that will take Serin back to the small cabin. She can feel her anger ebbing away, leaving her tired and heavy. When the doors open and they step out, Serin is surprised to see that they are not on the floor she expected. This corridor is wider and carpeted in a light grey. There are only three doors, one directly in front of them, and one to each side.

'Marianna?' Serin asks, looking around in alarm. 'Where are we?'

'These are the royal suites. His Imperial Highness D'Ruja A'Riman, The Crystal preserve him, wanted you to be escorted to your own rooms, as befits your status.'

'Which are his rooms?' Serin asks hesitatingly before stepping any further. He better have separate ones. She doesn't feel ready for that fight. Yet.

'Those.' Marianna indicates a door straight ahead. 'And these are yours.' She walks towards the door on the right.

'And that door?' Serin asks, pointing at the remaining door, hopefully.

'Those rooms are empty, Ma'am. They are spare guest rooms.'

The seed of hope inside Serin's dies. Not Myriad then. He has not come with their uncle. He must be still on Crystal Moon. He has been her only light in this sad affair, the one person she is really looking forward to seeing again. Not quite the only one, there is Zachary. But he will have forgotten all about her. In all likelihood, he's married with six children, balding and with a paunch. She gives a brief, sad smile at that thought, glad that Marianna doesn't see it.

Marianna places her hand on the wall to the right of the door. Silently it slides open, revealing a large, spacious room. Serin steps in and looks around at an area decorated in an expensive but bland style.

The unrelenting white of the ship's corridors have been replaced with cream. Cream walls, cream carpet, and a large cream curved seating area. The tables and chairs are gilded, the gold catching in the light of the crystal lamps. The room appears soft, fuzzy even, until Serin realises that the walls are padded. There are no sharp corners or malicious shapes that could rush up and strike her if the ship suddenly tilted in space. Like a nursery or a room for someone insane.

Serin barks a laugh at the sight. Marianna looks at her curiously.

'What a change this is from my last room,' Serin says, to cover up her real thoughts.

Furniture is bolted in place. Here and there is a splash of colour—a green cushion, a golden lampshade. Through an open door, Serin can see a massive bed covered in a richly embroidered cover - gold on purple silk.

She sighs. This is just a bigger, more richly decorated prison. She is still under his control.

The lavish room holds one delight, however - a bookcase full of books. Serin reaches up to take a book and realises suddenly that they are all fake - just a cleverly painted façade. The disappointment is physical. Her shoulders slump, and she lets her hand fall.

'It's just for show. Real books might be dangerous flying around when the ship is manoeuvring. I have some real ones in a chest in my room if you're interested.'

Serin spins around at the sound of his voice to find her uncle lounging in the doorway. His dark hair oiled back, every strand in place, accentuating his long nose. He watches her carefully, the blue in his eyes like the sky on a winter's day—pale, cold. He steps into the room, making a quick gesture with his head for her escort to leave. Marianna scuttles past him.

'Close the door on your way out and stay on duty. I do not want to be disturbed,' her uncle says without looking at the young cadet, his attention firmly on Serin.

She stays rooted to the spot, her back against the false bookcase. He strides over to the curved seating area and sits.

'You have no idea of the trouble I've been through to get you back safely,' he says, his expression blank.

Was he angry? She can't tell. Experience has taught her to say nothing, to wait. He gestures for her to sit. She perches on the edge of the seating area, as far from him as she can.

'You want to know why you are here,' he says, and her heart gives a flutter. Her mind screams at her to close her ears, to sing, to walk away, anything rather than listen to him, but she knows that is the way her younger self reacted to him.

She stills the chatter in her head and conjures up the flame, willing calmness and bracing herself to hear the tyrant's words.

'I'm going to explain my plans for the future and why you are so important, but first, I want to tell you about our people's journey from our planet to this moon.' He keeps his eyes fixed on her face.

She opens her mouth to speak but he raises a hand. 'I know you're going to say you've heard it all before, but you have only heard the version that we tell children, and you are no longer a child.' His eyes take on a glint of steel.

He pauses, and a faraway expression crosses his face, the muscles there going slack for a moment, making him appear softer, nearly human. But she isn't fooled. He is looking towards her but not at her, looking inward, remembering. She waits, resisting the urge to run.

'Do you remember Lakhth al-Dubb, Princess?' he asks, and when she shakes her head, he continues. 'No, I don't suppose a babe in arms remembers much.' He takes a deep breath. 'Well, it was beautiful. Take our city Oasis on Crystal Moon, and multiply it a thousandfold, ten-thousandfold. Higher, wider, bigger in every sense of the word.'

She represses a shudder. The calm, green vistas of Maa Erda flash through her mind. But he catches it and sees.

'Oh, don't think our world was devoid of greenery, Princess. All sorts of plants grew there. There were waterfalls everywhere - sunshine, colours, space. But your father, the king, my brother—The Crystal give him rest - was far too soft and thought everyone was like him, kind and generous. He couldn't see it coming. Wouldn't accept it. He argued with the rest of us that we could not possibly be right. Couldn't accept that our allies would rise against us. Luckily, we ignored him and prepared the mothership.'

He gets to his feet and pours two glasses of water from a pitcher sitting on a tray on the circular ornate brass table in front of him. He hands her one. She takes it without comment, both astonished and suspicious that he has served her and not called a servant. He remains standing, looking down. She frowns.

'We were under attack,' he says, mistaking her expression for one of incomprehension. 'Our nearest neighbours and supposed allies, the Warkamesh, had been waiting, watching. Just when they thought us at our most relaxed, they attacked. Belpold the Magnificent wanted it all, crown and country. He ordered all royals were to be killed. We barely had time to escape.'

He paces the floor, the contours of his face hard and sharp, the disgust at her father's weakness clear. She can see the muscles in his jaw tighten as he clenches his teeth, and she physically draws back against the seat, away from him, remembering his outbursts of old.

He sits down and stretches his long legs out in front of him. He uncurls his fists and smooths the material of his immaculate dark-blue trousers and plucks off a piece of hair or dirt. He has learned some restraint.

'Three years we searched,' he says, 'for somewhere suitable to set up a new home. Three long years in the black emptiness of space, looking for a suitable planet.'

He sighs and his face takes on that distant look again. 'Then the virus struck, and we were forced down onto Crystal Moon. Your father refused to let us land on V713. He said if it were inhabited, we would spread the virus.' Her uncle pauses, looking back towards her. 'And you know the rest.'

He watches her while taking a sip of water. She looks down, not meeting his gaze this time. She did indeed know the rest. It was the last memory that she had of her parents.

A darkened chamber. Two skeletal people staring up at her and her brother as they are restrained from entering. The eyes, staring over at them, sunken deep in their skulls. A clawed hand, bird-like, the skin stretched tight, rising shakily towards her. She had tried to go to her mother, had cried out, but they were dragged away by people she had considered cruel at the time. Later she understood that the only cruel thing present was the virus.

She wonders what her mother had felt, seeing her daughter pulled away like that. Had she understood? Had she been hurt? She wonders what Myriad had thought. They had never spoken about it. The heaviness she had felt earlier returns a hundredfold.

They sit in silence for a while.

'That doesn't explain why you need me,' she says quietly, meeting his gaze.

'You are—' A loud commotion interrupts him, raised voices arguing, coming from outside the room. In a flash, he is on his feet, striding to the door, his face like thunder. He throws open the door, and the row ceases abruptly.

'I said I was not to be disturbed. Under. Any. Circumstance.' He enunciates the last three words slowly and carefully. She cannot see into the hall but can well imagine the people there stepping back and swallowing.

'Sir, I apologise, but there has been an accident. Three crew members are seriously injured, and Doctor Ferkenwell said to alert you immediately,' a man's voice says timorously. Her uncle does not hesitate but walks straight to the lift.

'Where?' he barks.

'On the hov storage deck, sir. They were carrying—' The lift sweeps them away, and Serin does not hear the rest. She is on her feet and crosses the room to look out into the corridor. Her escort, Marianna, is still there, leaning against the wall, and she hurriedly straightens.

'Do you know where the hov deck is?' Serin asks her.

'Yes, Ma'am.'

'Then take me there.'

She knows the lift doors open straight into the hov storage area. She remembers it from when she'd made her escape. She takes two steps forward into the hangar, looking around at a very different scene from when she had been there last. The space is brightly lit, and it bustles with activity, people in every corner shouting and waving their hands. A group of men cluster around a hoist near one of the hovs, which is clearly damaged, lying at an angle, with debris scattered around it.

The men wear the all in one dark-blue suits of engineers. Behind the edge of the broken hov, she can see the white of medics kneeling by some figures on the floor. She makes her way towards them. Her uncle is there, deep in discussion with one of the white-coated men. Doctor Ferkenwell she guesses.

'There are several broken bones and at least one serious puncture wound,' the doctor is saying, 'I've made as many of them as comfortable with pain relief injections as I can, but we'll need to bring down the mobile medi-unit to assess injuries before moving them.'

A short, balding man stands nearby, his face full of concern. He glances at the people lying on the floor covered in the heat-retaining trauma blankets.

'What exactly happened?' her uncle asks, his voice brisk and authoritative.

'We were carrying out a routine inspection on the hov before stowing it back in the shuttle.'

Serin edges closer to the injured men and bends down, screening out the voices around her. She focuses solely on a man who lies in front of her. Only his face, white and waxy, is visible above the silver cover. She reaches forward and gently touches her fingers to his forehead.

His body is a mess. His internal organs are crushed and bleeding. There are cuts and tears in multiple blood vessels, and a large splinter of metal is lodged in the muscle of his heart, having first pierced through one of his lungs. He is fading fast.

She closes her eyes and slowly draws the metal out, then rebuilds the tissue behind it. She pulls the metal shard down into the chest cavity and pulls it out through the entry point. She mends the tear in his lungs and seals the larger vessels around it before moving lower down in his body and healing the crushed tissue of his liver, stemming the blood loss.

At last, satisfied that she has helped the injured man all she can, she lets her hand fall and opens her eyes. A crowd has gathered around, silently watching. There is a mixture of awe and disbelief on their faces as they look at the man on the ground. The cover has fallen away, and although he lies in a pool of blood, it is clear that it is old from its dark, congealed look. The man is looking up at everyone, smiling.

'Is someone going to help me up?' He says from the floor, and everyone begins talking at once, hands reach out to help him up.

'By the crystal, Eachan, I thought you were gone!'

'Here, up you get.'

'I can't believe it.'

'We haven't had a healer with this kind of power since— well, not even our good Queen, The Crystal give her rest, could have saved him,' the doctor says to Serin. 'That was incredible. Would you be able to look at the others, please?'

Another reason for you to return, Princess, her uncle says in her mind. *It is past time for you to take up your responsibility for your people. It is time for you to help me—to help us.*

She glances up to see him offering his hand to help her up. She turns away but thinks better of snubbing him in front of others and turns the movement into brushing her gown down. Then she raises her hand to him. He helps her up.

'The princess is tired now,' he says. 'I am sure you can deal with the other two men in the normal way.' He starts to steer her towards the exit. She pulls her hand free.

'No, Uncle. Let me help them.' She smiles sweetly up at him, seeing the flash of anger in his eyes. A small victory.

'He will need to drink lots of water,' she says to the doctor, nodding at Eachan, and crosses towards the other men.

'See that he drinks,' the doctor says to one of Eachan's friends.

'Thank you, Princess,' the doctor says in a whisper meant only for her as he walks with her. 'These two are not so seriously injured. They have several broken bones, and one has a head injury.'

She is already kneeling by the man with the head injury before the doctor has finished speaking. The man on the floor is pale and fighting sleep, his eyelids flickering. His head has been neatly bandaged, covering most of his light brown hair. His eyelids flutter again, and he tries to look up at her.

She gasps, her hand flying to her mouth. His eyes are a deep blue.

Zachary. Her Zachary. He's here.

'What is it, Princess? Is something the matter?' The doctor hunkers down beside her.

'No. I'm all right,' she says. Her hand trembles as she reaches towards Zachary, and she is sure everyone can hear her heart beating loud and fast. She never thought she would see him again. Was he married? Did he think of her as much as she thought of him?

She hears her uncle directing a crew to clear up the mess and clears her mind. There will be time to unravel her thoughts and feelings later, once she has healed him. Taking a deep breath, she focuses on healing Zachary.

By the time she is finished, her head is lolling forward with exhaustion, and she knows that she can't get up. Her legs are weak and shaky. A huge yawn envelops her, and she sinks down on her side. Her uncle lifts her gently up, and for once, she does not struggle against his touch.

She hears him speaking as though from a distance. 'Anyone who discusses what happened here, especially the part the princess played, will be dismissed and publicly flogged. Is that clear?'

A chorus of 'Yes, sir' chases her into a deep, deep sleep.

Chapter 6

Camis follows Tor down several sets of stone steps hewn, out of the natural rock that links the levels in Hill Village. Dropping down three tiers, they walk between two large huts and out into a wide space. The ground has been long devoid of vegetation from the countless feet that have flattened it.

There are people everywhere Camis looks, busy with everyday tasks. Children race across the open centre of the village, playing games, chasing each other and shrieking. They add to the hum of people talking and laughing as they clamour to be heard above the banging coming from the extensive stone-built forge that takes up one side of the open space.

'This is the centre of our community, our village square,' Tor laughs, deepening the crow's feet around his eyes. 'Though it is neither square nor in the centre of the village any longer. It is here that we hold our gatherings when the weather permits. And that'—he points at a low barn-shaped building straight across from them—'is our Great Hall, where we work and gather in the winter months.'

Camis is suitably impressed, knowing the time and effort that it must have taken the villagers to build it.

The ring of a hammer, rhythmically striking metal catches his attention, and he is drawn towards it.

Children run in and out of the smithy, bringing logs and coal to add to the piles that have already been collected. Several young men, stripped to the waist but wearing thick leather aprons which drop nearly to their boots, work the giant bellows each side of the fire encasement, sweat running in rivers down their bodies.

Two older men beat at a long strip of glowing metal lying across one of the massive anvils. Overseeing the whole activity is the largest man Camis has ever seen. His biceps bulge with veins, and his dark, curly hair lies flat and plastered to his head. Beads of sweat glisten in his beard.

'More air, you lazy lumps of horse dung!' he shouts, not even turning to look at the lads on the bellows. 'Quench!' he instructs the two men beating the metal, and they lift the heated bar across to dip it into a huge bath of water with giant tongs.

Past the smithy, a cobbler works leather on a lathe. Women sit together, knotting a mesh net of some sort, and above the din, he can hear the distant thwack of someone chopping wood. A large brown-and-black dog rises up out of the undergrowth where it has been lying and pads across to them. Tor steps away to talk with some children practising archery, and Camis is left staring into the dog's dark brown eyes.

'Hello boy,' he says and reaches out a hand slowly.

Camis keeps very still while the dog cautiously sniffs at his hand. The dog's tail wags briefly. He stretches out his fingers and gently scratches the dog's ears. The dog visibly relaxes into the scratch and sits down beside him.

Camis watches another group of older children who are waiting for their turn to shoot at the target: a slice of tree trunk painted in coloured circles and nailed, at a distance, to a tree. The children shoot with varying degrees of accuracy. This is something he has always wanted to learn.

With a start, he realises that the children are all looking towards him.

'Is there a problem?' a familiar voice asks coldly behind him, and Camis turns to find the girl who had attacked him– Nenna.

He scowls back.

'Ah, there you are, Nenna,' Tor says, striding towards them. He gestures back towards the children, beaming. 'You have them coming on so fast. Well done. Carry on.' He walks on, expecting Camis to follow.

Nenna steps away and clicks her tongue.

'Quarrel, come,' she calls, heading for the group by the target. The dog leaves Camis' side instantly. As he walks away, he is sure he can feel his back burning from her glare as he hurries to catch Tor up. What is that girl's problem?

Eventually, Camis and Tor reach the top level of the village, and the view out across the grass plains is breathtaking. The plains extend as far as they can see, a yellow tinge to the grass indicating the end of summer. Horses graze at a distance, but from here, they don't look much bigger than ants.

A cool breeze whips back his hair and cloak, and he can smell the ripe meadow grass, sweet and dusty in the wind. Tor points out the distant mountains on the left, and Camis is surprised to see how much closer he is to them now. A flutter of panic rises in his chest. Just how far away is he from the South Forest now? He looks where he thinks the trees should be, but there is only the clear, unbroken line of the plains on the horizon. It will take him days to make it back to the trail.

In the afternoon, Camis lounges near the huts watching some younger boys kick around a straw-filled leather ball. He'd found his cart, safe and secure, in an open barn. Everything seems to be there, and he has worked out a plan to get it out.

The problem isn't the cart, though. It is Misty. She is in a grass corral with half-a-dozen other horses. She seemed to be well cared for and was pleased to see him, but the corral is constantly guarded by a stream of children. They come and go, changing places and chattering. Reaching her unseen is going to be more problematic.

A shout goes up, cutting through the boys' play. Figures appear, climbing fast towards the village. Four men race past Camis, bows and spears strapped to their backs, they bear a man on a makeshift stretcher with leaves still clinging to the roughly-hacked wood. The stretcher holds another man. Two hunters follow behind.

A skinny lad calls out, 'Dree, what happened?' But no one answers him.

The injured man's back is arched. His head tilts upward, his mouth stretching wide in a grimace that shows every tooth. He makes no sound, yet Camis feels a scream rise in his own throat, and his hand automatically rushes to clutch at his neck.

The group passes quickly, heading for Martha's hut, and Camis follows. He scrapes his toes in the dirt outside the door. Should he enter? He bites his bottom lip and sighs again. Would they even let him in?

The bearers emerge without the stretcher or its patient. Others come from all over the village as word spreads. No one speaks to Camis.

He looks around at the villagers as they gather in untidy clusters, some squatting in the dirt, others standing. You can heal! Shouts loudly in his head.

He takes a deep breath and steps towards the opening just as Martha draws back the cowhide. He darts to one side, lowering his eyes. His face heats. Martha looks out at the people who have gathered and shakes her head slowly. As she turns to go back inside, she hesitates, looking directly at Camis. He waits, holding his breath, then she beckons him over.

'Can you help him?' she asks. Her lips twist as though there is a sour taste in her mouth.

'I don't know.' He ducks through the loose cowhide. 'What happened?'

'He was bitten by a Na-led. They usually remain underground and don't bother us much. The hunt must have disturbed it somehow.'

She looks down at the man on the table. His back is frozen in an arch, his mouth wide, his shoulders clear of the table where he has been placed. Canvas support straps dangle underneath him. The stretcher poles lay discarded on the floor.

Camis moves closer. He can smell a musty, dank odour like the damp of mildew. The man's arms and legs are rigid, the muscles clenched in flight, his hands claw-like. His lips have a faint blueish tinge and are drawn back over his teeth in a grotesque grin.

Martha's shoulders droop, and she sighs. 'Sorrel doesn't deserve this. No one deserves this.' She removes a bandana from around Sorrel's calf, tied there by one of the hunters, and shows Camis the bite. Four tiny puncture wounds.

'See here.' She pinches the muscle on Sorrel's calf to show how the creature has inflicted the wound. There is only a little inflammation. The bleeding has stopped. There is nothing to justify the horrendous reaction.

'Will he get better?' Camis asks.

She gives a small shake of her head.

He reaches out and touches Sorrel. At once, he is thrown into blackness, arms flailing, thrashing outwards, down into the dying man. His muscles stretch. He curves into a backward arc, feels fibres snapping, hears bones crack. His mouth opens wide to scream but no sound comes.

Something knocks his hand, and he finds himself on the floor, the stone hard and reassuring.

'Camis! What happened?' Martha's wrinkled face looms close, showing concern.

He struggles to sit up, reaching a hand towards her for help. Her face visibly pales. Fear flashes in her eyes, and she backs away. Camis looks down, a flush spreading from his neck across his cheeks.

'I do not know how a body can bear such agony,' he says, rubbing his back. He is surprised to find himself in one piece and stares wide-eyed at the sick man. 'I'm sorry,' he whispers, shaking his head. 'I can't help him. It is beyond my ken.'

Martha moves towards the shelves with the array of pots, her movements slow and heavy, as though she has aged a hundred years. She takes off several of the clay-stopper lids and shakes out different herbs. Camis clambers to his feet and crosses to watch her as she grinds them with a stone mortar and pestle. She lifts down a white pot, separate from the others, and once the lid has been removed, she uses metal pincers to remove a white root.

'What's that?' Camis asks.

'Wolfsbane,' she replies quietly.

'But that's—'

'Poisonous.'

'Is that all we can do?'

'Yes. That's all I can do, just ease him on his way.'

She wipes her hands on her apron, then stirs the mixture into a small, black pot on the stove and adds some oil. He can smell the acrid root infusing with the sweet nut oil. Martha pours the concoction into a small wooden beaker and crosses back to Sorrel.

She cradles his head, locked still in that unnatural position, his back and neck arched, muscles fixed. Martha tries to lift him, holding the beaker of medicine in her other hand.

Camis keeps his eyes fixed on Sorrel. The man's breathing is quick and shallow. There is bruising under his eyes and his tongue is noticeably darker. That's when Camis sees the swelling.

'Wait!'

He reaches his hand out towards the lump at the base of the man's throat. This time he is ready. He touches only the lump and is not entangled in the pain. He can feel the mass, soft and pliable. It begins to dissolve beneath his fingers, shrinking, disappearing. As it vanishes, a feral cry breaks from Sorrel's mouth. It builds in intensity and pitch.

Camis snatches his hand away as the scream fills his ears, vibrating the very bones of his face as he takes a step back. The hide covering the door is roughly shoved aside as others look in, but Camis is rooted to the spot, his hands and feet suddenly cold. The shrieking increases.

'Camis, do something! Help him!' Martha shouts above the noise. Immobile, Camis stares fixated on the mouth, dark and gaping, through which screeches the agony of the world.

Recoiling, he backs away, his eyes wide. He turns and pushes roughly through the people at the door, and once outside, he hurries away. Eyes follow him, judging.

Once at the village outskirts, he quickens his pace, climbing the hill into a small thicket of trees, blind and deaf to everything except the piercing scream that follows him.

He starts to run. He runs until his sides ache and he can't breathe anymore, then he sinks down onto a fallen trunk. A sob breaks from his mouth. He tries to hold it in, but the dam is broken, and he buries his head in his hands and cries.

Gradually, the sounds and scents of the woodland filter into Camis' consciousness. The quiet murmur of wind through leaves, gentle birdsong, and the comforting aromas of autumn—ripe berries, nuts, and wood smoke.

Rousing from his stupor, he listens, lifting his head, his hammering heart no longer pounding in his ears. His ragged breath is calm, and now that he is no longer crashing through the undergrowth, he hears the silence. The screaming has stopped.

Wiping his arm across his face, he gives a little shudder as his breathing settles. A darkness fills his mind. He could have done something. What would his mother have counselled? But her voice is silent, he can no longer hear her.

It is too hard to manage, this gift, this curse. Where is her guidance? Where is she? She wouldn't have let Sorrel suffer. She would have known what to do.

'I think it may be time to start your training,' she had said after he had healed the rabbit what felt like eons ago. 'The ache in your hands will lessen with time.' He had grimaced, and she had laughed, ruffling his dark blond hair.

Well, she wouldn't be laughing now.

A twig snaps, and he starts. When no one comes any closer, he says flatly, 'I know you're there.'

'I've been sent to fetch you back.' When he doesn't respond, she snaps, 'You can't strop all night.'

Twisting round, he glares at Nenna, his face hot. Of course, they would send *her* to search for him.

'I'm not stropping.' He glares defiantly at her.

Briefly, her eyes flare, flashing like burnt bark. He storms past her towards the village without looking back.

Chapter 7

'That boy is useless! Useless *and* rude!' Nenna says aloud as she crashes through the woodland, not caring who or what hears her. Quarrel slinks along behind her, picking up on the anger in her voice. She can't go indoors yet; Sorrel's screams still haunt her. She needs to keep moving.

Why couldn't someone else have fetched the stupid boy back? Whatever on Maa Erda had Martha been thinking letting him near Sorrel in any case? Saying he could heal! Phaw! If that is how he heals then she doesn't want him anywhere near her.

An orange, black, and white butterfly flits down to land on the path in front of her. It triggers an image in Nenna's mind as it flits away.

The scene replays, as it always does, as though she were a watcher, as if it had happened to some other child, some other mother. Over the past thirteen summers, the pictures in her mind have become more stylised, some of the emotion overlaid with the perspective of hindsight. But there is one thing that would never change. She would always, always blame herself.

***

The child splashes happily in the river, jumping from stone to stone when she can and wading between them when she can't. Now and again, the dark-haired woman on the bank looks up from her washing and smiles.

'Careful, Siena. Not too far from Mama now.'

'Yes, Mama,' she calls back, not looking up. She balances on one leg, the tip of her tongue sticking out between her teeth as she tries to judge the distance for her next leap.

After a while, bored of the river and the stones, she comes to sit by her mama. Mama hands her some sliced apple and a dried biscuit out of a leather bag. Then she unwraps some leaves and breaks off some of the soft, crumbly cheese from inside, fresh from their goats.

They eat, sitting side by side on the grass bank, their feet on the gravel at the water's edge. There is a pile of wet washing in one basket, and the girl sees that there is still a big pile left to do. She can see her brother's tunics tangled with one of her father's shirts, a sleeve stretched across the top of the pile as though it were carrying the washing.

She points. 'Look, Da's bringing you more washing!'

And they laugh together. Lying back, the girl watches the big fluffy clouds scud across the sky.

'Look, Mama, that one looks like a tree,' she says, pointing.

'Mine's a beautiful galloping horse. Can you see it, Nenna?' her mother says.

'No, no! Look at mine!' Nenna shouts. 'It's Hadders jumping over a rock.' And Mama agrees that it does look like her brother, all spiky haired and big feet.

Mama returns to the washing, and Nenna watches for a while, noticing how red her mother's hands become when rubbing the clothes in the cold water.

A spider runs over her bare toes, tickling and catching her attention. She watches it weave its way between the stalks of grass, its long, spindly legs expertly climbing around and over plants and stones. Fascinated, she stalks it, curious to know where it is going.

A butterfly alights on the yellow grass flower nearby and distracts her. It opens and closes its wings, flashing orange, black, and white, and as she moves closer, she sees its long, furry body.

A loud scratching noise has her turn on her heel in an instant, the butterfly flitting away in alarm. Was it a rabbit scrabbling?

Excitedly, she rushes forward, chasing the noise, but skitters to a stop at the edge of the bank.

She glances back at her mother and sees her dunking one of her Da's shirts in the river.

The mysterious sound seems to be coming from just around the corner of the bank and though she knows not to go too far from Mama, she just has to know what it is.

Her feet take her around the corner before she can stop them. A black shape darts away, too fast for her to make it out. But where it had been standing, she can see a hole in the mud bank with a tiny black stick jutting out from it.

She reaches up towards the shape. She can just touch it. A foot! A small, black foot with toes and toenails, everything. But standing on tiptoe, she can't quite grasp it or see any more of it.

Intrigued, she fetches one of the river stones that litter the mud and climbs up onto the flat surface. It gives her a fraction more height, though she still can't see any more. She can grasp the foot and tug.

A small, black doll slides out of the hole. She takes its weight but overbalances on the stone and falls. The doll drops into the mud, and as she picks herself up, she sees that its face is turned towards her. Its eyes are open, and they are big, black and shining. It blinks, watching her. For an age, they stare at each other.

'Nenna! Nenna! Sieeeeena! Where are you?' she hears her mama call, and she picks up the little doll creature and takes it around to show her mother.

Mama is standing by the baskets, both now full of folded, wet washing. She will need Nenna's help to carry them back.

'Nenna, you were told not to go—'

'Mama, look! Look what I found,' she interrupts, holding out the tiny black creature, its fingers tangled in her hair. She leans forward to show it to her mother, but as she looks up, she sees a horrified expression on her mama's face.

'No! Nenna, no!' her mother cries, rushing towards her.

A black shape, a fraction taller than Nenna, springs out of nowhere. Its long, spindly back legs rebound off her mother's chest, pushing her away from the living doll that Nenna holds out. Grabbing the doll from Nenna's arms, the creature flees. Nenna follows its movements, but it vanishes quickly. She turns back to ask her mother what had just happened and sees her mother sprawled on the ground.

'Mama!'

But Mama doesn't look at her or answer. Nenna kneels beside her. Why doesn't she get up? Suddenly, her mother twitches and arches her back.

Through clenched teeth, she says, 'Get Da.' And then her mouth opens wide in a scream, but no sound comes out.

Nenna stands still. Her mind has gone blank, and she can't move. Her heart is banging so hard she can't hear the birds or the stream. She stares at her mother when slowly-so, so, slowly, her mother turns her head to look at her, and she can see the fear and pain in her eyes.

Spinning away, Nenna knocks one of the baskets over and clean washing spews out into the mud. She runs for home.

***

The evening shadows stretch, making alien shapes from the trees and boulders. Elongated and angular, they expand, turning the world into a nightmare landscape. The whole village has turned out to climb the narrow path up to their customary funeral site. The wind blows savagely down the mountain, carrying with it the taste of snow.

Everyone is bundled into their own thoughts. Nenna looks up at the unlit pyre, massive, menacing, the unnatural arc of Sorrel's body standing stark against the skyline.

The villagers form a semicircle around the bonfire, waiting in silence. The pyre is built out on a bluff. Down below, beyond the village on the vast grass plains, a herd of horses moves steadily towards them. A white stallion is clearly visible, herding and fussing his mares into unwilling motion. As the sun dies—painting the sky purple—so do the gusts that had buffeted them during the climb up to the bluff, where all bodies are released to the stars.

The shadows deepen. Her Da steps forward and begins:

'When the world was made.

When the mountains were carved.

When the rivers were new.

The plants grew tall and green.

The creatures came to fill the world.

To fill the air, the land, the sea.'

Tor pauses and everyone joins in the next refrain.

'Look for the spark.

When it is our time to go, go gladly.

We feel, we hear, we see.

Look for the spark.

For it tells of life arriving.

Look for the spark.

For it tells of life leaving.

Look for the spark.'

The pyre is lit. Heads are bowed in contemplation. The flickering flames obscure and then reveal the body. Sorrel appears to writhe, the wretchedness of his death emphasised. Nenna watches as sparks shower the darkened sky and the smell of burning flesh drifts towards her.

The sharp pain in her chest threatens to explode. She blows out hot air into the scarf that covers her mouth, shrinking down within the folds of her cloak.

The remainder of Sorrel's funeral passes in a haze. Nenna stands quietly, staring into the fire, remembering other gatherings, other fires. She ignores the boy, his presence an irritation. He looks fine to her, the blow to his head couldn't have been that bad.

She shoves away the image of him sitting on a log in the woods, crying. What a baby. As for that hysterical old hag Martha saying the boy could heal—what a load of horse shit.

Hadders, I need you.

Mentally she packs—water, blanket, knife, bow and arrows. She must get away quickly and hide the things in the stable before her father gets home, while he's still seeing to his duties.

Duties. The word echoes around her head, and she looks down at her feet. She will only be gone until she finds

Hadders—for two or three nights at most, and she won't be out there alone but will join the hunters once they have set up camp.

She nods to herself, rushing carelessly down the hill, heading for her home as soon as the funeral party starts to break up.

On the path, she passes Ash. He is holding a guttering torch but catches her arm as she passes. His strong hold forces her to stop. Lean and muscular, he is everything she wants to be—a hunter and free.

'Nenna, your father has asked me to have another look at the area where Hadders went missing. It's near the black boulders, to the south of the lily ponds, right?'

'Yes, that's right,' she says, biting back what she'd really like to say. That he has no right to go instead of her. That he is not needed. But she pushes her thoughts down and keeps her words civil. Anger will not help find Hadders or persuade her father to let her go too.

'If you keep the plains on your right and the hills to the left and follow that trail around towards the little dip before the grey rock watering pool, that will be your quickest route.'

'Ahh, it would be,' he says letting go of her arm and turning away. 'But I'm taking the lad to search the area where his mother went missing first. But thanks.' And he waves as he cuts across the path, heading in the direction of the stables, leaving her staring after him, all thoughts of remaining calm gone.

She waits impatiently inside the door and doesn't even allow her Da to remove his cloak.

'You are letting that boy go with Ash?' Her voice is low and could cut the air between them like a knife.

'Yes, he needs to search for his mother.' Da avoids her eyes and fumbles with the ties on his cape. She can see the lines of tiredness on his face.

She presses on. 'So, he can go but I can't.'

'His mother is all that he has,' Da says patiently.

'So Hadders is not important.'

'I didn't say that. You had one chance already, and we know what happened then.'

They stare at each other. The candle flickers on the table, casting shadows on the scarred wood. Further down in the village, a dog barks, causing Quarrel to rise up from where he has been lying by the fire. He looks towards the door, growling softly.

'Only I know where Hadders was last seen. And also, of where I . . . I found the boy.' She fumbles over saying 'where she struck the boy' but rushes on. 'And you said I was to pay the boy back by looking after him. How can I do that from here?'

She can see him begin to waver and presses on. 'It's only three or four nights, and I'll be with Ash as well as with the boy.' She feels a thrill of elation shoot through her as her father looks away, rubbing his chin. 'Please. Please. I will never rest until I know. You have to give me another chance.'

'All right, Nenna. You've got your second chance,' Da says sadly, turning away from her to hang his cloak and to hide his anguish.

In bed that night, she fights the panic that threatens to overwhelm her, replaying the events of that last day with Hadders, again and again, looking for any clues as to what had happened to her brother that she might have missed. Something. Anything.

The scenes in her head reach their natural end. She cannot see anything new. She gives a huge sigh. It is going to be even tougher searching so many days later, but she has to try.

The night Hadders had disappeared, she had been waiting for him when she realised that the fire had died down. She hurriedly fed it. Flames had licked at the added fuel, spitting and cracking, sending up a few sparks.

For a while, she'd concentrated on rebuilding the fire and wondered, not for the first time, what was keeping him. Standing with her back to the heat, she'd stared out into the black. The glow from the fire had illuminated a small circle, making the distance beyond seem even blacker. She could hear the crunching tear of grass as the herd ate it nearby. In the distance, an owl gently hooted as it hunted. A cold gust of wind had swirled around her, buffeting the fire, making it gutter. She'd shivered and stepped closer.

Sitting on the groundsheet and wrapped a blanket round her shoulders, straining to listen out beyond the safety of a camp. Quarrel had growled low in his throat, coming to stand closer to her. His head level with hers, turned outwards towards the foothills, towards where Hadders had gone to check on the pregnant mare.

It was unusual for the herd to wander so far from an pregnant mare but not unheard of. The stallion, invisible in the night, had whickered softly, and Quarrel, a bundle of tense muscle, had relaxed, settling down beside her.

In the morning, Hadders had still not returned. She'd woken when the day was washed in that predawn grey colour, light enough to make out shapes, but not yet sharp and clear. Groaning, she'd sat up, rolling her head and shoulders to ease the crick in her neck. Quarrel had been curled into a neat circle; his thick brown tail wrapped over his nose. He'd opened an eye and watched her.

'Come on, boy. Let's see how Hadders is and maybe get some breakfast on the way.'

Quarrel had been up before she'd finished speaking, stretching his head up and then lengthening forward, extending each of his back legs in turn. And just like that, he was ready. Nenna had drunk some water, then splashed some on her face. She'd glanced over at the herd and had done a quick head count.

'Don't go far,' she'd said to the battle-scarred bay stallion standing a few feet away from his grazing mares. 'I won't be long.'

Scouting ahead, looking for signs of her brother, she'd hoped he would come riding towards them, holding a brace of rabbits. Nettle had peeled away from the herd and had trotted over and patting his neck with one hand, she pulled a rope halter over his head with the other. With a blanket thrown over his back she had mounted and headed in the direction that Hadders had gone the night before, Quarrel trotting alongside.

The further she'd ridden, the deeper the dread had grown in her stomach, icy and bitter, leaving a sour taste in her mouth. Even Quarrel had ignored the thrill of the chase and his hunger, picking up on her anxiety.

There was no sign of Hadders or his horse or the pregnant mare. She'd wondered if she'd missed something and called Hadders' name again and again. But there was never an answer.

Then Quarrel had taken off at a run, racing past her, his head up, scenting the air. His brown-and-black hackles had risen across his neck and shoulders. Nettle cantering after him.

The landscape rose and fell, becoming rockier. Quarrel had twisted out of sight behind a large boulder but didn't answer her calls. Her voice echoed off the surrounding hills. Following hard behind, she'd reigned Nettle in sharply.

Black carrion crows rose in a cloud into the air, flapping and cawing as Quarrel had torn into their midst, snapping and barking. In the chaos, her mind and body had frozen at the sight on the ground.

Nettle had whinnied, swinging his head up and down, and had taken several paces back. There in the small hollow between the boulders on the rock-strewn earth was a scene from a nightmare.

The bloated remains of the young mare had lain on the ground, entrails spread in every direction.

'No!' she'd shouted as she'd slid from the horse's back.

She'd feared the worse, her heart hammering in her ears, the bile in her stomach choking her. Her hand had flown to cover her mouth. The birds had flapped and hopped a little closer. Quarrel had frozen at her shout, but now he'd charged at them with a bark that had shocked Nenna back into the present. She'd moved forward, scouring the scene.

There was only horse—only horse, just horse. Had the mare died birthing or had she been attacked? The birds had bounded out of Quarrel's reach but dotted the higher rocks, waiting, looking like mourners, still and solemn.

With a rush of anger at them she'd screamed, jumping up the rocks and flapping her arms. The ones nearest took off, only to settle higher and eye her with beady distain.

From her higher vantage, she could see the carcasses, making out the remains of the fully-formed, half-eaten foal that had been dragged behind a rock. It was partially hidden, and she'd jumped down to investigate, her stomach turning summersaults.

Wolves? But what had scared them away? Had Hadders been here when it had happened? So many questions and no answers.

Only foal, she'd thought, and then stopped. Only a foal! At any other time, she would have been furious or in tears or . . . something. Sighing she scrubed her hands over her eyes and concentrated on her search.

'Hadders!' she'd called, her voice startling a few of the birds. 'Hadders! Hadders!'

Only the distant echo of her own voice had replied, nothing else.

Something else had nagged at the back of her mind. Then she'd had it. Where was Blade? Where was Hadders' horse?

She'd caught sight of Quarrel just then, casting to and fro, just beyond the spread of the blood and gore, his head wrinkled in concentration. He'd raised his nose to sniff the air, then had backtracked again, going back over the same area. She'd watched him for a while, frowning before joining him.

'What is it, boy? What can you sense?'

Quarrel had whined and padded backwards and forwards, but his action had given her some hope. He was picking up Hadders' scent, she was sure of it.

She checked the ground where Quarrel was scenting, and there, scuffed and partially hidden by the blood, was a partial footprint. Made by someone big. Someone who wore soft leather boots. Someone like Hadders.

Quarrel had sniffed every rock and in every crevice, but there was nothing. No more footprints. The panic that she'd managed to contain began to build, making her feel faint, and she'd sat down on one of the grey rocks to calm herself and to think.

She'd wished she'd thought to bring some water with her. It wasn't too far back to her overnight camp, and she thought of riding back to get her things when Quarrel glued his nose to the rocky ground and tracked away to her right. She'd followed him, hunger and fear warring in her stomach, churning everything inside. She ignored it. There was always hope. Always a little hope.

'What is it, boy? What have you found?'

Winding between the rocks and boulders, which increased in size, she'd followed her dog, nearly running into the back of him as she'd turned a corner. There was Blade with his bridle snared in a gap in the rocks.

The horse had raised his head, trembling all over. Sweat had dried white on his brown flanks. He'd rolled his eyes in fear and had pulled upwards against the trapped rope.

'There, there,' she'd said quietly, moving closer. 'It's me, Nenna. You know me, old boy.'

She'd reached out her hand towards the terrified horse. Gradually, Blade had calmed enough for her to unclip her knife from her belt and cut him free.

She had a choice to make—get her things and carry on searching, making camp nearby and putting herself in danger of whatever had attacked the mare and maybe her brother, or riding home to get help.

She rode hard for home, pulling Hadder's horse behind her.

Now in the warm comfort of her bed, regret threatens to strangle her. If only she had stayed with him while he went to check on the pregnant mare. If only she'd searched longer, further, and not panicked and raced for home.

Her breath stutters in her throat as she relives racing home without him, pushing her horse through the early evening, dragging Hadders' poor exhausted Blade after her. His halter rope dug painfully into her wrist where she had wrapped it tightly. She had forced both horses to their limit in her panic, galloping recklessly up the hill and into their village. People had appeared in their doorways, but she had raced straight to her hut.

'Da! Da, is he back?' she had yelled. As if Hadders would have left Blade. As if he would have come home without her.

She'd been restrained from riding straight out again. The only way to console her had been to promise that she could leave again at first light and show the search party where she had last seen him.

In the end, Martha had given her bitter herbs in warm milk, and Da had watched until sleep had dragged her down. She could do with those herbs right now.

Rolling onto her back, she is about to give up on sleep when her old cat jumps up onto her chest and settles there. It rumbles in cat contentment, and she lets her hand automatically run along the length of its soft, striped fur.

This time she would find something. There would be something, some sign to tell her where her brother might have gone.

Hold on, Hadders, she thinks. Hold on.

Chapter 8

The light from the funeral pyre flickers across the faces of the mourners. Camis clamps his teeth tight against the prickling in his nose and his eyes, pulling the hood of his cloak tight. He should have done something. Anything that would have helped that poor man. He should have tried harder.

He makes and unmakes a fist, tipping his head back. He wants to scream, to scream at the stars that glimmer impassively above. His stomach roils as the smell of burning flesh reaches the back row where he is standing.

Tor stands beside Sorrel's widow, close to the flames, a red wool headscarf draped over her head and shoulders. She steps towards the fire, unwinds the scarf, and casts into the flames.

'I will be with you, wait for me and I will come,' she says with quiet dignity and watches the garment burn.

Camis' chest aches. He looks down at his empty hands. What use were they? He could have tried harder.

Tor puts his arm around the grieving woman and walks with her down to the village. Camis steps around to the far side of the fire, hoping not to be noticed. The guilt he feels increased at seeing Tor. Before the funeral, he had told him that one of their hunters would take him to search for his mother in the morning and then escort him to the farmstead. He does not deserve their kindness.

Gradually, people leave until only Camis remains, gazing into the fire.

The central platform of the pyre collapses inwards, spraying a shower of orange and yellow sparks upwards into the night like fireflies dancing. He watches them twirl and flicker against the deep navy of the sky, only to wink out of existence. Like Sorrel, they are gone.

 The hairs on the back of his neck stand up. He is not alone.

He shifts his feet, uneasy. Someone, something, is watching. Cautiously, he turns. The rocks behind swarm with Na-led. They sit or crouch, barely visible. The fire is mirrored in their large black eyes, fluttering orange streaks, a ceaseless movement. The creatures remain utterly still. Slowly, he backs away, his throat tight, his mouth dry. They do not acknowledge him but remain transfixed on the fire.

His foot twists on a stone, and as he falls, all eyes swivel towards him, glinting. He catches his breath, his muscles tense.

A whisper rasps in his mind. *We are sorry for the loss of this man.*

He blinks and they are gone.

Three sturdy horses stand patiently waiting, and Camis sees with dismay that the girl, Nenna, is also there. She is checking the bags on a dark grey gelding that is loaded with possessions—a bedroll strapped on top and full water containers dangling to its sides. Tor holds the bridle of a rich bay with a splash of white on her nose. She is similarly loaded with items they will need for their search. He gestures for Camis to mount.

'I'm glad you're leaving your poor old girl to enjoy a bit of rest. Just look after Nutmeg here,' Tor says, and he pats the horse fondly. He glances towards the man mounted, ready to accompany them.

'Ash, do you hear?' Tor says. 'Five days, no more. Then you both see Camis safely to his winter homestead.'

Ash nods and Camis watches as the man skilfully settles his side-stepping black stallion.

'Just recheck the area where your brother was supposed to be and where the healer went missing. I'll expect you back for the Gathering.' Tor turns to look at Nenna. 'And remember, five days. No more. So no bullying Ash into staying away longer.'

Ash has the look of a hunter, lean, tanned and well-muscled, but Camis has no doubt that if anyone can bully him, it will be Nenna.

Nenna's face shows several expressions in quick succession—eagerness, displeasure, and sadness—as she glares down at the elder from her horse. Camis frowns. Is she going to argue?

'Yes, Da.'

She is Tor's daughter!

Camis' horse snorts and prances, keen to follow the others. He fumbles to catch hold of the leather reins—he is more used to driving a cart—and manages to get Nutmeg under control. He looks back at Tor. 'Thank you.'

'Go, lad. Go see what you can find and get home safely.' And he raises his hand in farewell.

'Are you sure this is the place?' Nenna asks for the hundredth time as she watches Camis and Ash examine the ground.

Camis grits his teeth and nods. He'd like to hit her on the head. See how *she* likes it. He bites down his irritability. The ground shows nothing, just like before. Nothing to indicate that his mother had even existed.

After a fruitless search, they walk back to the horses to make camp. Camis drags his feet. Nenna has used the time they were searching the woodland to hunt; he can see a brace of freshly shot rabbits. She is cleaning off the arrows as they walk back. Again, he feels an unexpected stab of irritation at her and at the sight of the rabbits.

After their third canter, Ash tells Nenna to slow down. 'We will get there soon enough. Spare the horses.' Nenna's face is set in determination as she leads them to where she had last seen her brother.

They all hear the hoofbeats behind them at the same time and turn their horses to wait for the rider. Ash slides out his bow and notches an arrow. Nenna does the same. Camis grips his reins tighter, fighting the instinct to flee. The rider is still indistinct, but they can hear a shout.

'What is it?' Nenna says, frowning, but she does not take her eyes off the approaching rider.

'I don't know, but I don't think an enemy would announce themselves in such a way,' Ash says, squinting hard.

The rider rapidly closes the gap between them. They can see his horse galloping hard, white and bright against the grass and low shrubs of the plains.

'It's Kitt!' Nenna says and starts to ride towards him, Ash close on her heels.

Camis walks his horse after them. A huge light-grey stallion slows and stops in front of them, its sides heaving. Steam rises from the animal as it lowers its head, blowing hard. The rider slides down. He is sweating like the horse, his dark hair plastered to his head.

'Ash! You must come back quickly. The babe is on its way and Lin calls for you.'

'Is she alright?'

'Yes, yes. Fine. Just a bit early, but she wants you there.' Kitt pulls out a flask and tips the water over his head. The large horse lifts his head towards the rider and tries to lick the pouring water. 'Oh, no, you don't. Sorry, old boy, but you have to cool down first.' And the man neatly sidesteps away.

Ash looks at Nenna. 'Sorry, but we have to go back.' His eyes are bright with a frantic worry and excitement.

'Of course, Ash. You go ahead, and we will walk with Kitt until his horse cools,' Nenna replies, smiling. All fathers should be there at the birth.

Ash doesn't need urging and kicks his horse quickly into a canter, riding away from their previous path, heading directly for Hill Village. They watch him go.

Nenna and Camis dismount, and all three of them grab handfuls of dried grass and rub the big stallion down. Only after he has been dried and rested is he offered some water.

They walk together slowly, leading their horses. Camis is surprised at the calm way Nenna seems to be accepting the situation. Why isn't she trying to persuade Kitt to go with them?

'This will be your first grandchild, won't it?' Nenna askes Kitt.

'Aye,' he replies with a sigh, wiping a hand across his brow and sweeping his dark, wavy hair back, the sides of which show streaks of grey.

'Why don't you take Nettle here and catch Ash up, and you'll both be there for the babe's first breath,' Nenna says, looking slyly out of the corner of her eye at him.

Kitt looks back at her horse and rubs his grey beard with his free hand.

'Don't doubt you could manage old Ice here,' he says, glancing over at his grey stallion. 'But not sure I should be leaving you two out here alone.'

'Listen, as soon as Ice has rested, we will ride after you. I know you'll be keen to press on, but Camis and I can survive one night's camping. We'll break camp at first light and be home before anyone has noticed. Reckon you'll just have the water boiling for breakfast when we get back, or maybe you'll be celebrating with something stronger.' And she gives Kitt a beaming smile.

The older man still looks troubled, glancing first at Nenna and then at the trail ahead. They walk on slowly.

'All right then,' he says, handing Nenna Ice's reins. 'But if you can't make it back to the boundaries tonight, you make sure you light a decent fire.' And he swings himself up onto Nenna's grey mare. 'Once you're within the boundaries, the watchers will see you or your fire and send riders out.'

'Been camping lots of times with Hadders, remember?' Nenna says, reaching for her pack and handing Kitt his. 'And the healer's son lived this way all his life. Also, we have Quarrel with us, so don't worry.' She slaps her horse on the rump.

They watch as Kitt vanishes into the distance, then Nenna calmly turns and walks in the opposite direction.

'Come on,' she says as smooth as silk. 'We should have time.'

Camis watches her, his mouth hanging open. He glances after Kitt, then back towards Nenna. 'Hey, where are you going?'

'To look for Hadders,' she calls back without turning round.

'But we . . . You told the others . . . '

'It's not far. Come on. We can soon catch up.'

'No, Nenna, we must . . . ' He trails off as she turns and glares at him.

'You! You had your look, and now it's my chance. What are the others going to do? We will be home tomorrow, and if there's any punishment, I will take it. I'm not giving up the chance to search now that I'm this close.'

She swings up lightly onto the stallion's back and gives Camis a look that dares him to argue, then she tugs the reins, pulling Ice round, and clicks him into a walk.

Camis watches her for the space of five or six steps, his emotions warring inside him. Should he go after her, be an extra pair of eyes, or head back to Hill Village and tell Tor . . . Tell Tor what? Maybe this is his chance to cut his losses and head for the winter's homestead. Luk and Anna will expecting them any day now.

His head twists back and forth as he considers which way to go. A little voice inside him whispers, how would you feel if you heard that something had happened to the wretched girl? An image of Tor being told that his daughter was missing or injured or dead flashes into his mind. He gives a big sigh, and with one last look in the direction of Hill Village, he mounts up and follows Nenna.

The grassland rises gently and gives way to black rock. A few clouds scud across the sky, and he can see more massing on the horizon near the mountains. The wind whips their hair one way and then another. The giant stallion suddenly raises his head and neighs. The hackles rise on Quarrel's neck, and he slows to a stiff-legged walk. Nenna pulls Ice to a halt.

'Lie down, Quarrel!' she commands. 'Camis, wait here with the horses.' And she slides down from Ice, throwing him her reins. 'There is something I want to check.'

She trots towards a small rise in the land. He watches her crouch, creeping to the top, lying flat in the long grass. He feels angry at being told to wait like a child. His internal compass tells him that the village is somewhere behind them, and he can see the plains spread out to the horizon on his right, full of early-autumn colour from berries and flowers.

Nenna jerks back suddenly and scuttles towards him, clutching at her neck.

'What is it?' he asks her as she takes back her reins and prepares to mount.

'Nothing,' she snaps and pulls herself up, turning the horse.

'I think you saw something.' He slides down off his horse, and she tries to block his way.

'No, leave it!' Ignoring the warning, he dodges around the horses and heads towards the rise.

'Camis, don't,' she hisses after him, but he is already on the slope, creeping forward, and she doesn't follow.

Peering over, he realises he's at the top of a sharp drop, possibly the height of three men. There on the flat rock below are two Na-led. They are nearly invisible against the dark grey rock, but he can just make out the shape of a smaller one lying twisted and still, with a larger one crouching beside it. A deep, keening grief engulfs his senses.

Without thinking, he stands and follows the edge of the rise to a point where he can scramble down. The adult creature raises its black face towards him, nostrils flaring, but it does not move. There is intelligence in those eyes, and there is care in the curled fingers, which caress the head of the smaller Na-led.

He hears Nenna cry out, but he ignores her. He approaches the Na-led slowly, carefully.

It's all right. I'm not going to hurt you. Easy. Easy.

He is only a few steps away when Nenna appears on the ridge. Her bow is raised and an arrow notched, ready to fire.

'No!' he cries, rushing in front to block her view.

He hears the twang of the bowstring and turns to see the arrow shaft buried deep in the creature's dark body. The Na-led drops heavily. Camis stares down. Black liquid oozes from the arrow wound, trickling slowly out, the viscous liquid staining the rock an even deeper colour.

He bites down hard, clenching his jaw tight, and feels the muscles in his neck bunch. He takes a deep breath and looks up. Nenna's eyes are wide and stormy, her face a livid red. Eventually she whispers, 'You stupid, stupid fool.'

Chapter 9

Riding through the rich grass plains, the air filled with birdsong, Camis catches up with Nenna, but she only stares straight ahead and spurs her horse faster, her back straight and muscles tight like the string on her bow. She doesn't speak.

They don't stop. Passing abundant wildlife—autumn bushes glow gold and flame red, and small birds flit busily to and fro, gorging themselves as they ready for winter. The air is a mass of insects, thick with their buzz and their bite. The horses flick their tails, their flanks twitching at the irritation, the soft thud of hooves on the hard, baked ground sounding a rhythmic beat.

'You need to listen.' Nenna angles her horse to block his progress and looks straight at him, her brown eyes dark and threatening. She glares and speaks in a quiet, level voice that scrapes the hair off his scalp.

'Na-leds are dangerous. Do not go near them. Ever.' And she kicks her horse forward so that he has to call out after her.

'But this was different! They were hurt. They asked for help.'

She reigns Ice around sharply, making him rear up. Camis flinches from her anger.

'Oh, so you had a nice little chat with them, did you? And they begged for your aid?'

'No, it wasn't like that. You saw . . . I felt . . . '

'You felt? You felt what? You shouldn't have been anywhere near them! They kill. You have never lived in the hills and know nothing about them.'

She turns her horse and spurs it forward. Clumps of mud fly out behind the stallion as he springs into a gallop, and Quarrel races beside her, his ears flattened back over his head.

'You don't know everything either,' Camis says softly, and yet again finds himself trailing after her.

His head pounds and his hands have that now familiar ache. He sways in the saddle and forces his eyes wide. Luckily, Nenna has left obvious tracks.

The Na-led's anatomy had been so different and yet familiar. Camis had stopped the viscous black blood flow of the larger one and the set bones on the smaller. Healing all their internal bruising, he had somehow found his way around their small bodies. He'd instinctively known that they were a mother and son.

Nenna had warned him to keep away, that they were dangerous but . . . they would have died without him. It was his fault the female had been shot, and he couldn't let her die.

And now Nenna was mad at him. But then, she always seemed mad about something.

Forcing himself to stay awake, he follows Nenna's trail.

He stretches his legs out in front of him and throws some thin brushwood onto the fire, making sure not to look towards her. Why should he apologise? She had been wrong. It was a useless, senseless waste of life. Why should he speak first? She was the one who had ridden away. Twice!

He lies awake, staring at the stars as they move across the sky. Across the black, a golden streak arcs, diving towards the ground. A falling star. Should he make a wish? Or is he too grown up for that now?

In the morning, they eat the remaining food, and Camis hugs a hot drink, watching the steam rise. Morning dew soaks their belongings, dampening their emotions as they pack up camp.

Tell her.

Nenna hasn't spoken to him yet and seems to be avoiding eye contact. He looks up from his horse to see her staring out into the distance.

'The last time I saw my brother was from that ridge,' she says.

Camis remains silent.

'Hadders was worried, a mare was about to give birth and she had dropped away from the main herd. He was torn between trying to help her or following the herd.' A gentle breeze carries the smell of horse dung.

'He told me to go with the main group. Said he'd catch up when things were done.'

She tightens a strap on her pack, her dark hair falling to hide her face. Camis waits.

'I went back later the next day because he hadn't caught me up. It was carnage. Blood and guts spread all over. It took all my courage to check it, to see if there was any . . . '

'Wolves?' he asks, but she shakes her head. 'What then?'

'I really don't know,' she replies. 'But I fear for my brother.'

Tell her.

Camis walks to where Nenna is loading her pack and places a hand on her arm.

'Nenna,' he says, taking a deep breath. 'Before I caught up with you yesterday evening, I, um, I healed the Na-leds.'

She frowns, looking at him mystified then her expression turns to incredulity, then to a cold stillness. Her eyes harden to rock. Without saying a word, she finishes her packing, stuffing things in with a ferocity that keeps him from saying more. Mounting up, she kicks Ice to a trot. Quarrel races out of some bushes after her.

He watches until she is a speck in the distance, then, with grit in his stomach and heavy limbs, he starts to pack up the remaining camp, extinguishing their small fire with the remains of his cold tea. The embers hiss and splutter, sending up a brief puff of white into the cold morning air. Neatly rolling his blanket, he adds it to his bundle.

Well, let her go. She can explain to Tor why she left him alone.

A bright flash of fire in the nearby hills draws his attention, followed by a boom he can feel through the ground. Nutmeg shies, shedding his bag and bedding. Camis catches the reins at the last second as her head jerks upwards.

'Whoa, girl, it's all right,' he says soothingly, but his stomach knots and his throat tightens as he looks towards the source of the sound.

He watches as black smoke billows upwards into the clear morning air.

Chapter 10

Ice is eager to get going but she keeps him to a fast walk. She cannot get the picture of Camis standing by the Na-leds out of her mind. The boy is insufferable! Did he listen to nothing? Na-leds were lethal, nasty, malicious . . . She runs out of descriptions. Nothing seems to cover exactly how she feels about them.

Her breath catches in her throat as she sees her mother fall, a black creature darting away. Her mother's mouth wide in a scream, Sorrel's mouth wide in a scream, Hadders' mouth . . .

Shaking her head, she dispels the images that torture her, concentrating instead on Camis, honing her anger on his stupidity. Pig's breath! What will her father say when she arrives back without that empty-headed boy?

Well, Da will just have to moan. He can deal with him because she . . .

Ice screams suddenly, rearing and spinning, throwing Nenna from his back, stamping and trampling the ground where she has fallen. She rolls away from him, glimpsing his wild, rolling eyes through the deadly hooves. As she scrambles away, something silver flashes above him.

She twists and turns, trying to stay clear of the horse's flailing hooves, but it is more luck than judgement that keeps her from being trampled. Shaking and bucking, he snaps at the air behind him.

In mid-rear, Ice stiffens, his scream of rage cut short. There is a strange moment of stillness, then, with a loud thump, the white stallion crumples, collapsing to the ground.

Nenna shuffles backwards just in time. The weight of the stallion hitting the grass sends shockwaves through her body, and she stares in disbelief at his still form. The horse's eyes are wide, white and staring. Froth and foam plaster his mouth.

As she pushes herself to her knees and starts to stand, she hears Quarrel snarl. Her muscles bunch, ready to run or fight or pivot.

She never saw the blow coming.

Feeling returns gradually. She is lying face down on a cold, hard surface. Rolling over onto her side, she feels bindings dig tightly into her wrists, which are caught behind her back. The movement causes her to cry out, but the sound comes out as a muffled sob. There is a cloth gag stuffed into her mouth, tied tight behind her head. It cuts cruelly against the sides of her lips.

'Quiet!' a male voice commands, and she tries to move her head to see, but her hair has come loose, straggling across her eyes. 'And keep still,' the voice continues as a boot connects with her thigh.

She bites down on the gag and holds in a cry. The ground tilts slightly and vibrates. She slides headfirst a short way. Her body pivots around and rests against something soft and warm. Another person? Where in Maa Erda is she?

A shadow looms over her, and she is jerked to her feet by her arms.

'Get up, prim,' a harsh voice commands.

Anger washes through her, and she tries to shake off the person holding her. A short, red-faced man stares at her with a sneer on his face, his eyes level with hers. She can smell his sour breath and twists her head away in disgust.

'Look at me when I'm speaking to you, prim,' he says, narrowing his eyes and giving her a shove.

She stumbles back, unable to gain her footing even though the ties around her legs are loose enough to shuffle with. Large hands catch her shoulders.

'Give it over, Adnan. Can't you see this one's scared stiff?' The hands spin her round gently, and she looks up into the face of an extremely handsome man. The man's smile is flat and doesn't reach his light hazel eyes. They shine in a predatory way.

''et 'o o' 'e,' she growls through the gag, and she tries to kick the man, but the kick is brought up short by her restraints.

Handsome-man steps back, his smile fixed in place. He is enjoying this game, she realises.

'Aww, she likes you, Vitrainy,' bad-breath-man says.

'Oh, yes. We got a feisty one here,' Vitrainy says, looking her up and down. Both men laugh.

'Right, Ad, slide open the hov's hatch, and she can watch me aim that mut of hers for the nearest rock. She won't be needing him to protect her anymore now she's got me to look after her.' Vitrainy laughs as his hands slide up to her shoulders, brushing her breasts on their ascent.

She shudders, shrinking inwardly. The man pretends not to notice her reaction, but a small half-sided smile curves his mouth. A hole slides open in the floor, and she can hear the wind whistling past. Vitrainy pushes her forward, and she can see the ground flashing green and black underneath them. Immediately, she feels sick. It is the highest she has ever been, and instinctively, she pulls back.

'Oh, don't worry, my lovely, I'm not about to lose you,' says Vitrainy, and he places an arm around her shoulders. 'Come on, Ad. Kick the brute this way, and let's see if he flies or just bounces.'

She can hear the short man huffing and puffing as he tugs something into view at the edge of the hole. It is Quarrel, unconscious, his tongue lolling loose, and one of his forelegs is bent at a strange angle. She tries to move around the hole towards her dog, but the man holding her tightens his grip and prevents her. The sick feeling spreads to her throat, and she feels afraid.

'Oh, 'ease,' she pleads through the gag, looking at Vitrainy but he ignores her.

'Hov! Slow,' the man restraining her says aloud, and abruptly, the ground below stops rushing past. 'On my count, Ad, lob the beast out.' And he leans forward, watching the ground below.

'One.'

Nenna feels as though her heart will climb out of her throat. This cannot be happening. It is some nightmare. Wake up. Wake up, Nenna.

'Two.'

She tries to look away, but he stops her. She closes her eyes, and he slaps her hard and unexpectedly.

'Open your eyes, bitch,' he hisses, and when she doesn't, she feels the arm around her shoulder lift up.

A punch catches her on the side of her head, and she spins away, falling. But there is no time to gasp for breath or shake away the stars that swirl around her as a hand grasps her hair and drags her towards the gaping hole.

'Look, you bitch, look,' he says quietly, twisting his fist tighter in her hair, and it is the quiet menace in his tone that makes her open her eyes.

The ground below is more rock than grass now, and she stares down, not daring to look towards Quarrel. She doesn't want to believe what is about to happen. She holds her breath, watching the black ground far below.

'Now!' the man shouts, and 'bad breath' kicks Quarrel out of the opening.

She watches him spiral down, turning over almost lazily. Her heart stops thudding. There is an endless silence, broken by a dull thump as Quarrel hits the ground. Nothing could survive that drop. If he weren't already dead before he was thrown out.

'Hov, stop,' Vitrainy commands, and the ground below stops moving, showing the broken body of her dog lying on the black rock framed by the opening in the floor.

Tears run silently down Nenna's cheeks and drop out of the hole. She cannot see them as they fall but feels that a little of herself will be left behind with Quarrel. That's all she can leave him with.

Abruptly, Vitrainy straightens, pulling her up by her hair.

'Right then, Adnan. Let's get this one back. I'll put my claim in for her later.'

'Don't know why you'd want one of those.' Bad breath Adan replies. 'Everyone knows they are not right in the head and go mad, killing anyone they work with.'

'That's after they've been to the mines, you idiot,' Vitrainy says letting her go, and she feels that he is disappointed in some way. Maybe his cruel sport hadn't lasted long enough or her reaction hadn't been what he wanted.

'Hov, return to shuttle,' he commands, and she rocks unsteadily as the floor jerks.

'Well I wouldn't trust one in my bed.' Adnan says pointing her to the floor against a wall. She crosses the short space to sit, but as she turns, she sees the two men disappearing through a door, which wasn't there a moment ago. The door slides shut, closing out their voices, which are discussing the meal they hope to have when they arrive at this 'shuttle'. She is already forgotten.

She leans against the smooth wall as she slides to the floor, and bending her knees, she lowers her head to rest on them. The strain on her arms and shoulders is painful, but she needs to hide her face as she allows herself to cry for her lost companion.

There is a shudder and the vibration stops. Adnan returns, and the hole in the floor reappears. He drags her to her feet.

''o 'o!' she cries as he forces her towards the opening. Jerking her arms up cruelly.

She looks at him pleadingly, her eyes wide with fear, but he ignores her. Despite his bulk and grip, she manages to twist around and hooks a foot behind his leg. He looks at her then, the nasty sneer back on his round, red face. Slowly, he raises his hand and gives her a hefty shove in the chest. With her leg raised and her arms tied behind her, she falls backwards through the opening, watching as he grins maliciously.

She hits the ground almost instantly, and it isn't the sudden impact that makes her shut her eyes, but the pain that jolts through her arms as she lands on them. When she does look up, both men and the contraption are gone, and she is left staring up into brilliant, bright blue sky. What happened? Is she free?

As her breathing calms, she curls around and pushes herself up with some difficulty into a sitting position. About twenty paces in front of her is a massive, metal mountain. Huge, black, and menacing, it dominates the dip in the valley, and she is sitting in its shadow. Her breath catches, and she shrinks back. What in Maa Erda is that?

Stunned, for a few moments, she doesn't move until the fear inside her unlocks her muscles, and she scrabbles backward.

'Sit still!' a voice commands, and she swivels round to see a man standing on the rocks above her.

He is at a distance, looking down at her. He looks relaxed— a man on duty but not expecting any trouble—and he wears that strange, jumper shaped black top and tight-fitting black trousers, just like the men who had bought her here.

Who are these people? She struggles to make sense of what she sees, her eyes homing in on his top, which has some sort of embroidered lettering on the left of his chest. The only other colour he wears is a triangle of red material worn loosely around his neck. He holds a long, slender silver stick in his right hand, which is raised towards her.

But more shockingly, she suddenly realises that there are others like her. Stretching back along the rock behind her are people, bound and tied like her. They are mostly men, but dotted in amongst them there are a few women. Some are asleep, and some of them are injured, their faces bruised and bleeding. Is this what happened to her brother? Is he here? She peers around carefully, hopefully.

No one moves. She cannot see anyone she recognises. A horrible weight sits in her stomach. What is going on? Why are they here, guarded like a herd? What do these people want with them? All she has, apart from the aches in her body, are questions and no answers. She needs to pee, and she needs water.

A low hum vibrates through the rock as a silver disc flies into view. It halts, hanging in the air just over her head, and terrified, she presses herself flat to the ground. Nothing makes sense anymore. Will this never end?

Her heart thuds loudly in her chest, trying to beat its way free. A hole slides open in the bottom of the disc, and a body is spat out, landing with a thump behind her. A man moans as he hits the rock, and she hears the wind expelled from his lungs. She sits up and starts to shuffle towards him when three things happen all at once.

The disc flies a short distance away, the guard starts towards her, and Camis shouts out loud and clear. *Nenna, sit still! I'll try to find a way to release you!*

She looks wildly around. Camis has come and bought help to rescue them all!

The guard is shouting and waving his stick thing. She frantically tries to get to her feet, looking around to locate Camis and the rest of the Hill Village that have come to free them. The guard's stick touches her lightly on her arm, and pain flashes through her body like nothing else she has ever experienced. It is a violent lightening, coursing through her limbs and up to her head in an instant.

The world flares white and she remembers nothing else.

Chapter 11

Camis runs his hands softly along Nutmeg's neck while keeping an eye on the hills.

'Shh. Steady girl. It's all right,' he says, watching the black smoke ripple upwards in an angry column.

Maa Erda! What was that? Quickly, he straps on his bag and picks up his bed roll.

Help! For the love of crystal, help!

The bedding drops from his hands as he twists his head sharply, trying to locate the caller.

Please, help me!

Mindspeak! Someone other than his mother is using mindspeak! For a moment, he is too stunned to react, then, forgetting her instructions, he reaches out. *Who are you?*

Please, come quickly. I can't reach Kestell to help him. I think he's dying.

The voice is distant and seems to be coming from within the black smoke that is filling the sky above the distant hills. Retrieving his bedding, Camis stuffs it under the strap of his bag and leaps lightly onto Nutmeg.

Keep calling, he projects, *so I can find you.*

I don't . . .

Who are you? What's happened? Hello? Keep talking. But there is no reply. Camis kicks his horse in the direction of the call.

As the ground becomes rockier, Camis allows the mare to pick the pace while he scans the area.

Where are you? he sends. But the voice is silent.

He can smell the acrid smoke now, and as Nutmeg squeezes between some boulders, he sees wreckage strewn over a large area. A fire blazes fiercely in the centre of the clearing, and he can see twisted metal and strange melting shapes flickering at its heart.

Foul smoke pumps into the sky. His eyes smart. Two men lie on the ground. He jumps from his horse and quickly crosses towards them. What in the name of Maa Erda happened here?

One man is arched into a familiar, rigid pose—a Na-led bite. The man is dead, his mouth frozen in a scream, his tongue blue. The other is . . . Camis watches closely, hardly daring to breathe, and lets out a sigh of relief as the man's chest rises and falls.

Camis looks around quickly, scanning the area for Na-leds. Why had one man been attacked and not the other? But there is no time to worry because the young man groans.

As Camis glances back at him, he realises just how gravely injured the man is. A pool of blood seeps around him, and his leg is twisted back at an unnatural angle. Drawing closer, Camis sees the whiteness of bone jutting through skin. Pig's ears! The man only looks a summer or two older than him.

Kneeling, Camis gently touches the man's broken leg. Instantly he is drawn in, down through flesh and blood, down to the hard white bone. In his mind, he stands there, tiny but powerful, surrounded by flesh and blood. He can fix this.

He moves his miniature self into a gap, a gap that shouldn't be there. Blood streams around him. He waves a hand over the damaged area, smoothing over a crack in the curve of a blood vessel. He concentrates on drawing the two cut ends of bone closer and closer, turning them slightly so that they align. He holds them together as ribbons of white float out from the bone, twisting sinuously, wrapping the two ends tight. The blood flow slows to a trickle, then stops.

He withdraws his mind, comes back into himself, and opens his eyes. He can see the swelling around the area of the break has reduced, and he carefully straightens the man's leg. He is satisfied that everything is back where it should be.

That's when the man gives a low moan and opens his eyes. Camis startles as blue eyes look back at him. He is used to comments from others about his own blue eyes, but he has never come across any others with the same colour.

'Who are you?' the young man asks, his voice feeble.

He needs water for the blood loss.

'Drink this,' he says to the young man on the ground, but the man pushes the flask away.

'Who are you?' the man asks again, his teeth chattering.

'I'm Camis, but we can talk once you have drunk some water. You have lost quite a bit of blood, and you need to replace the fluid. The shivering is shock and will stop once you give your body what it needs to carry on healing.'

He is relieved when the stranger raises the flask to his lips, then drains it.

Camis sits back on his heels and a wave of nausea hits him. Three healings so close together might not have been such a good idea. His hands sting to the bone. His mother would know what to do to alleviate it.

'What happened to my pilot?' the young man asks. Camis frowns. 'The other man with me. Kestell.'

Camis glances across at the stiffened body on the ground. The lad follows his gaze and gives a strangled shout, his hands flying to his mouth. 'No!'

'I'm sorry, I couldn't have saved him, even if I had arrived sooner,' Camis says.

Something is not right here. Why had only one of the men been attacked? Rising, he checks the area, expecting to find a dead Na-led.

'How did you find me?' The man struggles to his feet, gingerly testing the leg that had been injured. 'The last thing I remember was someone answering my call. Then I woke up, and you were here. Is there someone else with you?'

The question puzzles Camis, but he shakes his head. Does he mean Nenna? How can he know about her? Oh, pig's feet! He'd used mindspeak.

Camis scrutinises the stranger more carefully. Realisation slowly sinks in as he takes in the man's clothes, the deep black, the tight weave, and a distinct lack of seams. Could he be one of those his mother feared?

'Who are you?' they say together.

'I told you, I'm Camis, son of Serin.'

'Forgive my rudeness, Camis.' The young man puts his right hand on his heart and gives a small bow. 'I'm Tiberius, a Cadarch'—he frowns, searching for a word—'a new cadet with the fleet of His Imperial Highness, D'Ruja A'Riman, The Crystal protect him.'

Tiberius and imperial what? Camis stares, open mouthed. Tiberius looks back. The silence stretches awkwardly. Nutmeg dunts Camis in the back, and he lurches forward. They both grin, the tension between them gone.

Camis picks up the empty flask from where Tiberius has left it and glances over at the fire. there won't be much risk of it spreading, but just to be sure, he walks around, clearing things away that seem too close to the flames.

'Did you . . . did you fix my leg?' Tiberius asks, watching him move things back from the fire.

Camis nods. 'It might ache for a few nights. I don't have any pain relief to give you, and I'm too tired now to help, but there should be no lasting problem there.'

Frowning, Camis examines an object that he has just picked up—a broken cylinder, about the length of his arm, both ends jagged. It is black, smooth and shiny, like metal, but lighter, much lighter.

'But that's impossible,' Tiberius says with astonishment.

'Huh?' Oh. The healing. 'Why?'

'Because you're a prim,' Tiberius states, flexing his arm and rolling his shoulder.

'A what?' Camis glances up sharply.

'A prim. A primitive.'

'What does that mean?' Camis bristles.

'Prims. The people who live here can't heal.'

Camis feels a wave of anger flash through his body, heating him. 'You make it sound like you're superior in some way.' He reaches for Nutmeg's reins, ready to ride away from this rude individual.

'Please don't leave me here. I didn't mean to sound disrespectful. It's what my people call the natives here. It is the only name I know.'

Camis pauses, his hand on Nutmeg's mane, but his feet remain on the ground.

Tiberius hurriedly continues. 'We don't come from here, and I need to get back to my ship before they leave without me.' Camis can hear the anxiety in the young man's voice.

'Ship?' Camis repeats, turning to look at him and frowning. 'The sea is a long way off. Did you sail up the river?'

'No, we flew. But now the hov is damaged'—he waves a hand towards the still-smouldering wreckage—'and I have no way of getting back to my main craft.'

'Are you telling me that . . . that thing can fly?' Camis says, scrutinising the lump of twisted mess glowing on the ground. The smoke is less but thin tendrils continued to spiral into the sky.

'Yes.' But he doesn't elaborate.

They stand together beside the damage, surveying the jumble strewn around. Camis has a hundred questions but doesn't know where to start.

'Will you take me back to my ship, please?' Tiberius asks, cutting across his thoughts.

Camis pauses. Nenna will be worried. But she left him! The sun is not yet halfway to its peak. There is time.

'Yes.' Camis nods. 'Then you can answer some of my questions as we ride. But first we must deal with your friend Kestell.'

Camis rolls the body towards the centre of the smoking fire. Tiberius watches him briefly, then his hand flies to his mouth and his eyes widen. He rushes forward to stand in front of Camis.

'What are you doing? We must take him with us,' he says, gesturing to Kestell's body.

Camis shakes his head sadly. 'I'm sorry, but Nutmeg will struggle with the two of us, and I have to catch someone up as soon as I deliver you to your . . . your ship. We will have to burn him.'

For a long while, Tiberius blocks his way, his emotions high. Anger, fear, and sadness all cross his face. Suddenly, his shoulders slump.

'Is this your custom here?' Tiberius mumbles, stepping aside.

'Yes. By burning, we keep predators from digging up the body and scattering it all around.'

Tiberius turns pale and turns away.

'Can you find things that might burn?'

Tiberius nods, but Camis notes that he keeps his back towards the body and the fire. Camis rolls the body towards the fire, his hands aching.

Tiberius brings more wreckage, and they feed the fire. Finally, it flares, sending flames and smoke skyward. Camis gives the body one last shove and steps back. The smell of burning flesh reaches them, along with a caustic chemical stench.

Tiberius heaves, his stomach threatening to empty of the water that he had drunk. His eyes are red-rimmed and not just from the smoke. Camis cannot think of any words of comfort and stands stiffly, watching.

The fire burns fiercely, a furnace devouring everything in a swift roar. Kestell is consumed, gone. Just as Camis is wondering if he should say a few words, Tiberius speaks, his voice muted and shaky.

'Send him home. Send him to the stars. Return him to us. Return him to the crystal.' He looks up at the sky.

Camis slips away towards Nutmeg and waits, giving Tiberius time.

Nutmeg shows no sign of strain at having to carry two young men, but it is clear to Camis that Tiberius has little experience with horses. He bounces around alarmingly when Camis urges Nutmeg to anything more than a fast walk, clutching so tightly at Camis' jerkin that Camis thinks he might be strangled by his own clothes.

They don't speak much, though Camis has a thousand questions swirling around his head. What on Maa Erda was he doing? This man, this stranger, appears out of nowhere, alleges that he flew here, and here Camis is, ferrying him back to his 'ship' like a long-lost cousin. His mother would box his ears for being so reckless.

'What happened back there?' he demands suddenly, his tone sharp enough to shock Tiberius into talking.

'We were coming back empty handed when Kestell saw a dark shape on the rocks below. He shouted something about getting some sport in. Told me to buckle up and started swooping low over a strange, black creature.' Tiberius speaks in a strangely clipped tone, like he is reporting to an elder. 'I asked him to stop, to let it go.' He sounds grim. 'The edge of the hov caught an outcrop and flipped over. I was flung out and skidded along the ground. Then I saw Kestell running towards me. That's when something black darted out and bit him on the leg. I think I lost consciousness, but I called for help when I could.' Tiberius pauses, his voice breaking. 'It was horrible. Kestell just . . . ' He tails off.

'It was a Na-led. They live underground. Their bite is fatal,' Camis supplies.

The dead man's frozen face flashes in his mind. It morphs into Sorrel. Camis scrubs a hand across his eyes. But Tiberius's story answers one question that has been nagging at him. The Na-led knew which of the men had attacked it, and it left Tiberius alone.

Camis, can you mindspeak?

Camis stiffens. Pig's feet! He has remembered.

I thought I heard mindspeak, and then when I came to, you were there. I thought perhaps I'd dreamt it or been delirious or something, Tiberius says softly into his mind.

The horse plods on through the grass plains. Dry flower heads brush against their legs, stems snapping, brown, brittle. Camis can smell the dryness in the air. Should he go against her wishes? Or . . .

No, that was me, he says.

You can mindspeak! I thought . . . we were told—I mean—we never realised any of you could . . .

I've always been able to, but my mother said not to use it. She said others didn't have that ability. You are the first I've spoken to that way, other than her.

Camis, where do you come from?

I don't understand.

I was taught that prims can't mindspeak, and no one anywhere can heal anymore.

They ride in silence for a short distance. The term 'prims' echoes in Camis' head, making his mouth curl into a grimace. He feels insulted, though he had never heard the word before today.

Where do you come from, Tiberius?

I come from— But before he can finish, Camis gives a shout and kicks Nutmeg into a canter.

Tiberius grabs hold even tighter as the horse is pushed into a gallop. Camis pulls at the reins, trying to get Nutmeg to slow, but before she can stop, he swings his leg over her neck, dismounting at a run, leaving her for Tiberius to control.

He races towards a white mound barely visible in the long grass of the plains. There is Ice. Camis falls to his knees next to the fallen horse, quivering hands hovering over its broken neck. There is no sign of Nenna or her dog. Frantically, Camis searches in all directions, looking for a sign, any sign of her.

'I have to find her!' he shouts back to Tiberius who is sliding off the horse. 'I have to follow her!'

And he starts scouring the ground for footprints, but like his mother before, there are none.

'I don't understand it, people just don't vanish,' he says more to himself than to Tiberius. He looks across the grass plains in the direction of Hill Village. Should he get help or keep searching?

A light breeze flattens the grass. A dark cloud passes overhead, casting a shadow that glides swiftly away. He watches its pathway and shivers. What if . . . ? Turning back towards his horse, he is startled to find Tiberius standing behind him.

'I think I know where this person might be. Is she a friend?' Tiberius says, looking directly at Camis. His blue eyes unsettling.

'Yes, we were travelling together back to her village when we had a row,' Camis explains. 'She was angry and rode on ahead. That's when I heard your call. She could be out there somewhere, injured.' He looks out across the plains again. 'Goodbye and good luck, Tiberius. You'll have to make your own way from here.' He strides back to Nutmeg.

Tiberius shakes his head sadly and points back at Nenna's dead horse. 'Why would she leave everything behind? Her bridle, blanket and'—he crosses over to the body and pulls out Nenna's flask—'even her water?'

For a few moments, Camis just stares at the objects before Tiberius' words sink in.

'What, do you mean you think you know where she is?'

'Take me to my ship, and I'll show you.'

Camis looks at the dead horse, then back at Tiberius and out towards Hill Village. A wash of fear passes through him, making him shudder. It is followed closely by anger.

'This is ridiculous. You're wasting my time.' He mounts Nutmeg. 'You just don't want to walk.' He kicks his horse hard, turning her towards Hill Village, and doesn't look back.

It is clear, even when riding at speed, that no one has passed this way. Gradually, he slows Nutmeg to a walk and criss-crosses his path, double checking for any evidence of Nenna. Pig's ears. Tiberius is right. She wouldn't have left all her things.

Still, he clenches his jaw and keeps on looking. Hill Village is just too far. He won't reach it until dark, and then a search party won't leave until dawn. What if Tiberius's people do have her, and they leave?

It is late afternoon when he turns back. The light is fading when Camis spots the smoke from a small fire, and he urges Nutmeg to a canter. The knot in his stomach lessens a bit. He hopes she is safe somewhere. Maybe this man does know something. Maybe he'll get some answers.

Tiberius is sitting on Nenna's blanket, her pack lying at his feet. He is feeding the fire twigs and dried grass.

They look at each other in silence. Camis dismounts, removes his pack, and rubs down his horse. He pulls out some stale bread and twists of dried meat from his pack and hands some to Tiberius without speaking.

'Thank you,' the young man says and eats quickly.

Watching him, Camis' sour mood fades, and he returns to his pack to find more of the dried meat and a piece of wrapped cheese. He hands them to Tiberius.

'I am sorry I didn't think to offer you food earlier. You must be hungry.'

'You not eating?' Tiberius asks him.

Camis shakes his head. He doesn't think he could swallow anything. Where is Nenna?

When Tiberius finishes, he takes a swig from Nenna's flask. Camis looks away, squashing down another wave of anger.

'I owe you my life. Thank you,' Tiberius says.

Again, Camis' anger dissipates, and he flushes. He is being irrational and can't understand where these mood swings spring from. To hide his discomfort, he collects his blanket and sits on the opposite side of the fire. He looks across at Tiberius who is holding his hands out towards the fire, even though the night is mild.

He studies the young man. At first, his short, spiky hair had made him appear younger, along with the remnant of puppy fat that still clings to his cheeks, but the shadow of dark hair on his upper lip marks him out to be maybe two or three summers older than Camis.

'Will you tell me what you know, Tiberius? Anything that might help me find Nenna or even point towards . . . others that have gone missing?'

There is a long silence, and Camis is just beginning to wonder if maybe Tiberius doesn't know anything at all when Tiberius interrupts his thoughts.

'Did you notice the flat-topped mountain in the distance?' At Camis' nod, he continues. 'The ship is docked in a small valley not far from where the land starts to climb towards the mountain top. I really don't know how far it is on foot or on horseback as we flew everywhere. This is my first collection trip. Kestell was tasked with teaching me the procedures.' He pauses. 'Poor Kestell.'

Camis keeps quiet. Kestell had bought it on himself.

'We set off with instructions to do one last sweep, and that's when . . . that's when . . . '

'They will be looking for you, won't they,' Camis interrupts.

'Oh, yes. But only during daylight hours, when someone is free and not out collecting.'

'I assume that they won't leave without you?'

Tiberius shakes his head. 'The captain has instructions to take off at the set time regardless of whether everyone is back or not. We all know the risks. We are told when we first join up.'

Something Tiberius had said, something about . . . Camis replays the information in his head.

'Tiberius, what exactly do you collect?' There is a long pause. Perhaps he hadn't heard. Camis takes a breath to ask again.

'Prims.' Another long pause. 'People. We collect people.' Tiberius looks down at his hands and does not meet Camis' eyes. The colour drains from Camis' face.

'People? You come here and take people away?'

A reply whispers in his head. *Yes.*

Camis is stunned, his mind in turmoil. 'You take people back to your home and then . . . what?' His voice is hard.

Tiberius fidgets and keeps his eyes downcast.

'And then what?' Camis presses.

'They work in the mines for His Imperial Highness, D'Ruja A'Riman, The Crystal protect him.'

'What?' Camis is on his feet, his fists clenched, one is raised in the air. He sees Tiberius flinch back, the fire casting an orange glow across his face, his eyes wide. A deep all-encompassing rage sweeps through his body. 'Slaves!' There is a longer silence broken only by the crackling fire.

'Where is she?' he cries, and he doesn't know if he means his mother or Nenna or both.

His heartbeat sounds loud and slow in his ears. Time stops. All the frustration of the last few weeks coalesces, starting in the centre of his abdomen and spreading out to his arms. He raises his other fist, his veins prominent. Both hands glow a silvery white.

With a sudden rush of energy, he throws his fists forward. There is a blinding flash on the ground three cart-lengths away. The impact throws him backward, knocking the air from his lungs.

Time resumes its normal pace. Soil and stones shower down. Nutmeg screams. Hoofbeats sound in the darkness. He covers his head with his arms and gasps for breath.

What . . . what had just happened? His vision is bleached, and purple motes of light dance and flash across his sight. His fingers scrabble in the dirt. He feels heavy. His head droops, his eyelids close, and he rests his head on the ground, falling instantly into a deep sleep.

Camis wakes with a start. His heart pounds in his ears, and his chest is tight. He lies on his bed roll near the dying fire, covered in a blanket

Breathe, breathe.

A sharp pain stabs through both his hands, and he remembers the flash of rage that had torn through him. What is happening to him? Panic tightens his chest again, and he struggles to draw a breath.

Stop, you flea brain. What good will panicking do? Breathe.

He manages a ragged calm and pushes his fear to the back of his mind. First, he needs to find and free Nenna, then resume the search for his mother.

He feels hot and throws off his blanket, even though the temperature has dropped. There is the metallic taste of snow in the air. Creatures squeak and rustle in the long grass. He remembers hearing hoofbeats racing away, and he rises quickly.

A brief dizzy spell catches him unaware, and he stumbles. A fresh breeze gusts through the plains, catching strands of Camis' dark blond hair and whisking it across his face. He feels nauseous, and a deep, unreachable itch rises under the skin on his hands. It makes him want to flee and hide, but from whom? Himself?

What would his mother tell him to do? What would she say about . . . about this . . . this violence of his? Would she be expecting it and tell him how to control it? How to use it in a good way? He hopes there is a good way. He hopes it is a gift and not a curse.

But she isn't here. Tears prick his eyes, and he rubs a hand through his tangled hair, taking deep, gulping breaths. What if it isn't a gift? What if he is sick in some way? What if it kills him? Suddenly he feels old—a lot older than his fifteen summers.

He sees Nutmeg nearby. Her head is low, one back hoof tucked under, resting. Relief rushes through him, tinged with guilt. Camis clicks a call to her. Nutmeg comes towards him and he reaches up to stroke her. There is a faint line of light on the horizon. It is time to go.

Sighing he pushes away, giving her one last scratch behind her ears. Rolling up his blanket and gathering his pack, he glances across at the figure sleeping on the ground.

'Tiberius, it's time to go.' Camis leaves the horse, crosses to the fire, and kicks dirt over the glowing embers. Tiberius grunts but doesn't stir. 'Tiberius! Now!' His anger stirs, and his hands throb, but he closes his eyes and swallows it down, afraid of what he might do. Afraid of losing control. He needs Tiberius, for now.

Camis mounts Nutmeg and waits, watching Tiberius roll Nenna's bedding and walk slowly towards him, stopping a few paces away. He looks warily up at him.

'Are you . . . are you alright?' Tiberius asks, biting his lower lip. Camis feels the slow creep of red as it colours his neck and climbs up to his cheeks. He looks away, across the horse's head, then nods slowly. Hopefully. Maybe.

Tiberius looks carefully at the hand Camis offers him.

'I won't bite or explode,' he snaps.

Tiberius hesitates a moment longer, then accepts the hand. They ride for a short way in silence.

'Tiberius, tell me about the people you take.'

The silence stretches on, and Camis wonders if Tiberius is going to answer. Then the young man clears his throat and starts speaking.

'We come once a year for a full moon cycle, and we live here, hidden in our ships. We use hovs to scout the land and pick up people. We never take from the same area twice, but move around this world. We usually collect one, sometimes two at a time, but no more.' He pauses.

'And what happens to them then?' Camis asks him, gripping the reins so tightly his hands turn white. He feels Tiberius stiffen, hears him swallow.

'We take them back to work in the mines to find the sacred crystal, which powers our craft and gives us light and heat. It is said to be a great honour,' he adds in a rush.

'What? An honour to lose your freedom, your home, and your family? If it is so much of an honour, why don't you mine this sacred crystal yourself?' Camis is stiff with anger, noting with satisfaction that Tiberius does not reply to his question.

The terrain slopes gently upwards. The flat-topped mountain is closer. A fluttering starts in Camis' belly, and he resists the urge to make Nutmeg canter. Breaking the horse's leg now on the rocky terrain is not going to help.

He thinks again of Nenna and then of his mother. She had been trying to avoid this. He can see that now in all her warnings. She had known. Was she a prisoner now, along with Nenna and her brother?

'How long have your people been doing this?' he asks.

'Years and years, long before I was born,' he replies quietly, and Camis' lips compress into a thin, tight line.

The mountains are silhouetted against the soft charcoal sky in a pale blue line, heralding a new day. The grass plains whisper softly in the morning breeze. Birds strike up short practice refrains before breaking into a full-throated dawn chorus. Camis' hands and head ache.

'Camis, what happened last night?' Tiberius says from behind him.

Camis shrugs. He doesn't know what to say. He feels his face burn, this time he's the one who has no answer. What had happened? An image of a white flash, stones and earth thudding around him, flicker in his mind. A sharp spasm of pain flashes through his hands, making him jerk the reins. Nutmeg automatically slows.

A cold breeze blows Camis' hair back, cooling his face. Something tugs at his memory, and he turns his head in time to see something brown and furry lying on the rocky ground, partially hidden by the low shrubbery. He walks Nutmeg slowly back towards the shape, dread creeping in his gut. Nenna's dog is lying on his side, looking as though he is peacefully asleep.

For a long while, Camis doesn't move. He sees Nenna and Quarrel racing across the plains, Quarrel's pink tongue flowing out. He sees them sitting side by side on night guard, the flickering fire lighting their backs and silhouetting them against the night sky. He slides down to check Quarrel even though its clear what he will find.

There is no doubt now that Nenna is in danger. Her dog would have given his life to protect her.

Chapter 12

Serin is vaguely aware that she is being moved, but try as she might, she cannot claw her way out from the deep dreamless sleep. All she can do is turn over and nestle deeper into the soft mattress. She gives a long, contented sigh before sinking back down into oblivion.

Waking at last, she sits on the side of the bed and finds herself in yet another cabin. This room is stark white again, but with a desk and chair in muted wood tones as well as a comfortable brown settee. A second door likely leads to a wash and shower space.

She has moved from the mothership back into a shuttle. It is another blow to her heart—confirmation that she really has left Maa Erda and Camis behind. A heavy weight descends onto her shoulders, pushing down into her chest. It is an ache that reaches to her very soul. How in Maa Erda is she going to get back to Camis now?

Marianna looks in quietly and, seeing her awake, crosses over to kneel in front of her and look up into her face.

'I was beginning to worry about you, Your Highness.

'How long?' Serin tries to ask, but it comes out as a croak.

'You were asleep for two whole days. We are approaching home now, and Oasis is already visible on Crystal Moon.' Marianna continues talking while she gets Serin some water. 'We are nearly ready to land. I must report to his Royal Highness and let him know you are awake.'

She walks towards the door. 'I'll come back with some food for you.' Then she is gone.

Serin sits for a short while, trying to gather the strength to walk to the washroom. Her legs feel like they will never support her again, and the thought of food makes her stomach roil. She longs for home and for Camis. Poor Camis.

Please look after him, Anna and Luk.

An image of a man lying injured on the floor flashes in her head. Zachary! Her heart beats faster. Had she truly healed him? Or had it all been a dream? The room starts to spin, and she closes her eyes.

When Marianna returns, she sets a tray on the side table, and Serin can smell the warm yeastiness of fresh bread. Her mouth waters, and she finds herself reaching for the buttered bread, suddenly ravenous. The woman must have run all the way to the staff kitchens, and the thought fills her with gratitude.

'Thank you, Marianna,' she manages to mumble between mouthfuls and is rewarded with a smile that lights up the young woman's face.

After eating the food and drinking some well-watered wine, Serin stands up. She is still a little unsteadily, but feeling stronger, she walks towards the washroom.

'I'll take a shower now,' Serin says, and the young woman gathers the tray to go.

Trying to sound casual, she asks, 'I don't suppose you know how the men are. The ones that were injured in the accident.'

Over the tray, Marianna beams at her. 'They are all well. Two of them returned to their duties yesterday. They were so lucky. What you did was miraculous and—' Marianna stops in mid-sentence, her face turning crimson. 'Oh, my lady, we were told not to talk about it.' She looks stricken.

'Marianna, I'm sure my uncle did not mean we could not talk about it amongst ourselves—amongst the people that were present.' Serin crosses the floor towards the young woman. 'I expect he just wants to make sure that my work is not exaggerated. You know how men brag.'

She stops before Marianna. 'Before you know it, people would be saying that I healed a whole legion of men, all at death's door. Or even worse, that I brought them back from the dead.'

As Serin walks back towards the washroom, her smile, which was meant to reassure Marianna, disappears. Why *did* her uncle want her gifts kept quiet?

The black of space slides past the small window, pinpricked with stars. It is crowded in the cockpit as Serin stands with her uncle behind the seated pilots.

The ship rotates slightly to the left, as a moon swings into sight, gradually looming closer—their objective, Crystal Moon.

Serin never thought she would see it again. It shines bright, deceptively white and clinical, just like the rooms on the ship. But as the craft approaches, refracted colours glimmer and fade across the surface with the changing angle, like circular rainbows. Rainbows mean hope, but she knows there is no hope down there.

To her reckoning, they are at least five days away from Maa Erda, her home, and from her son. Five whole days. It is an effort, but she stands straight, holding herself tightly, keeping emotion in, locking Camis away behind the door in her mind so that her uncle cannot glimpse the truth.

This is how we first saw Crystal Moon, her uncle says, right on cue, as though thinking of him gave him permission to speak inside her head.

He moves to stand closer to her. *An unpeopled space for us on which we could rest and recover from the dreadful virus that had claimed so many lives. Far enough for quarantine, but close enough to a live planet ripe and ready for us, once the virus was no longer a threat.*

A twitch of a smile touches his lips. *That was the original plan, until the full structure of this moon was discovered.* He nods towards the windows where the approaching moon shines innocently in the black.

Finding crystal changed everything. He says so quietly into her mind she is not sure he meant for her to hear it.

I am surprised that you cared so much for the people there that you bothered to isolate, she says through mindspeak, mindful of his request to keep their conversations private.

Taking a deep, slow breath, he uses that tone, the one that seems reserved especially for her.

I would have thought even you could work that out, he says sardonically. *Spreading the virus would not have been in our best interest. There would have been no way to control it. Eventually, it would have reignited somewhere and spread back into our people.* He looks away towards the approaching moon. His mouth is tight.

After a while, he places a hand on her shoulder. She keeps a tight rein on her feelings, tense beneath his touch. *I wanted you to share our approach. To share your homecoming, and to see Crystal Moon in all its splendour before we leave it forever.*

What do you mean? she demands. *Where do you plan to go to?*

But he does not answer. Is he planning to settle on Maa Erda at last? She can't help the sudden stab of fear. It would solve her problem of getting home, but it would put others, especially Camis, in more danger. She sees a twitch of a smile in the corner of his mouth as he stares straight ahead, and a rush of anger fills her as she realises that he has snared her right back into his plans.

The features of the planet become more defined. Colours and shapes coalesce as they glide closer. Buildings, roads, and waterways materialise. Oasis stands out against the uniform whiteness, a multicoloured extravaganza, an exaggeration assaulting the eye.

From their perspective, the splendour of the palace foreshortens into a squatting toad. The green, red, and blue domes of the palace temple twinkle like jewels on its leathery back. In places, there are glimpses of the lake on which Oasis is built, showing between buildings, shining like a mirror.

Her brother will be there, retired and living a quiet life of luxury after the rigours of maintaining the Book for his allotted years. Despite her situation, she finds herself looking forward to seeing him again, having someone to share problems with, someone to talk with.

Their descent slows, and they slide away from the city and across the white expanse towards the safe landing site.

Memories flood and overwhelm her. Suddenly, she is four and swimming in the royal pool, surrounded by splashing, chattering children. Her brother is there, his red hair spiked by the water.

Another image suddenly takes its place. She is thirteen, alone in the pool, her twin already training for the priesthood. Moonlight glitters on the black water. She is proud and happy because she now knows that she has the power to heal. The recollections tumble, crowding her mind—family, friends, parties, ponies, games, glamour . . . laughter. The innocent girl with no clue as to what is to come.

He squeezes her arm, and the images vanish.

Serin, we are here. I will wait while you change, then I will escort you to your horse.

***

Her uncle rides in front of her on a showy black stallion. The horse has been groomed and oiled and gleams in the sunlight. He manages to look arrogant even in the saddle, as though no one in the universe matters but him. He keeps his chin lifted and his eyes fixed ahead.

The city looks the same, but it feels different. Is it only because of the passage of time? People would line the streets as for any royal parade, but this one feels staged. There are cheers but they sound forced. No one is smiling. Everyone is clean, but their clothes look patched and worn. A nasty smell reaches her, and she wrinkles her nose. The streets are clean, but they are tinged with the smell of decay. Strange. There aren't any children. She wonders vaguely where they all are.

101

Her white mare rolls her eyes, snorts, and skips sideways. She squeezes her knees, and the creature calms. Her riding clothes cling—they are already clammy. Sweat beads her face.

An old woman, her mouth collapsing inwards without the support of teeth, spits. The yellowing sputum flies towards her, a malicious missile that falls short, but she is stung inside. The people used to love her and her brother, and though she didn't expect dancing in the streets at her return, she had thought there would have been a warmer welcome.

A guard strikes the old woman with his riding crop. The horses speed up. Their procession passes quickly into wide avenues, where the crowds gradually dwindle, then stop. The company rides through the gates and into the palace grounds.

She feels more alone than ever. Marianna had been left on board the ship. Part of the ship's crew, she was never intended to accompany Serin permanently. Would she still know anyone in the palace?

The guards at the entrance are alert. Some watch their party, but most stare back towards the city, as if expecting a mob to suddenly rise up and storm towards them.

Disquieted and with a nagging pain in the pit of her stomach, Serin grips the reins and rides with muscles clenched, mind numb, heart aching.

They ride through a park, rich and green. The long, straight avenue leading up to the palace clatters with hooves, the creak of leather, and the jingle of harnesses. In the empty park, the palace on the hill shines, its domes fiery in the bright sun. The smaller domes are red, purple, and yellow but the temple dome looms from behind the palace buildings, dwarfing the others, gleaming emerald green.

She swallows a rising bile.

The sun is low in the sky when Serin finally steps out onto the balcony. Her uncle had her escorted straight to her quarters unceremoniously, and though she is glad not to have to make polite conversation with the nobles that live in the palace, she does find it strange that he had missed an opportunity to flaunt his success in getting her back.

She meets her maid—a motherly, grey-haired woman called Onora—who draws her a bath efficiently, leaving her soaps, shampoos, and towels before withdrawing. The woman has kept her gaze downwards, but Serin can feel . . . what? Anger?

Soaking in the bath, she dismisses the maid from her mind, concentrating on finding some sort of plan that will get her back to Maa Erda and Camis. She knows there are sometimes short, one-way windows in the winter months that can be exploited with a shuttle to get back up to the mothership and then down to Maa Erda, but they are few and far between. And dangerous. Something to do with planet angles and distance and their rotation relative to the sun.

Maybe her brother can help, or even Zachary. Zachary. Had he recognised her? Did he even remember her? It was all a long time ago now.

The sun glints on the smaller domes scattered throughout the city. They flash in the lowering sun and bring Serin's mind back to the balcony. From this height, the city beyond is beautiful. Slender walkways span the buildings and weave an intricate web of white stone, raising citizens out of the heat and the water.

Mature trees stand like sentinels in the gardens below, offering shade and shelter. Wild parakeets chatter and call, flitting like jewels through the gardens. The heady perfume of night-scented stock flowers wafts on the air, nearly masking the more subtle scents of jasmine and honeysuckle.

The sun sinks lower, dazzling her, and she blinks against the glare. The scene ripples and wavers, as though seen through rising hot air. Her vision blurs, and she blinks away the tears in her eyes, but that small movement causes the world to spin.

She grips the balustrade, closing her eyes, and swallows down the sour taste in her throat. Looking out, she gasps. The city has vanished.

Blackened, smoking ruins rise in its place. Buildings reduced to rubble, brick and plaster heaped in disarray. Domes split and shattered, laying splintered on the ground like giant mosaic tiles, slowly sinking into black bubbling water.

Pillars slant at dangerous angles or lie cracked and broken. Trees stand jagged below, dead and black. There is no green. The landscape is scorched and the clear water of the underground lake on which Oasis has been built oozes up dark and thick around the chaos. A spiderweb of cracks spread across the once delicate white bridges that span the water.

Her hand flies to her mouth, her legs refuse to hold her up, and she sinks slowly to the floor of the balcony.

Drawing her knees in tightly towards her body, she rests her forehead on them and takes deep, calming breaths. Her shoulders loosen. She looks up towards the safety of her quarters. Lamps glow through the diamond lattice shutters.

Just go in, and don't look back.

She forces herself to stand and look out again. The sun is nearly set. The city once more gleams in its splendour.

She stands for an age, her mind in turmoil. What had just happened?

Tomorrow you will resume your duties.

Her back stiffens as she realises that he has entered unannounced, unheard.

Turning to face him, her hair lifts in the breeze, tendrils fanning outwards, flaming in the setting sun. He is bronzed by the sun's glow—a brittle, vermeil figure. His tongue flicks to wet his lips; they gleam slick.

A gentle yearning softens his expression. He reaches a hand towards her. She shudders and pushes past him quickly to enter her rooms. She pours two drinks from an ornate silver jug. Her hands shake from what she has seen. Should she tell him or will that be another string to tie her to him? She takes a sip from her wine to give herself time to calm and think.

'I will be ready, but in return, I want a day to work in the city,' she says.

That will not be necessary. The people have managed without you and will continue to do so. He follows her across the room.

'I will help everyone'—she pauses and hands him the swirling wine, viscous and bloody, and holds his gaze—'or I will help no one.'

A small red patch forms at the base of his throat. She ignores this warning sign. She will not back down.

His eyes narrow; his lips stretch tight and thin. *You will obey.*

She shakes her head—a tiny, defiant gesture—and keeps her eyes firmly on his. She stops his hand as it flies towards her face just as Onora enters. His eyes flick towards the servant and back. He drops his hand but holds her stare.

'Everyone or no one,' she repeats.

The mark at his throat deepens to a murderous hue, but his face is blank, unreadable. Abruptly, he turns and stalks out.

Sinking down onto her bed, Serin tries to stem the fit of trembling that shakes her body. Onora crosses to her, rescuing the wineglass from her hand, and kneels at her feet, concern etched on her face. Gently, she rubs Serin's hands until they stop shaking.

At dawn, Serin joins the barefoot procession through the palace. Women, white-clad, walk in single file, each holding a tiny glowing crystal in their outstretched hands. They pass down the steps towards the temple and through those great doors in silence.

A heady, flowery perfume hits Serin as she crosses the threshold. There are massive lemon trees sitting in enormous black pots. They line the inner temple, sitting two to each side of the fluted pristine-white pillars. Each tree bears green-and-yellow fruit, hanging like tear drops.

But it is the flowers that dominate, their fragrance filling the air with an aroma so thick that Serin feels she should be able to push it aside like a curtain. The tiny, waxy pale pink-and-white flowers belie the sheer intensity of the odour that they produce, so strong that it can be tasted.

Heads bowed, eyes downcast, the women gather in the central atrium. Around a raised dais, as one, they look up.

Serin gasps and the scent of flowers is forgotten. For the briefest moment, the words of the Book falter.

Horror washes over her. He shouldn't be here.

Her eyes sting. Her brother is so thin. How is the city surviving?

A naked figure sits cross-legged atop the circular platform, running his fingers across a huge blank book that rests across his legs. His skin crawls, writhing in text, every inch of his body covered in a living black calligraphy, from the soles of his feet to the top of his bald head. It rolls across his torso, down his limbs, and vanishes.

Tomatoes, barley, peas, beans, yams, oranges, lemons, limes—an endless list of words flow down one arm, scrolling around him before disappearing, while spice and herbs march down the other—***chicory, sage, turmeric, pepper.***

She is momentarily mesmerised by the ceaseless flow. How these words manifest themselves into the food in the biodomes that feed the city, she has no idea, but she does know that if the words stop—or if he stops—the city will die of starvation. In fact, the whole city— buildings, pathways, bridges, *everything*—that has been created and maintained by the crystal, will be destroyed. Stop the Book, and the city will collapse.

His mouth moves ceaselessly, keeping the sacred text alive. She never thought . . . There is a silence, fidgeting. They are waiting—waiting for her.

Taking a deep breath, she sings a cascading note, rich and pure, surprised to hear that it does not waver. Another voice joins hers, then another, until the whole circle is singing in unison.

The figure and the Book on his lap glow. The music reaches a crescendo, harmonious, haunting. One by one, the singers step out of the circle to reach up and drop their crystal onto the huge blank Book, and it glows brighter. Then they return to their place in the circle and their voices fade out, until only her refrain remains.

She lets the music die, ending the Song of the Dawn. The Book, and in turn the city, is replenished.

The lists roll on, written large across his chest, the words seem darker, harder.

Bread, water, wine.

She drops her eyes, unable to bear his pain any longer.

The Book—that centuries old tradition, bought with them from their home planet with its ancient rituals and harsh training, repaid with honours, riches, and gratitude from those who recognise the sacrifice.

How is it that he is still here? Still serving as the Book? Still supporting the city and feeding the people? He should have retired years ago. Others should have been trained to take his place. Was there no one else capable or has her uncle kept . . . ? She lets the thought trail away. Surely not even he could be so cruel.

Lowering their heads, the women file out behind her, their feet shuffling a whisper on the marble. As she steals a glance, her heart lurches and her chest aches.

Brother, I am so sorry.

But there is no reply. The huge doors swing shut behind her, locking him away.

Watching the women walk away, she stands alone. Why hadn't she felt him when she returned? Why hadn't he reached out to her?

In the vast temple hall, cold and hollow, its beauty lost to her, the long-buried pain trickles down her cheeks. The carved leaves on the arching vaults overhead are still, solid, unmoved by the passage of time or her tears.

Chapter 13

Gradually the ground rises more steeply, becoming increasingly rockier. Camis slows Nutmeg to a fast walk. His teeth grind together, but he dares not risk the animal breaking a leg on the increasingly stony terrain. Even with both him and Tiberius riding, Nutmeg shows no sign of tiring.

The pale early-autumn sun has arced halfway to its peak before Tiberius calls out, 'Camis, stop! Leave the horse here. I think we are close.'

They dismount and clamber over some rocks. There is a small, rocky outcrop ahead of them, and Tiberius signals for Camis to drop low. A light breeze cools their faces, bringing with it a late-summer dust. They creep up over the ridged black rock, lying on their bellies to peer down onto a small valley.

Camis' breath catches in his throat. A huge black shape squats on the rocks below, stretching twenty or more cart-lengths and maybe half as many tall. It glitters in the early morning sun, reflecting the sky, clouds scudding across its surface, mirroring those above. The top is nearly level with their outcrop. It tapers slightly at one end and is bulbous at the other.

Sweat erupts on his forehead. His mouth hangs open. What in Maa Erda's name is that?

What— he starts to say, but Tiberius catches his arm, eyes wide with horror. He presses his fingers to his lips and shakes his head.

Camis chokes off his question as Tiberius wriggles forward and gestures for Camis to look over the edge. Whatever he wants Camis to see is directly below them.

Camis pulls himself further forward, the sharp ridges of the rock cutting uncomfortably into his chest. Keeping a wary eye on the black monster and another on Tiberius, Camis leans out over the edge. He stifles a gasp.

There are people sitting in a line on the rocks below. Their hands are bound behind them, and they are gagged. A guard wearing the same stark black as Tiberius stands over them, a triangular red neckerchief knotted loosely on his chest. He is holding a long, thin metal stick, which glints as the sun clears the rocks behind them.

A faint hum catches Camis' attention as a silver disc glides around the huge black structure, like a strange, flying plate. It moves towards the prisoners.

He shrinks tighter to the rock and feels the ground vibrate under him. Fleetingly, Camis smells quenched metal, and a thought slides in and out of his mind before he can catch it. Sniffing the air, he frowns, trying to remember, and breathes in, trying to capture the thought again, but the smell—no, the echo of the smell—eludes him. The breeze has died, and with it, the smell and the memory.

The thing hovers low. Abruptly, it spits out a body before drifting away silently. The rock under Camis continues to vibrate until the thing is out of sight.

He looks back at the body, which is now wriggling to sit up, hampered by bindings. One of the earlier prisoners twists around and tries shuffling across to the new person. The movement catches his eye. His mouth dries. It's her. She's here. Nenna is here.

Nenna, sit still! I'll try to find a way to release you!

Down below, he sees her turn wildly, looking left then right.

Stay still! You'll be noticed! But it is too late. The guard turns and stalks towards her.

'Oi, you! No moving!' the guard shouts and shakes the metal rod he is holding.

Camis holds his breath, willing her to calm, but Nenna gets to her knees. The guard reaches forward and taps her lightly with the stick. She stiffens. Her limbs jerk strangely as they are held in place by the bonds. She looks like a puppet just before the strings are cut, then she falls limply on to her side, eyes rolling upward, and lies still.

Camis doesn't remember standing up, but suddenly, he is.

They've got her! She's here! They've injured her and it's my fault.

Tiberius frantically tugs at his arm, dragging him back out of sight of the guard below.

'Be quiet!' Tiberius whispers, his eyes wide with fear. 'You mustn't use mindspeak!'

'I've got to help her,' he hisses directly to Tiberius.

'Yes, but don't use mindspeak.' He holds onto Camis' arm. 'She is too close to the guard, and I've heard that there are some people able to eavesdrop. He could hear you.' They stand together, glaring angrily at each other, but the young man holds his place.

Suddenly, Camis relaxes and indicates with his head for them both to move further back. He needs answers. As they step apart, a thought occurs to him. Camis looks at Tiberius.

'You didn't call out.'

'Of course I didn't call out. I said I would help you. The crystal only knows if someone from the ship would ever have found me if you hadn't.'

'So how do we get her back?'

The rock floor begins to vibrate again, and they both move towards the ledge, but before they reach it, Camis catches Tiberius's arm and holds him back.

'What in Maa Erda's name is that huge, black structure?' he whispers.

'That is our ship,' Tiberius states. 'That is how we flew here.'

Camis stares at him open mouthed, and shakes his head, but no words come. How could something that big fly?

They watch from their hiding place on the ledge. The strange silver plate has returned and is hovering in the air. Another person is deposited on to the ground.

Nenna is lying where the guard left her, she doesn't move, but he can see her chest rising and falling. He sighs in relief and relaxes a little.

The silver craft doesn't fly away but glides a short distance and settles on the ground. A tall, wiry man with greying hair steps out and looks towards the guard. No one speaks, but Camis can hear a distant whispering. It seems to be coming from inside his head. Mindspeak! He can hear mindspeak.

He locks onto the face of the guard facing him and concentrates.

Just a couple more, and we'll have our quota.

Yes, sir.

We'll be back by dusk. There will be no more hunting after that. Once the hovs are stowed and the pre-flight checks are complete, the captain says we leave.

Yes, sir.

Any news of Kestell's craft?

No, sir.

The tall man rolls his shoulders back and stretches, rotating his head and neck before returning inside. The silver plate rises off the ground and moves away. The guard relaxes, leaning back against the side of what Tiberius calls a 'ship', and closes his eyes. He clearly does not expect any trouble from the prisoners.

Sliding away from the edge, Camis sits back on his heels. What to do? Tiberius shuffles back to join him.

'They are leaving once they get two more. There must be something we can do,' Camis whispers.

'How do you know that?'

'I listened to the guard's conversation,' Camis states but moves back as he hears the whispering murmur start again. Tiberius is now staring at him with his mouth open.

A hole has opened in the side of the huge ship, sliding upwards, and a new guard appears, stocky and balding..

You washed out those pens then, Rik?

Yeah.

Well, don't rush to load them. He gestures to the sky. *Looks mild enough. Leave them out until the last minute. Enough stench on the journey, eh?*

Shall I feed them?

No. Don't worry, they'll be alright until they are released in the pens.

The first guard disappears into the interior, leaving the bald man on duty. The guard looks over the group sprawling across the rocks. He shakes his head, and Camis hears him mutter, 'You poor bloody animals.'

'I have an idea,' Camis says, returning to Nutmeg and retrieving the packs. He searches through them for the last of the food.

Camis and Tiberius sit on a boulder, chewing the tough dried meat. It has no smell and no real taste, but it stops his stomach turning somersaults. 'Can you rush down, yelling and distraught? Tell the guard what happened and convince him that you are hurt and need help. When he takes you in, I can rush up and get to Nenna.'

Tiberius nods his head thoughtfully, and they chew until the shreds of meat are gone.

Creeping quietly to the top of the ridge, Tiberius tenses, ready to play his part, but as they peer over the edge, there is already a raggedy line of prisoners on their feet, entering the strange ship. They must have already reached their quota!

Camis cannot see Nenna among the few remaining prisoners.

'Quickly! Move! Come on, we haven't got all day,' a guard bellows and prods at the line, roughly pushing at each one of the prisoners as they baulk at passing through the black opening. The last of the prisoners disappear inside.

A second guard comes out, and the two of them walk in opposite directions around the ship, checking the ground. They meet up back in front of the door.

Camis hears, *Well, that's all clear then.*

Yep. The new orders say to give them another span, then we're off. Poor sod. His first trip, and stuck on this dump.

Yeah. The guard sighs, looking around. *Let's hope it's not worse than that though.*

The two guards disappear into the ship.

Pig's turds! They're leaving! Camis looks at Tiberius.

'They've taken her in, and they say they are leaving in a span, whatever that is,' he whispers urgently and sees Tiberius's shocked expression.

'There is only one way I can think of that will get you inside and give us any hope of getting her away.'

'What's that?'

'You will have to trust me. You are going to have to be my prisoner.'

***

Ahoy, on board!

By the crystal, you're back at last! A bald, stocky man comes to the opening, and Camis recognises one of the guards. *Get in and get that one down to the pens. Where's Kestell and why's the hov not in the docking bay?*

The guard peers around behind them, hitching his black trousers up over his ample gut.

Kestell is . . . Tiberius looks down briefly, then takes a deep breath and continues. *He crashed the hov while I was out chasing this one.* He pokes Camis in the back. *He was having some sport, stupid imbecile, diving at one some strange, black creature.* He pauses, his voice breaking before continuing. *Kestell died; I couldn't save him. I had to walk back. Nearly thought I wouldn't make it in time and would be stuck here all winter.*

Crystal!

I'll just get this one down, and I'll be up to make a full report.

We don't have time to pick up the body, the guard calls out to them as they try to walk calmly away down the interior passageway.

There's nothing left to pick up. Whole thing exploded and burnt to ash.

113

Pushed roughly forward, Camis stumbles into the ship's interior. Luckily, the guard didn't question the lack of a gag. A door slides shut behind them, blocking the guard from view and any form of escape.

Camis fights down an urge to run. Tiberius lets out a rush of breath and leans heavily on the wall.

'Camis, there is no time left. Even if we could get down to the holding pens and find your Nenna, we won't have time.'

'Then I'll just have to come with you until you can find a way to get us back.'

'It's worse than that. This is the last shuttle of the season. We won't come back this way for nearly another year.'

'Fifteen moon cycles! How . . . ? Where . . . ?' His head pounds and his hands ache, but they are tied tightly behind him. He starts to sink to the floor.

'No! Don't sit down! Someone may come. They will have logged the time I arrived. If they come looking . . . You will just have to go down until I can find another way to get you out. There are people at home who might keep you both safe.'

A door slides open in the distance, and Tiberius steps away from him.

'Get a move on, you dog,' he says loudly and prods Camis back into motion.

They reach the wall at the end of the corridor. It seems like a dead end, but Tiberius reaches out and taps the wall with his fingertips. The wall slides open, revealing a stairwell. Camis goes to climb.

'No,' Tiberius says, pointing. 'We go down.'

The flight of steps leads to a short landing that twists back on itself and descends further. At the bottom, they meet another guard about to climb up. Dressed in a black uniform, he is tall, sinewy, with his dark hair swept back and tied at the nape of his neck.

He ignores Camis and looks directly at Tiberius. *Well done, Tiberius. This puts us over our quota.*

He puts out an arm to stop Camis from continuing. 'Wait!' he barks without looking at him. His long bony face is drawn back into a haughty sneer, as though a bad smell has just wafted past.

I'll take it from here. You go and get changed and have some well-deserved rest. He indicates with a silver stick for Camis to continue. Camis keeps his eyes forward, his face impassive, his heart thudding loudly in his chest. As he walks forward, he hears Tiberius re-climb the stairs.

Cadarch! the new guard calls out to Tiberius. *Why are you on your own? Where is your Archarya?*

My mentor died out on the planet, sir. There was an accident.

The guard takes a sharp intake of breath. *The Crystal protect us.*

Aye, sir. The crystal protect us.

'Get on, you prim scum,' the guard says, shoving Camis roughly forward. The stick digs sharply into his back, causing him to stumble.

They walk along a curving slope, down into the bowels of the ship. A door in the wall slides open at a tap from the guard. It lights up a large, cavernous space. Cages line the walls—cages full of people. Their faces are pale, petrified. They shrink back as the guard approaches.

Camis scours the cages in a desperate hope of seeing his mother or Nenna among the captives. No one looks familiar. In the last cage on the left, a small, slight figure darts forward,

'Camis!' two voices call out, and there is Nenna. But beside her is Ash.

No! Not Ash as well! His baby—oh, Maa Erda, his new baby. Camis' heart aches at the thought.

Nenna has a large purple bruise on her left cheek. The swelling nearly closes her eye. Blood has trickled down to dry on her chin. Her hair is wild and matted, and her clothes are muddy.

Ash looks worse. His nose is clearly broken, and the way he holds his arms carefully around himself and stoops forward indicates that he may have broken some ribs. Forgetting the guard, Camis darts forward, pleased to see them both alive if not completely well.

'Oi!' the man shouts, slamming the metal stick abruptly across Camis' chest, stopping him. 'No, you don't.'

The guard peers around at the cages on each side then. Sighing, he presses his hand to a small flat plate fixed to the metal bars of Nenna's cage. 'Well, lucky for you, the rest seem full, so you might as well join your girlfriend.' And he grins at Camis, a nasty sneering grin with no humour in it, only malice.

But Camis pays him no mind, and before the guard has a chance to shove or push him, he slips into the cage as the bars slide open. As he reaches Nenna, he instinctively reaches out a hand to touch the bruise on her cheek, but she steps back away from him. The cage bars slam shut.

'So they got you too,' she says. Her voice is flat and more than a little cold.

'Well, er, no. I mean—that is . . . ' he stammers.

The light goes out as the far door closes behind the exiting guard, but they are not in darkness as the area is lit with an eerie orange glow, which darkens the bruise on Nenna's face, turning it black. Her eyes glitter in the light.

'What do you mean, no? You are here,' she snaps. 'I thought you had brought at least half the village hunters with you the way you shouted to me out there. But instead, nothing. And now you're here. A prisoner like the rest of us.'

Ash places a hand on her arm, and she glares at him, then stomps to the back of the cell, facing away from them.

Camis stares after her, a small maggot of a thought eating away in his mind. Maybe, just maybe, this wasn't such a good idea after all.

'Camis?' The glow of the strange lighting casts deep shadows under Ash's eyes, making him appear four times his age. He winces with the effort of speaking. 'What happened? I thought you were free. Nenna thought you would be able to help us.'

'There was no time. They started loading you, and I needed to find out where they were taking you. A . . . a friend helped me to get on board this ship. He has promised to come and release us as soon as he can. He knows people who will hide us until we can get back.'

'Ship?' Ash says, confused.

'Yes. This is some kind of ship. I watched for a while and was just making a plan when they started taking everyone in. Ash?' Camis says frowning. 'I didn't see you with the prisoners.'

Ash smiles grimly, revealing a missing top tooth.

'The man who caught me needed treatment, so they threw me straight in here.' He pauses and looks back at the others. 'But it is worse than that Camis. They also caught Kitt.' He points to a figure lying at the back of the cage. 'I think they broke his leg, but it seems like it is more than that.'

A woman kneels by a man lying on the floor. In her middle years, she looks kind, with laughter creases around her eyes, but she is not smiling now.

'There isn't anything any of us can do for him,' she states. Her long brown hair falls forward as she looks down at Kitt. Another man stands nearby, his expression forlorn, lost. Kitt's features are cast in deep shadows. He looks gaunt, his large nose emphasised by the strange spectral light. His eyes are closed, his breathing rapid and shallow.

'Your friend?' the woman asks, looking up at them with sadness. Camis nods and drops down beside Kitt, touching the injured man's chest.

'He has a head injury. I'll see what I can do,' he says and moves a hand to Kitt's head. He focuses his attention on drawing out the fluid, passing it into blood vessels and reducing the swelling that has gathered in the man's skull. Then Camis checks on the break in Kitt's leg. It is only a crack that will be easily fixed. Kitt's breathing slows and deepens.

'He will be fine now,' Camis states, 'but will need water when he wakes. Does anyone have any? Is there any in this prison?'

He looks up at the group surrounding him. There is surprise and disbelief on their faces. The woman on the floor feels for Kitt's pulse and holds the back of her hand to his forehead.

'If I didn't know any better, I'd say he was sleeping,' she says to the group.

Everyone stares at Camis, their eyes wide, and more than one mouth gapes. There's no hiding his gift now.

Embarrassed, Camis stands up and gestures for Ash to join him. 'I didn't get a chance to explain,' he says quietly. 'We won't be going home anytime soon.'

'What?' Nenna has moved to stand behind him, her voice sharp enough to skin the hide off a cow. 'How do you know? Was that another of your—' She is interrupted as a deep thrumming vibrates through the floor of the ship and the room begins to tilt.

Around him, people grasp each other and cry out. A loud whine fills the air, reverberating off the walls and into his skull. An unseen weight pushes them all down and begins to build. Camis' legs buckle under the strain and give way.

All around them the people in the cages, fall to their knees. Lights flicker. As Camis crashes to the floor, he sees Nenna go down on the floor too, her hands pressed tight to her ears, her eyes wide and black. Her mouth is open wide in a scream, but he cannot hear her as the whine intensifies.

The pressure increases, forcing him flat. Then without any warning, the weight lifts, and for an instant, Camis feels light, lighter than a feather, and begins to lift off the floor. Others are flailing as they rise, arms and legs windmilling in the air. A sudden force drops them all like falling stones. Camis slams into the deck, winded, sucking vainly, desperate for air. Then, as air rushes in, he is abruptly sick.

Chapter 14

An age. An age of torment. Tiberius promised. He promised he would be back. What is going on?

Camis looks around in the dim, red light at the others, all sleeping, packed tight together against the back wall of the cell. Excrement is piled in another corner, festering, disgusting. The stench of unwashed bodies and human waste permeates his every breath. He can sense the underlying anger, overlaid with fear, which thickens the stagnant air.

He bites his bottom lip until he feels the skin start to break, the pain a welcome relief from what is happening around him. He breathes in deeply and slowly, trying vainly to calm his panic.

His dreams are full of darkness. He has never been indoors for so long, and he longs for the sun on his face, the rain on his skin, and the freedom to run. He could scream with frustration.

His arm has gone to sleep, and he carefully rubs the top of it, the only bit he can reach without disturbing Nenna. She leans against him, fast asleep, and strangely, he is flattered. Though her tongue can flay a pig, he still finds himself drawn to her.

He looks at her, her long, dark lashes and full mouth. His head slowly drops towards hers, his lips parting. Nenna's head lolls forward, breaking his trance.

What on Maa Erda was he thinking? He pulls her gently back against him, careful not to wake her.

Glancing around at the small cages nearby, he can just make out the huddle of people slumped in each one, like human flotsam washed up with the tide. All in the same fitful stupor, penned like animals. He wishes that he could help them but most are out of his physical reach. At least it is quiet now. The women weeping in the far cages had nearly broken him. His hands ache, but he doesn't know if it is from all the healing he has done recently or in sympathy with everyone's pain.

White light floods the area, blinding those who are already awake, waking the others. Food has arrived.

Two guards enter carrying trays, each stacked with bowls that steam lightly. The bowls are pushed through a slot cut in the bars at the base of each cage, and at a nod from one of the guards, one person in each of the cells steps forward to retrieve them and pass them back to the others.

Ash collects the bowls this time. Camis takes his and gulps down the contents greedily. There are no utensils, and the food is the same each time—a watery grey-green soup lacking both flavour and quantity. At first, plenty of it had been poured away, but now, nothing is ever left. His stomach growls.

Water is dispensed for a short period after each of the two feeding sessions. They fill their bowls in turn from the metal spout that dispenses a trickle into each cell and drink to try and fill the hole in their bellies.

Nenna struggles to her feet and shuffles across to collect a second bowl of water. She crosses to the open latrine and sluices it down. Others follow her example, and the stench dampens a little. The faeces and urine are gradually washed out and into the centre area, where a guard quickly hoses the mess down towards a metal grid in the floor. Camis watches. The man's face screws up in revulsion as he clears their waste.

'Filthy creatures,' he mutters, and people look down or away.

An older woman called Wynn sits at the front of the cage next door, heedless of the soaking floor. She reminds Camis of Martha, her greying hair tied in an untidy bun.

'Why? Why?' she starts to sob as she rocks herself.

A younger man called Herb kneels beside her his face lined with concern.

'Shh, Mother,' he says as he pats her shoulder.

'Shut up!' the guard snaps, and he swiftly crosses to the pen to jab at Wynn with the stun stick. Camis hears a crackle, and he can see that the young man has caught hold of the stick. Wynne cries out as the young man convulses and collapses.

'Pah!' the guard exclaims. 'You were lucky.'

He spits at Wynn and turns away to resume his sweeping. He doesn't see Camis step across his cage towards him, his fists clenched.

Nenna quickly blocks his path. 'Look at me,' she says softly, gripping his wrists. 'Don't be pig-headed. Don't engage. We need you.'

He looks down at his hands clenched tight into fists and bites on his lower lip hard to stop himself from doing something foolish. He wrenches his hands free and stalks away. She's right, but it doesn't make it any easier.

Once the guards have left and the lights dim to their usual eerie-red glow, Camis crosses over to Wynn who is cradling her son's head. She is crying silently now, mouthing 'I'm sorry' over and over.

Camis crouches down. How many more must he heal? He reaches out through the bars and touches the side of the young man's head. He pulls the now familiar charge of pain from Herb's body to his own.

Stiffly, Camis stands and crosses his arms over the front of his body, pressing his hands into his armpits. The energy makes him spasm, but he grits his teeth and forces the pain down to the soles of his feet, discharging it into the floor. When he stops shaking, he sees Wynn and her son looking at him.

'Thank you,' Wynn says sadly. 'I'm sorry. I just couldn't . . . ' Strands of grey hair straggle across her lined face. She brushes them back, revealing soft dark eyes. She should be sitting out in the sun, watching her grandchildren play. Why hadn't they left her in peace? What did they need this old woman for?

'It's all right,' he says.

Camis drops his gaze; his arms fall heavily at his sides as he turns back to the bare sleeping corner and crouches down. He scrubs a hand across his forehead.

Squeezing his eyes shut, he shudders. These people think he has a plan, a way to get them out, and he lets them believe it. Why had he come on board? Why hadn't he just gone to the village for help? Thoughts and questions swirl around and around not letting him rest.

'What about your friend?' Nenna whispers, crouching down beside him. 'Do you think he'll come?'

'I think so. I hope so.' Camis rubs his hands together, trying to hide the guilt he feels. His hands do not ache any more than usual, but the action is a vain attempt to distract himself and to draw Nenna's questions away from his growing concern regarding Tiberius.

'Here, let me.' And Nenna takes one of his hands and tenderly massages it. Her hands are small and cool against his. He resists the urge to pull away as his ears slowly heat up. He is glad the orange glow hides his discomfort. Gradually, the pain recedes, and his long fingers uncurl, leaving his hand tingling.

A shaft of light breaks the dim glow. Everyone looks towards the door, tense and silent. As the door closes, the chamber floods with white light. A young man steps forward hesitantly, twisting his head left and right, searching. *Camis? Where are you?*

'Here!' Camis rushes to the front of his cage and gestures through the bars so Tiberius can locate him. 'What took you so long?'

I'm sorry, Tiberius says as he stands in front of him, looking around nervously. *Camis, use mindspeak.*

'Why?' Camis says suspiciously.

I don't want everyone to hear. I can't help all these people. Only you and your friend.

Won't we be overheard? Camis says, glancing at the door and switching to mindspeak, not because he doesn't want to help everyone, but because Tiberius looks as though he might bolt at any moment.

No, no one will hear us here. This area is sealed. No one will come now until your next meal.

Camis narrows his eyes. *Meal! That stuff isn't food! I wouldn't give it to pigs.* Tiberius looks ashamed, his face colouring, and he glances away briefly.

Listen, he says. *Soon there will be a lot of noise and movement as they start processing. We need to get you out before then.*

Processing?

Yes, it's when—

'Camis, what's going on? Is this the friend you spoke about?' Camis turns his head to see Nenna standing beside him, looking at Tiberius.

'Yes, Nenna, this is Tiberius.'

'Ah, so this is, Nenna.' Tiberius puts his hand through the bars of the cage. Nenna ignores him.

'What's going on. Why are the two of you just staring at each other? Why isn't he unlocking the cages and getting us out of here?'

Camis turns back towards Tiberius. Others have gathered closer to listen. Tiberius still has his hand out. He hasn't taken his eyes off Nenna.

'Look, it's hard to explain, but he is talking to me,' Camis says. 'Trust me. Just wait.'

So what is the plan?

Tiberius looks at Camis and starts to withdraw his hand, but Ash catches hold of it and pulls Tiberius tight against the bars.

'Ash, no! He's come to help.'

'You don't think we're going to trust the likes of him, do you, lad?'

'Let him go. I promise you he is helping.'

'What? Like he has so far? No, Camis you listen'—and he pulls Tiberius towards the bars, twisting his arm, making him grunt in pain—'we can use him to make them let us go.'

Kitt steps forward, reaches through the bars, and clamps Tiberius around the neck. The muscles in Kitt's arm bunch. Tiberius gives a strangled cry.

This man helped me get on board! Camis cries in mindspeak. *I came in of my own free will to find Nenna and pretended to be his prisoner.*

Both men swivel their heads towards Camis, their eyes wide in surprise.

I can communicate with him in this way, Camis continues, *which is why you don't hear anything. We need him. They will never release us in exchange for him. They will just kill him, and then we will all be punished.*

'But why would he help you?' Kitt asks.

Because I saved his life. Ash and Kitt exchange glances. *And I trust him.*

'What is going on?' Nenna snaps, looking from Camis to Tiberius and then to the men holding him.

At first no one moves, then abruptly, Ash and Kitt drop their holds. Tiberius steps back, rubbing his arm, his eyes narrow as he glares at the men in the cage. Then he storms away.

'Will someone tell me what's going on?' Nenna askes again, looking towards Ash and Kitt.

'Camis spoke into my head. He says he pretended to be a prisoner and that this young man helped to get him on board,' Kitt explains quietly. Nenna's eyes flash in anger.

'He did what? Of all the stupid—'

As she swings around to face Camis, Kitt cuts her short. 'To come on board to save you,' he says, and Nenna stands with her mouth open, the words frozen on her lips.

Tiberius! Camis calls after the man, clutching at the cage bars, but Tiberius swiftly exits the chamber, taking the light and their hope with him.

After the next meal, the guards leave early, and shortly after, the floor begins to tilt again. This time, everyone rushes to hold onto the cage bars. Nenna grasps the ones next to Camis. A few are not so lucky, and he hears their curses as they collide.

The tilt slowly reverses and becomes level again. Some have already let go when the tilt shifts the opposite way, and they slip and slide across the wet, squalid cells, sliding through waste matter and tangling together before they can grasp for the bars. The chamber groans like a cart coming slowly apart. The floor levels off again, vibrating with the faint hum that he had first noticed when entering the ship.

People moan and rub their limbs, shaking their heads, thinking the worst is over. The hum becomes a loud whine, which gradually builds to an intense pitch, increasing beyond endurance. Camis clamps his hands over his ears. It is the end of the world.

'Make it stop,' he sees Nenna mouth in a scream, clutching her ears. Ash and Kitt are down on the floor, their arms over their heads.

Suddenly, the sound ceases, replaced by a metallic boom that shudders through the chamber, thundering like a thousand metal pails being banged together. It echoes around and around and through them. As it fades, Camis lowers his hands. He can see people crying, but he can't hear anything. Then his ears pop and sound rushes in, magnified, painful.

In each cage, prisoners sit shivering in a huddle, battered and bruised. They listen to the strange ticks and creaks coming from the walls and floor, like a house settling for the night, only louder.

The evening meal arrives. No one is hungry.

Nenna settles down beside Camis, the bruise on her cheek is fading. Both are wrapped up in their own thoughts, and Camis is grateful that she doesn't start on again about his fool idea to let himself be taken prisoner. Perhaps he shouldn't have trusted anyone.

'Will he come back?' Nenna's question echoes his own thoughts.

'I don't know.' He looks at Kitt and the man looks away. 'I hope so.'

In the time between one meal and the next—a time that might be the afternoon—two soldiers arrive. They unlock the cage opposite Camis, gesturing to one of the women inside. She looks to be about twenty-nine or thirty summers, slim and strong. Her long, dark hair is loose and matted, her eyes unnaturally wide. He can see her start to shake.

'You! Out!' the guard shouts.

The woman backs away, her face grey, etched in fear. They all watch, still and silent. What now?

One of the guards enters the cage.

'Do you really want me to use this?' he says, brandishing the stun stick and goes to grab her arm, but one of the men in the cage steps forward. He is taller than the guard, muscular and hard, and looks down at the slender man in his all-black uniform.

'What do you want with her?' he asks, but the guard doesn't even answer him. In a quick, almost dismissive gesture, he jabs the man with the stun stick and steps away from him as he drops to the floor, his limbs stiff and twitching.

Ignoring the man as he convulses on the floor, the guard signals again for the woman to exit. Tears start to run down her face, but she goes with guard without a protest. Others in the cage gently reach out and touch her as she passes.

The next day, after their first meal, the doors slide open, and the guards come to their cage. Wynn is selected this time. The guards separate Wynn from her son, threatening them both with their stun sticks. When she cries out and refuses to go, she is treated to a jab and dragged away, hanging limply between them. The anguish and helplessness in Herb's eyes tears Camis' heart out, and he can feel his temper rising as he balls his fists.

Nenna touches his arm lightly but doesn't speak. She gives a slight shake of her head. She's right. Don't draw attention. His shoulders sag.

Makes the processing easier this way, one guard says to the other.

Camis crosses swiftly to the bars at the front of the cage and grips them tightly, watching their backs as they take Wynn away. Luckily, the guards are too busy to notice him.

'What is it?' Nenna asks.

'Something Tiberius said. Something about . . . '

'What?'

'Processing. I'm not sure what it is, but I don't think it's good.' Camis starts to pace the small cell, rubbing the back of his neck.

'Processing?' Nenna asks, frowning.

'It's what I heard one of the guards say to the other just now in mindspeak.' He replies without turning.

Two more guards enter, and they walk towards their cage, looking straight at Camis, and one waves his stun stick.

'You! Out!'

Nenna steps between them.

'No! No, not him,' she says and is swiftly rewarded with a tap from the stick, just as Camis reaches out to her. At the same time, the other guard jabs him in the arm. Two jolts of pain shock through him from opposite directions. He doesn't see Nenna fall to the ground as blackness descends.

Nenna lies on the floor, her limbs twitching. Every particle of her body aches. Even her hair seems to hurt. And the worst thing about it is that Camis is no longer there to help.

Nenna wishes Kitt had twisted that Tiberius's neck until it had cracked. But those fool men had let him go, told her Camis had spoken to them, into their minds, he had said Tiberius was going to help them.

Maa Erda, the whole world has gone mad.

She squeezes her eyes tighter. She will not cry. She will use her anger to get her through. And she will not believe they are on some sort of 'ship' either, despite the screeching and the movement of the floor. The bloody ocean is days away! They might have fooled the men here, but she was going to stay sane and get them all out of this prison somehow.

She groans softly as some of the pain recedes, and her body begins to respond to her requests for movement.

She's still angry at Camis. Fancy walking into this, fool boy. He could have done so much more had he gone for help. And now they'd taken him. Taken him for this processing thing that he seemed so anxious about. And there was absolutely nothing she could have done to save him.

Her shoulders slump, and her head droops forward, away from the bars she is propped against. A wave of despair washes over her.

Just as she is thinking that it couldn't get any worse, the light snaps on. People around her stir and moan softly. The brisk, booted footsteps of two soldiers echo through the prison as Nenna rouses herself to stand along with those left in their cage. Others slowly climb to their feet, faces pale and fearful. An ice-cold stone sits in the pit of her stomach. This cannot be good.

Two soldiers escort a third person purposefully towards her. Her heart leaps. Are they bringing Camis back? The two at the front stop just short of the cage and stand aside to let a man behind pass between them.

'Hello, primmy,' he says. She recognises him immediately—handsome-man, the one called Vitrainy who ordered Quarrel thrown from their flying machine.

He looks straight towards her, his lips curling in that leering smile of his. She bares her teeth back at him, all tiredness forgotten.

He leans forward with an excited breath.

'Still a feisty little thing, I see,' he says. 'I'll soon break you of that.'

128

Chapter 15

A needle of anger drives Serin through the palace corridors towards her uncle's offices. How could he? The depth of his cruelty is shocking—a lifetime of torture. Her beautiful brother—that once long-legged, slender adolescent—made to suffer for so long. Made to serve as the Book for over fifteen years. It was unthinkable.

Her nose and eyes sting with tears for his pain. How has he survived for this long? His body must be held together with dried and withered sinew. Her brother had known the risks— but this! Myriad had always wanted this position—or had thought he did. She wondered now how much influence her uncle had in Myriad's choices.

The Book was the ultimate position to hold within the priesthood. The position came with much prestige and power, and after five years of service, a replacement would take over. The promised retirement held everything one could wish for. It was this Myriad had told her that he wanted.

It was a huge honour to be selected as the Book, using the crystal's power to create everything their people could ever need. But acting as a conduit for such a force required a strength and control that few possessed, and luckily—or unluckily, Serin thought—Myriad had the gift and the control.

'Then we'll be safe, Serin. Just the two of us, away from him. Living how we want, free to love who we want.'

Serin had nodded up at him but kept the disquiet she felt to herself. Even then she knew in her heart that their uncle wouldn't let either of them go that easily.

However, Serin had thought Myriad was safely retired. Why hadn't he contacted her as soon as they had landed? He would have been aware of her. But she knew the answer. Her uncle had forbidden it.

The last time they had been together, Myriad had begged her to stay. He was close to finishing his training and would soon rise to sit as the Book. The youngest and most powerful conduit ever to rise to such a position. He would be responsible for holding the city structure together, for growing food in the biodomes that fed the city, and for channelling the power of the mined crystals into light and cooling for their homes.

They had clutched each other, whispering as they snuck through the empty corridors, the red moon lighting their way and casting its cardinal glow. They had to find a safe place, away from their uncle's ears, the man who had controlled them since their parents had died. He was supposed to advise and guide them until one of them was ready to succeed. Only she knew that he had other plans. She was already well and truly caught up in them.

'I have to go, Myriad,' she'd said.

'Go? Go where?' he'd asked.

'I am taking a shuttle down to the world below.'

'But why?'

'It is best that you do not know.' But she had been shaking, and he'd held her, begging to know why she was leaving.

'Please, Serin. A few more years, and we will be free. I'll look after you, I promise.'

'I have to go.'

'You will not survive there alone; it is too alien. Please Ser—'

'I'm pregnant, Myriad. He will kill me or the baby or both of us – he will not allow the shame to become public.'

She remembers his expression in the moon-strewn corridor, his silence as he tries to process the information. She remembers holding him tight, hearing his strong heartbeat, just as she had heard it from their conception.

Now, reaching her uncle's office, she composes herself, takes a deep breath, and enters. Her uncle's secretary, a thin, officious little man with a pinched face and a thin line of moustache, is seated at a large black desk in the antechamber to her uncle's official study. The door to the room beyond is open wide, allowing sunlight to flood in through the expansive arched windows. The massive desk is empty, and shines, clear of all the paper and paraphernalia that used to litter it.

'His Imperial Highness, D'Ruja A'Riman. The Crystal preserve him, is not here.' She can already see that and clamps her teeth tight, swallowing back a retort.

'Where is he?' she manages to ask.

The secretary doesn't reply immediately, but shuffles through some papers. Selecting one, he takes his time and scans the page. She waits, muscles tense. Eventually, he raises his head to look at her and blinks. She is reminded of a praying mantis.

'His Imperial Highness is preparing for an assault on the insurgents in the northern mines.' His voice is dry and gravelly, making her want to clear her throat. He returns to his paperwork. The muscles in her hand twitch with an urge to slap the horrid little man.

'Where, exactly, will I find him?' She measures her voice and tone.

The secretary does not look up. 'He is on the practice field.'

The encounter fuels her anger, and she storms through the palace to the outside grounds. Servants curtsy and bow as she passes, but she does not see them, her face darkened in rage.

Reaching the practice area, she does not wait to gather her thoughts, but strides into the centre of the duelling men. The strong smell of sweat assaults her, along with the sound of clashing swords and the grunts of their fighting. She stands fast on the tightly packed ground, the white dirt smooth from training. Gradually, the action around her ceases.

Her uncle spars on with a soldier. In arrogance, he has cast off his face mesh. It lies abandoned behind him. His movements are fluid and confident, and he has his opponent slowly in retreat. Suddenly, his opponent is aware of her. As the soldier glances over, her uncle jabs him with the full thrust of his practice sword.

'Hakkaa!' Her uncle stands over the prone man, jubilant.

Serin ignores the crowd, ignores the crumpled soldier, and focuses entirely on her uncle.

'How could you?' she flares. 'He is so thin. A mere shadow.'

Her uncle clicks his fingers, and the soldiers flee, two helping the winded man. Her uncle turns, his face flat and expressionless. Alone, she faces him. Exertion drips in sweat from his face, but the hard glint in his eyes could dry all the water in Oasis.

'I cannot believe that you would be so cruel. All these years! It is unthinkable, unbelievable, that anyone could survive the rigours of the Book for so long. I don't know how he is still alive.'

Wiping the hot tears tracking down her face, she steps closer, jabbing her uncle in the chest. 'I had no idea that his life would be so harsh. You are an abomination.'

His face is blank.

'All this time in service to you!' she shouts. 'I want you to release him now. Right now.'

He grabs her hand. *You will heal him. You will heal the Book,* he states.

Her eyes open wide. The air solidifies, and breathing is suddenly difficult.

'I—I can't. It can't be done. It will kill him.' Her anger is drained away from the shock of his request—no, his demand. 'It could kill me. You know no woman can enter the Book. It is death. I won't.'

She shakes her head and backs away. One hand clutching her throat. She physically shrinks.

Then know this: I will force him to continue. He will never die, never stop reading, never be replaced. He will exist, but each day, you will be forced to view him at song and prayer, and each day, you will remember that you did nothing.

Crossing between palace and temple, she is blind to the beauty of the grounds, to the heat of the day, to the soft tinkle of the fountains. She stands outside the sanctum, fighting the impulse to flee, and clutches the doorframe, her legs weak. The great doors are wide open as though expecting her.

She leans her forehead against the cool, pale marble, cold to her core, her hands creased in sweat. Calming her racing mind, swallowing all emotions, she walks in towards him. The cloying perfume from the lemon flowers make her gag, even though the doors have brought fresh air in and lessened their scent. Their strong fragrance is being used to mask his decay, she realises in horror, and she remembers the foetid stench that permeated the city on her arrival.

He is as she had left him, cross-legged, naked, eyes closed, murmuring the words, the only movement his hand across the Book. Now she must betray him. Make him whole so he can continue this living hell. She holds her breath, hoping to be unnoticed.

Greetings, sister. I hoped you would not come. I hoped you would stay lost.

Appalled at his condition, she moves closer.

Brother. I . . .

You come to heal. I know, he says so quietly, it is like a breeze in her mind.

Reaching up, she touches his foot.

A whirlwind sweeps her up, throwing her into its turmoil. Her hair whips at her face; words swirl around her. She tastes bitterness, sourness, and regret, a bile rising in the back of her mouth. She wants to spit. The words the Book has conjured beat at her flesh, solid, vicious, pecking and flapping.

BATTLE   FIGHT   KILL   CONQUER   CONTROL ENSLAVE

They are not real, she knows, but they sting just the same. The Book tries to drive her off, away. It is like walking into the teeth of a storm.

She shields herself with her free arm. Her breath is snatched by the violence of the wind. She holds tightly to a foot she can no longer see. She strains and pushes with her free hand against an invisible barrier, one that tries to drag her back. More words beat and scratch at her back, clawing, ripping, tearing. She feels blood trickle from the gouges. Pain fills her mind and threatens to overwhelm her. It is not real. Don't let doubt in.

Closing her eyes, she refocuses, pushing her mind hard against the unseen obstacle. Slowly, bit by bit, she moves forward, and her hand breaks the barrier. The Book's tactics suddenly change. Her brother screams in pain in her mind.

Stop! Oh, Serin, please, stop! The last word is dragged out in an endless wail.

How could she cause her twin so much agony? But this is nothing compared to the suffering her uncle has caused him. Years of crystal has stretched him so thin. It is still eating into his body and soul; she can feel it. If only she can reach the centre, at least relieve the physical pain for him.

She strains, and without warning, falls through an invisible membrane, right into the centre of her brother's being. All is still and silent. Peaceful.

She pauses for a brief moment, savouring the rest, getting her bearings. Then she gathers information about his condition and wonders sadly how he is still alive. There is little flesh to see, and what is there is torn and ragged.

She is small in the vast space of his body. He is merely scaffolding now for the crystal, and the ravages of the wasting disease have taken its toll. He is now irredeemably lost. The crystal has permeated his very soul.

She wants to wrench him free but knows that will certainly mean his death and the death of the many others too, as the city will be unsupported. Unless there is another priest trained and ready. That is information she doesn't have yet. She will do what she can to help shore up his body for now, and hope to escape with her life, and his, intact. She must not touch the crystal herself or it will consume both of them.

She takes a deep breath. The healing begins.

The wind rises again to buffet and shake her as she reaches out to strengthen bone, make new blood cells, and repair his heart. The Book resists and twists, with viperous speed, ripping her away again and again. She can feel its anger—tangible, real.

Each time, it is as if they are being born again and again, ripped apart, torn from each other's arms, out of the womb. The Book flights to repel her presence, bucking and rippling as it tries to rid her from Myriad's body. There is strength and power lurking in the black of the words.

She tries to continue to work but is repelled from every angle. Finally, he twitches as a jolt of electricity crackles between them. The intensity of the wind increases outside. She hears the words beat against her physical body, slapping, stinging, spinning, reverberating, swirling faster and faster, a wild vortex. She must be close.

She hangs on, returning anew to complete the task, reeling from the roar, reaching into his soul. A scream fills the space, so shrill. Is it him—or her?

Stretching, she becomes unfathomably thin, a single strip of atoms. She slips between the particles, soothing the fibres of chaos. She gives him everything—her life force, her energy, her love—parting with it all to mend what she can. The tempest around her fades away. Finally, in the centre of it all, deep in the core of his essence, there is true calm, and she looks around, satisfied.

Slowly, carefully, she withdraws.

From deep with his core, she hears his voice whisper, *Did you find peace there? Did you find peace? Did you?*

With a snap, she is back. Crouched on the floor, she vomits, emptying her stomach. Opening her eyes, she sees with relief his wholeness, fuller, fleshier, a faint blush to his lips and cheeks. He is healed. It has never been done before, and she risked their lives to try.

A deep hatred for her uncle courses through her. She sits silently on the marbled floor, vomit soaking her white robe. Myriad's lips still move, but she cannot hear the words. Tenderly, she touches her ear, and it is wet and sticky. A profound sadness permeates her soul. There is no strength left for her to heal herself.

But a niggling thought tugs at the back of her mind. There is something that connects Myriad to their uncle's power. It slides away, fatigue weighing heavily in her limbs and head, but before she gives in to the welcome blackness, she says,

I am so sorry.

***

In the darkness a familiar disembodied voice floats in her mind. Her eyelids won't open, no matter how hard she tries.

Serin, I have to leave.

I will see you soon, my darling, and share with you some wonderful news.

She hears and doesn't understand, but she hears. The heaviness of a warm hand leaves her arm, and she gropes for some reference to tell her where she is and what is happening, but a sluggish sleep drags her back down into a deep dreamless void.

Her maid flits in and out of her consciousness, bringing water, clear broth, clean clothes. Time is punctuated by the smell of fresh bread, warm and doughy, the coolness of lavender scented water, and a gentle breeze blowing in from the open shutters. She doesn't want to leave her bed. A bone-deep lethargy overwhelms her.

Myriad, alone for all those years. Alone and suffering with no future while she— Tears leak, rolling down her cheeks silently.

Onora doesn't chatter or fuss. She is quiet and efficient. Serin is grateful for that. Eventually, sleep comes again, restoring her strength but leaving an ache, an ache deep and hard in her centre that she knows will never leave her for all the pain and torment her brother has endured.

I've come to see how you are. I've missed you.

An icy shiver runs through her. She feels his presence in her mind like someone pressing on a bruise. He stands there on the threshold of her room, the great and mighty imperial guardian, D'Ruja A'Riman, her uncle. He is hawk-nosed, arrogant, and regal, even in his riding clothes, his crimson-lined cloak brushing the floor.

He steps forward, smiling, bringing in the dust, along with his sword.

Serin, my love. I couldn't reach you. Your mind was closed. I am leaving for the mines to deal with. . . something. But I wanted to check that you were alright. I was worried about you.

'Worried? If you were so worried, why did you risk us in that way? My mind was torn in two, and Myriad was close to death.'

Serin, I . . .

'Get out of my head!'

He glares at her. His eyes are cracked ice, and he takes a deep breath in. *I do not discuss my business in front of servants.* He gestures towards Onora at the far end of the room. She is folding some clothes.

Serin feels his hand gently brush her hair back. *Serin, my sweet. I wanted to wait until you were stronger to share—*

Abruptly she looks up, interrupting him. *I would like to set up my clinic in the city.*

I cannot allow that.

I have upheld my end of the bargain.

No!

But—

There are no buts Serin. You are too important.

Important to you.

Yes, exactly. And important to the city.

How can I be important to the city when I am barred from helping anyone?

You are an important symbol of prosperity. You are royalty. Not one of them.

What if I come with you and help the prims, as you still insist on calling them. You will benefit too.

137

No. We have improved their conditions, and already, they exceed their working lifespan.

They are people.

A primitive form of people. Not intellectually developed.

Onora passes them, carrying an armful of bedding. Serin's uncle ignores the serving woman, keeping his attention firmly on Serin, who frowns and pinches her lips tight. She shakes her head and glances around, checking that they are alone.

'That is not true. I have lived there. I know all they lack is mindspeak.'

Mindspeak is evolution's next step. It sets us apart. We are not the same.

'They are people with thoughts, hopes, emotions, dreams.' Her nails dig deep into her palms.

They are a primitive form of human. You have no compunction using horse or dog. This is no different.

'It is a world of difference. The people you take have no choice. They are forced to work. It is barbaric. We could make a difference.'

Serin, what would you have me do? We have been harvesting prims for years.

Serin grinds her teeth.

We never lift a whole village or devastate them as a crop, her uncle continues.

'But they die. It is obscene and unnecessary.' Her voice is quiet and controlled.

We need the crystal.

'Yes, that's it, isn't it? It comes down to the crystal.'

Yes. What is your point?

'It is done at the expense of lives.'

Prims!

'People!'

Stepping towards the door, the discussion clearly closed, her uncle turns slowly, his expression hard and looks at her, his hand opens and closes on his sword's hilt.

You always make things so difficult. I wanted to do this in a gentler way. His look conveys anything but gentleness. His head is high and his jaw is tight. *You wanted to know why I need you. I want a legitimate link to your line, which comes through your mother.* He pauses. *And I want an heir to solidify my claim. I came back to release an important announcement to the city. We are to be married.*

Chapter 16

Nenna's muscles scream out for her to move, but she has learned that to even allow one toe to stray beyond the thin scrap of fabric she's been given to sleep on will elicit a beating.

The beast—she refuses to give that animal a name—always seems to know if some part of her has strayed beyond the boundaries of her 'bed', and he makes sure she knows he is in control.

Her left leg spasms momentarily, jerking out and back. She glances up fearfully at the bed, but the man seems to be sleeping. She bites down on the inside of her cheek. Don't cry. Don't.

She'd thought that the conditions in the cells had been barbaric, but now . . . those cells seem luxurious compared to how she is being treated.

In the beginning, she had refused to react. But that only seemed to excite him more. It was a game to make her scream, to break her. She learned to cry quick enough.

She squeezes her eyes shut, willing her cramped muscles to relax a little as she rubs them quietly.

Quarrel comes to her mind again—his long pink tongue hanging from the side of his mouth as though he were laughing at her, that warm, brown, comforting smell of damp earth and summer that clung to him after he'd been out hunting. His nose constantly checking the air for excitement or danger, his tail wagging, nudging her for treats. She smiles sadly.

'What you grinning at, you prim freak?' Vitrainy says, sitting up.

His bare feet slap the floor as he crosses the room towards her. His hand snakes out towards her head, grabbing a handful of her matted black hair, dragging her to her feet.

'You're obviously far too comfy down there,' he says, pointing at the fabric on the floor. 'Pick it up.'

She tries to reach for it, but he still has hold of her hair, and it tears her scalp as she tries to reach, stretching her arms out and bending her knees. He wrenches her head back hard, and then shoves her forward and lets her go. She stumbles but quickly recovers, grabbing up the material and holding it tight, trying but failing to hide her shaking hands.

'Fold it in half,' he says with that half-sided sneer of his. 'We'll see how you manage that.'

She stares at the folded cloth in her hands, her mind not fully able to comprehend the order.

'Fold it,' he hisses. 'And now. Put. It. Down.' He punctuates each word as though speaking to an imbecile. The back of his hand cracks against the side of her skull and she flies backward, hitting the wall. 'Put it down, you stupid prim,' he roars, spitting out the word 'prim' as though it were utterly disgusting, obscene even.

A beeping sound comes from the wall by the door, and a small, red light flashes.

'Bah!' Vitrainy spits, looking towards the sound. 'You better be sitting on that when I get back. And I want you to know that I can watch every move you make now.' And he grins his lopsided smile, pointing to a small square of shiny black material on his wrist.

She doesn't know what he is talking about, but she doesn't doubt him for one instant.

Sitting on the folded scrap of fabric, she finds that by bringing her knees up and tucking her feet as close to her bottom as she can get, she can just fit.

Her scalp stings. It feels as though her hair has been torn out at the roots. She rests her head on her knees. While he is away, she sleeps.

She wakes in the dark and finds to her horror that her legs are stretched out in front of her, while her back and head lean against the wall. In a panic, she sits up, drawing her legs back onto the thin material. She holds her breath, listening. There is no sound in the room.

She hopes that the darkness has hidden him from 'seeing' her on that device of his. Gradually, her heart rate slows, and taking a chance, she forces herself to stand. Her muscles scream in protest, and for a while, she works some feeling back into her cramped and stiff body, but she doesn't dare step off the material.

The room instantly floods with light as he enters, his face a blank mask. She freezes, expecting another beating, or at least some of the usual up-close shouting that he seems to enjoy, but he ignores her, throwing himself on the bed, fully dressed, and lies staring at the ceiling.

'Lights out!' he commands, and the room is suddenly dark again.

For a while there is no sound except for the beating of her heart in her ears and the distant hum that pervades the room. Vitrainy starts to snore gently, and she bites down again on the inside of the cheek to stop herself from screaming.

She must have dozed off and tipped back towards the wall. She wakes as he hauls her to her feet by handful of her matted hair.

'You fucking lazy whore. Sit up!' He slams her head against the wall and lets her go, the violence stopping as quickly as it had begun.

Tears blur her vision. How much longer can she endure this treatment? How long until he does something to seriously injure her?

She watches him cautiously, wiping her nose on her sleeve. He has opened a recess in the wall and is rummaging inside. He throws items of clothing out, scattering them behind him on the

142

floor, until eventually he grunts and, walking over the mess, lays a deep green cloak over his bed.

'You'll put that on when we land and not show me up,' he says and opens the door to leave. 'Oh, and tidy that mess up.' He waves his hand over the garments strewn on the floor. 'I won't be long.'

The last is said pointedly, and he looks at her with his leering half-smile. She hurries to pick up the clothes before he returns.

Her head throbs. Suddenly, the door opens again, and he stands silently, watching her.

'What the fuck are you doing?' he spits, spinning her round. 'They don't all go together! You really are fucking useless.'

His face is so close that it is difficult to focus, and she finds herself watching his thin, angry lips. A dot of white froth on his bottom lip rises and falls as he speaks.

'Look at me!' he yells, and she lifts her eyes wearily. There is a thin dark line around the edge of his hazel irises. His eyes are narrow and mean. The pinch of his mouth accentuates his long bony nose. How had she ever thought him handsome?

'Turn around and put your fucking, idle, useless hands on the wall.'

She does as she is told. Here we go again. Brace. She closes her eyes in anticipation. But this time, he kicks her legs further apart, spreading her stance wide and catching the bones of her ankles. She winces, but he doesn't stop there this time.

He wrenches at the all-in-one suit he had forced her to wear when she was removed her from the cell. He rips the fabric away in one violent tear. She sucks her breath in, tensing, waiting, but like the two other times he had done this, forcing her to stand naked with her back to him, he does nothing.

The first time, she had waited for the next inevitable move. She had been so petrified that she had wet herself, urine snaking down her leg and pooling on the floor. He had laughed and left her there with her hands on the wall. She had been too scared to move in case he returned. Shame and confusion battling inside.

Her face heats at the thought of his eyes on her back. So far, he has never touched her. He does nothing, but this time, he stands closer. Close enough for her to feel his breath, warm on the back of her neck. She shivers, her body pebbling with cold bumps, waiting. Why does he do this?

It is quiet for a long time—a lot longer than the other times. Then she hears the door hiss and his footsteps as he retreats down the corridor. There is never any rhyme or reason to these actions, but this one feels different—unfinished.

She sinks to the floor. Her arms ache. Her legs shake. She shivers, even though the temperature in his quarters is warm. But above all she is tired—tired of these attacks, tired of his games. Bone wearily tired.

She rubs the tops of her shoulders and looks around at the strange space again. There is his bed, and further over, there is a wall that moves to reveal an indoor privy with running water—magical things that under different circumstances she would have enjoyed finding out about. But this animal just throws her in there and screams at her to 'use the fucking toilet.'

There must be something that she can do. Get a message out? Escape? She wouldn't get far and who could she get a message to? The others are still locked up somewhere and that odd friend of Camis' hadn't been any help. But she knows that she can't take much more of this.

She must have dozed off again and is kicked into wakefulness.

'Get up, you lazy prim.' His boot slams into her hip.

She winces and struggles to get up.

'For the love of crystal, move!' She knows not to answer.

'Bathroom,' he barks, pointing at the wall, and she stumbles gratefully towards the sliding panel.

Twice a day, morning and evening, just like a trained dog, he takes her here. But now isn't the usual time. She moves over to the privy, which he calls a toilet.

'No, stupid! Not there.' His hand closes over the top of her arm and shoves her into the centre of the little room. 'Stand there.' He steps back.

She instinctively draws her arms around herself, crossing her breasts, and crouches lower, squirming to hide her shame. He isn't looking at her though. He is busy pressing a panel on the wall, which beeps at each touch.

She gasps as it starts to rain on her—only this water is warm. It cascades down from the ceiling and beats down on her bruises in spiteful spears. She looks up to see where it is coming from, instinctively stepping aside.

'Stand still!' he barks, and she freezes, water plastering her hair to her head and running in rivulets down her face, stinging her eyes.

The rainfall slows, changing from clear to soapy. 'Wash yourself all over, including your hair. I won't have you letting me down when we land.'

She does as she is told, trying hard to keep her expression bland. The painful stinging has stopped, and now the water feels incredible. She worries that it will all end in some unimaginable punishment if she is seen to be enjoying it so she schools her face to blandness. The water flows clear, rinsing off the suds, then stops.

'Stand still,' he repeats.

There is a cold feeling on her scalp, as though a small amount of water is being poured onto her head.

'Rub that into your hair,' he says.

She finds a thick, creamy liquid on her scalp and spreads it along the length of her hair. Miraculously, the tangles fall away, and she can now run her fingers through her hair without any resistance. More water pours from the ceiling, rinsing the excess substance away. She enjoys the sensation as it sooths and cleans. She closes her eyes for a few brief moments, trying to forget the awfulness of the situation.

The water stops and is replaced by flowing hot air blasted at her from all angles, taking her breath away.

'Right. There are some clothes on the bed. Put them on but leave the cloak until we exit the craft. Sit on your bed until I return.'

And just like that, he is gone.

She scuttles into the main room, feeling clean but lightheaded. Even though he has seen her naked before, she still feels exposed and vulnerable, so she hurriedly pulls the tunic over her head that he has left. The shapeless baggy garment falls to her feet, coarse and unpleasant against her tender bruised skin. It has a peculiar neckline with extra stretchy material hanging in ripples front and back. Her stomach growls, but there is nothing to eat, so she sits on the floor, careful to keep every bit of her on her scrap of fabric. She waits. Her eyes close.

She wakes slowly, her head down, resting on her knees. She resists the urge to stretch. Everything aches—her ribs, hips, legs, shoulders, everything. Her mouth is dry and sore. Tiny cracks and ulcers indicate the start of an infection.

In the time she has been with Vitrainy, she has lost weight. She isn't sure how long it had actually been. She remembers the bony feel of her ribs as she soaped herself earlier. To make matters worse, she can smell freshly-baked bread and the sharp citrus of fruit. She is so hungry that she is hallucinating the smell of food! A deep, overwhelming despair washes over her. She wishes she could die and end this nightmare.

Come on, Nenna, don't you dare give in. Don't let him break you. Don't let him win! She can hear Hadders' voice whispering in her ear.

A small seed of defiance returns, and she straightens up to find a full tray of food and water on the floor beside her. She freezes. Is this another of his cruel tricks?

Her hand hovers over the tray, but before she can stop, she is ripping off a chunk of the soft bread. What if this is a test? It would be worth the beating.

Wait! The voice in her head commands loudly, and she stops despite the hunger. Drink some water first. Then eat slowly. Remember what happened last time.

When he returns, she stops rubbing at her bruises in case it draws attention to them. He looks at the empty tray beside her but doesn't say or do anything. His hazel eyes are flat and empty as he points to the cloak laid out on his bed, walking to the door.

'Hurry up. Put that on and keep close. Pull the hood up.'

She hobbles over to the bed, her limbs screaming at the sudden change in position, swings the cloak over the coarse

146

cream fabric of the dress, and hurries after him. A small flutter of hope rises in her chest. She is leaving his room at last.

He strides down a wide empty corridor, and she limps behind, rubbing her hips, excitement helping to lessen the pain in her legs and the chaffing of the garments against her raw skin. They pass silver doors at intervals along the long white corridor lit by a harsh white light that seems to come from everywhere and nowhere. They enter a small white box, which gives her a strange feeling in her tummy, and she wonders if she is going to lose her food.

The sensation stops, and just as the door starts to slide open, he turns to her.

'Keep your hood up. Speak to no one,' he says sharply, and steps out onto a wide metal platform.

Nenna follows and finds herself looking out and down across the biggest indoor space she has ever seen. She stands on the platform at least eight-to-ten carts-lengths in the air, and yet the ceiling stretches far above her. She shrinks back against the now-closed door to the box, feeling sick. Where in Maa Erda is she?

Vitrainy just stands, staring down at something below. Slowly, curiosity overcomes her fear, and she creeps forward to clutch the rail that guards the platform and stands beside him.

The scene that spreads out beyond her is incomprehensible. In the vast space below, there are at least six of those enormous black metal mountains, like the one she had last seen sitting in the valley where she had been hit with the stun stick. Like the one she had been forced into, dazed and bewildered, before being taken her down into the cells. And now, somehow, she is still inside, but looking down on six more of these mountainous shapes. How can that be?

There are people the size of ants rushing around on the floor around the mountains. The dark metal catches the light on the edges and curves. There is a low murmur, like the sound of hundreds of people talking at once, along with a background hum, and a mineral smell mixes in with dust and heat.

Vitrainy turns suddenly to his left and starts to descend some stairs that seem to hang in space.

'Hurry up, prim,' he says as he disappears.

Chapter 17

The world zigzags back into view, flashing and flaring. A bright white light pierces Camis' eyes, and he shuts them quickly again. His body shakes, and he tries to push the floor away, but there is no floor under him. Instead, he touches what feels like a narrow metal shelf.

The pain throbbing through his body adds to his confusion, and he groans and tries to lift his hands up to his head, but they are locked to the bed with a short chain. He can feel the metal links in his fingers. Panic rises in his chest and threatens to suffocate him.

This one's coming round at last. Really thought those great brutes from security had killed it, a voice says.

Yeah, would have been a shame too, nice fit young specimen like this, a second voice answers.

Got a good year, maybe two, in him.

If the wyrms don't get him first.

Both men laugh, and the noise hurts so much that Camis tries to raise his hands to his ears. A hand restrains him.

'Lie still!' one of the voices says out loud, and then continues in mindspeak. *Sevac, you ready yet?*

Yes, just let me enter this one's details, and we'll get going. Er, Zigan, this one doesn't seem to be on the system.

Stop messing around, Sevac. I'm starving.

No. Really.

Let me see. Crystal bollocks, now the screen's froze.

Let's just do the procedure and then enter it later.

There is a pause, and Camis doesn't hear any reply, but there is a clatter of metal on metal, and someone takes hold of his hand. He tries to pull away and open his eyes, but the light sears his eyes, making him screw them tight.

He feels a sharp sting in the top of his hand. His brain registers the pain, but his muscles do not respond. He tries to call out. Nothing happens. He can taste metal. A slow, icy sensation creeps up his arm, spreading across his chest and down his legs, gradually numbing every part of him. He can hear the men talking, but gradually, their talk becomes a muted buzz until eventually even that fades. For a long while he is lost. Lost to himself and to the world.

Camis. Camis.

He can hear a familiar voice speaking to him but can't understand it. What does it want? Why can't it just leave him to this quiet oblivion?

Camis, please open your eyes. Come on, wake up. We haven't got long.

There is a hand on his shoulder. Someone is shaking him.

He can feel. And with that thought, the whole terrifying experience returns to him in a flood. He jerks up into a sitting position and opens his eyes.

The lights have been muted now, and the chains are gone. For a while, the world spins. A hand places a cup in his own and guides it up to his mouth.

Drink this and the spinning will pass.

He recognises Tiberius's voice speaking in his mind.

'Wha—what happened?' he manages to croak.

'I put a glitch in their system and told the technicians that it would take some time to fix. I told them I'd watch you and return you to your cell when you came round.' Tiberius says.

'Did they . . . did they?' He shudders, trailing away, not really knowing what to ask.

'They believed me. And no, you haven't been processed. You were lucky, but it was close.' Tiberius takes the cup away from Camis. 'But now we need to get you away from here. Put these back on.'

He hands Camis his clothes, crumpled and dirty. It is only then that Camis realises he is naked. He fumbles to dress and is surprised at how happy he is to see his own leather boots. His eyes fill with tears, and his face reddens as Tiberius looks back at him from where he has been checking the corridor outside.

'That's just the drugs,' he says. 'They'll wear off soon. Think you can walk unaided?'

Camis nods and concentrates on getting his legs to work. They shake, and several times, they threaten to give way. He makes it to the door and grasps it for support. His head swims, but he knows the danger and forces himself upright.

'Wait here while I check ahead to the lift,' Tiberius tells Camis and leaves him propped inside the room.

Camis looks around at the space. There is a metal bed in the centre of the room. It has chains attached to it and the whole structure is bolted to the floor. The floor itself is solid, smooth and white. His eye is drawn to a drain in the floor under the bed. He has watched enough butchers to instinctively understand its use. It makes him feel sick.

A long metal arm is suspended from the ceiling, and a huge round light hangs over the bed. He tries to swallow, but his throat is dry despite the water he has just drunk. His legs shake, and he wants to sit down, but he knows that if he does, he might never get up again.

Tiberius reappears. *It's not far, Camis. I can't help you. If we meet anyone, they will be suspicious if I'm supporting you.*

'I think—' Camis starts to reply but is cut short by Tiberius.

Dont speak, Camis. We will be passing other rooms, and they may be occupied.

They make slow progress through the long narrow corridor of the ship as Camis still feels weak and unsteady. Tiberius carries a stun stick and makes Camis walk in front of him.

There's the lift, he says, indicating an open door.

They enter a square windowless room. Tiberius taps the wall, and some numbers appear, which light up. The door hisses shut, sliding from one side. Camis feels a strange heaviness in his body and looks towards Tiberius for an explanation, but the young man just keeps his eyes forward, gesturing with the stun stick for him to exit when the door hisses open.

They walk down another wide corridor, which curves gently to the left and rises gradually. The corridors are bigger and longer than he remembers. There are door panels at regular intervals in the wall on both sides, which shine like the cream of milk.

A door opens and a man in guard uniform steps out behind them.

'Hey, you!' the man calls. 'Are you lost?'

Camis' heart hammers loudly in his chest.

'Stand still,' Tiberius barks, tapping Camis with the stun stick. 'Sir, my orders were to collect this one from the shuttle cells and take it up for processing in the labs.'

'This is floor fourteen. You've got out too soon. Come, I'll show you the way. First time?' says the guard. He has short, spiked hair and what looks like a badly-mended broken nose.

'Yes, sir. First time on my own, sir.' Camis is prodded into motion. 'Did a few with my archarya. Thought I knew the way.' They enter another small room, and Camis watches from the corner of his eye as the guard presses the wall and some lights appear as before.

'Bit young, aren't you?' the man states.

'Yes, sir. Youngest ever to pass the cadarch exams.' Tiberius stands up straighter, and Camis can hear the pride in his voice. 'I'll be seventeen short-cycles in eight moons' time.'

The guard whistles in appreciation. The door slides open.

'Well, here you are, young man. What's your name?'

'Tiberius, sir.'

'Right, Tiberius. You see this one safely delivered. I'm impressed that you never took your eyes off it once. Continue to be on your guard. Even just a twitch in the wrong direction, and you use that,' the guard says, nodding towards the stun stick. 'Nasty, tricky lot, never mind the stench.'

Camis stiffens, but it is pointless to react, and he isn't sure what he could do anyway with his limbs still feeling like water.

He is pushed out into another corridor. The door hisses shut behind them, and Tiberius lets out a long breath.

'By the crystal! That was close. And now we're on the wrong floor. Come, we've got to go back.' They wait for a while outside the door to the small box room, but Camis can see the agitation building in Tiberius. Tiberius slaps the wall with a hand and pushes Camis into the now-empty room as the doors slide open. He presses the wall again.

If anyone comes now, I'll just say I'm taking you back because of a delay in processing. It's not far to the hold, so hopefully we'll make it without any more incidents.

Again, Camis feels the strange sensation in his limbs, but this time, his stomach feels as though it is trying to get out of his mouth. When they exit again, it is into another identical corridor.

Tiberius, Camis says. *It feels to me as though your ship has grown bigger.*

What do you mean?

Well, the ship you took me into back near the plains, that was only three or four floors, and the walk to the cells took no time at all. But this—this seems huge. And that guard mentioned fourteen floors.

You are no longer on that first ship, Camis. We docked with our mothership, and when you came out of the cell and up for processing, you left the shuttle and entered this one. This ship is too big to land, so we use the smaller shuttles to fly down to your planet.

They keep walking, and Camis tries and fails to imagine the sheer size of the structure, let alone the fact that Tiberius has told him that they 'fly' everywhere and in something the size of a dozen barns. The idea is just too alien. Too difficult to imagine.

They stop at one door, indistinguishable from any other, and Tiberius holds his hand on a small panel to the door's right. It slides open, revealing a black interior. As Tiberius walks into the room, it is flooded with light.

Camis gasps. It is the largest indoor space he has ever seen; the light does not penetrate into its depths or reach its ceiling. There are huge, strange shapes clustered under a dark tarpaulin and wrapped in a criss-cross of rope. Tiberius leads him a long way before wriggling between two of the mounds and around to the back.

'Right, you can rest here for a bit,' Tiberius states, talking out loud again. 'We are back on one of the shuttles and this is its storeroom. These are the supplies that are left after our current mission.'

Close up, Camis can see that the mountainous shapes are covered with a canvas-like material, not unlike the tarp that he and his mother had used to cover their herbs on their cart. They even have the oily smell of weatherproofing.

'Tiberius, what about Nenna?' Camis says, holding Tiberius by the arm, but he can see that the question has unsettled the cadarch.

'I'—he says, backing away and allowing Camis' hand to fall free—'will see what I can do, but when I went to the holding cells to find you, I had to act fast. That's the thing, Camis. Nenna wasn't in the cell anymore and . . . you see . . . ' He wrings his hands and looks genuinely upset. 'It might already be too late.'

'Tiberius, please, you have to find her,' Camis says, his voice almost a whisper, surprised at how much he cares, and surprised at himself for asking this young man for more help. But it isn't as though he has much of a choice. It's Tiberius or nobody.

'I have to go back on duty and put back the recorders I disabled just before my break. I've manipulated the numbers, and as far as the system is concerned, you don't exist, but it won't be long before they get the labs up and running again. Hopefully, I'll find her before . . . '

He looks at Camis and doesn't finish. Camis' stomach knots.

'I'll be back later and let you know what I can find out,' Tiberius says. 'There's some food and water in here and my spare uniform for you to put on.' He gestures with the stun stick to a bag set on the floor.

Camis stares at the stick with a sour expression.

'This one isn't live,' Tiberius says. 'It's called a training taze. It's just for show in case we met anyone out at this time of night.' He tucks the Taze down the back of his trousers, pulling his tunic over the top of it. Walking back to the corner of the massive stack, he pats the Taze shape before vanishing out of sight, leaving Camis with his thoughts.

Camis leans against the huge, covered shape where he is hiding, vaguely wondering what is in the boxes tied under the thick net that is fixed to the floor.

How much can he trust Tiberius? Saving his life was something he would have done anyway, but now, surrounded by his own people, it would be easy for him to betray Camis. But why go to all this trouble disabling some thingamajig and hiding him here?

Camis sinks to the floor, the adrenalin rush of meeting the guard in the corridor wearing off, and he aches all over. He is about to close his eyes when the lights wink out, leaving him in total darkness. He tenses, ready to run, but apart from the odd clicking of the ship's structure settling, he hears nothing. Gradually, despite—or maybe because of—the darkness, he sleeps.

Light suddenly floods the room, and he is on his feet, peering carefully around the covered mound. Tiberius appears and sits down on the floor, leaning against the block. He looks tired. Camis slides down to sit next to him, and Tiberius hands Camis a leather cord.

'You are allowed long hair on ship, but it must be tied back.' Camis nods. Tiberius has short dark curly hair. The rest of the soldiers he has seen all have short hair. Sweeping his blond hair back like a horse's tail, he knots the thong firmly.

Next Tiberius hands Camis a smooth metal container, and though he examines it carefully, Camis does not know what it is. Tiberius reaches across and smiles, pressing down the top, which slides back to release a puff of steam and a waft of meaty soup.

'Drink it.' Tiberius reaches into the bag on the floor and hands Camis bread and an apple.

Camis crams the soft brown bread smeared thickly with nut butter into his mouth. He finishes the soup and crunches on the sweet apple. Life! Food never tasted so sweet. An image of the others still in their cages flashes into his mind. Suddenly, it is hard to swallow. If only he could get some of this to them.

'What did you find out about Nenna?' he asks Tiberius. When the young man doesn't answer straight away, Camis' stomach contracts, and he stops chewing. Tiberius lays a hand on his arm.

'She hasn't been processed. But she has been chosen.'

'Chosen? Chosen for what?'

'She has been chosen by a Nauarch, one of the ship's officers, as his reward. She is now his property.'

'And what does that mean?'

'She belongs to him, for him to do with as he pleases, and she will not work in the mines but will end up . . . working at his residence in the city.'

'But that's good, isn't it? She won't go through this processing thing.'

Camis detects a tightening in Tiberius's shoulders. The young man doesn't turn to look at him when he replies, 'That all depends on who has taken her.'

'Can we get her back?'

'Maybe. But first we need to get you safely off the ship. I do have a plan for that. You need to change into one of my uniforms.' He points at the bag on the floor. 'I think I can hide you and sneak you out when everyone is busy.'

'But . . . '

Tiberius looks at the inside of his left wrist, and Camis sees small black numbers. The numbers change. Camis' eyes widen. His mouth opens in surprise, but Tiberius is on his feet and already disappearing into the gap.

The crystal save me, I'm late! No time to explain, Camis. When we start the landing procedure, just hook your arms through the cargo nets. Camis can hear him panting. *And hold on tight. I'll be back as soon as I can.'*

Tiberius, how will I know?'

Know what?

That we are landing.

Oh, you'll know.

The background whine of the craft builds in intensity. Camis understands immediately what Tiberius meant. He grabs hold of the cargo net, but as the noise increases, he hooks his arms through the mesh and clamps his hands over his ears.

A strange lightness lifts his stomach into his mouth, but unlike before, this does not settle quickly. He feels queasy. The canvas covered mountains on each side of him lift, pulling on the stays that fasten them to the floor. His body hangs in mid-air, and his feet rise of their own will. The sound grows, multiplied a hundredfold, reaching an unbearable pitch.

His head feels stretched thin and swollen at the same time. His mouth is open, and he thinks he might be screaming. The pitch and screech is joined by a burst of hammering. The noise is ear-splitting, and he feels the vibration in the very depths of his body—in his bones, his skull, his teeth.

The noise ceases abruptly, leaving a deafening hum, but he has no time to feel relieved as his body slams into the floor at the same time as the mountain of cargo. The jolt jars hard through his spine, slamming his shoulders forward against the rope around his arms. Breath explodes from his mouth.

It is a few moments before he realises that the craft is still and silent. As he swallows, his hearing returns in a painful whoosh just like before. He rests, leaning forward, arms still entwined in the net, and an image of a freshly caught fish flashes through his mind.

Chapter 18

Sitting alone in silence, Serin stares, unseeing.

We will be married, we will be married, we will be married.

All at once, she bends over the side of the chair and retches. No. *No!*

She shivers. His hands, dry and cold, pinning her shoulders, nails digging into her flesh, his breath hot on her face, his lips on hers. It can't happen again. She won't let it.

Her hands drop down to her belly, as her stomach bucks. The shock of his betrayal, the shock of him inside her head and in her body—images, long suppressed, surface.

Her teeth clench, biting down on the scenes that whirl through her mind, biting down on him. Of him laughing. Her biggest fear at the time was that he would find out that it wasn't her first time. That he would find out that she wasn't a virgin, that she wasn't the prize he thought, that someone else had been there before him.

She grasps the arms of the chair, trying to control the hysteria. An image flashes in her mind, that conquering thrust of his chin and the lust in his eyes. Again, the gut-wrenching twist in her stomach.

We will be married.

The pain in her chest is suffocating. Her body responds with a deep shuddering breath, and she draws her knees in tight to her chest. The pain moves to her throat, choking. She screws her eyes shut.

A light touch on her arm causes her to jolt. Her eyes fly open. Onora. Oh, Onora.

Clutching at her maid's hand, she sucks at air, tries to breathe, tries to speak, and fails at both. Onora's soft brown eyes radiate concern, and she gently strokes Serin's clasping hands.

'What is it mistress? It will be all right.'

But Serin can find no comfort in her touch.

'He says we will be married,' she whispers into the silence.

Onora's eyes fly open wide. Serin moans—jagged, bereft. The tears flow at last, hot and angry, as her handmaiden hugs her close and rocks her to silence.

The greatest pleasure is finding that when he is gone from the city, he is also gone from her mind.

A faint orange glow lights her way as she flits through the palace grounds on bare feet, aware that this was how it used to be, sneaking out at night. In the early days, it had been to swim with her twin in the black, still water of the lake, then later to—

She can't torment herself with thoughts of him, of what might have been. He is another forbidden male, another that she must keep secret, closed away in the depths of her mind. Locked away not only from her uncle but also from herself.

Myriad, let me in. She calls out, trying to reach her brother, but the huge marble doors remain firmly closed. They glow faintly red from the light of the moon, as though heated with fire.

She glances up. The Papa moon, as it is called on Maa Erda. It is visible in the deep plush of the sky, shedding a coppery light down onto a distant blue planet, the one that she thinks of as home, the one with Camis. Her eyes prickle, and she turns quickly back to the doors.

Myriad, if you can hear me, I need to speak to you.

But cool and solid, the doors remain firmly closed.

The next morning, she begs the priestesses of the Book to forgive her as she doesn't feel up to leading the procession. News had spread quickly in the temple, and she is well respected after healing their beloved Book. They can see what it has cost her in her pallid complexion and the dark sunken circles under her eyes.

As they file past her, each maiden smiles and touches her lightly on shoulder or arm, their gratitude clear. No one is surprised when she slips away. She waits until the procession moves into the inner temple and follows, sliding behind one of the two tall pillars that flank the massive doors, waiting for the singers to leave.

Listening to the closing incantation as it echoes around the chamber, she holds her breath. It is so beautiful. Camis would have loved to hear it. Thinking about him makes her smile.

The women glide past her hiding place, their bare feet silent on the marble, the faint swish of their gowns fading, leaving her alone with him at last.

'Myriad,' she calls out, slipping into the main chamber. She catches the gentle *shush* of his reply.

Looking up, she sees him lit from above, the circular crystal dome allowing the first shaft of morning light to angle down, lighting his nakedness. Dust motes swirl and dance above his head like stardust. His sea-green eyes mirror her own. He holds a slender finger to his lips. The doors swing shut silently.

Sister, are you well?

And she hesitates, momentarily taken back by his concern for her, at the compassion in his voice. Tears threaten to overwhelm her.

I couldn't speak last night, he says. *He has me watched.*

'He is going to marry me!' she blurts out.

The sunlight blinks out, revealing the black words that writhe over his torso. They jump and judder to her announcement, and she sees 'married' briefly scrawled in amongst the usual litany. He concentrates on his breathing; the words slow and resume their regular pattern.

That cannot happen, Serin. It must not! He will take full control. With me safely out of the way in the priesthood, you are his only obstacle. While you were missing, he could not legitimise his claim until he produced your body. This way, he will have everything he wants . . . including you.

'If it is the words that you speak that keep him in power, just stop,' she says rashly. A jagged laugh—a thin mirthless sound—rings in her head.

And that would kill everyone. D'Ruja, you, everyone.

His lips continue to mouth the flow of words that keep their world alive, words she once saw as miraculous. But now she sees them as a prison, as the abomination that they really are. She shudders and wraps her arms around herself. The Book, their source of life, of survival, has become the garotte around their necks.

'What can we do?'

Again, he places his finger to his lips. *We must find a way together. I have an idea.*

He gestures for her to sit, but she looks around fearfully, expecting to see spies leap out from behind every pillar, before sinking down onto the step that surrounds the dais.

Over the years of dealing with . . . with D'Ruja, I've explored every option, and each and every time, somehow, he knows. He feels a shift in the pattern of my reading and puts a stop to it. He has loyal spies within the priesthood who keep him informed if he is out of the city. He knows exactly how to hurt me.

He pauses, and Serin sees the writing stutter and fade on his torso. A tremor vibrates through the marble floor, and he looks up, momentarily confused, before the writing continues and the ground quiets.

I had a friend. A very good friend. Another priest, he says. The words flow back across the Book briefly, then resume their fluid motion off the page and across his body. *We shared the night watch when we were children. Kanta and I have—*his mindspeak falters—*had a . . . close relationship. Once I was selected to become the Book, he would wait for me every night, content to sit beside me whilst I slept.*

He stops talking and closes his eyes. She looks up at his face, holding still. *We hoped to be together when I was released.*

Myriad, what happened?

A whisper brushes her mind. *I refused to keep the wyrms away from the new mining area that our abomination of an uncle had found. I told him we had enough of the stuff and did not need it. That using slaves needed to stop. That it was barbaric.*

It is a while before he continues. *Kanta was dragged into the temple. He had been beaten. His face was nearly unrecognisable, eyes swollen shut, blood . . .*

She sees his tears fall, and her arms ache to hold him, but it is forbidden to touch the Book, and it would be dangerous for both of them. She remembers the pain she'd felt when she'd healed him, and the way they had stretched out nearly into oblivion. They had been lucky.

D'Ruja held Kanta's mind closed and put a knife to his throat.

A chill sweeps the chamber, and she hugs herself.

He called me an abomination and threatened to expose my sin to the priests and to the people. He said Kanta would be kept safe so long as I did as I was told. Once a year, he is paraded before me, as proof that he lives. We are not allowed to speak.

Now, sitting in silence, unable to physically comfort her brother, she can't see any way out. She thinks of Camis, glad that he has no idea of this life, and she prays that he never will.

Some of the priests were shocked by D'Ruja's actions. They knew of our friendship. They know that it is no sin to love in the way we love each other. But the people have been brainwashed by that man's regime. His voice is barely a whisper in her mind.

As time went on, the priests realised what D'Ruja was doing to me. That he had no intention of releasing me. There are a small number already spreading dissension. A tiny smile touches his lips, and a flame of hope flares in her chest as she watches him intently.

I don't know all the details of their incursion. I dared not to know in case he . . . in case he somehow senses the information, or I let it slip. He looks directly at her. *I know it's silly—I know*

I can block and hide things from him, but I cannot bear anyone else to suffer like . . . He trails away.

I will get news to them of his plans and let them know that you are on our side and that you will be needing their help, he continues. *I'm sure between us all, we can find a way to make life better.*

They sit in silence for a while.

Myriad, where are the children? I did not see any on my ride through the city.

He looks down at her. *There is a sickness,* he says sadly. *One that the Book cannot reach. There haven't been any children for years now. A few are stillborn and some are born very badly deformed, but these do not survive long. He punishes these women and their families. Tells them it is their fault. He keeps food from them, telling them that there will be rewards for those who follow his guidance.*

She stands up. *I must help. I will start by reaching out to the ordinary people. Let them see me helping them.*

They talk and plan, and when she walks to the doors, it is with a much lighter heart filled with determination. There are two of them now. They can spread the seeds of dissent against her uncle's actions.

The people also need to be able to return to the temple to see you, Serin says, turning back around to face him. *To question his decision of keeping you as the Book for so long. I will try to delay the marriage for as long as possible.*

Serin . . . He has a second Book. One that ties me to him. He forces me to read from it each evening, and it gives him power. He keeps it on him at all times.

She turns back, her eyes wide. There is a long pause.

There must be another way to defy him. I will watch for him using this second Book. I'll sneak it away when he sleeps and destroy it. Squaring her shoulders, she stands taller.

No! He says sharply. *He has tied his Book to me and to Kanta. Destroying it will kill us both.* He continues more softly.

I tried to defy him by trying to die but he knew and sent you to heal me.

His fern-green eyes are a mirror of her own, pools of sadness.

Myriad, I'm sorry that I left you in that position. I am just so grateful that my son has never been part of this world. Though I wish he could meet you.

The blood drains from Myriad's face and his eyes lock on hers. *A boy! The baby survived. You didn't speak of him before, so I was afraid to ask. Does he—?*

No. He is safe, Myriad. My boy is safe. That monster doesn't know of his existence. But her brother's last words turn her blood to ice.

For now.

***

'Move out of the way and open this gate.' Serin looks down her nose from her horse, with the haughtiest expression she can manage.

'I can't do that,' a sweaty, round-faced guard says nervously, stepping across their path.

'You do know that His Imperial Highness, D' Ruja A'Riman, and I are to be married.'

'Yes, but—'

'I wish to choose a surprise wedding present for him, and I cannot do that from here, can I?' And she gives him a scowl.

'I—'

'Well? What is the problem?'

'I, er, we . . . we were told to keep you safe.' He pulls off his red neckerchief and mops his balding head.

'Well.' She moves her grey mare backward, pretending that the horse is misbehaving. 'Be quick then and get me an escort.' The horse twirls and dances around, but the man is already sprinting towards the stables. She ignores the remaining guard and settles her horse.

'I am not sure the master will like this,' Onora says.

'Stop worrying, everything will be fine.' Serin's horse lays back her ears and tries to nip the maid's placid bay gelding.

164

Serin concentrates on bringing the mare under control. 'First, I'll spend money in the market, and then we will find a suitable corner for me to see people.' She sees Onora's frown and laughs. 'The winds will change.'

The market is crowded—colourful, noisy, and familiar. They leave the horses on the outskirts of the market, in a quieter side alley. Two of the younger soldiers mind them. Four dismounted guards help to push a pathway through the thick, bustling throng.

Onora catches Serin's arm, nervously glancing around. A cacophony of sounds and scents assault her. Serin breathes deeply, savouring the spices from nearby stalls. Cooler floral aromas fight to be noticed over wafts of hot, peppery smells. She recognises lemongrass, juniper, cloves, cumin, fennel, and turmeric, and the warm, fruity undertones of liquorice from star anise.

The confusion of colours brings back memories of trips to the market with Myriad a lifetime ago. Her mind soaks it all in—the pale yellow to deep gold of the ground spices, the greens of the herbs: rosemary, thyme, bay, and mint. There is barely time to recover when her senses are hit with the sugary-sweet scent from the next stall, mixing with warm malty bread are aromas of freshly-baked pastries, sweet and sticky. Serin's mouth waters.

Hawkers cry from their stalls, which display leather, silver, and wood. 'Come try—' 'Buy my lamps!' 'Best you'll find!' Cries from infinite voices.

And there are the people—from pale pearly skinned, like herself, to the shining mahogany of the Alakay Ajakai. Music bursts through in fits and starts, flowing through the crowd, filling the gaps between the shouts and smells. She glimpses the swirl of scantily clad dancers, silken and sensuous. Peddlers shout their wares, and beggars call for coin. There is laughter and music, bells and tambourines; drums, flutes, and harmonious voices capture the rhythm of the market.

But there are no children, just as Myriad told her.

They stop to admire a carpet weaver working on a rug. His brown, spindly fingers deftly weave an intricate pattern, using a long slender bone shuttle, he tugs a length of thick purple wool into place. Around him hangs his craft. Rugs are stacked in an untidy pile each side of his wooden loom.

The heat stifles and the shimmering air sticks clothes to legs and hair to necks. A faint smoke hangs in the air from the variety of foods cooking on a hundred braziers. A snake charmer sits cross-legged on a corner, a black-hooded cobra rising out of the basket in front of him, swaying to his music. Two fakirs, faces and heads covered apart from their vivid violet eyes, sit one above the other. They hover in the air, nothing holding them up, their yellow kaftans billowing. She throws them some coins.

Serin calls Onora to 'look at this' and 'can she see that?' She loads her maid with forgotten treasures—a bamboo flute, some coconut cake in pink and white, and a crystal dome of purple bathing oil—even though her wash area has enough products in it for fifty people. Laughter bubbles just below the surface, and she is a girl again. Stallholders rush to wrap her purchases, but she misses the fact that they are not smiling.

The deeper they walk into the market, the more people seem to knock into her, and she stops. Now she sees the clothing patched and patched again, colours washed and faded, eyes that never directly confront. The glares, the scowling faces. The guards drop back and surround her.

'Mistress, let's go.'

Deflated, she turns to leave, but a material catches her eye—a bale of shimmering fabric that seems to deceive, flashing first blue and then green with hints of purple. She fights towards it and points, indicating the fabric.

'How much?' Her attention is fixed on the beautiful cloth.

'Not for sale.'

Serin looks directly at the stallholder. The woman is about the same age as herself but a little shorter. Her brown hair is piled in an untidy bun, long curling strands escaping. Folding fabric scraps into a basket, she pointedly does not look at Serin.

'I'm sorry, but why is it on display?'

166

'I changed my mind. It's not for sale.'

Onora tugs at Serin's arm, but Serin shrugs her away.

'I will pay double.' The woman ignores her, turning away and stacking the basket she has been packing on top of others.

One of the guards steps forward and barks, 'Woman, do you know who you are addressing?'

'I know well enough. I don't need her money or her charity,' the woman replies.

She turns and faces Serin, who is taken aback to see a flinty anger in her blue eyes. The market around them stills.

A man's voice calls out from the gathering crowd. 'She don't want to sell!'

There are murmurs of agreement.

'Yeah, just go back to your palace.'

'We don't want your money.'

'You were never here before.'

'Go home.'

'Why come out now? You never bothered before.'

More voices join in.

Serin's cheeks colour, and she faces the crowd. 'I'm going to start a clinic! A healing surgery.'

The silence is cloying. A ripe tomato sails through the air in a graceful arc. It strikes Serin's white gown just below her breasts, bursts, sticks for a moment, and then slides slowly to the floor, leaving an orangey-red stain in its wake. Someone titters.

'Good shot,' a voice calls as one of the guards roughly pushes his way through the crowd, looking for the perpetrator.

Serin stands motionless, a small frown on her face, and Onora moves to stand in front of her. The crowd erupts. They surge forward, one screaming mass.

Serin and Onora are pressed back against the table as the stallholder frantically begins shoving her wares into baskets, trying to clear her goods as the press of the angry people surges forward.

Serin can see their ill-fitting clothes, their scowls, their angry mouths, can hear their shrill voices and the pulse of their rage.

There is sweat, hate, and anger in the air. The crowd surrounds her and Onora, only the few remaining guards holding them back.

'Quick, under here!'

Serin turns in disbelief to see the stallholder gesturing for them to slide under the table.

The remaining guards force the horde back a little, but they field a barrage of flying objects—old shoes, stale bread, stones. The two women crawl under the stall and to the relative safety behind. Moving some baskets to make an opening, the woman gestures for them to go and closes the gap behind them.

A bestial howl rents the air, followed by a splintering crash. Serin glances back, but the baskets block the view. The stallholder is shouting, but she can't make out the words as Onora tugs her away.

Chapter 19

Pressing herself tight to the wall, Nenna follows Vitrainy down the steps, her bare feet gripping the open-meshed stairs. The hum below gradually increases to a loud buzz until they reach the bottom, where it becomes a cacophony of noise and confusion.

People shout, boots ringing out on the odd pale flooring as they scurry in every direction. Strange objects are hauled, shoved, or carried towards a large gaping hole in the side of each of the strange black mountains. Wide black ramps lead to the holes.

Nenna hurries to keep up, scared of becoming lost and attracting Vitrainy's anger. He crosses the space towards one of the openings as a young female, wearing the same black uniform as Vitrainy but without the red neckerchief, approaches them.

'Sir, you asked to see the inventory report for your shuttle,' the woman says, handing Vitrainy a black rectangle, which lights up as he takes it.

Vitrainy looks at the object he is holding and scowls. 'Why are there only one-hundred-and-fifty personnel allocated to shuttle four?' he says without looking up.

'I . . . I don't know, sir,' the young woman replies nervously.

He hands the black object back with a grunt, waving her away, and continues towards the nearest mountain.

'Wait by that shuttle,' Vitrainy says, pointing to the side of the huge black object. 'Don't move or talk to anyone.

Understood?' He waits for her nod, then walks off. She watches him stride away.

At first, she stands exactly where he has left her, free to gawp and stare around, but gradually, she is forced back as people hurry past her, carrying boxes, books, stacks of clothing, and crates of food. Some climb the ramp beside her and disappear inside the mountain. What had Vitrainy called it? A shuttle?

No one speaks to her. They are all intent on their work. She feels invisible.

'Oops, sorry,' says a young dark-haired girl as she bumps into Nenna.

The girl hurries away, adjusting the large bundle of folded cloth she is holding so she can see better. She isn't wearing a black uniform but a long plain dark skirt and white blouse. Nenna frowns. Was that fear she had glimpsed in the girl's dark brown eyes?

Conversations swirl around her.

'—wants a full report on water for the horses and the prims on board.'

'He's got shuttle four's stats now, so it won't be long—'

'Lec, have your tents got enough ground roll?'

The noise and number of people increases, and Nenna is forced to the side of the ramp. There seems to be no order.

She stares about her, looking, hoping for a glimpse of a familiar face. Where were the others? Ash or Kitt or even Camis? She can't recall how long it's been since she last saw them. Three days? Five? More?

Perhaps this processing wasn't as bad as Camis had feared. She hoped he was all right.

Unconsciously, she rubs the bruises on her arms and a thought hits her. What if Hadders is here? What if he has been taken too and is somewhere inside one of these mountains? She can't believe this hasn't occurred to her before.

She looks up at the black monstrosity she is standing beside. Hope springs alive in her

A man and a woman approach. They stand on the other side of the ramp, close together, and they do not seem to be aware of her. She draws back slightly into the shadows.

'How long did he say you would have to be at the mines?' the woman asks, looking up at the man. Even holding her hood tightly and discreetly glancing over, Nenna can see the concern etched on the woman's face. Her light hair is tied back in a tail, and her eyes never leave the man's face.

'We haven't been given a time span, but I promise you, Beadria, that I will ride straight for the city the moment I'm relieved.'

He smiles down at her. She leans in and rests her head on his chest. Nenna can see tears on the woman's face. The man bends down and kisses the top of her head. His own hair has streaks of white running through the dark blond, giving him a distinguished look, strong and dependable.

A stab of pain shoots through Nenna's chest at the tenderness they display to each other. It seems an age since someone looked at her that way. An image of Camis with his arm around her in the cage flashes in her mind, to be replaced immediately with her brother standing at the corral looking at the horses again with a strong reassuring arm around her. Tears spring to her eyes, and she dashes them angrily away, then returns her attention to the couple on the other side of the ramp.

'I'm worried I'll be posted to the new Mastership without you,' she hears the woman say, but she doesn't hear the reply because Vitrainy is suddenly beside her. He pushes her roughly forward by the shoulder.

'In there,' he growls, gesturing for her to climb up and into the shuttle.

She stumbles and puts out a hand to catch herself, holding on to the edge of the ramp. He smacks her hand hard, knocking it free. His face is dark, thunderous. She shrinks back.

'Move!' he spits, and she scuttles to the end of the ramp and begins to climb.

The couple watches them silently, partially hidden by the ramp. Vitrainy has not seen them, but as she passes, Nenna thinks she sees pity in their eyes.

Vitrainy leads her inside, taking her quickly through the white corridors. He nods and smiles to some men as they pass, not all smile back.

They enter a long room filled with seats in rows. At the front are two chairs set apart from the others. The chairs are padded in a rich deep-red material, with soft armrests. They appear to be bolted together and fixed to the floor.

Vitrainy gestures for her to sit on one of the red chairs, interrupting her thoughts. Leaning over her she has to press herself into the high back of the chair away from him, waiting for one of his shouting bouts or a blow, but he just gently sweeps her hood from her head, pulls a strap across her stomach, and clicks it into a slot at her side.

'Don't speak to anyone,' he hisses in her ear, then he stands up, turns on his heel, and leaves.

She sits, looking down at her hands for an age, afraid to move in case he is watching from somewhere. The strap across her lap frightens and confuses her. She feels a rising panic and swallows several times. There is nothing she can do, so she closes her eyes and thinks of home—of Da and Hadders, of riding Nettle with Quarrel beside her.

People start to enter in twos and threes, filing passed her to the seats behind. The room slowly fills with the soft gentle murmur of conversation.

Vitrainy returns and sits down next to her. He draws another strap from somewhere she can't see, across his own body and clicks it into the slot at his side. He doesn't speak, but a quick glance at his face tells her all she needs to know. He looks as though he has chewed on some bitterroot.

A background hum begins, and a strange pressure forces her whole body back against the seat. The last time she had heard that sound, everyone had . . . She screws her eyes shut and grips the seat arms, bracing herself. But nothing happens except a very brief feeling of lifting off her seat, the strap holding her in place, and then the noise fades.

Gradually, she lets go and opens her eyes. The chatter behind her has continued, and from the corner of her eye, she can see that Vitrainy hasn't moved. His face like a thunderhead, he stares straight ahead at the white wall in front of him.

Suddenly, the room tilts sharply forwards, flinging her hard against the belt. She gasps, her hands flying back to clutch the sides of the seat. The room is silent. She holds her breath. Her stomach rises into her throat. It is similar to the sensation she had felt in the box that had taken them between floors, only magnified a hundred times.

A loud *whoomph* resounds through the room, shaking the floor and her seat. Her ears pop, taking all sound with it. The silence is primal, and all thought leaves her. She scrabbles at the belt that holds her. She wants to flee, which is ridiculous because the belt is the only thing keeping her in place. Undoing it would slam her into the wall in front of her.

But she doesn't care. She has to get away, to escape this nightmare. Her fingers fumble along the belt, and on one side, she finds a metal catch. A hand snatches her own away, twisting it painfully.

Vitrainy holds her hand tightly, his nails digging spitefully into her wrist. It is the pain in her hand that reaches through the panic. She stares at him and slowly lets the immediate fear fade.

He isn't panicking. The people behind her are not fleeing in terror. Slowly, she relaxes, just as the room tilts back and there is a jolt that shakes her chair. Everything is still.

She takes a deep breath and swallows, her ears popping again, returning sound at the same time. It comes back in a rush, greatly inflated, surreal. People are louder, sounding more excited, but it seems like a good excitement, not one of panic or fear. Some are on their feet, chatting as they leave the room.

Vitrainy stands, turning his back to her. He greets people as they pass.

'And no extracurricular from you two, mind,' he says to the last of the couples. They laugh, and the young man gives Vitrainy a grin and a nod as he passes.

'Keep your eyes down, and don't speak to anyone,' he snaps to her without turning around. He strides away through the corridor briskly, expecting Nenna to keep up.

Walking down the ramp into the bright, warm sunshine is a shock. The heat hits her like a wall and overwhelms her.

She stops, drawing back into the relative safety of the shuttle. Vitrainy turns, looking at her but saying nothing, his eyes hard. She hesitates a little longer, allowing her eyes to adjust to the glare, then steps gingerly onto the ramp and into a strange new world.

Extending from the ramp is a long thin mat. The ground on either side is a bleached white sand. Vitrainy walks away from her. Squinting in the glare, she hurries to catch him up.

Horses and soldiers mill around a short distance away. Younger people dart in and out, dropping bags in the sand and running out of sight, returning moments later with more bags. Where had they come from?

Sounds reach her in a strange, muted way—the jingle of harnesses, the shouts from the boys. People are talking, but words are indistinct. She puts up a hand to shield her eyes and only just stops before she collides with Vitrainy, who has abruptly bent to clip on some strange wires to the undersides of his boots.

'Wait there,' he says, and stepping off the matting onto the white ground, he walks towards a soldier who holds a skittish chestnut stallion.

Elegant and fine boned, the horse tugs and jerks his head upward, trying to snatch his reins from the soldier's hands. Nenna does not follow, although she itches to look more closely at the horse. Something familiar at last.

The stallion is a far cry from the stocky solid horses she is used to. Much taller, it has four beautifully-matching white socks and a narrow blaze of white that tapers down its nose. It stands out on the white sand, magnificent, gleaming in the sun.

'I don't care that your orders only allow one horse per man. I'm telling you to find me a second one. I'm taking all my belongings with me,' Vitrainy says, making a gesture over his shoulder towards her.

The soldier glances at her and back to Vitrainy, shuffling his feet. 'Sir, with respect, I . . . '

Vitrainy speaks over the soldier, his tone containing that hidden menace that she recognises so well. The muscles in her bladder clench. 'We have orders to take what we can carry. Isn't that right?

'Yes, sir.'

'Then I intend to do just that. So unless you want to be digging latrines for the whole of this trip, then you will find me another horse.'

The soldier salutes, sweat beading his brow, and trots away.

Nenna watches as Vitrainy checks the horse over. He runs his hands down the horse's front legs, picking up the feet, and checking the shoes. He speaks softly to the animal in a reassuring way as he works, patting the horse gently. He adjusts the horse's bridle, loosening a strap here and tightening one there. He checks beneath the soft white sheet that covers most of the young horse's back and seems satisfied with the blanket that he finds underneath. He checks the back feet just as carefully.

Finally, he pulls down a strange leather hood attached to the top of the bridle, covering the whole of the stallion's head, which makes the horse prance sideways and snort. The hood has mesh eye and ear openings, and Nenna can almost feel the claustrophobia of the young horse. Vitrainy rolls the hood back up and fastens it into place behind the horse's ears.

A lad dashes past, dropping a backpack behind Vitrainy who turns at the noise. The lad doesn't wait but runs on, depositing one of the many bags he has slung over his shoulders to the next soldier.

Vitrainy sees Nenna watching, and she lowers her eyes quickly, but he just grabs the bag and slings it up behind the horse's saddle, then he fiddles with some straps, blocking her view. The horse dances sideways, its head swinging towards her. Automatically, she reaches out and catches hold of the reins. Vitrainy looks at her, and she flinches under his cold stare, but there is no blow.

'Glad to see you're not totally useless. Stand there and hold him,' he says, walking off.

She watches him weave his way between the long line of men and horses until she can't see him anymore. She strokes the chestnut's soft nose, and her own shoulders relax.

The soldiers around her busy themselves with their packs, equipment, and horses. A low rumble of chatter envelopes her, along with the comforting smell of horse, dust, and dung mingling in the air.

The young stallion paws the ground and shakes his head. His bridle rattles, adding to the strange, muffled din around her. It is a bit like being underwater. Vaguely, she wonders where the horse has been stabled.

Youngsters race past with urgent messages. People call and laugh, slapping each other on the back. Men and women bristle with excitement. She can almost taste the anticipation.

She watches them all and remembers her first hunting party—getting ready, the anticipation, willing everyone to hurry up. Remembering home makes her eyes sting and her stomach clench. This isn't a hunting party, and this isn't her home.

Mount up and go, a little voice urges her, while another internal voice screams, Where would you go? How far would you get? You don't even know where you are.

The stallion suddenly swings his head high, snatching the reins from her hands.

'Whoa, boy,' she says, reaching up and catching hold again.

A cry goes up in the distance, and the soldiers around her start to mount. The stallion prances, trying to pull himself free, picking up on the excitement of imminent departure. Then, stretching out his neck and baring his teeth, he tries to bite. Instinctively, she gives him a flick of her hand, catching him on the soft whiskery part of his upper lip.

'Ah-ah!' she says sharply. He snorts and draws back, respect in his eyes.

'Nauarch! Lower your hand.' A soldier is looking down on her from his mount. Is he speaking to her? But he seems to be looking past her, over her shoulder, and she turns to find that Vitrainy is behind her, his arm raised to strike.

'Commander,' Vitrainy says. 'With all due respect sir, the prim struck my horse.'

'The horse was about to bite, and she corrected it,' the man on horseback says.

Nenna recognises him as the man who had said goodbye to the woman beside the ramp. Vitrainy takes a breath to speak, but the man continues, 'Your horse could do with some discipline, and you could do with some restraint. You are in uniform and no longer on the shuttle or in your hov. You are under my command. Remember that.'

He guides his horse around to face the other soldiers. 'Mount up!' he calls, and the cry is taken up and passed down the line.

Men, quietened by the scene, quickly grab the last of their packs and swing themselves onto horseback. The chatter returns. Vitrainy stands ramrod still, the muscles at the side of his jaw bulging. Others pass them as mounted soldiers begin to move forward.

So, he is not as high up as he believes. Interesting. But from the set of his jaw, she knows she will pay for his dressing down.

She sees the tightness around his eyes as he moves around behind her. His previous cruelty makes her tense, and she waits for the blow. Suddenly, he lifts her up and throws her belly downwards across the back of the horse, his hand firmly on her back. She is so shocked not to get a beating that she doesn't struggle to sit up and lies on her stomach, looking at the white ground.

He leans down close to her head and whispers, 'You will pay for that, you shrivelled scab.'

And she doesn't doubt it.

Chapter 20

Camis stifles a groan, waiting in the pitch blackness. His mind works overtime. Had his mother been captured too? Had she gone through . . . He imagines all sorts of dreadful situations and works himself into a state of anxiety, his heart pounding at all the improbable things that he concocts.

He bites on his lower lip, not feeling the pain. At last, he remembers the candle and the deep breathing exercises she had taught him. Gradually, he focuses on the flame in his mind. Its soft glow calms him and his body relaxes.

A thought drifts across his mind—Nenna in chains. Immediately, the oasis of calm he has built shatters, and he is back in the eternal black of the huge room with new tortures running through his mind.

The front wall of the room begins to rise slowly. White light and heat flood in. Camis shrinks back into the shadowy space behind the mounds, partly to avoid being seen, partly to help adjust his sight to the glare. Two figures appear in the open wall, black against the brilliant daylight. They untie sections of rope and Camis holds his breath. They each slide out a large box and carry it out of the craft.

The men reappear and disappear again with the boxes, and the pile on his left dwindles. What would happen when there were no boxes left? What would he do?

He is dressed now in the uniform that Tiberius left him—an all-black shirt and stretchy trousers that are a little baggy on his wiry frame. There is a red triangle of cloth that the other soldiers wear tied around their necks, he fixes it in place, but doesn't think anyone will be fooled for long, especially if they ask him any questions. Where is Tiberius?

The men are just coming back in when a voice outside shouts something indistinguishable, and they both turn away, disappearing back outside. When they do not reappear, Camis edges along the narrow passageway towards the front of the boxes. There is a ramp leading up and into the storeroom. It rests on what appears to be white sand, but he is afraid to go closer to the opening to get a clearer view. There may be guards out there.

Other than the boxes, there are no other hiding places. Someone climbs into view, and Camis darts back.

'Camis?' a voice calls in a loud whisper, and Tiberius appears at the end of the boxes. Camis breathes out in a rush, relieved to see him.

'Did you find her?' Camis asks him, moving forward.

'No, not exactly.' Tiberius places a hand gently on his shoulder. 'But I have some news.' He looks Camis in the eye and continues. 'I have found out who has chosen her. She was taken by a Nauarch named Vitrainy. He has her in his quarters.

'But we can get her back, can't we?' Camis stares hard at Tiberius, who drops his hand along with his eyes.

'He is one of the top Nauarch's. I am not permitted onto his deck, and I couldn't get close to her.' He shakes his head sadly.

'Well, I'm not leaving without her,' Camis says, turning for the back of the ship.

'And what exactly do you expect to do?' Tiberius asks as he steps in front of Camis. 'You do not know your way around the shuttle, and as we speak, most have disembarked. She has probably accompanied him to his home.'

They stand for a moment, Camis tense and ready to tear the place apart, and Tiberius watching him sadly.

'Our only hope is to find out where the Nauarch lives in the city and watch and learn the movements of his household and see if we can reach her,' Tiberius says softly.

'What does he want with her?' Camis asks, his eyes narrowing. 'Will she be treated well?'

Tiberius doesn't reply straight away, and he has an odd, sour twist to his mouth.

'I'm not going to lie to you, Camis. The rumours are not good. They say he is a hard callous man.' Tiberius swallows, and his eyes flick away and then back to Camis. 'She will be used for his pleasure. They say his 'rewards' don't last long.'

An icy cold sweeps through Camis' body. Clenching his fists, he glares at Tiberius. 'We can't let that happen. We must get her out. Now!' He pounds his fists against the tarp covering the boxes.

'All I can do is try to get you off the ship safely and into the city. If we make a move now . . . ' He trails off, backing away as Camis continues over him.

'You consider yourselves superior to us and call us prims, but you behave like animals. No, not animals—savages!'

'Oi! You two!' A shout causes them both to freeze. Tiberius's face is white, emphasising the dark shadows under his eyes, and Camis realises just how much danger he has put them both in.

A man is silhouetted, standing halfway up the ramp. The man is not dressed in the black uniform of the crew but wears a grubby once-white vest and a pair of tan trousers.

'Come on, lads. I haven't got all day. If you're all the replacements I'm going to get, then get to it. If not, then piss off.' He pulls out three of the boxes, hoisting them up. His arm muscles bulge, veins snaking over them. As he walks away, they can see the sinews around his neck stand out, and they both let out their breath. He hadn't heard Camis' outburst.

'I'm sorry,' Tiberius says quietly as he crosses to the huge pile of boxes. He slides the top box closer. Straining to lift it, he waddles away towards the opening. Just before leaving, he looks back. 'Come on.' He hisses. 'Get a box. He thinks you are one of us.'

The bright light blinds Camis, who squints at Tiberius's back as he manages to struggle after him to a nearby cart. Tiberius hauls his box up onto the cart floor, but Camis has to lean back and strain in order to reach the back. His mind is blank. The man is up on the cart and slides one of the boxes to the front. He stares down at them, sweat trickling down his cheeks. He is short and muscular with an open smile. His skin is tanned and his light brown eyes are edged in laughter lines. He takes out a cloth and mops his bald head.

'Right, then, what do I call you lads?

'Camis,' Camis replies automatically.

'And you?' says the man looking at Tiberius.

'Er, um, Tiberius.'

'Jump to it. I gotta deliver this lot to the mines. This surplus is needed. Quick.' The man wipes his arm across his forehead and carries the remaining box back to add to the stack at the front of the cart.

The ground crunches under his feet, and Camis looks down. Tiny white stones litter the floor. He glances to each side, seeing nothing but white. Where are they? He looks towards Tiberius who is walking slightly in front of him.

At the boxes, Tiberius pokes him. 'Whatever made you give him your real name?'

'Where are we?' Camis asks, ignoring Tiberius' question.

Tiberius looks puzzled. 'On the shuttle, helping to unload it after landing,' he says. 'We docked with the mothership, which flew us closer to home here, and then we came down on the shuttle.' He hoists up another box and turns to leave.

'Oh,' is all Camis can say, his brow furrowed.

They return to the cart, passing the man going for his next load. Once they are back collecting their third box, Tiberius continues.

'As for where we are, Camis,' he says hoisting a box into his arms, 'we are now on my home planet, Crystal Moon. I think your people call it the Mama.' And he shuffles away towards the cart with his load.

Camis staggers back into the stack of boxes, his stomach roiling. It is impossible. He feels sick and dizzy. He closes his eyes and tries to swallow down the rising panic.

'You alright?' the man asks him, coming back up the slope. 'You look as though you're about to throw up.'

Camis nods but doesn't move away from the pile of boxes that hold him upright. How in Maa Erda has he ended up here? How is he going to find his mother now? He tries to suck in air, but his lungs won't work. The light around him dims, and he hears the others talking, but they seem far, far away.

'How much water you drunk today?' the man asks.

'Not a lot,' Tiberius says as he joins them. 'We didn't even have time for breakfast because Cammy here got us a section six for laughing during the briefing.'

'Working in this heat will make anyone a bit wobbly. Hang on here a bit in the shade and I'll be back.'

Camis slides down the boxes to the floor. His head sags to his chest.

'Camis, what is it?' Tiberius stops speaking as the man climbs back up the slope. He might be solid muscle, but he is quick.

'Here,' the man says, giving Camis a flask of water and handing the sack to Tiberius. 'Help yourself. I'll pop over to the mess before we leave and get some more supplies. Name's Arture, by the way. My job is to see supplies reach the soldiers at the mines, and there's a lot of them there now, as you'd expect.'

Tiberius rummages in the sack and pulls out a leg of cold chicken, which he stuffs in his mouth. Camis passes him the water and looks quickly away, his stomach somersaulting. How is he going to get home from here?

'Why's so many soldiers being sent to the mines?' Tiberius mumbles through a mouthful of chicken.

'Some sort of trouble, I heard. Insurgents freeing prims or some such thing,' Arture says, exiting the craft and disappearing to the side. They hear him relieve himself noisily onto the crystal sand.

'So, young cadets, how many trips you manage to make in this old bucket?' he says, coming back in and picking up the discarded sack.

Camis frowns, turns his head so only Tiberius can see his face and mouths, 'What?'

'Oh, this was our first trip. We only just passed selection,' Tiberius says with a mouthful of chicken.

Arture looks over at them sharply. 'How the devil did you manage to get a section six on your first trip?' Arture says, laughing.

'Didn't hear briefing start and carried on talking and then he'—Tiberius nods at Camis—'laughed at my joke, and we got thrown out.'

'Oh well, lads, my gain. You've been assigned to unloading duty as your punishment.'

Tiberius doesn't correct him.

Arture starts pulling out boxes, selecting three to lift.

'Well come on then you two, let's get on with it.' He grunts beneath the weight of the boxes. 'Got a couple of days ride ahead once loaded.' He walks away.

Tiberius looks across at Camis. 'We might have to go along with this, Camis, sorry. But we'll get away as soon as the boxes are off-loaded.'

Camis nods. 'Let's hope he doesn't check the ship's log for a Camis.'

'Oi! You two! We got work to do,' Arture calls.

In the white glare and heat of the day, they haul box after box towards the covered wagons until at last they are all loaded. Three cartloads stand waiting for the next stage of their journey. The three men stand out in the open, drinking from the water flasks that Arture has handed them. The flasks are made of some sort of lightweight metal, and the water inside is cool. A warm breeze dries the sweat on their bodies.

'Well, lads, if you just wait here, I'll get the horses and some supplies, and we can get off,' Arture says.

Tiberius lowers his flask hurriedly, choking on the water. 'You want us to come?' he splutters, splattering water down himself.

'Aye, lad,' Arture calls back over his shoulder. 'I can't drive three carts by myself.'

'But what about your regular carters?'

'All working soldiers, lad. All called by his Imperial Highness, D'Ruja A'Riman, the crystal protect him, to help with the insurgents. We're all that's left. So, I'll have to make do with you two.' And he laughs, disappearing around the ship.

'Crystal! I'd not expected this,' Tiberius says once Arture is out of sight. 'I thought after we'd done this job, we could get away into the city.'

Camis looks at his feet. 'I just wanted to find Nenna,' he says. 'And then find out if my mother is here.

'Well, if all leave is cancelled, Vitrainy will not be in the city. He'll also be at the mines. So, she'll be safe at his villa until his return.' Tiberius clamps Camis on the shoulder.

Camis straightens and looks at him. 'Well, in that case, I could go to the mines to see if my mother is there and if I can find Nenna's brother.' He turns to watch Arture reappear, leading two huge horses.

Arture nods towards the boys. 'Any of you ever hitched up a horse?'

'Yes.' Camis replies as Tiberius shakes his head.

'Well, Camis, you can show him how it's done. I'll fetch my lad and the rest of our food.' He hands one set of reins to Camis and ties the other horse to the back of one of the loaded carts. 'This brown 'n white's called Scout, and the pretty little mare there is Spirit. Back in a bit.'

Camis leads the huge gelding towards the nearest cart and clucks him slowly back, expertly positioning him between the traces. The horse is the biggest he has ever seen—a good head and shoulders higher than any back home. The horse has thick long hair hanging part way down its legs to its hooves.

Camis shows Tiberius each of the straps and how to secure the cart firmly but comfortably. Tiberius stands a good distance away, fidgeting from one foot to another. When Camis is finished, he moves to the front of the horse.

'Come say hello to your charge,' Camis says, grinning. 'He won't bite.'

'He might,' Tiberius says, taking a step away.

'No, not this big old softy. Hey, Scout not you, eh?' Camis replies, rubbing the horse's broad white nose.

The massive horse lowers his head and half closes his eyes. Tiberius tentatively steps closer and reaches out to touch the soft brown-and-white hair. The horse swings its head upwards, and Tiberius steps away hurriedly.

'Whoa, boy, gently.' Camis moves his hand to tickle one of the horse's ears, then he hands Tiberius the reins, leaving him staring nervously at the horse. Quietly, Camis withdraws and confidently hitches up the other horse.

'Where did you learn to do all that?' Arture asks. Camis hadn't noticed he'd returned. He continues tightening the cheek strap and glances towards Tiberius.

'Worked in the royal stables, didn't you, Cam?' his friend says quickly. 'Soldier's orphan.'

And Camis nods and turns towards the horse to hide his reddening cheeks.

Arture slings two large leather packs over his shoulder and backs his horse quickly into place, clicking his tongue to encourage him to move. He nods approval at Camis.

'I like to test new boys to see if they can handle my drays. They can tell if someone is useless. Can see you know your stuff, youngster,' he states. 'You'll do.' And Camis feels the glow in his cheeks which had started from the lie, now deepen from the praise.

Once his horse is set in the traces, Arture pulls a lightweight sacking material over the grey's head and fastens it in place. Camis can hear him talking quietly and soothingly to the animal. He does the same for the other two horses, then climbs up onto the front bench of his cart, slinging the pack behind him into the covered wagon.

'Right, lads. Let's be off.'

Masked by the ship, Camis does not immediately see the strange globe in the sky until they have ridden a short distance.

Gradually sliding into view from behind the massive craft, the orb hangs there, revealing itself in frightening-but-unbelievable splendour. It is breathtakingly beautiful. His horse knows the routine and plods on behind Arture's cart, leaving him to gawp. The blue-and-green jewel in the bright white sky makes his heart lurch and fills him with awe.

He turns to look back at Tiberius and points to the planet. 'What's that?' he mouths, slowing his horse a little to wait for Tiberius to catch up.

'That is where you came from,' Tiberius says. 'That is your home planet.'

Chapter 21

'He cannot keep me locked up like some animal!' Wringing her hands, Serin paces the floor. 'I won't be treated this way!'

'Mistress, come and eat.'

'A few bruises and a knife wound to his precious guards - which I healed - and for that, I'm locked up. Onora, the people, their poverty . . .' She rounds on the serving woman. 'Why didn't you tell me? You could have warned me. I had no idea.'

Onora looks directly at her. 'You were gone for over fifteen years. I was sworn never to discuss you outside of the palace. We all were. I value my job, my life.' Onora starts to clear the plates of untouched food, stacking the dishes noisily on a silver tray. 'The people in the city didn't know that you had returned because' She looks across again at Serin, annunciating every word. 'they didn't even know that you had left.' She picks the tray up and walks to the door.

'I know exactly what your uncle is like. The young girls he sneaks into the palace then discards. The beatings his guards carry out under his instructions for any perceived crime. The staff that mysteriously vanish.' She takes the tray and leaves the implications of what she had just said to sink in. 'He can treat you this way because he can.'

Later, washed and dressed, Serin indicates for Onora to join her on the balcony. They sit with untouched embroidery hoops on their knees, staring out over the city. Should he arrive, they will look busy—a princess and her ladies' maid, sewing and relaxing in the fresh air.

'Please tell me more,' Serin says, her own problems seeming petty compared to what she has just heard.

'The people think the only one in the palace on their side is the Book. They think that he still reads the words for them. They don't know the changes that *His Imperial Highness* has made for his own benefit.' Onora spits out his name as she pours them both a glass of water.

'What do you mean? Of course he still reads the words.'

'Yes, but only a token amount of them. Your uncle has claimed the rest, making another secret book that he uses to shore up his power. In that second Book, *he* writes the words and forces your brother to read them every evening. We are not meant to know about it. But some secrets cannot be hidden.'

Onora slams down the empty water jug, making Serin wince. 'Most of the food the Book grows goes to feed his army. The rest of the people go hungry. Your uncle's strength, speed, and spite is enhanced through this second Book. It channels the power of the crystal and the words for his own good. He thinks only a handful of the priesthood know, but not everyone is on his side.'

Serin's heart feels heavy. 'I had no idea how bad things had become.'

'He has managed to divert some of the power that the crystal provides through this secret Book and away to . . . well, we don't know to where. There is talk that he's up to something north of the city, but the soldiers that return from duty there are tight-lipped. No one with even a pinch of talent can oppose him.'

She hands Serin a glass. 'We don't know exactly what your uncle is capable of, and none of us really want to find out. The priests have told the people of what you did to heal the Book. The city hears their whispers. Give it time. The news will percolate deeper. There will be others on your side, and maybe, once you are married to him, you might even be able to help us more.'

Serin looks out across her balcony to the city, hope and horror waring inside her.

'Mistress! Mistress, wake up!' Serin opens her eyes to her maid bending over her, a crystal lamp glowing.

'What is it?' she says, sittings up. The light silk sheet falls away.

'There is someone here to see you. It is urgent.' Onora passes her a lightweight wrap and waits while she slips her feet into her sandals. Serin follows Onora to the door, stifling a yawn. They walk down the dark corridor.

'What time is it, and where are we going?'

'It has just passed into the next day,' Onora says and leads Serin down the servant's stairs towards the kitchens. The stairs are unadorned stone and spiral around endlessly.

'Someone is waiting. She needs your help.'

The kitchens are lit from a score of wall sconces, the white crystal illuminating everything brightly. As they enter the vast kitchen area, a woman moves to greet them. She is petite, wearing a plain blue headscarf with strands of her dark hair escaping from it. Serin recognises her immediately—the stallholder from the marketplace.

'It's you,' Serin says in surprise.

The stallholder bows her head. 'I am sorry for what happened. I never intended . . . '

'Mistress,' Onora says, 'this is Jai. She wants to ask you something.' Onora smiles encouragingly at the woman. Serin glances back to the stallholder and realises with a shock that the woman is crying. Large tears roll silently down her cheeks.

'There is a child—she is only five, maybe six, and she is very sick.' She scrubs a hand roughly across her face. 'There are others too, but I don't think this young one will last much longer. We heard that you can heal. Please, will you come and help her? You are our last hope.'

'A child? I was told . . . I thought . . .' Serin trails off. The questions can wait until later. 'Of course I will help. Can you bring the child to me?' Serin crosses closer, placing her hand on the woman's shoulder. Jai shakes her head slowly, her eyes pleading. Serin drops her hand.

'I am a prisoner here. Every move is reported back to my uncle.'

'There are ways out, mistress,' Onora interrupts. 'Ways unseen, and there are those who will help us in the palace to get out and back safely. We couldn't share this with you before because'—she looks over at Jai— 'we didn't know if we could trust you.'

Onora points to a door in the corner. More stairs lead down into a cavernous cellar. As Serin descends, she glimpses the uniformed legs of two soldiers waiting below. With her heart pounding, she turns to run back up. Onora and Jai both reach out to stop her.

'Mistress! They are with us. They will see us safely into the city and back.'

Slowly, she steps down into the cellar, and there he is. The man she had healed on the shuttle deck. The man she thought she would never see again. The man—no, the boy—she had left all those years ago. Zachary. Alive and well and here.

Her heart stops beating and her legs fold beneath her.

He catches her before she falls, holding her gently in his arms, his breath soft on her face. Spirals of light blue spin across the azure of his eyes. She can see the universe, the ocean, the love, the ache.

'Hello, Serin.' And he places her softly back on her feet. She touches his shoulder to steady herself and to check if he is real. Her pulse races. She holds his gaze.

Her breath explodes outwards, carrying his name. 'Zachary.'
 And he smiles.

She is back, swimming in the pool at midnight, riding out across the white desert, hiding in the palace gardens, always with him, always laughing. And she breathes in, capturing a long-forgotten familiar scent. An image of limbs, naked, tangled, soaked in sweat, flash through her mind, and she blushes.

Letting go of his hands, she steps back, awkwardness pushing its way between them.

'Thank you for your healing back in the shuttle hanger,' he says. 'I couldn't come before without raising suspicion.'

The boy she knew is gone, and in his place is a man—confident, with startling blue eyes, still someone she would know in a crowd. But the trusting smiling person she had known has been replaced by a harder version, as though the soft edges have been knocked away and replaced with stone. She wonders if he'd thought of her in the years she was away. She takes in the uniform.

'You work for him,' she states. But of course he does. She'd seen him, healed him on board the shuttle.

'In a way,' he says, his eyes hardening. 'Your uncle leaves very little work for people other than soldiering.'

There is a hand on her shoulder. 'Mistress, we must go.' And Onora gestures for Serin to hurry.

Lightheaded, she walks without seeing; emotions, thoughts, memories whirl. She knows he is behind her from the feathery sensation that prickles her spine. This can't be, not now, not ever. And she shakes her head, trying to clear the conflict in her mind. She had left those childish dreams behind when she'd fled—dreams of a normal family life, dreams of him. Her uncle would never have let him live, let alone the child.

Onora places a dark cloak around her. It smells faintly of orange blossom. They walk down into the city. The other two women wear similar cloaks with the hoods drawn up. She does the same.

They move quietly through the side streets towards a huge building. There aren't any windows. Wispy, tattered clouds streak across the Papa, black against the vivid red and orange. Maa Erda is not visible in the night sky. They climb the stone steps, passing under wide graceful arches flanked by grey fluted pillars, and into a vast atrium. It is deserted and smells musty.

'Isn't this a water purification plant?' she asks Onora softly.

'Abandoned as the population shrinks,' Onora replies as she uncovers a crystal from the basket she is carrying. It throws up gigantic shadows around them, which spread out across the wide echoing space. It is as though they are surrounded.

Jai and Onora hurry forward. Before following, she steals a quick glance at Zachary, and her heart flutters. He is busy scouring the hall. His light brown hair is shorter, his curls cut away. He seems more solid than she remembers.

Some instinct makes him look across at her. Again he smiles. Her legs shake, threatening to give way once more. Then the light fades as her maid vanishes into a stairwell, and she hurries after her. They climb to the roof, and once at the top, she has no more time to think about him. On the flat roof are children. Lots of children.

The whole rooftop is covered in pallets and bedding, with makeshift canopies over many of them. Children swarm around the two women, and Serin realises that they are giving out food. She recognises her own untouched supper coming out of Onora's basket—cold meats and cheeses, tomatoes, bread, and fruit. A meagre allowance for the number of children. Her eyes fill with tears. How could she have been so blind? So selfish?

Jai hands Onora her own basket of food to give out, and beckons Serin to follow her to one of the beds. A child lies on top of some rags with her eyes closed. She has a fever, and the light cotton shift she is wearing is plastered to her thin frame. She is restless and agitated, her eyes flickering, as she fights monsters in her fever. Serin kneels beside the child.

'What is her name?' she asks as she places her hand on the child's forehead. But she doesn't hear the reply as she is already immersed in the healing.

The child has a pervading odour that clings to her, cloying and yeasty, like a bad wine. Serin draws the heat up and out of the child and into her hand, channelling it through her body, bringing the temperature down. Gradually, the child's flushed complexion calms, and she relaxes into sleep.

Serin keeps one hand in place and passes her other gradually down the child's body, holding it first above the chest area, waiting for the rapid heartbeat to slow. Moving her hand lower, she presses on the child's abdomen, checking the liver, gut, and kidneys. She does a rapid check all over, finding only a slightly swollen hand, and a small cut on the child's right palm, about the length of a thumb nail, it is angry and red.

She sends a force through her own body, across and into the child. The area with the cut swells briefly as blood floods in, sweeping away the last of the infection. Serin knits the edges of the cut together, growing fresh tissue up and out, until there is a barely-visible white scar. Sighing, she sits back on her heels, looking down at the sleeping child.

Becoming gradually aware of her surroundings and the silence around her, she looks up to see the other children and three older women, along with Onora and Jai, standing quietly in a ring around her. Their faces show astonishment and awe. She scrambles to her feet.

'Right, are there anymore that need help?' she says quickly, wiping her hands on a wet cloth that Onora holds out to her.

There are only minor scrapes and bruises among the remaining children, and other than needing a good feed, the children seem in remarkably good health. The women are settling the children back to their beds when a young boy catches her eye. He is supporting his right arm by the elbow protectively, and his right hand is lying on his chest curved into a claw.

Crouching down, she brushes the boy's dark hair away from his face.

'What happened?'

'A cart crashed into me,' he whispers.

'And who set the bones? Your mother?' The boy shakes his head. 'Your father?'

'Ma'am, we bought the boy back from the mines,' Jai says. 'No one set his arm. After the accident, he was discarded. The few soldiers who are on our side risked their lives to rescue him and the others that you see here.' Jai gestures to all the children.

Serin straightens up to look at Jai. 'What do you mean, the mines? Children don't work down in the mines.'

Jai looks towards Onora. 'Mistress, these are children of the prims. Some have been born here, some arrive with their parents. Some are born from soldier-prim . . . relationships.'

'But . . . ' Serin looks around at the children and notices the brown hair and eyes, their shape and size—slightly heavier, shorter. She kneels back down to the boy and lightly touches his thin stiff fingers.

'I will be back tomorrow night. You will need to take a sleeping potion because the healing will be painful.' The boy's big brown eyes fill with tears. 'It's all right. I'll look after you.'

'No,' he says, shaking his head. 'I'm not scared of the pain. I'm just frightened that you won't come back.'

'What's your name?' she asks, smiling sadly.

'Two-seven-two.'

Serin whirls towards the other women, her mouth open, green eyes flashing. 'What is the meaning of this? Have you no humanity that you number a child?'

'That is D'Ruja's doing! Your uncle will only allow them numbers,' Jai retorts angrily.

'Mistress, they are numbered at the mines. It is all he has known,' interjects Onora. 'And in time, he can pick his own name, and we will honour it.'

Speechless, Serin stares at them. Even his horses are given names! She cannot comprehend the devaluing of a life so that it is just numbered for convenience. Her mouth feels dry. She had thought she had made Camis' life hard, depriving him of the privileges of the palace and the things she could have given him. But this boy has nothing, not even a name.

She crouches back down to the boy. He must be only about nine or ten. 'Well, I promise you, I will be back tomorrow night, and you will be the first one I see to.'

The boy throws his good arm around her neck and hugs her. She can feel the withered arm pressing into her chest, and her throat tightens, tears stinging her eyes as she hugs him back.

'Thank you,' Jai says.

As she walks back to the palace, Serin knows that she has found a purpose, a reason to stay and help. She sees her son in her mind's eye, sitting on their cart, clicking the old pony onwards. She prays to the Book that she has given him enough skills to survive with, prays that he uses his gift wisely, prays that one day she might see him again.

'Onora, how is it that the'—she cannot bring herself to call them prims—'the people that work in the mines can have children. I thought that they'—and she shudders at the thought—'were processed.'

Onora is quiet for a long while, walking briskly and staring ahead, her hood up. Then she turns and says, 'Your uncle only has the men castrated. There was a sickness that took the women early if they were sterilised. He found that they could work for longer if left whole. 'Besides, leaving them whole gives him an additional source of manpower, as the children are set to work alongside their mothers picking the mined crystal.'

Serin's mouth opens but she cannot speak.

'There is also the added bonus of his men getting some . . . sport with the women.'

Once in the palace gardens, Onora slips into the building ahead, leaving Serin alone with Zachary. She is so wrapped up in her thoughts that she does not notice that the other guard has left too. They stop before the doors.

'I waited for you.'

'I . . . ' She doesn't know what to say. The years drop away, and she feels awkward. Why did he wait? Did he still love her after all this time? She is too scared to ask.

They stand close, and she can feel the heat of his body. She can feel his longing. Or is it hers? His fingers stroke her cheek, and she tilts her head towards his caress. The door in her mind, where she has locked him away, doesn't just unlock and open, it flies wide, splintering into tiny pieces, exposing emotions, thoughts, and longings she had thought safely buried there.

They stand for an age just looking at each other. Then he closes the gap between them quickly, and his lips brush hers, a feather caress. A tingle spreads slowly through her body from that touch, reaching from the roots of her hair through to the nails on her fingers, down to the soles of her feet. Her arms are around his neck, and she kisses him back with the desire of fifteen lost years. They break apart, a burning glow heating her face and her belly. She wants him so badly.

'I have missed you,' he says, keeping his eyes locked on hers. 'You vanished, and I searched until your brother got word to me. The palace never admitted you were even missing.' She doesn't answer, and he continues. 'You wanted to know why I wear his uniform. Well, I worked my way up through the ranks and onto his ships. My plan was to train as a hov tech and sneak onboard to get down there, to find you again.'

Her heart goes out to him. He had never forgotten her, and all this time he had been actively trying to reach her.

'Did you think of me?' he whispers.

She looks up at him; her chest aches with love for him, and she starts to nod, then hurriedly shakes her head. The hurt in his eyes as he steps back cuts her like a knife.

'No, you misunderstand,' she says quickly. 'I had to survive in a strange world on my own. I had to shut all thoughts of you away, or I would have gone mad. And I left because...' She watches his face closely knowing the enormity of what she is about to say. Pain flashes through her. She has to tell him the truth, but how will he react? He leans towards her.

'Zachary.' She stops him with that one word. 'It isn't as clear cut as that. You see . . . ' She fumbles for the exact words. Looking up, she sees again the indigo ring that outlines the deep ocean-blue of his eyes, and an image of Camis flashes in her mind. His deep blue eyes and his intense passion. Is he their son or is he. . . ? She wipes the thought away quickly, reaching up to touch his cheek.

With a shock, she suddenly realises that she can see clearly. Zachary's face glows gently with a soft light. It is dawn. She has to go.

'Go,' she tells him. 'It is dawn, the palace is waking! Go before we are seen.'

***

You took your time.

And something hard slams into her stomach, knocking her breath away. Doubled over she tries call out in alarm as she sees her maid lying like a discarded rag on the floor.

'Onora!' But the sound is a gasp.

Who were you talking to? Why were you out at this hour?

Her uncle lunges towards her, his face contorted in rage.

'I couldn't sleep,' Serin snaps aloud at him. 'I was bored and went for a walk around the grounds. I tried talking to one of the guards, but as per your instructions, he wouldn't answer. I sent Onora ahead to run me a bath and then to go to her bed.' She clutches her throat, glaring, defiant.

I thought…

'I don't care what you thought. I'm sick of you and your controlling ways.'

All the anger of the night and what she now knows boils inside of her. She hisses and takes a few wobbly steps towards Onora, her knees weak and shaking. Before she reaches her maid, he pushes her roughly towards her bedchamber.

I know you are hiding something. Stay in there. His eyes are a wide flat grey. They pierce her mind and are as sharp as his words.

'Guards! GUARDS!' he bellows.

Three guards clatter to a halt outside the door, their sides heaving, their swords drawn. More swarm up the stairs and down the corridor towards her room. Their boots thunder on the marble floor. She glimpses Zachary among the early arrivals. He does not acknowledge her, and she lets out her breath.

Her uncle points at the maid on the floor. 'Remove her! Lock her up.'

'No!' Serin cries and pushes past him to protect Onora. Her uncle catches her by her wrist and wrenches her hand back. A needle-sharp pain begins to build in her head. The guards hesitate.

'What are you waiting for? Take her and go!' her uncle shouts, his face dark.

197

Helpless and angry, her eyes cling to Onora as the guards lift the maid away.

'Close the door,' he bellows after them.

The instant they are alone, he pulls her to him and kisses her savagely. His lips are hard and dry as bone. The pain in her head increases as she squirms against him, vainly pressing her hands on his chest to push him away.

'I hate you!' she screams as she breaks free from him, and the pain stops.

Expressionless, he stares at her, holding her at arm's length. Then he pivots on his heels, his scarlet riding cloak swirling around him, and leaves her alone.

Chapter 22

The legs of other horses passing by stir a cloud of low dust, tickling Nenna's nose and stinging her eyes. Vitrainy's legs tighten in a squeeze, signalling the stallion to start moving. The dust increases. She splutters, choking.

'Pull up the neck of your dress, you stupid prim. Use it to cover your mouth.'

At first, the movement is gentle, soothing even, as she lays face down across the back of the horse. Despite the strangeness of the position, she feels herself begin to drift. The hood of the cloak falls over her head, covering her hair and flopping around her face, masking her view of everything except the occasional blurred glimpse of the horse's hooves. The steady rhythm lulls her into a doze.

She is leaning across the curved branch of a tree, its knobbly bark digging into her chest and tummy. She swings out and back across the river, laughing, hearing the other children on the bank behind, egging her on. If she twirls right around, she might be able to see them and wave. But when she does, they've vanished, replaced by a man clad all in black.

He is grinning at her. The rope holding the branch spins her slowly around, and she looks down to see Quarrel falling through the air away from her, spinning counterclockwise to her movement. His tongue lolling, his eyes shut, he hits the ground below with a thud that makes her gasp.

She strains to get off the rotating log, but looking up, she finds that the landscape beyond is stark, white, and devoid of life. The river is a dust bowl. Languidly, she continues to revolve, turning a full circle.

The man is still there but closer. His grin is more of a leer, his hazel eyes dead. Her heart thuds in her chest, and she wants to look away, but she can't as he opens his mouth wider and wider, and she is sucked towards the gaping hole.

'Lie still, bitch,' a muffled voice growls, and a hand slaps her backside.

Vitrainy kicks the stallion into a trot, jolting Nenna relentlessly, bouncing her up and down, clashing her teeth together so that she has to clamp her jaw tight. She tries to cough and clear her throat, but the pressure on her chest and the thud, thud, thud action made it difficult, agonising.

The rest of the day passes in a blur of pain and gasping breaths. She tries wriggling and pushing herself upward with her hands, but each time, Vitrainy feels her movements and whacks her hard across the rump, not even bothering to yell at her.

There are brief breaks in which the horses and soldiers are refuelled, and more importantly, even she is fed and watered. In the short periods of respite, she is lowered to the ground and made to stand on a strange, flat mat that Vitrainy unrolls from his backpack.

'And don't you dare move,' he snarls, his face close to hers. 'Or you'll find there's worse than my hand.' Instinctively, she cows away from him, and he barks a laugh.

Vitrainy carefully removes the stallion's protective hood, and dampening a cloth from his pack, he gently wipes the horse's face, all the while talking in a low, soothing murmur, his metal boot guards clicking strangely as he walks around the horse.

He offers her some water, and she takes it and gulps it down.

'Would you like some more?' he says.

Shocked, she looks up to see him baring his teeth at her in a kind of smile, and she doesn't immediately hold the cup back out, fearing some trick. But he reaches over and refills the cup from his flask, continuing to smile.

But then the commander passes by, nodding and stopping to check on the men and horses. Vitrainy walks away after the commander has moved off.

During the ride, she hears another man talking to Vitrainy.

'You need to calm down, Vitrainy, or the commander will revoke those privileges that you worked so hard to regain.'

Vitrainy stiffens. 'That insufferable prick winds me up. I just can't help it. He likes to lord it over me now. I could smash—'

'Shh! Keep your voice down.'

'You know he doesn't have any right to tell me how to treat my property,' Vitrainy says, slapping Nenna's backside.

'You know that's not true. After your last one and the, uh, accident, you know he's going to watch you.'

Vitrainy doesn't reply to this last remark. An icy band grips her heart. The last one? An accident? Horse shit.

Night falls, and they ride on, alternating short periods of walking the horses with a rib-crunching trot. When they finally do stop, the sun is full in the sky, her clothes stick wetly to her back, and she is numb from neck to hips.

Vitrainy scruffs the back of her cloak and dress and pulls her down, dropping her onto the strange mat. Her legs crumple, and she sits down hard, unable to rise. She rubs the grit from her eyes, blinking, exhausted, and sore.

People around her begin to set up camp. The horses are seen to, watered and rubbed down. Gingerly, she touches her chest, numb from the ride, gently rubbing some feeling back to the area, watching the activity. High poles are hammered into the ground and canopies are unfurled, giving both soldiers and horses a necessary respite from the sun.

Thin pliable groundsheets are rolled out, like the mat she is sitting on. Once in place, the soldiers remove the metal clips from the soles of their boots. Small campfires are quickly lit in strange metal buckets. The buckets have holes puncturing their sides, and she can see a white glow coming from stones placed in the bottom. If there is any heat, she can't feel it from where she is sitting. It isn't long before the smell of cooking pervades the air—roast meats and flatbreads mingled with an unusual sharp tang that she can't place, but it is spicy and makes her mouth water.

'Don't move off that,' Vitrainy says and lowers his red bandana to give her a malicious grin.

She stays on the ground mat, trying to stretch the kinks from her neck while rubbing her ribs and abdomen. She will be a mass of bruises the next day and hopes that they are not far from their destination. By the third day, she realises that was wishful thinking.

A slim young man with slicked-back brown hair joins Vitrainy after supper. He stands very close, looking up at him. Both men ignore her. When he speaks, she recognises the voice. It is the man who had spoken to Vitrainy while they were riding.

'We need to talk,' says the younger man, placing his hand on Vitrainy's arm, 'but not with her here.' And he twitches his head towards Nenna.

'Oh, she can't do anything, Eachan.'

'I know, but she makes me uncomfortable.' The young man scratches the wispy brown hairs on his chin.

Vitrainy laughs. 'What's with the beard fluff anyway?' He reaches out to tug the hair on the young man's chin, but Eachan draws back, scowling.

'Seriously, V,' Eachan says, staring with obvious dislike towards Nenna. 'You know we can't talk with her here, and you know I can't mindspeak.'

His voice has taken on a whine. Nenna keeps her head down, slowly chewing the last of her food, careful to look as though she is not listening even though the two men are within touching distance of her.

'You!' snaps Vitrainy, looking down at her. 'Go take a walk. Keep to the mats.' And with that, he waves her away, and taking Eachan's arm, leads his friend to sit beside their unusual campfire.

Nenna cannot believe her luck, but she is careful not to look too excited or move too quickly or too slowly. What if he changes his mind? She places her bowl on the floor beside her and pushes herself up stiffly. Although every muscle aches and every rib feels bruised, she walks away from them deeper into the camp, expecting at any moment for him to wrench her back and beat her for leaving.

She is a long way through the camp before she begins to believe she really is free, for a while. Most of the soldiers, men and women, ignore her, but a few glare at her with open hostility, while one or two regard her with what looks like pity. Maybe they know the real Vitrainy.

The camp is orderly and clean. With their suppers cleared away, many of the soldiers are settling to sleep. Some are mending clothing or polishing saddles; others play games of cards or dice.

The camp snakes over a wide area, all of it covered over with matting underfoot. Lines of horses are picketed at intervals between the tents and have clusters of people gathered around them. Men and women in their black uniforms, with their essential red dust scarf, sit or lie in twos or threes, eating, sewing, polishing harnesses, or dozing. There are far more horses than people. Indicating what? That they're pack horses? A change of mount for each man? That would indicate a long journey.

She stops by a line of horses to think, drawn to them. They remind her of home, and she reaches up to stroke a dark bay mare.

'She's lovely, isn't she?' says a voice, making Nenna freeze.

A scruffy young man with a long face and a shock of blond hair emerges suddenly from behind the mare. He is holding a thin metal hoof pick in his hand. His smile is the first open warm smile she has seen from these people.

'Oh, don't panic, miss. Nothing wrong with saying hello to the workers, is there, girl?' He pats the horse on the rump as he walks towards her.

'Name's Finstar,' he says, looking at Nenna and brushing his hair back out of his eyes. 'But my friends just call me Fin.'

'I . . . I'm Nenna. Short for Siena,' she replies nervously, stepping back and looking around, checking to see if anyone is watching.

'Don't worry about this one,' he says, misunderstanding her action. 'She wouldn't hurt a fly.' Then he laughs. 'Well, maybe a bite-fly, but we don't get many of those, thank the Book.' His hair has flopped untidily back onto his face again, covering one eye. Nenna wants to brush it back for him. Instead, she reaches up and strokes the mare's nose.

'She is beautiful,' Nenna says, looking into the horse's deep brown eyes, seeing intelligence looking back at her, along with trust.

Oh, Quarrel, I couldn't protect you. Her eyes fill unexpectedly with tears.

'I'll just finish her back hoof,' Fin says, turning away.

Nenna's face flushes. He'd seen. She closes her eyes and swallows. She used to be stronger than this. She rests her forehead against the mare's. The horse stands still, solid and warm, giving her strength. They stay that way for a long time.

Taking a deep breath, she pulls away and strokes a hand gently down the front of the bay's dark brown face.

'Thank you,' she whispers to the horse and looks around for the young man. He must have moved on down the line to check more hooves because she can't see him.

She walks past a few more horses, noting that these are heavier, sturdier, with feathered fetlocks, more like those she is used to.

'Do you ride, Nenna?' Fin says, appearing suddenly and making her jump again. 'Sorry. I seem to be making a habit of that.' He grins and nods to the horse they are standing by. 'I was just checking old Patch here. He's getting on in age, and I like to keep a special eye on him.'

Fin is closer this time, at the front of a parti-coloured horse, which has a white face and a huge brown patch over one eye. Fin bends over, tapping the horse's front leg, and Patch obligingly lifts his foot for him to inspect.

'Has to work hard, this old veteran.' He scrapes the compacted white powder from inside the hoof and tests the shoe by tapping at its edges.

He efficiently completes both of Patch's front feet. Straightening up, he gives her a quick glance before turning to the next horse in line. She follows, happy to watch him, happy to let her mind empty for the moment.

The horse next to Patch is a young light bay mare with a mean streak. Her ears are laid back, and her head is turned towards Fin, stretching the holding rope as far as it will go.

'Oh, it's you, is it, Blossom? And how are you today? As kind and gentle as ever?' Fin grins and ducks down out of reach of Blossom's teeth, tapping her leg. The horse deliberately changes her weight so the hoof Fin has asked her for is firmly planted on the mat.

He laughs. 'Right, I see you're up for a battle today.' Still crouching out of reach, he lifts himself up a little and shoves into Blossom's side. This has the desired effect, and the horse is caught off balance, causing her to transfer her weight.

Fin immediately snatches up the hoof, swings himself around so he is partly under the horse, and brings her foot up between his legs. He starts to clean the hoof out. Immediately, the fight leaves Blossom, and she relaxes.

'Tries this every single time. Become a bit of a game, I think,' Fin says, snatching a glance at Nenna.

He expertly works his way down the line of horses, cleaning, tapping, and talking to each animal.

'Some of these horses seem built for heavier work,' Nenna comments.

'Oh, yes,' Fin replies, happy to explain. 'Normally, they pull supplies to the mines, but His Imperial Highness, The Crystal preserve him, wants us there as quickly as possible. So, this lot have been pushed to work harder and faster than normal. Arture, my boss, is following with the extra supplies, but I was sent ahead to keep an eye on this lot. You can't rely on the soldiers to do it.'

And he scowls over at a group a little distance away, sitting around their fire container and mutters, 'Lazy, good-for-nothing dogs.'

'Why?' she asks.

'Why what?' he says.

'Why the rush? Why is your imperial whatsit wanting you there so fast?'

He starts at her words. 'Shhh!' he says, looking around frantically. 'You cannot, must not, ever insult His Imperial Highness, D'Ruja A'Riman, The Crystal preserve him.' He hisses, drawing an *S* shape in the air with his free hand. 'In fact, don't even think ill of him.' He says, his face pale. He gestures for her to come closer. 'Not anywhere, not ever.'

There is a silence, and she watches him scoop out the gritty white stones from the hoof he is working on and thinks that perhaps he has said all he is going to say when he continues in a low voice.

'You lot—well, the ones that are not lucky enough to belong to someone—the prims are needed to work in the mines. The soldiers are travelling with us this time as there has been some sort of disturbance, and they are being sent to sort it out.

'Prims?' she asks, hopeful and afraid at the same time.

'Yes,' he says, straightening up and wiping the hoof pick on his trousers. Moving on, he taps the leg of the next horse. 'The carts over th—'

'Oi, you! Horse-face!' a voice interrupts him. They turn to see a soldier glaring at them. He is a squat man with a couple of days' stubble on his double chin. 'What you doing. talking to her?' He glares nastily at Fin. 'Nauarch Vitrainy won't be best pleased hearing that you're talking to his prim.

'Oh, I . . . ' he stammers, eyes wide. 'Sorry, sir.'

'Get back to your work, boy,' the soldier says. 'And you.' He spits on the ground near her feet. 'Get back quick, before I tell him who you've been talking to.'

A commotion makes all three of them turn. There are men cheering and converging on a flat wooden wagon holding a large heavily-meshed cage. The wagon is right at the edge of the camp, barely in the shade of the overhead canopies.

'At last! They've let one out! Now, let's have some fun,' the soldier says, turning away and ambling towards the gathering soldiers.

'I'm sorry, Nenna,' Fin says in a quiet voice, but she doesn't hear him as she walks after the soldier, her eyes fixed on the wagon and the increasingly excited group. She stops on the outer edge, peering towards the cage. It is hard to make out anything distinctly, but she can see dark men-shaped shadows inside.

A door is wide open at the back of the cage, and a soldier emerges, jumping down off the cart onto the white desert. She hears the metal jangle of his boots as he lands on the sand. He turns and gestures roughly at someone inside, and a naked man clambers out and stands still.

The sun is high in the sky, making their shadows short. Nenna recognises the man from one of the other cells when they were on the ship, but she can't remember his name. He is slick with sweat. Slowly, he raises a hand up to shield his eyes from the glare. The open white desert sand stretches out to his right, and soldiers stand in a silent line on the mat to his left.

The soldier who has released him points at the desert and says something. After a moment, he steps towards the prisoner. Nenna sees the sharp glint of metal in his hand as he raises the stun stick towards the naked man. The prisoner regards the soldier for a moment longer, then sets off at a stumbling run out into the desert. The soldiers start to chant, 'run, run, run,' and then they cheer. Nenna's hand flies to her mouth. There is something bad about this. She takes two faltering steps forward.

A hand catches her arm, and she tries to shake it away.

'Nenna, no!' a voice whispers fiercely, and she glances quickly at Fin.

'What is going on?' she asks.

'Stay here, Nenna. There is nothing you can do now,' Fin whispers urgently back, his hand still holding her.

The escapee staggers in the desert's shimmering heat. The crowd of watchers 'ooo' collectively and fall silent, but he recovers, lurching back into a run. The soldiers count.

'Twenty-eight, twenty-nine, thirty.'

She realises they are counting the man's steps. Her heart pounds in her throat.

'Thirty-six, thirty-seven, thirty-eigh—'

The ground erupts under the runaway's feet, and something indescribable shoots upwards in a shower of dust and white stone, taking the prisoner up high into the air, lifting him above the cloud of dust it has created.

The man shrieks once, a spray of red shooting upwards as he is crushed in the maw of a gigantic, snake-like creature. The monster falls, landing with a loud *whoomph*. Another cloud of dust billows towards them. Raising their red bandanas, the soldiers wait in silence.

The silence screams in her ears. As the dust settles, she can see that the man and beast have vanished. A cavernous hole is all that is left, along with a stain of red splattering the once pristine desert.

Chapter 23

Nenna stands with her mouth open in shock. Fin is speaking and tugging at her arm.

'Go back to him,' he hisses beside her, pulling on her arm. 'Go back, Nenna. Forget this happened.'

The words slowly infiltrate her mind, and she rounds on him in fury. 'Forget?' she shouts. 'Forget that?'

'Shh!' he interrupts, dragging her back towards the horses. She tries to resist, but he is stronger than he looks, and she has had days of inactivity with little food. She glances over her shoulder towards the soldiers who are laughing and slapping each other on the back. She sees coins glint in the light as they change hands.

'That was a good one.'

'Wow, did you see the size of that wyrm?'

'Biggest yet.'

'Well done, Luconius, you crystalline beggar. You win. You got closest.

'Never thought the old man would make it that far.'

'Come away, Nenna. Go back.' Fin gently shakes her shoulders. The scene flashes back into her mind, and she opens her mouth to shout at him, but then abruptly doubles over as her last meal spews out.

'Go back, Nenna. You can't do anything now for that poor soul,' Fin repeats quietly, blocking her from the soldiers.

They are nearly at the horse line, and he shoves her under the main tether rope and back behind the horses where they won't be seen. In her head is the picture of the man held high in the air by that *thing*, his screams halted as his blood sprays outwards. It plays over and over in her mind.

Eventually, she stops heaving and wipes the back of her hand across her mouth, looking up at Fin. There is sympathy in his eyes.

'Wha—what was that thing?' she croaks, her voice dry and cracking.

'That was a wyrm,' he says, handing her his water flask, but he doesn't elaborate. 'Nenna, go back.' He takes her hands gently. 'I need to try and find out who was responsible for opening that cage door, and I need to do it now while the prisoners are as shocked and angry as you and more likely to tell me.'

'And what good will that do?' she whispers, handing him back his leather flask, untouched. 'You're not any more respected than me.'

She sees him flinch, but there is no way to take the words back. Something inside her wants to lash out, to hurt someone else.

'I heard how that soldier spoke to you and how you reacted,' Nenna continues, turning her head away from him not meeting his eyes. 'I'm surprised you even dare to speak to me now that you know I'm one of them. A dirty prim.' There is a moment of uncomfortable silence.

'Nenna, I am sorry. Really, I am. But you're wrong. A word in the right ear can make all the difference. All I need is a name.'

She walks away, regretting her spite but not trusting herself to say anymore, her emotions warring inside her. The sheer cruelty of this strange place and its people are overwhelming.

Weaving her way slowly back through the camp, she keeps her head down, the foul taste of vomit in her mouth. What are these people? They treat others like animals and yet believe themselves superior. They play sport with lives, as though they are worth nothing. And that . . . that thing! What on Maa Erda was that? Fin had called it a worm or something, but it is like no other creature she has ever seen.

Vitrainy and his friend Eachan are still sitting around the fire container. They both look up as she arrives. Vitrainy's hand moves off Eachan's knee and he shifts away a little. Eachan gives her a vicious look.

'Ah, here she is. All safe and sound,' Vitrainy says, sounding just a little too bright. She stops nearby, unsure of what to do next, and looks down at the ground, biting the inside of her mouth. Waiting.

'Go, sit with the horses, I'll be a short while yet.' He gestures towards a group of picketed horses. 'And watch out for Drazin. He won't have forgotten your slap.' The two men laugh.

She finds Drazin, Vitrainy's stallion, tethered slightly apart from other horses, and reaches out to stroke him, not caring if he tries to nip. In fact, if he does, it might give her some respite from the numb, dull ache inside. But the young stallion has accepted her previous discipline and is now content to let her be.

She replays the experience again in her head, trying and failing to make sense of it, to get some meaning. One thing is clear. There'd be no escape for her across the desert now.

Sinking down, she sits on the ground cover, near to the stallion, and closes her eyes. She is lost. This is a new world, a place that she doesn't understand. The rules have changed, and someone has forgotten to tell her. Worse than that, it's a place of human monsters and nightmare creatures.

The horse nuzzles her. His warm breath is on her neck and the gentle feel of his whiskers tickling and prickling her face helps to smooth the knot in her stomach.

The next afternoon when they finally stop to rest, she is again dismissed after supper when Eachan arrives. She has formed a plan of sorts during the night ride, and although keen to implement it, she is wary of letting Vitrainy see any spark of purpose to her movements or anything that might arouse his suspicion.

She drops her shoulders and wanders over towards the long picket line of horses nearest to them and stops to rub Drazin's nose. The stallion is restless and throws his head up, away from her outstretched hand.

'Gently, boy,' she says. 'What's got into you today?'

'I expect one of the mares is ripe, and he can sense it.'

The familiar voice makes her jump as Fin straightens up from behind the chestnut gelding, which is picketed nearby but out of reach of Drazin. He flicks his blond hair out of his eyes and smiles at her. She is the first to drop her eyes, her mind confused at the mixture of emotions that he has stirred. She turns to walk away.

'Nenna,' he calls softly after her. 'Wait!'

And something in his voice makes her stop.

'Walk along the line with me and talk to the horses. *He* can't see me from this angle, and if anyone else looks, they will just see me working and that you happen to be nearby.'

It is the soft emphasis he places on the word *he* that has her attention. Does Fin know more than he is letting on, or is she imagining it? She likes Fin, but he is part of this vicious place and that makes him complicit in their actions.

The thoughts war in her head. Stay and talk—she sorely needs a friend. Walk away, have nothing to do with him.

For a time, they move down the line, and as she strokes each horse's muzzle and gently scratches behind the ears of those who lower their heads, Fin just scrapes out hooves and doesn't speak for a while. It is his gentle and expert handling of the horses that wins her around. That and the thought that she might learn something to her advantage.

'I am not in His Imperial Highness's army, The Crystal preserve him,' Fin says eventually. 'But I am part of the royal stables. Some of the soldiers look down their noses at us, but the commander and a few of his officers do respect us and know that the work we do is just as important as theirs. Most of this lot, though, come from the ships. Some of them are from the hov team. Those flying boys consider themselves above everyone else.'

He moves on to the next horse, and after a moment's pause, so that anyone watching would think she is just casually talking to the horses, she follows.

'I've let the right ears hear about . . . about what happened yesterday.' Fin straightens up, flicking his fringe back and wiping the hoof pick clean on his trousers. 'It won't happen again, and the men responsible have been dealt with. Proper guards have been posted now.'

She looks at him for a long while. It doesn't help that poor soul, and again, she sees the image of the man being hoisted in the air, his life's blood spraying out over the pristine desert. But it is something, and she gives a little nod.

She leaves Fin and returns to her plan. It's not much of a plan, but it gives her purpose, and she works her way towards the prison carts, hoping to get closer and maybe speak with Ash or Kitt and find out how they are.

She is disappointed. It seems Fin's word in the right ears has doubled the guards around the prisoners, and though she is pleased to see their dedication to stopping any further sport, she is frustrated that she can't get any closer.

The days fall into a pattern, with travel in the afternoons and at night. There is a regularity to the routine, bringing with it a strange limbo existence. Vitrainy pulls her up to sit behind him now, under the watchful glare of the tall thin commander. So things do improve, a little.

Each evening after supper, she is set free to wander so that Vitrainy can talk in private with Eachan. The round-faced young man still eyes her with hatred. Does he hate her because she is 'one of them' or because she sits behind Vitrainy on his horse and shares his meals and tent?

There are things of beauty to see, even amidst the horror of knowing what lies under the crystal sand. The first time she witnesses the desert dawn, with its myriad of colours and its magical tinkling call, she is entranced. She asks Fin about it.

'Oh, that,' he says, sounding relieved at her question. 'That's just the crystal warming up and expanding in the light.' He continues with his hoof cleaning as he speaks. 'But my Da'—

he pauses briefly, then hurries on—'my Da used to say that it was all the angels of the universe singing to us through the crystal. In fact, His Imperial Highness, D'Ruja A'Riman, The Crystal preserve him, still insists on the Acknowledgment of Dawn and sends his priestesses to sing a response, which is supposed to keep us all safe.

He finishes the back hoof of the horse he is working on and moves along to the next. 'None of us have ever seen the ceremony, but not for lack of trying as the rumours are that priestesses are naked as they sing.' He looks up suddenly from his work. His face has turned crimson. 'Not that I—I mean . . . ' His embarrassment makes her smile briefly.

On the third evening, Nenna receives another shock. Sitting behind Vitrainy, trying not to hold on to him even though she is petrified of falling onto the sand and attracting the wyrms, she glances up at the darkening sky and gasps. There on the horizon is a massive blue-green ball slowly rising above them. She stiffens and clutches hold of Vitrainy's tunic.

'Say hello to your home dear,' Vitrainy says nastily.

'I don't understand. What is that?' she asks, but he does not answer.

Nenna watches the globe as it climbs higher. Her mouth is dry. It is both beautiful and terrifying. Where has it come from? Where in Maa Erda is she that she can see . . . whatever that is in the sky?

When Fin explains later that what she had seen is her home planet, the place she calls Maa Erda, and that right now she is on Crystal Moon, she feels sick and lightheaded. Her breathing quickens, shallow and inadequate, the air not reaching her lungs, and her knees buckle. She drops to the floor, not feeling the pain. Fin leaves his work and is beside her in an instant.

'What can I do?' he asks her, his eyes full of concern. But all she can do is shake her head. It is too impossible.

'Can I give you some water?' he asks, and at her nod, he pulls the leather strap holding his water flask over his head and hands it to her. She takes a drink of the tepid water, feeling it drop into her stomach and threaten to come back up. She shakes her head and hands the canteen back.

'No, I'll be alright. I just need a moment,' she manages to whisper.

Fin stands up and checks that no one has been watching before returning to his never-ending job of grooming the horses. Nenna joins him after a while, still pale and unsteady on her feet.

'You feeling better, Nenna? I never meant to—'

She interrupts him. 'Please, can you tell me what is going on? He'—she says the word pointedly—'won't tell me anything.'

Fin looks up sharply at that. 'Don't ask me to tell you things that he doesn't want you to know. It's more than my life's worth. I can't go against his orders.'

'What orders, Fin?' she says, her voice starting to rise. 'He hasn't given you any, so you won't be going against anything.'

'No, but if he found out that I've been telling you things that he wanted kept from you for some reason then . . . ' He trails off.

'The only reason he keeps things from me is spite. He is a nasty vindictive man and not the man you think he is, or the man he shows to the world.'

Her voice starts to rise. 'You all think of him as some sort of hero. I've been with him behind closed doors. I know. He's foul and cruel and a liar. And who's going to tell him? I'm certainly not. And anyway, do you really think he cares?'

'Keep your voice down, please.' His face white. He stops his work to look up at her, the horse's hoof clamped tight between his knees.

Nenna looks towards the main camp, and though the tents are not that close to the horse line, she can see that some soldiers are looking in their direction. She moves back behind the nearest horse.

'All right,' she says quietly, deflating. 'But please, please tell me what is happening, Fin. I need some answers so I can try to make sense of what is happening here.'

Fin continues to scrape out the hoof he is working on, tapping the compacted crystal off the scraper onto his trousers, where a mark has long since stained his tan britches. He flicks his head back to get his blond fringe out of his eyes, and she sees a muscle on his face twitch.

'I like you, Nenna, but I need this work more.' And he shakes his head slowly, then moves onto the next horse without looking at her.

She watches him for a while before sighing and turning to go. There was a time, not so long ago, where she would have shouted more and bullied Fin into telling her what she wanted, but people got hurt here for no reason, and she was as sure as Maa Erda not going to give Vitrainy a reason.

It takes Nenna a few more tries before she manages to get close to the wagons that hold the prisoners. Sneaking quietly behind a tent, she observes the soldiers on guard more carefully. They watch the rear of each of the five carts, making sure no one unauthorised gets close.

She watches in surprise as the prisoners are released from the carts—for exercise, she realises. They follow the actions of an instructor, who takes them through a series of stretches and movements, all under the watchful eye of at least twenty guards. Some of the guards look bored and uninterested, but others look on with intent. All of them are naked. Nenna feels a spark of anger at their predatory gazes.

She can make out Kitt and Ash in the middle of the group. Her heart lightens at the sight of the men from home. For a moment she dares to hope that they all might be freed.

She watches them stretching and sweating in the heat of the day. Suddenly, she freezes. Shock rolls through her body in waves. They have been gelded. All the men have. The breath leaves her body, and she feels rooted to the spot.

Gelded! It is so unthinkable, so horrifying. She sinks slowly to the ground, her hand clasped to her mouth, tears streaming down her face. What about Hadders? Where was he? For the first time, she hopes that he has died on Maa Erda.

Exercise finished, the prisoners are given water and led back to their respective wagons. Once safely on board, the rear door is shut, and the excess guards are dismissed.

Nenna takes a deep breath, wipes her face on her sleeve, and with her heart hammering loudly, she walks quickly to the front end of the nearest wagon. It is facing out into the desert, and the guards are watching the rear, facing towards the camp.

Slowly, she inches her way towards the wagon with her friends in it. Perhaps now, with her on the outside, the others can help her plan a way to escape. She wonders where Camis has gone. She doesn't see him among the exercise group. She blinks back threatened tears, surprised by her emotion. She has tried hard not to think of him at all. It just makes life harder.

Stepping over the cart's traces, she makes her way to the second wagon. Quietly, slowly, she sidles to the side and peeks in through the bars and mesh. It is the stench that hits her first— sweat, urine, and faeces. It reminds her of the cages on the ship.

There are ten or twelve prisoners, men and women, crammed into the space inside, sitting on wooden benches on each side. It is dark and surprisingly quiet. The prisoners are not bound or gagged, and it takes her a moment to locate the two men from her village.

'Ash,' she whispers. The people inside jump. 'Ash.'

He is sitting on the opposite side of the wagon, a little to her left, and he rises to cross the aisle between the benches. The others scrunch up to let him through.

'Ash, is everyone all right? Do you know where Camis is? Have you seen him?' She waits, but Ash does not reply. He flicks his hands at her. She looks from him to his hands and back.

'I don't understand,' she says quietly, on the verge of tears. 'Tell me what to do, please, Ash. There must be something.'

Suddenly, Ash is shoved roughly out of the way, and Kitt is there. He also makes a series of hand movements at her and motions her closer.

'What is going on, Kitt?'

Kitt leans close to the mesh and gestures her closer. She leans in and he opens his mouth. It is a black, gapping empty hole. His tongue has gone.

Chapter 24

The shadow from the cart falls long across the desert floor, and Camis begins to wonder if they will ever eat or sleep. Arture makes no sign of stopping but seems determined to press on. The water from Camis' flask is long gone, and in any case, drinking while moving is not pleasant. As soon as he pulls the neckerchief away from his mouth and nose to drink, he finds himself breathing in the fine dust in the air. The grit is even in the water itself.

The white gravelly stones on the ground twinkle and shine gold then orange, reflecting the setting sun. It is a welcome distraction after the long tedious day.

At first, he had been glad to be alone on his own cart. It has taken time to come to terms with the sight of his home in the sky. So far away and so unobtainable.

Disbelief has gradually settled into acceptance and longing. The whole situation is unreal. For peace of mind, he gives himself up to the rhythm of travelling, seeking the candle flame to help calm his mind. There is nothing he can do now but press on.

The slowly disappearing sun reflects off the ground, producing an orange glow that deepens to violet in the twilight. Even in this harsh landscape, there is some beauty. The colours wink out as the sun finally sets, returning the land to white, which glows softly, making it light enough to see by. In this strange night light, Arture presses on. Camis' eyes start to feel heavy.

He jerks awake as the cart stops. Camis sits for a moment, still in that stupefied state between sleep and reality. He watches as Arture angles his cart back towards him and stops when the horses are in line. He gestures for Tiberius to join them. Everything—the carts, the horses, and all three of them—is coated in the desert dust.

'Good. Well done, lads. I think we'll stop here for the rest of the night. Let's get this lot fed, and then I'll see to our food.' Arture stands up and stretches. He then rummages behind him, pulling out three nose bags for the horses, but as he turns back, he gives a sudden bellow. 'No!'

Camis stops in his tracks with his left foot hovering just above the desert floor. 'No, lad! Have you taken leave of your senses? It's night.'

At Camis' puzzled look, he explains, 'The wyrms will be rising. Stay in the cart.' Arture's face is pale in the strange glow from the ground. His expression is one of shock.

'Sorry,' Camis blusters, returning to his seat. 'I wasn't properly awake.'

'You city folk. You forget the danger. Maybe this will wake you up. Watch!'

Arture pulls out two leather buckets and a long wooden pole with what looks like a foot carved on the end. He glances up at the others.

'Either of you ever seen a wyrm close up?' he asks.

Camis and Tiberius both shake their heads.

'Watch, then.' Arture pounds the ground on one side of his cart with the end of his long stick. 'Three stomps should do it.' He waits, staring at the ground.

After a short while, he repeats the three thumps, and just as the last one finishes, the ground erupts. A snake-like creature rears out, grabbing the end of the wooden foot. Arture waits for the creature to get a firm hold of the stick. Its long sinuous body writhes out of the hole, and its circular gaping mouth clamps down on the stick.

Arture deftly pulls the creature out of the ground, flicking the tail end up towards him. Letting go of the stick, he works his hand up to hold the wyrm just behind what Camis assumes is the head. It hangs from Arture's grip, reaching nearly to the ground, writhing and thrashing, but it is still biting the stick, which swings wildly with the creature's thrashing. The mouth contains a multitude of tiny jagged teeth, which are grinding the wood that it has latched onto.

Arture holds the wyrm out for them both to examine. It is the thickness of a man's muscular arm, except it is pure white. He moves it closer for Tiberius to inspect, and the boy instinctively shrinks away. Arture gives a grim smile.

'Just imagine if this were someone's foot,' Arture says. 'And don't think you can outrun the disgusting beggars or pull yourself free. Once latched on, they inject a paralysing venom.'

They both stare at him in shock.

A knife appears in Arture's free hand, and he splits the creature's belly swiftly to the tip of its tail in one quick, efficient stroke. He holds it over one of the buckets as a clear liquid pours out.

'Thank the crystal that they're good for something,' he says, tipping the bucket to show them. 'Clean, safe water.'

Camis' stomach spasms. He's not sure how desperate he would have to be to drink that.

Arture reaches across and removes the hood from Spirit's head, offering her the bucket. She gives a quick shake of her head and drinks long and deep.

Each horse is watered before Arture retrieves the nose bags from his cart. He clips one of the bags over Spirit's nose, and then repeats the action with Scout. Camis can't help but smile at the image of the three horses with their true colour only visible around their heads, the rest of them in perfect camouflage with their surroundings.

'Think you can reach Traveller's dinner to him without falling off 'n getting ate?' Arture asks Camis and tosses the remaining bag across to him.

'Yes, of course,' Camis says and quickly attaches the feed bag to the big grey.

Arture hands around the evening meal—soft bread rolls, hard cheese, and a red fruit, about the size of a small apple. Camis watches Tiberius bite into his first before trying it. It bursts open, full of sweet juice that squirts pips and liquid down his chin.

'Bet you two missed tomatoes down on that crystal-forsaken planet. Good to be back home, eh?' Arture says, looking across, smiling.

'You're not wrong,' Tiberius says, while Camis busies himself swigging water from his flask. 'I couldn't wait to get back to some decent food. Arture, could I ask why you are not up front with the other soldiers? If every last man is needed, why are you driving supplies?'

'Honourable discharge,' Arture says tapping his left leg below the knee, which raps with a metallic ring.

After they have eaten, Arture pulls a leather case out from underneath his seat and takes out a strange musical instrument. Sitting back down, he lays the rectangular box across his knees. He gently runs his thumb across the strings. He twiddles metal pegs that run along one end of the instrument with his other hand. He notices Camis watching him.

'You ever played a zeppy?' he asks, and as Camis shakes his head, he begins to play, strumming and plucking simultaneously.

He coaxes out the most beautiful music Camis has ever heard. Camis closes his eyes, sitting back on the seat of his own cart as he listens. The music rises and falls, richly complex. It sounds like two instruments being played together.

Then Arture begins to sing. His voice adds a deep melodic bass to the tune. He sings of love—love lost, love found, and love lost again. He blends one song into another, and Camis is astonished to find that he knows the next one.

He opens his eyes to watch Arture play, and then joins in quietly at first, then with more confidence. It is a song his mother had sung regularly around their own camp. Tiberius catches Camis' eye and frowns. Camis gives a small shrug and carries on singing. Tiberius eventually joins them, and Arture switches his voice to harmonise. When the song is finished, he grins across at the two lads.

'The old ones are always the best,' he says, and he places the zeppy carefully back in its case. 'Time to water the horses, then we can get some shuteye.'

Camis watches in horror as Arture jumps to the ground and crosses over to the front of his horse. A writhing mass of wyrms appear from the ground a few paces away. Camis' throat is tight, and he tries to shout. Arture looks up.

'Don't worry, lad.' He taps his left leg, which gives a hollow ring. 'Leg's metal.' As if that explains everything. 'I can't sleep until I've checked the horses are still covered, but it means putting on this bloody thing,' he says, lifting his good foot to show a metal contraption strapped to his boot. 'It's awkward to put on, and damned heavy to walk in.'

He taps Traveller's front left leg, and the horse dutifully lifts it, revealing a metal shoe. The shoe reflects the red glow from the Papa, which is a lot closer here, oppressive.

'Got a few spares for each of them,' Arture continues. 'But as you know, working in the royal stables an' all, nothing's better than a proper forge.'

Camis watches him check each of the horse's feet, tapping and twisting the shoes to check if they are loose. Pieces of the puzzle begin to fit together. Camis realises that none of the terrifying wyms have drawn close to the horses or the carts all day. So in some way metal is important then.

The days fall into a pattern. Arture rides well past dusk, and Camis feels that they only stop for the horses' sake.

Their night stops are filled with Arture's stories. Some nights, he teaches them how to sign—to speak without words. He says it is just a bit of fun, but that it might turn out to be useful. He looks at Camis in a peculiar way when he says it.

Other nights, he teaches them more about the wyrms.

'You know what they feed on?' Arture asks one evening when they stop for the night. 'They grind up crystal below the surface, extracting minute amounts of water and spitting out processed crystal. It's processed crystal that is the most powerful and so is the most sought after. It is what his Imperial Highness prizes above all else.' He waves his hand to take in the barren landscape around them. 'It is the Wyrms size that determines how fine their jaws can mill the stuff and how big the waste material is. Over time, they have created subterranean lakes deep, deep underground. It is one of these that has overflowed and broken the surface that our city Oasis is built on, but I expect you both know that.'

Luckily, he doesn't expect an answer and carries on. 'They make their burrows and nurseries as they travel, looking for more unprocessed crystal. It's their abandoned shafts that we now mine. It is rumoured that a giant queen lies at the centre of their den or hive or whatever you want to call it, though no one has actually seen her. They are not above eating each other on occasion though, when they are really hungry, but given the chance, they prefer a tasty dog or horse or . . . human.' Both Camis and Tiberius shudder.

The next night, lying in the footwell of the cart, Camis thinks that sleep will come swiftly. It has been another long tedious day, and again they have ridden well into the night, travelling by the eerie light from the crystal desert. Yet sleep eludes him.

His shoulders and neck ache from sitting so long in one position. He rolls his head gently from side to side to try and relieve the tension. A strange prickly sensation creeps down his spine between his shoulder blades. The stays creak as Spirit relaxes into a rest position. He inhales her familiar oaty smell and is immediately transported home.

He remembers long wakeful summer nights lying by the fire with Misty snuffling softly nearby. Stars shining overhead and the comforting sound of his mother nearby, her breathing deep and regular. Noisy crickets climbing high on the grass stems, sawing loudly, desperately calling for a mate. Owls hunting and screeching in a nearby wood. Bats flitting silently across the night sky, their blackness briefly blocking the stars, the only sign they are there. The wood settling on the fire causing the embers to briefly glow more brightly. The endless boredom.

How he had longed for something, anything to happen, to break the relentless and unchangingness of it all.

Now he longs to be back there, his mother safe, the stars tracking their ageless path, the days spent trekking between remote communities, the time spent herb gathering, learning their names and uses. He would even put up with the agonising tongue-tied sensation he gets when faced with others his own age. If he squeezes his eyes tight and counts slowly and wishes hard, maybe he'll wake up and find it has all been a strange dream.

Water flows, slowly meandering through the green countryside, and Camis floats on his back, watching the scenery—green trees, green grass, green. Relaxed.

Suddenly, the river dips down, swirls between two rocks, speeds up, tugs him faster. He tries to turn and swim, but the current swells and has him in a strong grip. He flounders, splashes, on the edge of panic. The water is deeper, wider, wilder. A whooshing sound builds in intensity as the water sucks him down into its black depths, and he sits up gasping, to hear the sound of the wind whipping over the desert. It had risen while he was dreaming.

He turns his head, still half asleep, and sees Arture down on the ground, unfurling a large sheet of canvas. Another blast of warm air shakes his cart. He staggers to his feet, holding the cart edge.

'Arture! What are you doing?' Camis watches as Arture scrabbles about under his cart, pulling out more strange items.

'No time to explain,' Arture shouts above the rising wind. 'Just turn your cart that way, Camis, and you bring yours alongside, Tiberius, but angle it away.' He points in the directions he wants them to take. 'Keep one back corner of the cart close to Camis', and I'll get Traveller to back up into the gap.'

The carts are hurriedly arranged in a rough triangle with their backs facing inwards. Arture starts to unhitch the horses.

'What can we do?' Tiberius calls from his cart.

'Just tie down the front canvas,' Arture shouts, 'and I'll—'
But his words are whisked away in a sudden strong gust of
wind.

Once the front canvas is secure, Camis makes his way to the
back of his cart in time to meet Arture with Spirit. Arture throws
her reins to Camis and hurries away with the other two horses.
Gusts whip Camis' hair across his face and Spirit's mane and
tail into the air.

Arture hammers some metal pegs into the ground behind the
horse, and he points up to the cart roof where Camis sees more
neatly rolled canvas. He knows what he must do.

Camis makes the sign for wyrms, and Arture shakes his head
to let him know they are safe from them. Pulling up his bandana,
Camis jumps down and is immediately hit by the wind, the dust
replaced with larger gritty bits of crystal that sting as they hit.

Together, they secure the canvas in place, pulling it down
and over the horse in a kind of lean-to tent, and as Camis ties
the edges, the force of the wind reduces. Arture touches Camis'
shoulder, gives a little wave, and vanishes, sliding between the
cart edge and the canvas. For a brief moment, the wind increases
its roar like a beast kept from its quarry, then quiets, leaving
Camis alone with Spirit. He ties the gap Arture has left and
secures all the ties around the floor, then climbs back up onto
the cart.

The wind rages, and gusts shake the cart, making him worry
that they will be blown over. Spirit has knocked the lid of a box
off and is contentedly munching on some oats. The noise of the
storm outside is deafening, and Camis spends some time
rubbing and stroking Spirit's head, more to reassure himself
than the horse.

Camis removes the lid from another box, finding some basic
provisions. Next to the box is a bucket of water. Emergency
supplies had been on board the whole time and he had never
even noticed. He pours out some water for the horse and keeps
some back for himself.

Fetching his bedding, he makes himself comfortable at the
back of the cart with the horse.

Do you know how long we are going to be here? he asks the horse and is astonished when she gives a start and raises her head, blowing cream-coloured oat flakes from her muzzle.

You heard me?

They stare at each other for a long while, and Camis can see himself reflected in her dark liquid eyes—a spectre of white covered in crystal dust.

Then Spirit lowers her head, returning to her food, leaving Camis to the noise of the storm that rages outside and the turmoil of thoughts that rage inside.

Chapter 25

Sitting on her balcony, staring into space, Serin is blind to the splendour of the sunrise with its deep flush of reds and orange. Her mind in a whir, she hears the rattle of the door opening, followed by the sound of boots on the marble floor.

Two black-clad soldiers cross her chamber, carrying trays of food—fruit, cheese, and bread. They lay them on her table. A third guard holds the door open. In the corridor, she can see another. No one looks at her. No one speaks to her.

She walks briskly to the door guard as she has for the past several days. 'Where is my maid?' she says as she stops in front of him, partially blocking the exit.

The guard, a short, portly man, older than the others, doesn't answer.

She turns to the two who had bought the trays. 'Can you tell me where my maid is?'

The men shuffle their feet, their faces reddening. They glance towards the older guard, who gestures impatiently at them. Quickly, they sidle past her and leave. The guard can't close the door without physically knocking her out of the way, so he walks around her to the outer threshold, his lined face sad, his eyes downcast, and turns his back to her.

Serin waits for a moment, her mind in turmoil, then reaches out to the solid wooden door. She slams it shut. She stomps over to the table, sweeping the trays onto the floor. They clatter loudly. A pitcher of wine shatters, spraying blood-red liquid onto the mess. It pools around the fallen food. A bread roll meanders across the floor, coming to rest by her bed, leaving a trail of red that fades to pink.

No one comes.

She stands for an age, staring unseeing at the mess, her arms limp by her sides, her jaw tight. Slowly, her eyes focus. The children won't be getting any of this food—or her help. That boy, the one she'd promised she would fix his arm—she clamps her arms to her stomach, her throat tight, and quickly crosses the room back to the balcony.

Soldiers leave more trays of food, their boots crunching on the shards of the broken pitcher. There are purple-red footprints where they have walked, and now there is silence.

She stays on the balcony, staring down at the palace grounds, while up in the slowly-changing sky, the night dresses itself in a sparkle of stars, mocking her. Unhurriedly, dawn blooms— magenta, coral, and violet.

Shivering, she pads barefooted across her room and throws herself across the bed. Eventually, she drops into an agitated sleep, unaware of the cuts on her feet that stain the bed linen red.

She reaches for the dress. It shimmers, tantalising, first blue, then green, shot through with a purple that is at first lavender and then scarlet. She has never seen such beautiful material before. The gossamer-thin garment glows, lit by the full moon behind. Its bodice is a lattice of fine cobwebs, the finest embroidery and weave. Her hands pass through the material.

Frowning, she tries again, reaching for the top, but again, her hands pass straight through. She stands back, surveying the dress in all its beauty, tilting her head to one side, a finger resting lightly on her bottom lip. She closes her eyes, and when she opens them, she is wearing the dress.

She surveys herself from all angles in a mirror. She twists first one way and then another, the dress flaring out in a fan of colour. Her hands caress down her sides. But as they sweep downwards, she feels the dress tighten.

Scowling, she peers more closely at her reflection, and as she steps forward, the material tightens again, shrinking, squeezing, contracting close against her. The straps of the bodice cut into her shoulders. The laces are lashed hard against her back, slicing into her skin. She wriggles and squirms, trying to lift the dress overhead, but the silky material slips through her hands and draws even tighter. The bodice bites deeper, the skirt binding her legs together. Blood seeps through at her neck. She gasps and thrashes, crying out, but like quicksand, the spiteful material increases its hold.

Serin, wake up!

Her eyes fly open. Her uncle is there, clasping one of her hands. His face is full of mock concern, his eyes cold, grey, and empty.

Are you awake now? You had a bad dream.

He is smiling, gently, slyly. How long has he been there? Thank Maa Erda it was a dress she was dreaming about and not . . . He looks at her more sharply.

'Yes, I . . . ' She snatches her hand from his and pushes herself upright, aware that she is still fully dressed, her clothes crumpled, the bed in disarray. 'Where is Onora?' she asks to mask her thoughts.

Who? He frowns.

'My maid, Onora. Where is she?'

His face hardens, and though he doesn't physically move, she feels a blast of cold air sweep between them.

I have removed her. You do not need to concern yourself about it. Now go wash and put on travelling clothes. It is time I showed you something.

He waits, clearly expecting her to obey. She opens her mouth to argue and feels the familiar pressure start to build in her mind. Slowly sliding off the bed, she disappears into her bath chamber to dress, too tired and worn down by her isolation and imprisonment to argue.

Outside, an escort awaits them. Her uncle has bought her the showy white mare, Crystal, for her to ride. The horse throws her head up and nickers, shaking her mane. Her uncle crosses to have a brief word with one of the palace guards.

The soldier holding Crystal comes around to offer his cupped hands for her to mount. Her heart lurches. It is Zachary. He keeps his head down and his hands out. She holds the saddle, and as she places her foot into Zachary's waiting hands, he leans in and whispers, 'Onora is safe.'

He steps aside as she settles onto Crystal's back.

'What was that, soldier?' Her uncle is standing a few steps behind Zachary, glaring at him.

Zachary turns to face him, but Serin manoeuvres her horse between the two men, using the horse's high spirits to look as though she doesn't have control.

'I asked him if Crystal had been exercised regularly. He said that she has.' Serin looks down at her uncle. Calm and unruffled on the outside, she does not look at Zachary. 'But you wouldn't think it as she's so keen to be off.'

And giving Crystal a light squeeze of her knees, she encourages the horse to leap forward, heading for the archway that leads into the palace grounds. A quick glance back shows her that Zachary has used her distraction to vanish into the mounted troops that are turning their horses to follow, leaving her uncle scowling after her.

They ride through the palace grounds, green and empty. The only sounds are the ringing of the metal hooves and the jingle of harnesses. Even the parakeets are silent.

Leaving through a gate, crossing straight into the barren white desert, she feels the tension begin to drain away. She knows Zachary rides somewhere behind. Her heart feels lighter than it has for days. Riding brings her a sense of freedom, and if she closes her eyes, she can nearly imagine herself home—except for the fine white dust that billows up, rising from the horse's hooves.

Serin coughs and pulls her travel cloak over her hair, wrapping the extra material tightly around her mouth and nose. Her uncle sets a fast pace after locating the first sand marker—a bright red flag with a blue stylised flower denoting the house A'Riman on it. It hangs limply from a long slender pole, and they turn right.

She wonders how far they are planning to go. This part of the desert is flat and empty for tens of cycles. It doesn't even have a viable mine that she can remember.

I found a large expanse of solid ground, her uncle says, making her jump. Had he been listening to her thoughts again? She shivers despite the heat.

A rarity, you'll agree, he continues. *And just suitable for my purposes, with none of that forsaken honeycomb of tunnels underneath to ruin my plans. I couldn't use any of the existing sites, as they are already full of shuttles and other craft.*

Both she and her horse are sweating by the time they glimpse their destination. The grit stings her eyes as she squints into the white light.

A tiny speck of black grows steadily bigger on the horizon, resolving into a vast canopy spread out across the desert with long low buildings to the side. The covering protects the biggest spaceship she has ever seen. They cross from light to shade, from heat to relative coolness, and dismount. The horses are led away.

My Mastership, he announces dramatically. *This is my plan for the future. Our future.*

He waves towards the giant black spaceship that squats on the white sand. They climb a ramp into the cool interior and stand in a vast central atrium.

Not finished yet, but it will be soon. He points upwards and Serin follows his gesture. *The ship can house about eight-thousand people with all the usual facilities—a medical centre, a hospital with state-of-the-art equipment. Down here, there is room for a thousand horses, along with an animal husbandry unit and veterinarian hospital. But we've been concentrating on the control hub. Come, I'll show you.*

He leads her to a set of ladders on the far wall and turns to let her climb first. His eyes are dark grey, igneous. She pulls herself swiftly up the rungs, away from his help. Breathless, she reaches the top. A white-clad arm reaches down to help her over the rim of the opening. Gratefully, she seizes hold and is hauled up and into the control hub.

It is swarming with technicians, scientists, and other fleet staff. There are wires, pipes, consoles, display monitors, and machines everywhere. She stands at the opening, panting, gaping around at the activity and noise. A white-clad technician hovers near the opening

'Princess,' he says respectfully and gives her a small bow.

Isn't it incredible? Hard to imagine that in little over a cycle, we'll be on our way.

Her uncle steps up behind her and places his arm around her shoulders, making her shrink inward, and she doesn't immediately register his words.

'On our way? On our way where?' She uses the question to pull away from him, twisting around to look up at him.

Serin, use mindspeak. This is a private conversation. And he moves towards her, but two more technicians cross between them, pushing a contraption on wheels.

'Sorry, sir,' says one of the men, waving apologetically as they pass. 'We are checking the power to one of the panels.' They hurry away, and D'Ruja scowls after them. She uses the moment to cross to a console, putting it between them, looking at the dials and forcing a look of interest.

So, uncle, on our way where? she asks.

Back home. Home to Lakhth al-Dubb. Back where we truly belong.

He steps around some boxes on the floor and presses a button on the console in front of her. The panels around the outside of the circular hub slide upwards, revealing the outside. *We cannot stay here. This moon is dying. Our people are dying. And before you suggest it, I refuse to start anew on that primitive planet.*

He doesn't need to tell her which planet he is talking about. Through the reinforced crystalline glass, she sees tiny people moving about below. The white canopy flaps lazily overhead, a light breeze gusting gently from the south, blowing gentle swirls of dust that uncover some of the tiny gem-like crystals that shine and sing at dawn. It covers others up as it twirls on its way.

I mean for us to return to civilisation and take back what is rightfully ours. For me to rule with you by my side. He gives her a hard stare. *Together.*

Her throat is tight, her mouth dry, and her mind full of questions and protest. He cannot possibly mean to retake their home planet. It has been years—things will have changed. The journey is long and arduous. Last time, sickness had nearly wiped them all out.

She opens her mouth to speak, but the technician that helped her up into the control room steps forward with an electronic notepad, which he hands to her uncle.

'Sir, I'm sorry to interrupt, but could I ask you to look at the latest . . . '

She tunes the conversation out, gripping the console, looking out but seeing nothing. He must be mad. She loathes the thought of him down there on Maa Erda, and she certainly doesn't want him finding Camis, but to leave forever . . . The people deserve a choice. She deserves a choice.

The knot in her stomach doubles. She hears him dismiss the man and turns swiftly to face him, to challenge him, to tell him she doesn't want to leave. She takes a breath in, but he holds his hand up to silence her.

You do not have a choice.

She stares back at him, colour draining from her face as she remembers just how much he has strengthened his ability to intrude on her mind.

Not everyone will want to go back to Lakhth al-Dubb. Some of us do not remember it. Some were born here. She tries hard not to sound desperate to stay.

I do not intend to take everyone, Serin. I will take soldiers, the technicians you see here and all their families, the temple priests and trainee Books, and a few loyal palace retainers, along with you and your brother.

Then what will happen to those left behind?

He looks at her, his expression flat. He shrugs dismissively, moving away, frowning down at something on the screen he holds in his hands. His normally slicked-back hair falls forward across his eyes, and he chews on his lower lip. A clear picture of her son flashes unbidden into her mind. Camis does that. The memory shoots a pain so ferocious through her stomach that she doubles over.

Instantly, her uncle is by her side, full of concern, shouting for someone to get a chair and fetch some water. What if he had seen? The question weakens her knees further, forcing her to lean on him.

What is it Serin? Are you unwell? he asks with surprising tenderness.

She tries not to shudder at his touch and resists the urge to pull away from him.

'I'm fine,' she says aloud. 'I just feel a little dizzy, that's all.'

With an effort, she forces herself upright, taking the water that one of the white-coated technicians holds out. She doesn't meet her uncle's eyes. He holds her elbow and gently steers her back onto a waiting chair.

I am sorry. What was I thinking? I was excited to share my plan with you and forgot that it was a long hot ride without food or rest.

He starts shouting orders for refreshments to be taken to his quarters and looks back at her. *Come, I'll help you. We will rest a while and continue our discussion.*

She tries not to cringe as he helps her up. Supporting her arm, he leads her out of the command centre.

His quarters are directly below. Close, she assumes, so he can immediately be informed of any incident that affects the ship. His rooms are already furnished, and through an open door, she can glimpse an enormous bed, which has yet to be made, piled high with folded covers and cushions. Rugs are rolled up and stacked on the floor. Several picture frames rest beside them, their faces turned to the wall.

Gratefully, she sinks down into one of the luxurious divans, leaning back against the cushions. She deliberately slides her legs up, forcing him to let go of her and to find another seat. Two young women, clad in the skin-tight black uniform that he keeps all his general staff in, are laying out dishes of fresh fruit, cheeses, and soft bread rolls. Two pitchers stand on a tray, condensation beading on their sides, with two clear crystal goblets beside them.

She waits for the women to leave, waits for him to speak first, unsure if he has already seen the image of Camis that flashed in her head. She closes her eyes and brings the candle flame to the front of her mind, blocking out all other thoughts and images, attempting to calm herself and to give him nothing to see or hear.

Opening her eyes, Serin gives a start. He is standing over her looking down, his expression schooled to give no indication of his thoughts. He hands her a glass of ice-cold water and gestures towards the food.

Eat, he says and crosses to the nearest chair.

How long had he been standing over her, watching? They eat in silence for a while. Serin forcing herself to take tiny bites and to swallow them down with the water, the food sticking in her throat. She wants him to speak. She wants him to stay silent. He drains his water and reaches for one of the jugs. A deep red liquid swirls into the glass, thick and cloying.

We haven't stocked the ship's galley yet, but luckily the mess hut has the basics and sent this up. I wasn't planning on loading food and livestock until the final fittings are complete and least one test flight has been done. Still, it won't be too long now before I have filled the crystal store and can have it moved out here to be loaded.

She half listens, trying not to let her relief show too clearly on her face. He hasn't seen Camis. Thank Maa Erda.

The crystal should provide enough power to get us home. It will give enough energy for our weapons, at least until I can get into the treasury and check what supplies haven't been plundered by those thieving Warkamesh.

Serin sighs inwardly. She had heard so much about the Warkamesh and their evil greedy ways from him growing up that she had even started to feel sympathy for them. It seems little has changed. Her uncle, for all his titles, could not let it go.

I have a few couples on the list—trained cooks, cleaners and the like—but mostly I have chosen young, fit fighting men, their families will be welcome too but you know young men so if you could find me a hundred or so women that . . .

Her mind wanders. She remembers the stories her mother had told her and Myriad at night, tucked up safe in their own private cabin on the ship when she was little. She can only recall brief flashes of her parents now, before the flux that ravaged the ship took young and old, leaving a bare third of the crew alive. Leaving her and her twin brother to the sole care of their uncle.

He was still speaking.

Most of the city think I'm readying a force to move to the planet below.

But what about those left behind? she asks again. *The people who don't want to leave or who don't want to fight.*

What about them? he says, annoyance flashing across his face.

Will you give them a choice? Unlike me, she thinks. *Will you drop them down onto Maa Erda and let them start again?*

Where?

Maa Erda, she says. *It is what . . . what the prims call their home planet.*

He snorts into his wine. *Don't be ridiculous, Serin. No, the people do not have a choice. I don't know what will happen to those left behind. They will mostly be those too old to fight or to be useful. I have made my selection and along with the women that you will pick out for me . . .*

The what?

The women that you will make sure are fertile, he says, scowling openly now.

What do you mean?

Did you not listen? I will take only those women able to bear children. This moon is dying. There are no children born now. I—we—will need to repopulate our home. I intend to wipe out all opposition. I want you to examine the priestesses and the palace for fit and fertile women.

237

Serin stares back at him open mouthed, her mind momentarily blank.

Breeding cows! she snaps.

Oh, do stop being so dramatic about everything, Serin. I can't afford to take everyone. I need you to make sure the women lucky enough to be chosen are fit for the purpose. The anger in his voice hardens his eyes to stone grey, a sign she knows she should heed.

'So you are leaving them to die, taking the Book and condemning them to starvation and disease?' she shouts, standing up.

Abruptly he is in front of her, his back-handed blow knocking her from her feet onto the settle behind. Her hands fly to her stinging cheek, her breath checked. He looks down at her, and she cringes away. She has seen that look before, once for real, and a million times in nightmares.

He reaches out, and she tries to bat his hands away and push herself deeper into the soft cushions. He grabs a handful of her hair and yanks her to her feet, dragging her silently towards the open door and the unmade bed.

'No!' she cries. 'No, no! Please, no!'

He throws her onto the bed, holding her neck with one hand while he wrenches down her divided riding skirt with the other. She beats at him with both hands, clawing and scratching at his face.

He pins both arms on the bed. Her hair sprawls over her face. Rolling her head from side to side only makes things worse as it tangles across her mouth. Through the mess of her hair, she sees his face—a scratch on his cheek oozes blood. A drop forms at one end, and she watches it, mesmerised to stillness, as it grows bigger and then falls towards her, deep red.

Spinning, it catches the light, and horrifyingly lands on her forehead. Her breath catches in shock. Her eyes widen as the drop splits in two, running into both eyes, clouding her sight.

Then he is on her, hard and unyielding, and she is fifteen again, small and helpless.

Chapter 26

He rolls off her with a sigh, and Serin's tears wash the blood from her eyes. He sits up and takes one of her hands in his, placing it on his cheek over the scratch.

Heal this, he says into her mind, all business, not expecting her to refuse. But when she delays, he turns his head to regard her lying on the bed. *Heal it now!*

She tries not to look at him but to focus just on the cut. Her hands shake, bile rising in her throat as she softly skims the scratch with one finger. It vanishes, and she closes her eyes. The muscles of her jaw are so tight that she is not sure she will be able to open her mouth ever again.

He pulls her to her feet, handing her the ripped riding dress from the bed. *Make yourself presentable,* he says, adjusting his trousers and doing up his sword belt. He hadn't even removed the bloody thing when he . . . Her mind refuses to name it.

She watches him cross the room to the tray of wine and pour himself a drink. He drains the wine in one gulp and pours another glass, which he brings to her where she is tying some fabric in place as a belt to hold the skirt together.

She shakes her head, but he presses the drink into her hand. She slams it to the floor. The crystal goblet bounces twice, chiming musically on the ship's floor, the wine spinning out in glistening red drops. He slaps her and her hand flies to her face, her hot temper evaporating, replaced with fear as he steps closer.

Placing a finger under her chin, he jerks her face upwards, bringing her eyes up to look into his. He is close, so close that she can feel his breath and smell the musky scent of sex.

An urgent banging echoes through the semi-empty chambers. A voice calls out on the other side of the door.

'Sir! Your Imperial Majesty! We are being attacked!'

He whirls away from her, the sudden movement jolting her, making her legs give way so that she sits back on the bed. Her hands and legs shake uncontrollably, and her teeth chatter, but he doesn't see.

Turning to quickly glance at her, he says, *Do not leave these rooms until I come back.* His face is all hard lines. There is no concern, just a certainty in his voice that she will do as he says.

She waits for a long time, sitting on the edge of the bed. Staring, unseeing. Some of the piled bedding has spilled down onto the floor, a tangle of blue-and-green silk. There is no change in the shadows in the room as there are no windows, just the soft glow of the crystal through gold-coloured lamps, so she has no way to gauge the time.

The attack or whatever is happening outside does not concern her. She has no doubt that her uncle is well equipped to deal with whatever it is, and her luck isn't strong enough that he will be killed, whatever she wishes.

He has told her she will be wed to him in as little as six days and then . . .

Her legs are sticky where the wetness has dried, and the riding skirt catches as she moves. She climbs onto the bed and curls up, letting go of the flood of emotion inside her, tears flowing as freely as the fluid that trickles down her leg, soaking her skirt.

She lies there long enough for the tears to subside and dry in tight streaks on her face. Long enough for her to be aware of her tangled hair caught under her, pulling at her scalp, catching at the tender spot where she had been yanked up. She feels dirty in more ways than just physically.

Sitting up, she wipes her hands over her cheeks, sweeping back her hair, and starts to rise. She pauses as an image of his

240

face leering close to hers flashes in her mind, the scratch on his face oozing blood, and that one drop hovering just before it falls. She shoves the image away. She thought there would be months, full cycles, before she had to be ready.

Wrapping her arms around herself, she rocks backwards and forwards and tries to think of other things, but all she can hear is his voice in her head—*you are mine, you are mine, you are mine.*

Without any warning, the door slides open, and footsteps hurry towards her. Fear and anger war with each other, and she is ready with an angry retort on her lips to flay the skin off the person who dares to enter without knocking, but she is also afraid, expecting that it might be her uncle. But the man hurrying towards her is not her uncle or a soldier or servant. It is the last man she'd expected, the last man she wants to see her this way—the only man she has ever truly wanted.

Zachary stops in front of her, his eyes sweeping over her, taking in everything, then looking at her so fiercely and with such anger that she shrinks back.

'Serin?' His voice is so tender, so full of concern, that she wonders if she had imagined the fury that she just glimpsed.

'I . . .' She works her mouth, but no sound comes.

He reaches out and takes her hands gently in his, and then she is in his arms, sobbing, when she thought there were no tears left.

'I will kill him,' he says, stroking her hair, and she looks up to see the anger returned, not at her but for what he suspects and for what she cannot deny or hide from him. Strangely, there is relief. A weight lifts, and she sighs, leaning tighter into his chest. They stay like this for an age, for an instant.

Pulling away from him, she looks towards the open door to the area beyond, seeing the remains of the meal she had shared earlier with her uncle.

'Zachary, what are you doing here? You will be caught. There was a disturbance and fighting, and he has gone to—oh,' she says, suddenly understanding. 'You are the disturbance.'

She pauses. 'But unless you have killed him'—and she waits expectantly, but he gives a tiny shake of his head— 'then you must go. If he finds you here, he—' She breaks off as he smiles.

'I expect he is halfway to the eastern mines by now. Charging after my men, with no water or change of horse. He will regret his haste as he only has a few men with him who survived our attack. He did not expect anyone to know of this secret ship, so he was ill prepared and only had a small escort.'

Zachary looks down at her and his smile fades. 'I got a message to my friends, asking them to bring their attack forward, hoping that I could find an opportunity to speak with you. To warn you.' He stands and walks towards the open door. 'I knew he would keep you safe from the fighting, but I never thought he was the one you had to be kept safe from.'

He half turns back, his teeth clenched, and his hands bunch into fists. She nearly doesn't catch his whisper. 'I will kill him.'

Serin gets to her feet, her legs shaky. Marriage. Six dawns. Her uncle's face leering. Zachary here. Slowly, something that he'd said filters through.

'Warn me?' she says. 'Warn me of what?

'In six days, we will attack the city.' It is his turn to be startled as she starts to laugh. A rough hiccupping laugh that turns to more tears, and he is back holding her tight.

Through the tears and the choking laughter, she manages to croak, 'In six days, he intends to marry me and later take this ship back to Lakhth al-Dubb. He intends to attack and take back what he believes he is owed.'

They stand facing each other, between the threshold of the door to the bedroom and living area. Zachary is stunned to silence. She waits quietly now, her hysteria gone as he absorbs the information.

She can almost see the plan forming in his head, and it is then that she tells him.

'I have a son.' She is shocked at how calm she sounds, at how easy it is to tell him about Camis. 'He is nearly fifteen summers, but he is alone down there on Maa Erda. Zachary, I cannot leave with no hope of ever seeing him again.'

There is a silence in which his face shows a multitude of emotions, shock and puzzlement fighting together.

'I . . .'

'We could have been married. I would have looked after you both,' he cuts over her, his blue eyes bright as a summer sky.

'We were children, and he would have killed you and the babe, you know that. He wanted me even then. We would never have stood a chance.' She says sadly. 'Besides,' she says, looking away from his intense gaze. 'I don't know if you are his father.'

He tenses as her words sink in and their full implication strike home.

'What do you mean? You . . .' He trails away as the conclusions hit him. 'You mean there is someone . . . another . . .'

She shakes her head quickly and reaches for his hand. 'No. No one else, Zachary,' she says quickly.

'You mean, he . . . that it happened before? That he . . .' He can't form the words.

'I'll kill him,' he says quietly. She expects him to push her away in disgust but instead he hugs her tight. 'Oh, Serin,' he breathes. 'I had no idea. I thought I'd done . . . That you'd . . .' He trails away. 'Down there, on your own.'

'I wasn't always alone. I met people—good people who helped me. Kind people who took me in and helped with Camis.'

Her mind roils in a multitude of images of Camis—of Luk and Anna feeding them, of helping on the farm, of the journeys they'd made looking for healing plants and herbs to sell to repay the couple. Of Camis learning to walk, of him riding Misty, and the tall grass, bees, birds. Camis laughing, Camis finding his healing gift, and now, alone with no one to guide him.

Oh, Camis, I have failed you.

The shock hits her. Once her uncle has her back here on board his Mastership, they will leave this galaxy, and she will never see Camis again, never instruct him, laugh with him, or hold him. They will never ride through the lush green countryside, or pick herbs, or sit in the warm sun of Maa Erda.

He will be lost to her, six days is not enough time. Tears slide down her face. She can bear the pain and humiliation, the loss of freedom, of not being able to love a man freely for herself, but to never see her son again, to never hug him, to never scold him, or to not even be able to let him know she is alive . . . It is too much. The tears start anew, and Zachary holds her tight.

'Listen,' he says when she is calm again. 'It doesn't really change anything. In fact, it makes it more urgent that we attack and, in the confusion, whisk you away. Don't you see that will really hurt him? His soldiers will be split guarding the parade and guarding this ship, and before he can reunite all his soldiers, we can hit him hard. Another group also plans to take control of the shuttles.'

'But surely all that will do is enrage him and make him move things here more quickly. Maybe even escalate his plan to leave.'

'Precisely! Once he has moved some of his forces he will be divided and weaker. We can attack where he least expects it. I need you to get me the exact parade route.'

'I'm not sure he will take my disappearance lightly,' she says, troubled. The plan has too many flaws, and her uncle has never been one to back down or relinquish anything he considers his.

'Oh, I'm counting on it,' Zachary says with a grim smile. 'As he searches, we will hit him hard and from all angles. Starting here, disrupting the supplies that he moves in, making it look like this is our objective. That we plan to take or ruin his Mastership.

'What he doesn't expect is an attack within the city as well. He has no idea how many of his own people are willing to oppose him. Especially when we expose that his little scheme is not to settle on the planet below, but to travel for years and then to start a war.'

'Zachary,' Serin says, a tiny seed of hope blooming in her chest. She reaches out for his hands, 'Do you think . . .?'

244

A whistle sounds in the corridor, and Zachary holds his hands up to stop her mid-sentence. Quickly, he crosses to the main door and slips out, pressing the wall to close the door. She can hear voices and steps forward part way across the room, her hand to her throat.

The door slides open only moments later, and her uncle stands there. He is covered in the fine white powder of the desert, and his face is a storm.

'You can stand down now, thank you soldier,' he calls over his shoulder, stepping into the room and crossing to the pitcher of wine.

Zachary salutes and marches away as the door slides shut, and a huge sigh of relief escapes from her before she can stop it. Her uncle stops drinking and looks at her.

'It's okay, Princess,' he says. 'The danger is over, but I will feel happier when I can get you back to the safety of the palace.' He drains the rest of his wine and holds his hand out for her. 'Come, I'll escort you back, and then I can concentrate on crushing these stupid scum.'

He leads her through the unfinished ship and out into the heat of the late afternoon. They ride in silence back to the palace.

When they arrive back at her apartment, he closes the doors and with a curt, 'Wait outside,' dismisses the two young girls he has replaced Onora with.

You will not talk to anyone about my Mastership or about my plans. He does not release her arm. *Not to anyone, including your brother.* His eyes are flat grey slate, and he waits until she nods before continuing. *You will find the women I need, Serin, so have the names ready for me.* He turns to leave, but she holds onto his arm.

'I—' she says, and swallowing, she switches to mindspeak.

We will need to start the plans for our wedding. Seeing him frown, she continues, making her voice matter of fact. *The parade route to plan, the holiday to announce, alms day to prepare, guests for the feast, my dress . . .*

A small smile tugs at the corner of his mouth. *When I return, we will talk about the wedding.*

She leans back against the door once he is gone. She had done her best to get the information that Zachary needed, but anymore would have made him suspicious of her intentions. She holds back a shudder and looking towards her open shutters sends out a silent prayer.

'Stay safe,' she whispers, but whether it is for Camis or Zachary or both, she does not know.

The two new maids fuss about getting her bath water ready. They look so similar that Serin wonders if they are cousins or even sisters. They must have seen twenty summers but seem naive compared to the young adults she'd known on Maa Erda. They each have curly hair and are constantly playing with it, twisting fat ringlets into shape. It makes Serin want to slap their hands. She wants them to leave as soon as they arrive. She really misses Onora.

In the pool, she uses a rough cloth to scrub herself clean, soaping and rinsing, again and again, trying to rub away anywhere that he has touched her, scrubbing her skin red and raw. With a sigh, she gives it up. There is no way she will ever be rid of the taint or the feel of him inside her.

Lying back, she rests her head on the tiled edge of the bathing pool and closes her eyes, glad of the peace, and thinks over Zachary's plan. Will it work? But it is all they have.

A faint scratching sound catches her attention, and she sits up, turning her head in its direction. It is coming from her bedroom area. Someone is in her quarters. She opens her mouth to scream for the guards, her maids, anyone, when a small hand appears from under her bed and then an arm, followed by a dirty little face.

The cry freezes on her lips as she recognises the child that scrabbles slowly out, his eyes fixed on hers. Reaching for a towel to wrap herself in, she ignores the dripping water and crosses to the boy, the boy whose arm she had promised to heal.

Chapter 27

Nenna dry heaves one more time and slowly straightens up, wiping the back of her hand across her mouth. Carefully, she looks out from behind the tent that she has run to and stares back at the wagons. Her limbs are weak and floppy, nearly unable to support her. Maa Erda, Maa Erda, Maa Erda, what have these cruel beasts done? Thoughts swirl and tangle like brambles in her mind.

Her hands make fists and clamp tight to her sides as she tries to think. How could they? Why? Whatever reason can they have for such mutilation? Her stomach roils again, but there is nothing left inside to bring up.

Her eyes stare unseeing ahead as she stumbles away, lost in the suffering, the sheer brutality of it all, the pointlessness. What can she do now to help them? Nothing.

Purposefully avoiding looking at the carts, she slips between tents and horse lines. Once she is a good distance away, she stops and breathes in deeply.

Drawing closer to Vitrainy's tent, she hears raised voices coming from inside.

'Look, you don't understand,' Vitrainy is saying, and Nenna hears the chink of glass.

'Oh, I understand well enough,' Eachan spits back. 'I understand that you need to keep your precious image. The big tough man, the man who takes any woman he wants, especially his prim prizes.'

'Eachan, you know that's not true,' Vitrainy's voice reasons. 'I only keep the prim females so that I'm not pestered by other women, and so that my . . . my preferences are kept hidden.' There is silence.

'Why?' Eachan eventually asks.

'Why, what?'

'Why do you keep it hidden? It's not against the law.'

'No, but . . .' Vitrainy's voice trails away. 'But you know the army. I want to continue flying, but I also want to climb the ranks and this . . . it just won't help.'

'Please, V. Just get rid of her,' Eachan pleads.

'Are you really worried that I'll bed an animal like that?' Vitrainy replies. 'Come, sit with me. We still have time before she's back.'

'Exactly what I mean,' Eachan says, his tone petulant. 'Can't you just give her up? I don't like her hanging around, watching us all the time. I want you for myself.' There is a silence filled with a rustling and the creak of wood.

Eachan, his voice slightly muffled, begs again. 'Please, V. For me.'

'No!' Vitrainy snaps, and she hears the tent flap opening.

Quickly, she ducks around the side of the tent and hopes no one has seen her listening. Thankfully, the camp is quiet. Most of the soldiers are sleeping or resting out of the sun.

'I've has enough of this conversation,' Vitrainy says roughly. 'In fact, I've had enough of you and your whining. Leave!'

'Vitrainy, I—' Eachan cries.

'Get! Out!' Vitrainy shouts, emphasising each word.

Nenna waits a few moments before weaving her way back to the path. But when she steps out, she finds Vitrainy still standing, holding the tent flap open and staring after Eachan. He is stiff with anger, and a part of her shrinks inside as he motions for her to enter the tent. He moves aside to let her pass, immediately letting the canvas door fall closed behind her.

'Strip!' Vitrainy hisses quietly, crossing to sit down on the bed. 'And be quick.'

It has been days since he has asked this. Not since they'd landed, and she'd almost begun to relax. She complies, thinking that anything that he does is preferable to being processed, but at the same time, she remembers the beatings and her stomach knots. Her knees threaten to collapse, and she hurriedly drops her cape and pulls the loose dress over her head. She lowers her chin down to her chest, and, standing naked before him, shivers. Others have fared far worse than she, and she braces her knees, willing them to hold her up.

'Get over there,' he says, indicating a large ornate chest on one side of the tent. 'Turn around and put your hands on the chest.' She does as she is told, and bending over, places her hands on the carved wood.

'Wider,' he says, his voice low. Not knowing if he means her hands or her feet, she quickly moves both. She hears the bed creak and is aware of him coming closer. He stands behind her as before, close but not touching. She can hear him breathing, and goosebumps pebble her skin. Her hands feel wet.

'Vitrainy,' Eachan says behind them at the tent's entrance, 'I'm so—' He stops speaking. 'What in the crystal is going on?'

'I told you to leave!'

She can hear the ice in Vitrainy's voice. She dares not move, knowing that quiet tone too well.

'And you told me you weren't interested in your prims,' Eachan says, his voice rising.

'Shh!' Vitrainy says sharply. 'I don't want the whole camp to hear you.'

'Oh, yeah, your precious reputation. Well, I'll tell you—'

But Vitrainy cuts across whatever he is about to say. He speaks softly, but this time, each word can cut stone. 'I want you to leave. And I want you to do it now. We will never discuss our relationship again, and you will never speak to me again unless it is to do with work. Do I make myself clear?' The last bit is said in a whispered hiss.

Nenna chances a glance under her arm, surprised to see that Vitrainy has moved away from her and is standing close behind Eachan, holding a knife to his throat.

'Is. That. Clear.'

There is fear on Eachan's face as he nods. The two men stay frozen together, then slowly, Vitrainy lowers the knife. 'Get out,' he says and removes his arm.

Lightning fast, Eachan turns, thrusting forward with his arm. Vitrainy's eyes open wide, and he clutches a hand to the spot where he has been hit. Blood seeps through his fingers, and Nenna gasps, moving back against the canvas wall. The two men do not move— their eyes remain fixed on each other, locked in a strange tableau.

Suddenly, Vitrainy gives a guttural roar, and still grasping his own knife, he lurches towards Eachan. He stabs high, puncturing the side of Eachan's neck. Blood sprays across their faces, arcing out into the air. Vitrainy thrusts again and again. Eachan screams and staggers back. Their eyes never leave the other. Once again, they are still.

After what seems an age to Nenna, Eachan's knees begin to buckle under him, and a single tear tracks down his face, gathering blood from the spatters on his cheek. He falls, one hand slick with blood clamps to his neck, his expression full of disbelief and fear. Falling forward he reaches out, but Vitrainy takes a step back with a blank expression. Eachan makes a tiny sound, almost like a sigh, and crumples to the floor.

Vitrainy slumps down beside his lover, then slowly lies back. Afraid to move, Nenna watches his chest rise and fall, one hand holding the wound in his abdomen, which still trickles blood.

Vitrainy turns his head and looks at her. Her pulse races, and she wraps her arms tight around herself. His breath is coming quick and shallow. She wills herself to breathe more deeply, but the breath sticks in her throat under the stare of those hateful eyes.

'Get help, you stupid prim,' he croaks, but when she doesn't move, he tries to raise his head, but a spasm of pain wracks him and he drops back.

After a few moments, he looks back at her. 'What are you waiting for? Go and get help.'

His voice is more urgent now. This foul monster wants her help. Her eyes flicker down to the wound and back up to his face. A war rages inside her head.

Do something, Nenna. Stop the bleeding. Run for help.

Finish him off, Nenna. Make sure he doesn't live. No one will know.

'Get help, you stupid bloody prim, or by the crystal, I will make you pay!'

An image of Quarrel falling flashes into her mind, and she takes a step towards him. 'You already have,' she says flatly.

'What?' he says.

'What I want to know,' she says, looking down at him, just out of his reach, 'is why?'

'Look, you filthy prim—' He tries to raise a hand towards her, but it just flutters up a short way before it falls back. He is so weak now, and the realisation hits him. 'Please,' he begs. 'Please, get help.'

'I did nothing to you,' she says. She thinks of her friends in the carts. 'We've done nothing to you, but you treat us like animals. No, worse than animals. Why?'

He looks away and stares up at the ceiling, not answering her for a long time. The blood pools in the dip of his stomach and slides down in small rivers to the floor. 'This can't be happening,' he whispers. 'Please, get me some help.'

'Tell me why you hate us so much?' she demands.

'I don't have to tell you anything, prim,' he snarls. 'You are inferior.'

She stares down at him for a long time. 'Well, I'll tell you something,' she says at last. 'In the morning, I will still be here, but you will be dead. How's that for being inferior?' And she walks back to the trunk and sits down to wait.

Vitrainy's breathing becomes ragged and irregular. He hasn't spoken to her for some time, just mutters incomprehensibly a few times with his eyes closed. He takes one more ragged breath and lies still. Everything is still. She continues to sit, looking numbly towards the two dead men.

Distant shouts slowly filter into her consciousness. The camp is waking, and this galvanises her into action. People will come soon to load things onto wagons and take down the tent. They'll find Vitrainy and Eachan and . . . her. And then what?

The noise outside the tent increases. She retrieves her dress from near Vitrainy but drops it instantly. It is wet and sticky, soaked in blood. She looks down at it, frowning, seeing the strange red patterns drying on it. As her brain tries to make sense of it all, a loud *thwomp* shakes the ground. Debris patters lightly on the outside of the tent.

She looks again at her clothing, instinct urging her to move, to dress, but she can't bring herself to pick it up. Cautiously, she moves away from it, as though it were a live snake, and looks around for something else to wear. She rubs her palms roughly down her naked thighs, leaving smears of blood.

Her heel strikes against the chest behind her, and she whirls. Another *thwump* outside vibrates through her bare feet. Somewhere deep inside her, something tries to warn her, urging her to move faster. That is not the sound of camp breaking.

She reaches forward to lift the lid of the chest. Vitrainy's spare uniforms are neatly folded inside, and she grabs the trousers and tunic top, pulling them on. He is taller than her, and she has to roll the top of the trousers over several times to keep the legs from dragging. The top is baggy, but it hides the folded trousers and at least she is not naked anymore.

She keeps her long tangled hair inside the tunic, tying the red dust scarf around her neck, keeping the triangle at the front as she has seen others do and using the knot to keep her hair back.

All the while her mind roils. What should she do? Where can she go? What should she say? Will she be put in for processing now that that beast is dead?

The commotion outside increases. The shouting seems more frantic, mixed with the sounds of hooves pounding and horses screaming.

Quickly, she moves past the bodies. There are more thuds from outside, one very close, and something about the sound tugs at her memory even in her frightened state. She reaches the tent flap but is afraid to draw it back.

A loud *thwack* shakes the tent, causing her to stagger and grab at the flap. The sound, along with an image form together in her mind. Wyrms! They are being attacked by wyrms!

She draws back several steps. She can't go out there, she just can't. Frozen with indecision, she hesitates when Fin bursts into the tent, screaming her name. 'Nenna!'

Relief flashes briefly across his face as he steps forward. Then he sees what she is wearing and looks beyond her to the dark mounds lying on the floor.

'What's going on?' And he pushes past her, looking more closely at the bodies. 'What have you done?'

'No! No, Finn. I never . . . it isn't what . . . Oh, Ma Erda, what am I to do?' She reaches out an arm towards him. He backs away, circling back for the tent opening, then turns and flees.

Things are worse, much worse than she had imagined. She'd not even considered the possibility that they would think she were responsible for the deaths. Her mind reels with questions. It will mean her death if they think she'd killed Vitrainy and that stupid little Eachan.

She forgets about the wyrms outside and pushes herself to action. She has to catch Fin, stop him and explain. He has to believe her, help her.

She rushes to the tent flap and pulls it open.

The world explodes.

Chapter 28

'Right, lads, I think that's it. Clip your metal sand grips on and start digging out the worst side.' Arture's voice wakes Camis with a start.

Camis is surprised to find that the sun has risen. He must have dozed off. He did not hear the crystal sing in the dawn—perhaps the wind had been too loud. The day is fresh and cool, the desert flat and calm, apart from the piles of dust that have blown against the carts.

Camis pulls the springs on the boot grips and checks that they are firmly in place, only hesitating for a moment before jumping down. Once the bottom canvas is loose, he leads Spirit outside to give himself more room to roll the material back up. The other carts have all but vanished under a drift of fine crystal particles, and he stands for a moment to stare at them.

'No good just gaping, lad. Tie her to the front and start digging.' Arture comes around from the far side of his cart leading Traveller.

Tiberius appears, yawning and rubbing his eyes, his usually spiky hair flattened.

Securing Spirit to the front of the cart, Camis reaches under the driver's seat for the shovel. Pulling up his face protection, he starts scooping away the windswept crystal that has lodged against his cart. Piled high, the whiteness reminds Camis of the snow drifts in winter at home. He remembers digging out the piggery at Anna and Luk's homestead. Tears prick the backs of his eyes, and he bends quickly to the task of clearing away the drift from his cart.

'You'll need these to clear around the axle and wheels, or the dust will get in the smallest of cracks and start damaging things even quicker than it normally does,' Arture says, handing him some leather gloves. 'You all right, young Camis?'

'Yes, thank you,' he replies a little too quickly, putting on the gloves and crouching down to inspect the underside of the cart. 'I just . . . I'm just glad that storm is over.' Camis runs his hands around the inside of one of the wheels, checking for damage. 'The crystal cuts so easily, not like a fresh soft snowfall.'

After the carts are free, Camis helps Tiberius hitch up Scout. Tiberius is still nervous with the horses. Before long, they resume their journey as though nothing has happened. They stop and eat together in Arture's cart.

'Why were there no wyrms about before or after the storm?' Tiberius asks.

'Don't really know, lad. They just seem to know that a storm is coming, and they stay away for a day or two after. My theory is that they can sense it and go deep underground into their burrows, and then it takes them time to travel back out again.'

The next morning, Arture tells them, 'We are only a day out from the mining camp now. Soon you will be sleeping in a comfy bed after a cool shower and some hot food.'

The news lightens everyone's mood except Camis'. Part of him longs for a bath to get rid of the wretched dust, but another part knows that he will be caught and exposed for who he really is. They complete their routine of checking the carts and feeding the horses Camis feels himself dragging his feet, delaying the inevitable as he helps Tiberius hitch Scout to the traces. As he backs Spirit into place a low rumble makes him pause. All three of them straighten from their tasks and look around. There is nothing in sight. The rumbling increases: the ground begins to shake.

'Get Spirit secure, lad, and get going!' Arture shouts, panic in his voice. 'The wyrms are rising. Get out of here now!'

He clicks Traveller and shakes the reins vigorously to get his horse to move, not waiting for the other two. Camis catches Spirit's halter before she takes off after them and soothes her, patting her gently.

Whoa, girl, he says softly into her mind.

Quickly, he pulls the leather fastenings through the cart's stays and glances up to see Tiberius and Scout already following Arture at a good pace, dust billowing up from both carts.

The rumbling increases, joined by a low hum. Camis jumps into the driver's seat just as Spirit jerks into motion, tipping him off balance and into the back of the cart. He catches his shoulder on one of the boxes and cries out. He tries to stand up but has to grab the sides of the lurching cart. He raises his eyes and forgets the pain in his shoulder as his heart leaps into his mouth.

Behind him, the desert floor writhes and undulates as far as the eye can see. Hundreds of wyrms have risen out of the desert floor, some breaking through the surface not far from where he had been standing moments before. The wyrms reach their gaping mouths to the sky, standing upright, rigid, their bodies still anchored in the ground. They wave and sway to some unheard rhythm.

More and more of them break through the ground, and he is transfixed, staring, until a wyrm crashes upwards just behind the cart, almost underneath them.

He scrambles for the driver's seat and unties the reins from the foot rail. Shouting at Spirit to speed up, he flaps the reins. She doesn't need urging. She is already pursuing the others at a canter, before breaking into a gallop. Her ears are flat back to her head, and Camis can sense her fear along with his own.

He hears the boxes behind him tumbling around, rattling and banging. An image flashes into his mind of a gigantic wyrm rising up, throwing the cart into the air, of his legs being ground to dust by those spiral teeth, of the horse's frantic screams, of the pain. He can't shake the image clear and concentrates hard to stay in the middle of the wooden bench, bouncing and thumping just like the boxes in the back.

He coughs and squints ahead to try and see the others, unable to pull up his neckerchief against the rising dust. He risks a quick glance back in time to see a huge beast launch itself out of the ground, towering above the sea of wyrms that surround it.

It unfurls massive wings and flaps them forwards, once, twice, and he glimpses whorls of brown, beige, gold, and white in an intricate pattern on it's wings before the creature vanishes from sight in a billowing cloud of dust.

Camis' arm throbs where he'd knocked it. He feels battered and bruised all over. Spirit slows to a fast trot.

'Pull over, lad,' Arture shouts as Spirit overtakes Traveller.

Reluctantly and yet also glad, Camis halts his horse. In the dry still air, the dust settles almost immediately. Camis can see that Tiberius and his cart are already waiting. All three horses stand with heads bowed to the desert floor, their sides heaving, and Camis realises just how hard they have been driven.

His bones ache. His mouth and eyes feel as though they are filled with grit. He realises Arture and Tiberius are drinking water, spitting and washing the dust away. He follows their example.

'No, lad,' Arture is saying to Tiberius. 'Leave the horses to cool for a little. Water is not good for them after such an extended run. We will rub them down first.'

Camis looks around, seeing nothing in any direction but flat white desert. 'I thought we would be near the camp by now,' he says.

'The wyrms have blocked the way, and we are now well off course. We will rest up and take a wide berth around that area tomorrow. I'm afraid it will take us another two or three days to get back on track, if we don't have any more problems.'

They eat a cold meal, chewing quietly on the dried meat and hard stale bread, wrapped in their own thoughts and too exhausted to discuss the day's events.

'We have enough food and water for a day or two, if we are careful,' Arture tells them. 'After that, I will have to draw out wyrms for water.' He looks across at them and grimaces. 'At least to get enough for the horses.'

Camis uses a backpack as a pillow and lies down across the seat, pulling his cloak over himself. The night seems a little colder. He is reluctant to leave the driver's seat, as Arture's instructions to feed and water the horses and leave them in the traces has him wondering if things are really over.

The attack, when it comes, is swift and silent. But it isn't the wyrms.

Camis is dragged off the cart and dumped painfully onto the desert floor. His arms and legs are quickly and expertly bound, and his mouth gagged. He is trussed up like a winter hog before he can gather a thought.

Camis twists and stains against his bonds, watching as dark figures swarm over the carts. The sound of boxes being ripped opened is loud in the silent desert. There is no sign of Arture or Tiberius.

One of the carts rumbles away, and a spasm of fear lurches in his gut. What if they leave him here? He shuffles his feet closer, trying to stand. Someone jumps down from Camis' cart, silhouetted by the glow from the ground, and crunches away out of sight.

There is a short pause, and then a second cart begins to move away. Panic envelops him, and he struggles to his knees just as hands grasp him from behind and another figure lifts him up by the legs. He is swung into the back of the moving cart just as it passes him, and he catches a glimpse of the two painfully thin men as they heave him up. They are wrapped in an odd assortment of ragged clothes, and their heads and faces are covered in dirty scraps of material.

Camis lands hard, his breath knocked from him. One man clambers up after him and scrambles over the boxes to the front of the cart, flapping material making him look like a living scarecrow.

Camis lies still, catching his breath, and listens for any clue as to who these people might be. The cart lurches downhill, rolling him against the nearest box. What is happening now? Who are these people? What have they done with Arture and Tiberius?

Frantically, he thinks of what might be stored near him that might help him get free, but anything useful is under the driver's seat. There is nothing sharp that he can use to cut the binding— only the boxes, shut tight with their heavy clasps. Heavy clasps!

He wriggles around and pulls himself into a sitting position, slowly shuffling his back along the box to find the clasp, but the box has been turned, and he is leaning on its back. Biting down a frustrated cry, he pushes himself along to the next box.

His progress is extremely slow, and he has only managed to feel the edge of a box when the cart takes a sudden tilt sideways. Everything slides a short way towards the front of the cart, but it is enough movement for him to become painfully trapped between two of the boxes.

Camis cries out, but the cart continues to tilt. It feels as though the whole thing, horse and all, will roll over. The boxes crush him, making it hard to breathe. He strains to try and bring his legs up and kick against the box, but it is pressing too tightly against him, pinning him like a wolf caught in a trap.

The floor of the cart continues to tip downwards, but suddenly, it tilts to the left and the box slides away from him, freeing him. He bends his knees inward and lies panting on the floor, desperate to rub at the ache of his ribs, but his arms are still tied.

Gradually, his breathing slows. He feels the cart change direction, and he slides along with the cargo to the right. He uses his feet to keep the boxes back. Closing his eyes, he concentrates on the pain in his ribs and gently massages the area in his mind with his healing skill. The pain eases slightly, enough for him to be able to breathe more deeply. He can sense that there are no broken bones, just bad bruising.

He opens his eyes to study what he can see out through the back of the cart, frowning in the dim light as he tries to make sense of it. The desert appears to be rising up on one side, as though the cart is sliding along the ground. It also seems to be getting darker. With a jolt, he realises that they are travelling downwards. They are somehow moving down into the ground, twisting and changing direction every so often.

The cart levels out and comes to a halt. The white light of crystal floods everything. A scarecrow figure appears, and Camis, shielding his eyes against the glare, makes muffled sounds in an effort to communicate. The figure ignores him and lowers the back of the cart, pulling Camis out and onto the ground.

He lands awkwardly, nearly on his feet, but the bindings catch around his legs, and he loses his balance, falling to his knees and blinking tears away. Scarecrow-man jumps down beside him and walks away. After a moment, the cart moves on.

All Camis can see is a white wall. Looking up, he cranes his neck to see the top. It is impossibly high, vanishing in a small circle of darkness that might indicate the night sky.

He shuffles round in time to see his cart, pulled by Spirit, disappearing into a tunnel. There are two large lumps of glowing crystal sitting on the ground to each side of the opening. Light illuminates the cart as it passes and disappears into the darkness beyond.

Camis shivers. A wyrm hole. They are inside a burrow.

Panic grips him, and he can't think, every fibre of his being telling him to flee. It is a little while before a strange sound draws his attention.

Far to the left of the tunnel is Tiberius. He is bound and gagged like Camis and is making muffled grunts, trying to get his attention. Lying flat on the ground beside him is Arture, unconscious, blood crusting the side of his head with dried stains that have run down onto his gag.

Camis can you help him? He hisses.

Camis shuffles painfully over the coarse crystal towards them. Arture's breath is ragged and shallow. Camis slides closer, turning around so that his hands can make contact with Arture. As soon as he touches the man, he closes his eyes and delves.

Arture has a nasty head wound. Camis carefully knits the tissue together after dispersing the fluid that has collected around Arture's brain. The man would not have lasted the night with that injury. He also has a broken arm. But dealing with that is straightforward, and when complete, Camis is satisfied to find Arture breathing deeply, asleep.

Camis shuffles around to face Tiberius and gives him a nod. Relief floods over the other boy's face.

Three men appear out of the tunnel—two of the flapping scarecrows and a more neatly-dressed man who doesn't wear the layers that the others do. He has no head or neck wrap to protect him from the desert. His neatly trimmed beard is tinged in grey.

Camis wonders what these people do to keep themselves safe from the wyrms because none of them are wearing metal clip-ons on their footwear. In fact, only the smartly dressed man has boots on. The other two have layers of cloth wound around their feet.

The smartly dressed man kneels by Arture, removes the gag, and examines Arture's head. He runs his hands expertly over Arture, then he stands abruptly, making quick gestures with his hands to the scarecrow men.

Camis recognises some of the hand signals from Arture's lessons. Smartly-dressed man points at Arture and signs 'where?' Camis doesn't recognise the final gesture, but it is then that he realises that during this whole ordeal, from their attack to the carts being driven away, he has never heard a single word spoken by these people.

Both scarecrow men check Arture's head, turning it from side to side and waking Arture in the process. They point at Arture and have a fast hand-waving conversation with smartly-dressed man. Camis cannot follow all the signs, but it seems as if they are arguing. He can make out the signs for, 'nothing there' and 'arm broken.' Smartly-dressed man shakes his head vigorously before kneeling back down by Arture and offering him a water bag. Arture drinks greedily.

'I know who you are,' Arture croaks. 'My wife is . . . was a prim.' He takes another mouthful of water. 'She taught me the signs.'

There is astonishment in the men's expressions. Their hands flick and sweep in a fast series of gestures.

'I'm fine,' Arture says, 'no thanks to him.' He nods towards one of the scarecrow men, who scowls back. 'Help me up and let me see to my boys.' The two standing men say nothing but gesture quickly to each other.

'I know you find it hard to believe that I married a prim. I loved her until the day she died.' He looks away into the distance, grief etched into his face. One of the men gestures again, and Arture turns back to follow the movements. Again, they are too fast for Camis to follow.

'I don't know anything about that,' Arture says as one of the scarecrow men lashes out abruptly and smacks him hard across the face. All Arture can do is glare back at him, while smartly-dressed man puts a restraining hand out, pulling the scarecrow-man back a step and signing for him to stop and makes a quick gesture.

'I am not lying,' Arture says, his face red where he has been slapped.

Tiberius and Camis are pulled to their feet and prodded towards the tunnel entrance where a tall young man in a bizarre collection of clothing is standing quietly, regarding their slow shuffle. Smartly-dressed man helps Arture up.

'Cut their ties,' the man at the entrance signs. 'Hurry up, you are needed.'

Their leg ties are cut, and they are led in silence through the tunnel entrance and down a side turning. A short distance down the sloping path, Arture is held to one side while the two boys are shoved roughly forwards into a small cell. Before Arture is pushed in to join them, the bonds tying his arms behind his back are cut. A bared metal door bangs shut, and the two men hurry off.

Arture unties Tiberius and tells him to help Camis.

There is barely enough room in the cell for all three of them to lie down on the floor. The walls are smooth and white, giving off a faint glow that is enough to see each other by. There is a damp smell as though they are near stagnant water.

'What is going on, Arture? Who are these people? Why do they sign and not speak?'

'They can't, lad,' Arture replies distractedly, running his hands around the outer edges of the door.

'What do you mean, they can't?' Camis asks him.

'They can't speak, Camis. They have been processed.'

'And what exactly does that mean?' Camis asks.

Not meeting his eye, Tiberius looks down at the floor and says quietly, 'They have no tongues, Camis. They were removed, along with their manhood, to accommodate working in the mines.'

Camis is stunned to silence. He thinks back to the hard table and white room that Tiberius had rescued him from. Maa Erda. Bile builds in the back of his throat, and he shakes his head in disbelief.

'Is this true?' he demands, turning from Tiberius to Arture.

'Aye, lad, I'm afraid it is,' Arture says.

'I have to tell them,' Camis says, stepping over to grip the metal bars of the door. 'I'm not from here. I'm one of them.'

'Camis,' Tiberius says in a low, warning voice, but when Camis doesn't respond, he repeats it more urgently. Camis glances back over his shoulder. Arture is staring at him. Too late, he realises what he has just said.

Taking a deep breath, Camis turns back to the cell door and bellows, 'Guard!' He waits and then shouts again. 'Guard!'

A guard appears, wearing a rag tag of clothing. He looks sourly at Camis, waiting a short distance away for Camis to speak.

'I know it doesn't look like it, but I need you to understand that I am one of you,' Camis says.

The guard's eyes narrow.

Camis rushes on, 'I was born on Maa Erda. I was captured and bought here just like you.' The guard turns away, disgust on his face. 'Tiberius helped free me before . . . before . . .' He can't bring himself to say it.

The guard stalks away before Camis has a chance to say anything else. With a heavy sigh he leans his head against the bars. After a while, a hand rests gently on his shoulder.

'What do you think you are doing?' Tiberius asks.

'I think it is time you explained exactly who you are and how you got here, don't you, lad?' Arture says. He does not look annoyed or threatening, just a little puzzled.

Resting his back against the cell wall, Arture slides down to sit on the floor. With his knees bent and his arms resting on them, he looks like he is sitting by a campfire, waiting for a story.

Tiberius gives Camis' shoulder a squeeze, and with a small nod, he moves back a couple of steps to join Arture. They both look up at him. Camis isn't sure exactly how much of the story he should tell Arture. The man has been nothing but kind to him and Tiberius, but he doesn't want to get Tiberius in any more trouble.

Camis gives a brief summary of searching for Nenna, of seeing Tiberius's hov crash and rescuing him from the wreckage. He tells Arture about finding that the ship was about to take off with Nenna onboard, and that he forced Tiberius to sneak him on so they could get to Nenna and free her.

'. . . and then you turned up to unload the boxes, and you know the rest.' Camis trails off. 'I don't think we thought things through that well,' he finishes lamely.

There is a short silence, and then Arture turns to Tiberius. 'Is that how it happened?' he asks.

Tiberius nods. 'More or less. He missed out the bit where he healed me from horrendous injuries, and how he gave Kestell, my archarya who was killed in the crash, a send-off that he really didn't deserve. The fool had been showing off just before he crashed the hov. Oh, and I caused a major data crash on the mothership to steal Camis out of the processing lab and into the loading bay.'

'Oh,' says Arture.

'And that he healed you of a head injury that would have killed you,'—Tiberius points out of the cell towards the way the guard had gone— 'after that stupid lot attacked.'

There is a longer silence this time. Camis looks at Tiberius, who in turn looks down at his hands. What a mess.

None of them hear the guard return. Suddenly, an arm snakes in through the bars and loops around Camis' neck. Startled, Camis pulls ineffectually at the man's grip as two more guards appear. Arture and Tiberius both get to their feet.

One of the men unlocks the cell door and gestures to them to stay back, waving a stun stick. The first guard drags Camis out, and the door bangs shut and is relocked. Without any warning, the guard holding Camis swings him around and punches him hard in the stomach.

All three of the men set about Camis systematically, raining punches on his head and torso until he falls to the floor. Gasping for breath, Covering his head with his arms Camis curls into a protective position. He can hear Arture and Tiberius yelling.

A well-aimed kick to the side of his head produces a loud crack, splintering his jaw. The pain is excruciating, radiating out from the impact up the side of his face into his mouth and up into his ears. His yelp only spurs the men into a greater frenzy. Suddenly, the blows and kicks stop.

Camis is a mass of pain. He can only manage painful shallow gasps, otherwise his ribs send shooting spasms throughout his body. He can already feel an eye swelling and closing up. Blood trickles from the corner of his mouth, which hangs open awkwardly. His hands and arms are numb where they have been repeatedly kicked.

He wishes he were dead but concentrates on getting air to his lungs. He doesn't know what has made the blows stop, but he is grateful that they have. He can hear Arture and Tiberius frantically calling his name, but he can't lift his head and his tongue feels thick and swollen against his shattered jaw. Blackness curls at the edges of his vision, slowly enveloping him.

Chapter 29

Slipping in and out of consciousness, Nenna watches blurred shapes drift past her vision. Muted thuds and thumps shake the ground beneath her. Dust hangs in the air, making breathing difficult and smoke stings her nose, strange and acrid.

The dark shape of a man silhouetted against the late afternoon sky flits across her sight. He is tall and thickset. His head and shoulders are covered with some sort of cloth, which billows in the desert wind. He isn't there long, but he walks as though searching, crouching now and again. He reminds her of someone, but her mind won't focus.

She tries to move and call out to him, but her body won't respond, and fighting down a rising panic, she closes her eyes for a moment and tries again. Nothing in her body responds, and what is more frightening, she can't feel her arms or legs.

'We've checked all the bodies and collected our wounded, which will make our claim of attack look more authentic,' a voice says.

The speaker is out of her line of sight, but his voice is vaguely familiar. She doesn't hear anyone respond. Her head won't turn.

Inside, she screams, Help me! Help me! Please.

'The remaining ones will be eaten by the wyrms,' the voice continues. 'The more damaged tents will be left for D'Ruja's scouts to find. May the crystal take him.' The man spits, and she hears footsteps moving away.

Clamping her teeth tight, she works some saliva into her mouth and tries to swallow down the grit and sand.

Suddenly, pain explodes through her and she is coughing and convulsing, her body spasming, filling with life. Every muscle screams as hands turn her gently over.

Her head is raised and a skin of water is brought to her mouth. She gulps greedily. Brown eyes peer at her through an opening in black material, which completely wraps the person's head and face. The eyes smile. Then the water is pulled away. She tries to hold onto the skin, but the effort causes another wave of pain to shock through her, and more coughing. When it subsides, the person is gone.

Helplessness and fear overwhelm her and she cries out, a guttural animal-like sound—a sound of absolute despair. Instantly, the person is back, looking down, and there are two more people lifting her gently up.

Pain lances through her body, sharp and unbearable. A darkness consumes her. When she comes to, she is lying flat on a wooden surface, staring up into a white canopy spread above her. Everything aches, but it is a distant pain now, and she struggles to rise.

'Hey, there, soldier, calm yourself. You're safe now.' Firm hands help her to sit up.

'Wha—' she croaks and immediately starts to cough again. A water skin is held up to her lips, and once again, arms support her.

'What happened?' she asks once the coughing has stopped and she has drunk away some of the dryness. She nods her thanks at the old soldier crouching beside her. He is frowning.

'Wait there,' he says, jumping down off the back of the cart. 'I'll be back in a bit.'

She looks around. She is on a large cart with four others. No one meets her gaze. They are all far more wounded than she is.

The man returns, bringing someone else with him. The second man is slight with a hard thin face and white streaks in his hair. Nenna recognises him and her stomach knots. Oh, Maa Erda, the commander. The man who had disciplined Vitrainy after his horse had tried to bite and she had corrected it. It is his voice that she had heard earlier.

He'll know who she is. Scenes from the tent flash through her mind—the bodies on the floor, pulling on the black uniform, Fin. Fin!

The older soldier climbs up and takes her arm. 'Can you get up?' he asks.

She nods. Her heart starts to pound. Getting up is painful but she doesn't cry out. Once she is up, a wave of nausea hits her, and she sways, closing her eyes.

'Sit on the edge of the cart,' the commander says. His voice has a neutral tone, giving nothing away.

The soldier helps her forward and lowers her down. Her legs hang off the edge of the cart. Her head feels off balance, as though she is listing to the left, and she closes her eyes. The commander leans in. She can feel his breath on her cheek, his mouth close to her ear.

'Whose side are you on?' he whispers.

Her eyes snap open. 'I—I don't understand.'

'Did you come off the hov or the ship?' he asks, his face close, his brown eyes locked on hers.

'The hov,' she says quietly, and the commander swings away from her. 'And the ship,' she finishes.

He turns back. 'Which command unit are you under soldier?'

Nenna's mind whirls. Nothing makes sense. Nothing has made any sense for a long while, but she feels that her life may depend on the answer.

'I'm with the horse unit, sir,' she says.

The commander looks at her, taking in the dust-covered black uniform and the red bandana. And in a rush, she understands.

'Oh, the uniform. I took it. I was sleeping when all the commotion started and the tent collapsed. I could only find these in a trunk that I found in all the chaos.' At least it isn't all lies.

The commander raises his eyes to look up at the soldier standing behind her. They both let out their breaths at the same time.

'Why did you say you came off the hov and the ship then?' the commander asks.

Realising her mistake, she looks down, her face heating. 'I . . . I was confused by your question,' she says, bringing her hand to her head.

'Maybe the lass is concussed, sir,' says the old soldier behind her.

'Aye, Angus, perhaps you're right. I just thought . . . ' He tails off, staring out over the white desert.

'Sir?' she asks. 'What happened? I thought it was a wyrm attack.'

The commander glances up at the old soldier again and then back at her. He is just about to reply when a group of men appear, and the commander turns to watch them approach. They are dressed in strange clothes in multiple layers and colours. All have head and face wraps, which leave only their eyes free.

A short distance from the cart they stop, and the commander walks the remaining few steps to meet them. One of the men moves his hands, and she hears the commander speak but can't quite make out the words. Again, the man makes intricate signs with his hands. The commander raises his hand up to shoulder height, palm outwards, fingers spread and all the other men do the same. He turns to walk back to the cart.

'Right, Angus, get going,' he says, looking up at the man still standing behind her. Then he walks past the cart.

'Aye, sir.' Angus jumps down and pats her leg reassuringly. 'Don't worry, lass. We were attacked by rebels and not wyrms. They got what they wanted and are letting us go.'

Then he disappears around the covered side of the cart, reappearing at the front and climbing up into the driver's seat. A few moments later, the cart lurches forward. She watches the strangely clad men still standing on the white sand. They shimmer and blur in the dust that still hangs in the air.

The cart passes the commander, who is now mounted on his huge bay stallion. The horse stands proudly, head raised, ears pricked forward, the hood on its head giving an alien appearance. The commander calls out to the men watching from the camp once the cart has trundled past, and though he is a distance away, she hears his words.

'Goodbye, Hadders and good luck.'

The words strike her like a blow. Hadders. He'd said Hadders!

'Stop!' she yells, and though the commander and Angus both look around at her, the cart trundles on. 'Please, stop!' But the cart continues, and she watches the figures in the distance turn away. Then she is down and running.

She doesn't think, just runs as hard as she can back towards the camp. She staggers over the rough, uneven ground, her feet bare and her limbs still weak. The fine powder that coats the surface crystal starts to puff up around her feet. Someone shouts behind her, and she hears hoof beats.

'Hadders!' She tries to yell, but the sound is feeble, and it starts a coughing fit. She keeps moving back towards the camp.

The horse is close behind her, the bridle jingling, and she doubles her efforts to reach the camp when the ground erupts in front of her.

A wyrm explodes upwards. A huge column of segmented flesh rises past her, a reverse avalanche, streaming onwards, a blur of cratered cream. The head bows down. Rows of teeth revolve in a gaping maw, looming over her. The strange smell of sweet fresh rain envelops her as the creature starts to fall, the black hole of its mouth widening to consume her.

Firm hands wrench her upwards, swinging her away. The stallion gallops past, veering to the right as the wyrm crashes down. Dust envelops them all.

Nenna coughs and splutters, clinging to the commander. Tears and sweat streak her face, turning the white powder to a paste. She can't stop shaking. What in Maa Erda was she thinking?

The commander slows his horse, walking them back to the cart, which has stopped to wait. The commander allows her time to compose herself. The dust haze has already begun to settle in the strange still air of Crystal Moon.

'What, by the crystal, were you thinking?' the commander asks, echoing her thoughts as they stop at the waiting cart. 'Did you forget all your training for the desert?'

The commander manoeuvres the stallion to the back of the waiting cart and lowers her down. She holds on to his hand.

'I—' she whispers and stops, takes a long deep breath, and takes a chance. 'I'm not a soldier.'

'You're from the horse team, but even they do the basics.'

'No,' she says, looking up at him. 'No, I'm not even that.' She takes a deep breath and tries again. 'I think that man you were talking to back there'—she indicates the direction of the camp—'I think that he might be my brother.'

The commander frowns, lowering his dust scarf, white powder falling like snow.

'I'm a . . . a prim.' And she reaches up, untying her own scarf and pulling her hair free. He stares at her for a long time and then starts to laugh.

Nenna looks at him incredulously. The commander wipes a hand across his face, smearing the dust in a weird swirl across his cheeks.

'Sorry. Er, sorry, lass,' he splutters, unhooking his water flask and taking a swig before passing it to her. 'By the crystal, that's the last explanation I expected, and I'm delighted. I recognise you now. You're Vitrainy's trophy, aren't you?' Not waiting for an answer, he continues on. 'I'm so glad you survived. What happened to that cruel swine? We didn't find him amongst the survivors.'

'He . . . I . . .' She tails off, not fully understanding the commander's reaction.

'Don't worry, I just hope he met a nasty end. What is your name?' the commander asks, his brown eyes crinkling in a smile. He thrusts out a hand, pulling off his glove. 'I'm Commander Domerantry, but you can call me Dom.'

'Nenna,' she says, taking his hand. He clasps it firmly but gently, not shaking it in the fashion she has seen these men do but holding on and looking straight back at her.

'Please,' she says, a sudden panic swelling inside her. 'I just want to find my brother.'

'Right,' says the commander. 'That is something I can help you with.'

He dismounts from his stallion and hoists himself up onto the side of the cart and sits with his legs dangling over the back. He pats the boards beside him. 'Get this lot fed and watered, Angus, and tell the men to settle again for a short break.'

Nenna glances towards Angus and sees a number of troops mounted, waiting in pairs in a line stretching out in front of the cart. Nothing makes sense anymore, and she sighs, sitting down beside the commander. He hands her his water skin, and she drinks, swishing away the grit in her mouth and throat.

'My brother . . .' she says, looking back towards the camp longingly.

'Aye, we'll catch them up soon enough and have you reunited, if it is him,' the commander says. 'But for now, we'll have to wait a little while and make sure that'—he points at the crater left by the wyrm— 'was just a rogue.' Nenna shivers.

Angus busies himself quietly on the back of the cart, holding water out to those able to fend for themselves and gently supporting others to drink. The sweat dries on her skin, caking the dust to a tight powder. She scratches her cheek, loosening patches, which flake off. Her heart rate slowly returns to normal.

'You were taken from your home to work in our mines by order of His Imperial Majesty, D'Ruja A' Riman, the crystal burn him,' the commander says. 'But Vitrainy'—he spits the man's name with a scowl— 'took you for his personal use. The hov team officers are allowed rewards.'

She nods. None of this information is new to her.

'D'Ruja plans to return to our home planet. And for that, he needs an enormous amount of crystal. It powers our crafts, lighting, and heating. In fact, it gives us just about all our energy needs.'

Nenna frowns, looking out over the white desert. 'But what about food? Nothing grows here.'

'Indeed. Our city is built over the only land lake on this moon. The Book provides the glue that holds the fabric together.' She takes a breath to question him again, but he holds up a hand to stop her. 'There is much you will not understand, but I'll explain as much as I can before I have to get you back to the others.

'D'Ruja will not waste any more of our people in the mines. He needs them—all able-bodied men—for his return coup. You have to understand, Nenna, we were just following orders. The things I've seen . . . that's why I help the rebels, when I can.' They sit in silence for a while until the commander stands up and dusts his trousers off, making very little difference in the amount of dust covering them.

'Come, I'll take you to them now. I think we have waited long enough, the imminent danger is past.'

Nenna allows herself to be lifted onto the commander's stallion, and he mounts up behind her. They cross to the camp in silence. He has given her plenty to think about. They skirt around the outside of the blasted area, and a thought occurs to Nenna.

'Commander, why haven't more wyrms come? There is enough disturbance to attract them.' She indicates the damaged tents and shattered cook fires.

'Good question, Nenna. This was a pre-planned, orchestrated attack. Most of the adult wyrms are taking part in the rising of the queen. But to make sure we weren't disturbed; we planned a second diversion a few leagues away at another mine entrance. We made enough noise to draw any stray wyrms towards that instead of here.'

Before she can ask more, he kicks his horse into a canter, and they head straight for the largest hole that Nenna has ever seen. It had been hidden by the angle of the camp and extends wide enough to hold her entire village. The commander does not slow the horse as they approach.

As they reach the rim of the enormous hole, Nenna looks down. Far, far below, miniature wagons, horses, and people are lined up and are slowly disappearing into a narrow opening in the wall of the canyon. They look like the ants she had watched as a child, scuttling across a twig that spanned a small brook, vanishing into the undergrowth on the opposite bank. How had they gotten down there?

'Walk on, Major,' the commander says to the horse, clicking his tongue.

Nenna tightens her grip on the saddle in front of her and holds her breath as Major turns suddenly right and steps out onto a broad ledge that drops below the rim. The ledge slopes downward, and after a while, switches back on itself, dropping even lower. The horse navigates the slope with confidence, even when his back legs slide a little on the incline, causing Nenna to suck in air. They continue down the path as it drops lower and lower, twisting and winding its way down the wall of the gigantic hole.

'This was originally a queen wyrm burrow,' says the commander. 'We use entrances like these to scour the underground wyrm network, looking for any rich seams of crystal that remain behind after the wyrms have excavated an area. The road was carved out by the first captive prims, who were then used to mine the underground shafts and tunnels below.'

Nenna watches as the people below spot their descent and stop to watch, hands raised to shield their eyes against the glare of the sky.

'This one has long been abandoned.' The commander squeezes his right leg against Major's flank, and the horse dutifully turns right.

One of the men moves away from the tail end of the group below and back towards the edge of the path. Once he is within hailing distance, the commander calls out, 'I need to speak to Hadders.'

The other man nods and moves back to the slow-moving line and disappears into the cliff face. Major reaches the bottom and joins the end of the train of people before stopping.

People glance back at Nenna as they continue their slow shuffle towards the opening. There is a mix of men and women in a strange assortment of clothes. They all have some form of head and face covering, which hangs loose around their necks and shoulders. They keep moving towards the arched opening in the wall, the scuffing of their bare feet the only sound.

The path continues downwards for some way, disappearing from view. She cannot see the bottom, even from her vantage atop the horse, and she has no inclination to get down for a closer look.

'Won't be long now, Nenna,' the commander says kindly. 'Let's hope this Hadders and your brother are one and the same and you can be reunited with him.'

Major stamps a foot and snorts, and for a moment, Nenna's attention is on the horse. When she looks up, a figure is approaching through the curved archway. People smile as he passes them and some clap him on the back or shoulder.

It is Hadders.

She is down and running to meet him, shouting his name again and again. He pauses, frowning, then he realises who she is and spreads his arms wide, sweeping her up off the floor, holding her tight. He burrows his head in her hair and makes strange grunting sobs that mingle with her own cries.

'Had! Hadders, it's really you! I thought I would never find you. When you disappeared like that, I thought'—she fights a stream of words and tears—'I thought you were . . . ' She can't bring herself to say it.

She pulls away and struggles out of his grasp, stepping back to get a better look at him. Like everyone around him, he is coated in the white dust of the desert. Tears streak his face, but he is grinning widely at her, touching her hair, her face, her shoulder, as if to reassure himself that she is real. She catches hold of his hand.

He is thin—so very, very thin. His cheeks are sunken, and his eyes are deep dark hollows with wide shadows underneath. She wants to howl, to scream, to shout!

'He says, don't be cross or sad. He is fine and strong and alive,' says the commander quietly from behind her.

And with a shock, Nenna realises why the commander is speaking for her brother. Hadders can no longer speak. He has been processed.

The shock roots her to the spot. Her brother, her capable, dependable big brother, mutilated. Her breath won't come; her limbs won't move. She stares at him in silence, and he gives her a small smile, his eyes so full of love that she can't bare it. A white-hot anger courses through her, and she rounds on the commander, still on his horse, thumping at his legs.

The commander tries to back Major away, but she follows, beating and screaming in rage. Strong arms envelope her and hold her close, lifting her gently away from the horse and rider. Hadders holds her tight, letting her anger dissipate. The passion drains away, leaving her weak and shaking from its intensity.

The commander looks down sadly from his horse. Major had not reacted to her outburst, remaining calm and standing solidly, a true war horse.

'I am so sorry, Nenna. You have every right to your anger, but when you are rested and more settled, please know that we are not all monsters.' The commander says sadly.

'How can you ever right what you have done?' She glares up at him.

'We are trying to help the rebels and are doing our best to disrupt the plans of D'Ruja. We are prisoners, too, of a sort.'

Hadders releases her and makes a series of gestures towards the commander.

'Your brother asks me to tell you that you must come with him now. There are urgent plans that must be put in place. He will teach you how to sign so you can understand him and work with them.' The commander barks a laugh. 'He also says to tell you that he will teach you some manners.'

Nenna looks up at her brother's smiling face and feels all his love looking back. Her brother, her insufferable annoying brother, he is *here*, and she hugs him tightly.

Hadder's arm rests reassuringly across her shoulders as she watches the commander ride up to re-join his troops. It is only once he has disappeared that Nenna realises that she hadn't asked him if he knew what had happened to the horse boy, Fin.

Hadders gestures for her to follow him. She hurries to catch him up.

Whatever she'd imagined was on the inside of the wyrm hole, it is nothing like the reality. A short wide tunnel opens into a wide expansive cave, which is brightly lit and full of people. The long line of people she had followed in walk down an incline and disappear into the melee. Horses and carts are being led away; people are smiling and hugging.

There is a whole village—no, a whole town—inside. There is even the rattling clang of metal as a blacksmith works. Cooking smells emanate from the strange metal containers that she had seen back at the soldiers' camp—a meat stew and warm bread. Her mouth waters.

All around, the walls, doors, and windows are carved out of the rock, indicating rooms beyond. The cavern glows from the crystal. People sit mending pots or clothes, sharpening knives, polishing leather, or rush around carrying clothes, horse tack, food, or wood.

Hadders nudges her and moves his fingers. She watches them, then looks up at him sadly. 'Sorry, Hadders. I don't understand.' He points and she looks towards a raggedy group sitting on the ground, while others hand out water and food. It is a moment before she recognises Kitt, Ash and all the others from the cages and with a shout she rushes forward.

Hadders turns to a man sitting nearby mending a bridle and signs briefly at him. The man nods and gets up, going through an opening behind him. He returns with a charcoal stick and some paper.

Hadders leads a small group through a tall arch and into a wide plain room, gesturing for Nenna to join him. There are

277

sconces of crystal set at intervals around the walls. The only feature in the room is a solid stone table, on top of which are lots of miniature buildings, intricately carved and beautiful.

'What is it?' she asks Hadders, who writes on the paper

A copy of their city; Oasis.

One of the men is signing frantically and grinning.

Hadders scribbles another quick line, and she can't help smiling too. Turns out that his royal what's-his-face is getting married and is holding a parade in the city. They plan to attack. Perfect.

A young woman enters and signs quickly at Hadders. He frowns then, and shaking his head, waves the woman away.

'What now?' Nenna asks him, curious.

He shakes his head and signs, 'Nothing.'

She touches him on the arm. 'Tell me. Let me know what's going on. I want to help.'

He reaches for the paper again and scribbles quickly.

Some prisoners. One was injured but now he's not. I don't have time for this.

He signs to one of the men standing around the table, and they point at something on the city model. Nenna watches, unseeing. Something . . . something . . .

'Hadders,' she says suddenly. 'Take me to these prisoners.'

Chapter 30

Hands gently turn Camis over.

'Camis? Camis, can you hear me?'

Nenna tenderly brushes his hair back from his face. One of his eyes won't open and the other won't focus properly, but he is sure it is Nenna. She is kneeling next to him, but looking up, away from him.

'Get some water for him to drink and more water with a cloth for me to clean him up with,' she says briskly. 'Let's see what damage you stupid brutes have done.' Camis closes his eyes and tears leak unbidden, sliding down his temple and into his hair.

'Hadders, I can't believe your men did this,' Camis hears Nenna say while she gently dabs a wet cloth to the side of his head. She holds out a water skin then helps to support his neck. 'Can you drink something?'

He is desperately thirsty, and the water is cool and refreshing. But most of it trickles out past his broken jaw.

Nenna and Hadders glare at each other, brother and sister, neither looking as though they will give ground.

'I don't care what they did to you. We are a more civilised and caring people than the savages that bought us here. You know what Da always says,' Nenna snaps, wiping more of the blood away. 'Be kind to others.'

At last, Hadders lowers his eyes and looks abashed.

Nenna moves around to kneel behind Camis and gently lifts his head into her lap. He winces at the movement. 'Right,' she whispers down to him, 'time to do your magic.' He stares back up at her. How did she get here?

'Sometime soon,' she hisses.

He closes his eyes and delves down into his own body, starting the healing process. He can hear Nenna remonstrating with the men, but closing out the words, he concentrates instead on the ache in his jaw and face.

'For your information,' Nenna says, looking to the side, 'Camis was born and bought up on Maa Erda.' One of the guards wriggles his fingers at her. 'Look, I haven't been here long enough to learn all your hand signals yet.'

'Ee 'ed . . .' Hadders tries to explain.

Arture speaks across him. 'He said, "How on Maa Erda was he supposed to know that?"'

***

Around him people speak aloud or sign while Camis ignores it all. Two healings in close succession have left him drained and all he wants to do is sleep. His eyes droop closed. He is aware of footsteps leaving at a run, and Arture hauls him to his feet.

'What? What's going on?' Camis says, he hasn't had time to rest or deal with the fact Nenna is here with her brother. He really needs to sleep. He twists out of Arture's grasp and starts to sit back down.

'No, lad.' Arture says. 'It seems like someone else could do with your services. Come on.'

They follow the others, pausing only when they reach a divide in the tunnel. Nenna comes towards them, shouting and waving.

'Quickly! A woman has had some sort of fit and knocked something over, starting a fire. There are women and children trapped!' She runs back the way she has come.

The fire isn't big yet, but the smoke it produces is black and acrid. People cough and cover their mouths, hurrying to rescue possessions. It is chaos.

Nenna grabs Camis' arm and drags him away from the fire. 'It's too late!' she shouts, pointing towards a side room and coughing. Camis shakes his head. No one could survive the smoke billowing from the open arch.

'STOP!' Arture bellows, and surprisingly, people do. 'Get out and stay out! Do not collect anything, just GO! You, fetch water. You, get blankets. Quick!' People rush to follow his commands.

The smoke is thinner at the top of the ramp. Only thin whisps form tendrils high on the roof, following the fleeing people. Buckets of water arrive at Arture's feet. People return with armfuls of blankets and other material.

'Wet your face coverings. Then splash some on these and smother that fire,' Arture commands, grabbing some bedding and heading towards a doorway. Arture takes a breath, bends down low, and rushes into the smoke-filled room, disappearing briefly and then coming out, his eyes streaming.

'To the right!' he says to the people behind him. 'Go to the right!'

The material and buckets have been bought closer, and those remaining work quickly and efficiently, getting the fire under control and reducing the smoke. Some men carry out unconscious women and children, rushing them up the ramp and out to safety. Camis follows those, leaving the firefighting to Arture.

Camis works quietly, gently checking the injured women and children to see what he can do. There are eight of them all together—three women and five children—and he manages to save six.

Clearing and repairing lung damage, he finds it is all smoke inhalation and that no one is burnt. Two children are beyond his skills, and he cannot do anything for them. They lie there on the white powdery sand at the tunnel entrance. Their bodies perfect, and apart from some soot stains on their small faces, they look as though they are asleep, peaceful and curled together.

A large group stands silently around, faces grimy and solemn. As Camis stands, people reach forward and touch him on the arm, meeting his eyes and nodding their thanks. He sways and strong hands catch him before he falls. Someone places a water skin to his lips and tips the cool water into his mouth. His eyes are heavy, and there is nothing he can do to keep them open. The last thing he sees as he sinks to the ground and into sleep are a circle of concerned faces.

He wakes on a pallet of stuffed sacking, which feels soft and scratchy at the same time. His mouth is so dry it feels as if he has eaten the desert and then glued his tongue to the inside of his mouth. He props himself onto his elbows and tries to swallow, which starts a coughing fit. Small hands hand him a water skin, and he drinks greedily, gratefully. Once the water is all gone, he sits up properly and swings his legs over the side of the makeshift bed, looking at a small boy crouching beside him.

'Is Nenna about?' he croaks.

The boy dashes away. He realises he has been left to sleep outside, close to the wall. The boy must have been left to watch him.

'Camis! Thank Maa Erda you're awake. Come quickly,' Nenna says, appearing in the tunnel entrance and then disappearing again.

Camis stares after her. 'Good day to you too. I hope you are feeling better and that you are fully recovered,' he mutters to himself while struggling to stand. His legs are weak and shaky.

'Do hurry up,' Nenna says, reappearing. 'You might be able to help her. No one can get near her, not even Hadders, and she is his girl. She is threatening to jump.'

That stops his self-pity and he hurries after her. She leads him down a smaller side tunnel, one he hadn't noticed before. It branches off from the cell he had been in. The tunnel is barely tall enough to stand up in and angles steeply down.

Nenna reaches out to steady herself on the tunnel wall and Camis copies her. The smell of dampness increases, but there is also a tinge of stagnation to it now. The tunnel walls gradually widen.

Abruptly, they step into a huge cavern. Camis shivers. Three steps further and they would have dropped into the dark calm water below.

The cavern extends for as far as he can see. It is lit by the white glow of crystal embedded in the cavern walls, clusters shining down like stars on the black water. Nenna looks to her right, and following her gaze, Camis sees two figures sitting above them on a ledge cut in the cavern wall, high above the water. One of the figures is Hadders, he is gesticulating wildly to a thin young woman sitting a little distance away from him.

The woman is ignoring his signing and stares off into the distance. She is poised, ready to jump. Underneath them, the water roils and swirls as something swims just beneath the surface. Camis watches the black undulating water and shivers.

Nenna moves closer to her brother. 'That's Sage,' she says quietly to Camis. 'She blames herself for the death of those two children and says no one is safe around her anymore, now the fitting has started.'

She turns to face Camis. The water laps the cavern wall — waves caused by whatever swims in the water. 'She helped Hadders when he was taken so he is very fond of her. Can you do anything to help her?'

Camis looks up at the distraught woman, wondering if his healing can help her mental anguish. After all, nothing can bring the children back.

A faint *whoomph* sound is heard in the distance. Camis looks towards the noise. The sound comes again, a little louder, and even the creature, or creatures, in the water stop writhing. Then again, another *whoomph*, much louder, as a creature flying low over the water comes into view.

It glides towards them on gossamer-thin wings. Its long neck is stretched out and colours flicker, reflecting in rainbow shimmers from giant scales spiralling down its body. Crystal light gleams through rips and tears in its wings. It opens its mouth and gives an ear-splitting screech as its wings flap, causing the air to blast towards Nenna and Camis.

Nenna falls to the ground, her hands over her ears. Slowly, the creature glides in a wide circle, its wings brushing over Camis' head . He glimpses white, brown, beige, gold, before the beast deposits a large white object into the lake as it skims the

283

water. The water dips around the object, then silently closes over it, sending ripples outwards. With one more circuit, the creature flies back the way it came. A deep contentment washes over Camis as he stares in awe across the wide empty cavern.

Nenna gets up. 'What in all the stars was that?' she asks, her voice shaky.

'That was a mature female Wyrm. A queen. Or even *the* queen,' Camis replies.

'How in Maa Erda do you know that?' she asks, looking up at him incredulously.

'I've seen it before,' he says, turning at the sound behind them to see Hadders helping Sage down from the ledge.

Sage walks with a strangely stiff, angular gait towards them. Camis smiles and stretches out a hand towards her.

'I'm Camis,' he says. 'I have the gift of healing. Will you let me see if there is anything I can do to help the fits?'

Sage looks up at Hadders and at his nod, holds out her hand. Camis grasps her arm with one hand, his other reaching up to touch her head.

A cold icy blast washes over him as he carefully slips between the tissues of her brain and finds them solid. Gently, he pushes into the nearest structure and finds the gaps between cells packed with a substance that is gradually solidifying, like flour and water drying, only harder. Tentatively, he scrapes at a section. It takes all his effort to break a few crumbs away which crumble immediately. She slumps to the ground, and he loses contact.

This is something outside of his ability to fix. Something he still has to learn, and wonders for the hundredth time where his mother is and whether she is safe on Maa Erda or if she has been captured too.

'Camis?' Nenna's voice says. 'Have you found the problem?'

Camis looks at Sage. She is stretched out, her chest rising and falling, her short dark hair sprinkled in the ever-present dust. She looks like she is sleeping.

'I can't help her,' he says and walks away back up the tunnel. How is this woman still alive? She will be dead in days, he is sure. The situation is beyond him. A hollow emptiness swells within his chest. He had thought that apart from death itself most things could be healed.

He only takes a few short steps before Hadders appears in front of him, waving his arms for him to stop. Gritting his teeth to stop the sting in his nose from reaching his eyes, Camis walks around him. Hadders crosses in front, again placing his hand on Camis' chest to stop him.

'I can't do anything,' Camis says angrily. 'She is hardening inside like stone, and I can't heal that.' He tries to walk around Hadders again, but the young man blocks his way and glowers down at him.

He signs slowly and carefully, and this time they are words that Camis knows, words that Arture has taught him. 'Please. I love her.'

'I can't!' Camis says and pushes passed Hadders, keen to be away from those pleading eyes and away from what he knows now is not anger in the man, but a desperate hope.

He runs, a sob escaping, tears blurring his vision. He cannot take all this responsibility. He's just a boy looking for his mother. He just wants to go home. In his blind flight, he thumps headlong into something solid, something which holds him tight.

'Hey, lad,' says Arture. 'Whatever is the matter?' But overtired and overwrought, all Camis can do is cry.

Arture leads Camis back up into the main chamber. It is filled with activity again, the events of the night before nearly erased. Some soot streaks the high vaulted ceiling, and there is still a pervasive smoky hue in the air, but otherwise, people look busy and relaxed. Some even smile and nod towards him, but he's not up to returning that gesture yet.

Arture takes him to a side room that has a couple of pallets with a mishmash of coloured blankets scattered over them. Tiberius is snoring gently, sprawled in the centre of one.

Arture points at the empty bed. 'Sit down, and then you can tell me what happened.'

He turns to scoop out a mug of water from a nearby bucket and hands it to Camis. Camis takes a long drink, still shuddering from his tears. Arture sits next to him and waits patiently. Camis spills it all out, from the healing of the rescued women and children, the ones he could not help, and then waking up with Nenna dragging him down to the cavern with the lake.

'And when the creature flew away, I was left feeling calm and strong. Thought I could fix anything and anyone,' Camis says, looking down at his feet. 'But I can't. I tried, but Sage has something. I don't know what it is, and I don't know how to fix her . . . ' He trails off.

'I can't even begin to understand what it is that you can do, Camis,' Arture says, 'but whatever it is, maybe between the two of us, we can figure out a way forward. Can you explain exactly what you saw or felt that makes you so sure that you can't help her? Maybe, by explaining it, we can figure it out how to proceed.'

Camis hears a noise and turns. Hadders is standing in the doorway, holding a sleeping Sage in his arms. He pushes between them and lays the girl down on the bed. She doesn't wake but rolls onto her side and snuggles down into the bedding. Hadders lightly brushes Sage's cheek with his fingertips.

Nenna appears. She looks from her brother to Camis, anguish in her eyes.

'Not you as well,' Camis snaps, rising to his feet. 'I've told you I can't do anything. I don't know what she has. I've never seen anything like it.'

Arture's hand is on his arm. 'Whoa, there, lad. Just slow down a little.' Arture's gaze is steady and calm, as though talking to one of his horses.

Camis hesitates. How can this man possibly help? Only his mother would know what to do, and then even she may never have witnessed anything like what he'd seen.

'It's like she is hardening from the inside. Turning to stone,' he says slowly. 'And when my mind touched the hardness, some of it crumbled away, but I don't know what breaking off parts of it does to her or where the crumbled bits go in the body, and that's when she fell to the floor. For an instant, I thought that she was . . .'

He glances across to Hadders and sees tears on his cheeks. Hadders signs something and Arture nods.

'Yes, lad, I'm afraid it is,' Arture says in response to the signing. He turns back to Camis. 'I've seen this before, and I think there might be something that you could try. It won't cure her, but it might help.' He looks at the sleeping girl. 'She has the crystal sickness and will slowly harden from the inside out, just like my beautiful wife Iris.'

'I don't want to hurt her,' Camis says, a sickly churning starting in his stomach as he wrenches his arm from Arture's grasp.

'She is dying anyway,' Arture calls after him, 'and it is a slow miserable death. She will be unable to move but will be able to see, hear, and think until the hardening consumes her. Do you know I heard my wife's heartbeat for nearly a year after she stopped being able to respond to anything? The crystal kept her living, trapped within a useless body.'

His words freeze Camis to the spot. Acid erupts into his mouth. His mind can barely comprehend a person actually turning to stone. He glances towards Nenna and sees his horror reflected there, her face ashen, her eyes wide. He swallows the bile that has risen in his throat and turns back to find Tiberius awake, shock etched on his face too.

'Just reach out, lad, and take a little of the hardening away from her every day. A small amount will let us gauge the effects,' Arture says. Hadders gestures beside him. 'He says that she will end it before she becomes a burden or a risk. She is near the end stage when she must choose to sit, stand, or lie for her final position.'

'How do you know she is near the end?' Tiberius asks.

287

'Because that's when the fitting starts,' Arture replies. Everyone looks at the sleeping woman.

'Please, Camis, do something.'

'If Arture's approach is right, then I have already removed a little of the hardening for today. I don't want to send her body into shock by loosening too much. She is sleeping now and that is the body's best healer.' Camis looks around at everyone. 'I will try again tomorrow.'

The expectation and the gratitude in their eyes is too much to bear. He needs air.

Out at the tunnel opening, the air feels cooler, clearer. He sinks to the ground with his back to the canyon wall and closes his eyes.

Chapter 31

Serin reaches out to touch the boy, but he shies away, his brown eyes glittering in anger.

'Don't touch me,' he hisses and moves in a circle around her, hugging his withered arm to his chest. 'You promised.' The words hang in the air between them like a wall.

'I did,' she agrees, looking down at the cool marble floor and keeping very still. Life on Maa Erda had taught her that scared skittish animals will not run if you remove your gaze. 'And I'm sorry.'

There is a long silence, but the boy stops circling her.

'I want to know,' he says hesitantly, 'if its cause you can't or cause you don't like me.'

She looks up sharply at that. 'No! Not that. Never that.' She reaches out a hand towards him. 'I was locked in here until today.' He looks across at her, frowning. 'I was punished for being out late at night.'

'But you're a grown up and a princess,' he says indignantly, his anger and fear forgotten. And despite the situation, she smiles, but it's a sad little smile. She crosses slowly to the bed and sits as he watches her warily.

'Yes, but sometimes there is someone bigger and stronger than you trying to make you do what they want.'

He nods, looking older and wiser than he should as he scrubs his good hand through his tangled brown hair. There is a deep scrape on the palm of his hand.

'What did you do to your hand?' she asks, resisting the urge to reach out and touch him. She will have to let him come to her if she is to regain his trust.

He looks at his hand. The cut is angry and red, and the hand is slightly puffy. An infection starting.

'I slipped getting over the wall,' he says, flexing his hand slowly, and she can see pain and worry in his expression.

'Will you let me look at it?' she asks.

For a long time, he stares at her, a little frown creasing his forehead as he considers. Then slowly, he steps towards her and reaches out his hand.

The infection is already in his system and spreading. It won't be long before a temperature will start, and he will begin to feel ill. She closes her eyes to concentrate. Stimulating the body's natural defence system is easy, but directing cells to ingest the bugs that are breeding in the cut is more difficult.

Eventually the main infection is cleared, and she can let the defence cells scatter and mop up the rogue bugs. She smooths and calms the disrupted tissue, knits the skin together, and opens her eyes. The length of the procedure makes her think that night should have fallen, but only moments have passed.

The boy's mouth is open, and his brown eyes are wide as he looks down at his hand. The palm is smooth. All traces of the injury have vanished.

'That is . . . that is . . .' he stutters, not finding the words. 'Can you help fix this?' he asks, holding out his other arm towards her.

It is thin and twisted, but she takes it gently and smiles up at him. 'You will need some herbs, as I said before, to help you sleep while I work as it will be very painful.'

'I can—' But whatever he was about to say is interrupted by a loud rap on the door. The boy is down on the floor and wriggling under the bed in the blink of an eye.

She gives him a moment and pulls the bedding down to cover the gap where he has vanished and slips a clean shift over her head before calling, 'Come!'

290

The seamstress enters—a large matronly woman with an impressive bosom and a commanding air. Seeing Serin in the bedroom, she sails towards her, her long dark gown swishing. Picking up a white silk robe and hurriedly throwing it around her shoulders, Serin intercepts the woman before she reaches the door.

'Princess,' the woman says, giving an elegant curtsy. 'You sent for me?'

'I'm choosing material today for my wedding gown,' Serin says, nodding to acknowledge the curtsy. Passing the woman, she picks up some papers from a nearby desk. 'When I've chosen, I will send the material down to you. It needs to be ready in six dawns.'

The woman doesn't even blink.

'Will you give me some indication of how much material to get?' Serin asks. And she hands the papers to the seamstress. 'These are sketches of what I want.'

'May I just recheck some measurements?' Not waiting for Serin's permission, she claps her hands. 'Girl!' she calls.

A rake-thin older woman enters. She has to be at least ten years older than the seamstress herself and is hardly a girl. Her hair is a short-and-fluffy white, reminding Serin of the seed head of a dandelion flower. The woman holds a flat leather tray in front of her with an array of items on it, including scissors, string, pencils, and a notebook.

The seamstress measures Serin efficiently, using pieces of string that are cut into suitable lengths and marked accordingly. Each piece is then threaded through a hole in a strip of leather that has a notch at the top, and each measurement is carefully recorded in the notebook. These, Serin knows, will be used to size the pattern for the dress. It's not the first time that Serin has been fitted for clothing, and she allows her arms to be held up and her body twirled around.

It is hard not to wince when the woman unknowingly presses the hidden bruises through Serin's shift. The seamstress purses her lips and frowns down at the figures she has written, tactfully avoiding Serin's eyes when the shift drops over one shoulder, revealing the marks his hands have left.

While the seamstress has her back towards her 'girl', Serin meets the assistant's eyes. The woman nods down at one of her hands holding the tray. There is a corner of folded paper peeking out, which is deftly concealed as her mistress turns around to write in the book.

'You'll need two full bolts of your chosen fabric, plus the same again in a suitable lining,' the woman states. 'Do you intend to have a veil?'

At Serin's headshake, she closes her book and places her things neatly back onto the tray. 'I'll await your material then, and we will get started on your undergarments.' She gives another curtsy before leaving.

Serin crosses the room to hold the door. As the older woman passes, she slips a note into Serin's hands before quickly following her mistress.

Looking down, Serin unfolds the message. It reads, 'Everything is ready.'

Serin stares after the departing women. Suddenly, things are beginning to feel far too real. What if the note had been intercepted? But the wording is so vague, she could just say it had come from a city merchant. Can Zachary really get the rebellion going in the city before she has to marry?

She jumps at a light touch on her hand. She hadn't heard the child climb out from under her bed.

'You are getting married?' he asks, looking up into her face. 'Is he nice?'

It's such a strange question that Serin doesn't answer straight away, bending to pick up the robe she'd discarded when being measured. Her first thought is to plaster on a smile and say, 'Yes of course,' but his face is so serious and older than his years that she sighs. 'No.'

'Someone older and stronger making you do something you don't want to again,' he says. It's not a question, but a simple statement of fact, of the inevitable.

He grips her hand tighter, his face full of sympathy. She nods, not trusting herself to speak. This little broken soul is trying to comfort her when she should be the one being strong and helping him. She swallows down the tears that threaten, not sure if they are for him or for herself.

'Come on.' She says. 'Let's find those herbs and get organised before someone else comes.'

Serin only has time to fetch the ornate tin she keeps on a table in her living area and place it on the bed before there is another knock. The boy vanishes again back to his hiding place.

'Your Highness,' one of her maids says, bobbing a curtsy and dropping a large basket down. 'Mistress Jai, as you requested.'

The market stallholder curtsies low, keeping a hand resting on a second basket.

'Thank you. You may leave us,' Serin says to the maid.

As the door closes the two women look at each other, smiling, and move to embrace. But before they meet, the small whirlwind that is the boy, hits Jai full on, grabbing her around the waist.

'Mistress Jai!' he says, grinning and hugging the stallholder tight. 'I found her. I found the healing princess.'

'You did, child, you did,' she says, hugging him back, surprise on her face. 'But you should never have gone out on your own. You worried us all to death. You might have been caught or—'

'But I wasn't,' he interrupts her. 'And she's gonna fix my arm.' He stares back at Jai defiantly.

'Yes,' Serin says. 'We are going to do it right now, before there are any more interruptions. Please lock the door for me, Mistress Jai, and I'll get started. If anyone comes, we can say we are discussing wedding plans and are tired of people barging in.'

***

Serin and Mistress Jai both look down affectionately at the little boy sleeping on Serin's bed. His crooked arm now lies straight on the covers. It is much thinner than the other arm, and he will need to do exercises to strengthen it, but it is no longer deformed and useless.

'We need to get him safely out of the palace,' Serin says.

'I think I can help,' Jai replies. She gestures towards the large baskets of material that she has bought with her. The two women rummage through the piles, waiting for the boy to wake.

'Oh my, oh my, oh my!' the boy cries, holding up his arm and sitting up. He twists it around and clenches and unclenches his hand, wriggling his fingers. 'Look! Look, Mistress Jai! Look what she has done! Look at my new arm!' And suddenly, all three of them are hugging and crying on the bed.

'Why don't you eat?' Serin says to the boy, gesturing to the tray of food she has in the living area.

'Really?' he asks, rushing away without waiting.

'He is a bit of a force of nature,' Jai says, smiling after him. 'By the crystal, I don't know how he managed to get here unseen, let alone into the palace.'

'No, he is a breath of fresh air,' Serin says, crossing to watch the boy eat. 'I wish I could have gotten some of my herbs from Maa Erda.' She says to him. 'They will help your arm to recover fully. You are going to have to exercise it for it to strengthen.'

The boy's eyes opened wide. 'You've been down there. To Maa Erda?' he whispers. 'That's where my mum came from.'

'I was lucky enough to live there for a while.' It takes all her willpower to not tell him she has left her son down there.

'What are the plants like on Maa Erda? Is it as green as my mum said? Have you seen'—he yawns widely— 'a tree?'

'The plants are beautiful,' she replies. 'And yes, it is very, very green, and yes, I've seen a tree. I've seen lots of trees, all different.'

'What was your favourite?' he asks.

'Oh my, that's a hard one. Oak, willow, beech. But if I were to plant one that I could see every day, I think I would choose a rowan with its orange berries,' Serin says, herding him back towards Jai, who has a large basket tilted for him to climb into.

'I've picked a name,' he says solemnly, looking at each of them just before they close the lid on the basket. His dark brown eyes are serious and his untidy, curly hair needs a good wash. 'Rowan. I want to be called Rowan.'

***

'Well, I like the blue pearls, even if it does restrict the colour of one's dress. What do you think, Princess?'

'Huh?' Serin tunes back into the inane conversation. 'I'm so sorry. I was just thinking of His Highness and wondering how the trouble goes.' Her cheeks ache from the smile she has fixed on her face. These women prattle and preen, and she doesn't think that they have done a single day's work in their lives.

'I was saying,' says the plump young woman whose name Serin has forgotten, 'that although pearls in themselves are considered old fashioned, personally, I would prefer them for my own wedding, especially the blue, and was hoping for your opinion.'

Serin stifles a yawn. The woman's hair is piled ridiculously high on her head. It had probably taken some poor serving girl hours to sculpt it. What a waste of time these afternoon teas have been. As she greets each woman at the door, she takes the time while clasping their hands to briefly delve down inside them. Her intrusion is so swift and light and the women so preoccupied with the queen-to-be taking a personal interest in them that no one notices the intrusion. In all of them, she has found only one fertile woman, and she is a lady's maid.

'Pearls are nice,' she says, and seeing the woman's self-satisfied smirk, adds, 'but I think I will keep to the crystal.'

She rises to indicate an end to the afternoon, and the three young women get to their feet in a flurry of dresses, fans, and feathers. They tattle on as she escorts them to the door, reminding her of the chickens on Anna and Luk's farm. With a rush, she remembers Camis. Oh, please, let him be safe.

The last of the three women is slender and pretty. She turns as the other two link arms and stroll away, chattering down the corridor.

'I nearly forgot, Princess,' she says in a conspiratorial whisper, leaning closer. 'His Imperial Majesty is already back in the city. He arrived yesterday to great acclaim, bringing most of the men with him, ready for the parade.' She has a slight mocking smile on her face as she turns away. 'There was a great deal of celebration in the city last night, which went on for hours. I was surprised you didn't know.'

Serin resists the urge to slam the door. That would give this snide young trollop the satisfaction she was obviously after. She probably wants His Imperial Nastiness for herself. Well, she is welcome to him.

She leans her head back against the closed door. What game is he playing now? Why return without coming to see her? Or send some word of his return? She sighs. She really hasn't the energy left to fathom him out or play his petty games. All she can do is pray that Zachary's plan works and that she can escape tomorrow out of that monster's clutches for good. If not, she will end the day living her worst nightmare—as his wife.

Chapter 32

It isn't easy persuading Hadders to let them help, or to leave Sage. Camis understands Hadders' need to keep his sister safe now that he has her back, but he and Nenna had made a convincing proposal. By using them, Hadders could free up more of his men to fight and cause disruption in the city. After all, he and Nenna could drive the wagon that was picking up the children and women from the hospital and drive straight out again. They would only be on the outskirts and nowhere near the palace or the fighting. What could possibly go wrong?

Camis wanders through the crowds with Nenna. Oasis is like nothing he could have ever imagined. It is beautiful; there are wide streets and tree-lined avenues. The first trees they have seen since being wrenched from their world. Camis stands transfixed at the lush green surrounding him and feels homesick.

Blend in, they had been told, mingle with the crowd, but don't go too far from the courtyard where the horse and cart are hidden. Wait for the signal. But this is difficult, for even in his wildest dreams, nothing could have prepared Camis for the sheer splendour, the magnitude of such a place.

'I'm here to take supplies out to the eastern mines,' he had said to the gate guard as they rode into the city.

'Really?' the gate guard had replied suspiciously, holding his lantern high and peering at Camis. 'You're a bit young to be soldiering.'

'I'm in the ship cadets,' Camis had said with as much authority as he could muster, even though his heart was pounding. 'I've delivered one load from the ship already and was sent to collect another. Every fighting man is tied up, putting down the rebels, or here at the parade, so I'm afraid it's all hands on deck.'

The guard hadn't replied but had walked to the back of the cart and peered in. 'What's in the boxes?'

'They're empty,' Camis had said, climbing over the driver's seat and into the back. 'Here. Look.' He'd grabbed one of the boxes and dragged it towards the man. 'Ready for more supplies.' He'd tilted the chest forward, lifting the lid to show the guard. 'The boxes help to keep some of the food separated and protected. That can help if you've got to speed up to get away from things.' Camis had managed a kind of laugh, his stomach-turning somersaults. 'Do you want a hand up so you can check the others?' he'd asked the guard. 'Save me dragging them all over to you.'

'No, that's fine,' the guard had said, walking back around to the front and waiting for Camis to clamber back into his seat. 'On your way, son.'

Camis had resisted the urge to make the horse go faster than a walk, plodding slowly towards the barracks' stores, just as he'd been instructed. He'd felt the guard's eyes burning holes in the back of the cart. Once he'd been out of sight, he'd let out a long slow breath.

Now, here they are. The cart is stored safely in a side turning. Camis had helped Nenna out of the box she was hiding in.

People brush past, dressed in their best, chattering excitedly. Today is a holiday, as His Imperial what's-his-name is marrying someone special—a princess or royal lady or something—so everyone is here for the parade, hoping to glimpse the royal couple on their way to the ceremony. Suddenly, the crowd surges forward, towards the main thoroughfare.

'Come on,' Nenna says, taking his arm and dragging him along. 'Let's take a look.'

'But we were told not to go far from the cart,' Camis says.

'We won't go far. We'll stay near the back, ready to go as soon as we are needed,' she replies, clearly infected by the crowd's excitement.

Hurrying after the crowd, they find the junction into the main parade route clogged with people. Even standing on tiptoe, they can't see over the heads of the crowd.

'I'm going closer,' Nenna says. 'I'll be quick,' she promises to his disapproving frown.

She pushes her way forward and disappears. Camis bites his bottom lip, looking after her. The crowd lets out a roar, which bounces off the buildings on either side of Camis. Looking left and right, he sees nothing but the backs of very excited people.

He looks up. There is a narrow ledge running around the nearest building right to the corner. He has an idea. The building is decorated with fancy scroll work—trees and plants and birds are etched into the plaster—and it doesn't take him long to scale the side up to the ledge, using the relief for hand-and-foot holds. He hugs the building, edging himself along to the corner. Now he can see clearly across the mass of people to the parade.

A stream of mounted guards ride four abreast in perfect formation. Camis is mesmerised. The men wear the same stark black uniform as he is, but these have an extra stripe of red down the outside of each leg. Along with their red neckerchiefs, they wear lightweight red capes that flutter and billow as they pass.

Here in the city, it is dust free, and the horses step high in absolute time together. What is even more remarkable, however, is that each horse matches its neighbour. There is a row of chestnuts with their white nose blazes and matching white socks followed by a row of greys all in a similar shade, then bays, their points darkening to nearly black, then finally a row of matched blacks, their coats gleaming in the sun. The pattern is then repeated over and over.

Camis gapes in astonishment. On and on the riders pass, keeping their horses in unison, bridles jingling, metal gleaming. He nearly misses the two figures that ride in the centre he is so engrossed in the sheer size and splendour of the display.

A large black stallion passes, arrogant and proud, just like the face of the man who sits upright on its back. His angular jaw and hawk-like nose are visible even at this distance. His beard is black and oiled to shine like the coat of his horse, trimmed to a neat point. A powerful commanding man, remote and hard. His hands are low and loose on the reins. He controls the animal with his knees and willpower.

The stallion tosses its head and dances a few paces sideways, enough to give Camis a view of the second horse. The horse is fine boned and delicate, the whitest grey he has ever seen. It glows, shining like fresh snow in sunlight. Breath-taking.

He has the merest glimpse of the woman that rides the horse as she turns to watch the man and the stallion. Her red hair is nearly obscured by sparkling jewels, curled high on her head. Her colour-changing dress is spread wide over her horse's flanks, shining deep purple, then glimmering green. The stallion moves back into formation, and the woman and the white horse vanish from his view.

But it can't hide who she is. Camis has found her. He has finally found her.

They ride past, the moment is nearly lost. He cannot lose her again! His mouth won't open but his mind can.

Mother!

Time slows to a trickle, but she doesn't hear and carries on away from him. Slowly, she turns her horse. There is undisguised shock on her face as her eyes sweep across the crowd, searching.

Their eyes meet, and he sees fear there, just as time rushes back with a *whoomph*, bringing with it the sounds of the crowd, the fading hooves of the rapidly vanishing troops, and the jingle of the stallion's bridle as the man swings his horse around to join her.

She breaks eye contact and tugs her horse's head back around to resume the parade, but the man reaches out and catches hold of her reins, stilling the white mare. He must be talking to her because she shakes her head and laughs.

The man gestures to the guards that line the streets, keeping the crowds back, pointing at the area below Camis. The people move back, but the guards are quick, shoving people closer together and moving around to block their escape.

Camis starts to shuffle back along the ledge. Maybe calling out in mindspeak had not been such a good idea. He should have waited until the parade of dignitaries had passed and just followed. Waited until after the high imperial king person had married his woman, and then he could have sneaked in to speak to his mother and find out what is going on. Maybe she is a trophy slave like Nenna had been with that despicable man Vitrainy.

He inches along the ledge until he is nearly back to where he climbed up, nearly safe, when a voice explodes in his head.

Stand where you are.

Strong hands grasp his ankles and jerk him from his perch. Arms windmilling, he falls, and Camis expects to hit the ground, but the soldiers catch him and drag him towards the man on horseback. The crowd has fallen silent.

'Who are you?' the man barks, looking down icily at Camis.

Camis gasps. His mouth dries, his tongue sticking to the roof of his mouth. The man's eyes are a pale blue! He does not answer. He can't answer, and that's when the nearest guard kicks him in the back of his knees, causing his legs to buckle.

'Answer His Imperial Majesty, dog!' the guard hisses, sending Camis sprawling on the floor. There are a few more moments of silence.

'Kill him,' the man says dismissively, waving a hand to one of his guards and turning his stallion's head roughly. The casual way the remark is spoken catches Camis off guard, and it is a moment before the impact of it hits him. As a nearby guard draws his sword, Camis panics and starts to rise, a shout ready on his lips. This cannot be happening.

The sword gleams in the light. The polished ceremonial blade looks sharp and entirely capable of taking his head off. His legs refuse to hold his weight.

'No!' His mother's cry is sharp and pained. 'No! You can't!' The blue-eyed man turns back. The silence now is absolute, as solid as the heat.

'And pray, why is that?' His eyes narrow slightly, suspiciously. 'Do you know this boy?' he asks her.

'No, I do not know him,' she says, kneeing her mare closer to the black stallion. Reaching out a hand, she lays it gently on the man's arm. 'But it would not be an auspicious start to our marriage with a death, and besides, today is meant to be a joyful occasion.'

What? She is—No! She cannot mean to marry this man. He shakes his head and opens his mouth, but nothing comes out.

The man on the stallion looks over at Camis still kneeling on the ground with two guards flanking him, his expression stone hard and unreadable.

'Uncle,' his mother says softly, 'you are frightening him. He is just a boy. Look at him. He wears your uniform. Let him be. Interrogate him tomorrow or the day after. Surely you will want to speak to one capable of such strong mindspeak.' She waves a hand dismissively. 'Or execute him if you deem fit, but come, we will be late. The Book is waiting.'

'Have him taken to one of the palace dungeons. I will deal with him later.' And dismissing Camis from his mind, he straightens his cloak and waits for his bride-to-be to join him.

Camis staggers to his feet. She has not acknowledged him in anyway. No 'hello, son.' No hugs or tears. Nothing. Anger swells, blocking out the warnings he should have heard, his face flushing. It takes a moment for her words to penetrate.

Husband to be. She really is marrying this arrogant man . . . and . . . and . . . she'd called him uncle. The guard had called him Imperial Majesty . . . Who? . . . What? His thoughts are clogged, but just as speech reaches his lips, a blinding flash cracks through the air, followed by the boom of an explosion.

Once again, he is knocked from his feet. People around him are flattened like wooden skittles from the impact of the blast. A building on the other side of the parade route is gone. It has dropped where it stood, leaving a gaping hole and a pile of rubble, dust drifting outwards and upwards in a cloud. A woman lies on her back near where Camis has fallen, her eyes open, staring at him, shock imprinted forever on her sightless gaze.

Mounted troops surround his mother, already hustling her away. Distant sounds of screaming, of horses, of people shouting as they scramble to their feet. Camis is lifted, his hands swiftly tied, and he is thrown, stomach down, over the back of a horse, which gallops away from the chaos.

He is pushed roughly into a long low cell, five time larger than the pens they were kept in on board the shuttle. There is straw on the floor, which smells surprisingly sweet and fresh. There is a bucket in the corner for toileting. It seems that even the criminals on Crystal Moon are kept in better conditions than the captives from Maa Erda.

When the guards leave, slamming the outer door behind them, they take all sources of light. Stooping in the dark with the low ceiling skimming his hair, Camis clutches the bars of his new prison.

'No, I do not know him.

I do not know him,

I do not know him.' Again and again, he hears her voice.

Why had she denied him? Why? The hurt lodges in his throat, threatening to suffocate him. All this way, all this effort and worry to find her . . . and for what? She did not want him. Maybe she had even left with these people on purpose, abandoning him to his fate. Maybe she had wanted her freedom and this grand lifestyle. She had seemed so pleased when his gifts had come in. Maybe she'd known that he could now survive without her.

Maybes and whys swirl around in his head, mixing with a deep, underlying anger. He grips the bars tighter until the anger boils up and bursts out, blasting the bars away from their holdings and raining stone and dust and debris down on him.

Instinctively, he crouches, covering his head with his hands and holding his breath. The main ceiling holds. He has only dislodged the few stones that hold the prison bars in place. Coughing from the dust, he gropes his way down the passage towards the door, listening for the sound of running footsteps or shouts, for anything that indicates that someone has heard and sounded the alarm. Nothing.

Slowly, carefully, he feels his way up the short stone passage. Finding course wood beneath his fingers, he reaches out to find the latch. He pushes against its weight and is relieved to feel it give and open. The passageway beyond is dimly lit by a few crystal lamps set into the wall.

He climbs the seemingly endless stone staircase that not long before he had been forced down. It twists around and around, leading up to another door, which also miraculously gives way, opening into a guard room.

The room contains a long wooden table with beer mugs, a couple of clay flagons and a set of playing cards strewn across it, as though the players have thrown them down, leaving in a hurry. An overturned wooden chair lies on its side, adding to the picture that the occupants have left in haste.

'Ah, there you are,' says a voice.

Camis freezes. A tall man, clean-shaven and dressed in the black uniform of the imperial guards, stands in the shadows on the threshold of a second door. He does not seem surprised to find Camis entering the guard room. The man steps forward into the light. Camis backs down a couple of the steps that he has just climbed. His heart thumps loudly in his ears, and his muscles tense, ready to flee, as the man holds his hands up, palms out to show he is unarmed.

'Camis, your mother sent me to free you. Please, don't be alarmed, but we only have a few moments. My name is Zachary. You must follow me.'

'Why?' Camis stutters.

'Because your life is in danger, and your mother wants you safe,' the man answers calmly.

Camis steps back as he notices that this man too has blue eyes. What if he's with the other man, the one who ordered his death? What if he is that man's brother or some relative and has been sent as a trap. Another thought occurs to him.

'Why?' he croaks and coughs to clear his dusty throat. 'Why does she want me free?

The man who calls himself Zachary looks puzzled, so Camis continues, 'Why does my mother want me free? She didn't even acknowledge me out there in the parade. She hasn't even made contact with me since she disappeared.'

'Camis, I promise to answer all your questions once I have you hidden safely in the temple with your uncle,' the blue-eyed man says, crossing to the table and peering into one of the flagons. He picks up a mug and tosses the contents onto the floor, then pours out some water and slides the mug across the table towards him.

'So, you are with him! You want me to go with you to that monster, so you can say I brokefree and you had to kill me.' The outburst causes a fit of coughing.

'No, no. Camis, you misunderstand. Not your mother's uncle, not the monster who ordered your death, but yours. Your uncle. Your mother's twin. Her brother. He will keep you safe until we can get you on board a shuttle and hopefully back down safely to your own planet.'

Camis' head whirls, and still coughing, he steps forward and grabs the mug of water, downing it in one gulp.

'We have to be quick. That bastard D'Ruja will be marrying her any moment. My men are keeping him busy, but I am needed.' He turns towards the door and waits again in the shadows for Camis to follow.

'Who are you?' Camis manages to pluck the words from the confusion in his mind.

I'm . . . I'm Zachary.' He faulters, as though he is about to say something else. 'Come on, it may be too late.'

He does not wait but vanishes into the darkened corridor beyond. Camis hesitates a fraction longer. For some unfathomable reason, he trusts this man, and after all, following him is the only way to go unless he wants to return to his ruined cell below. He steps into the darkness.

Chapter 33

Nenna worms her way through to the watching crowd as soldiers rush towards Camis. What on Maa Erda had he said to anger that man on the horse? What will happen to him now?

She pauses for a moment to gather her thoughts. A muffled boom rends the air and people begin to scream. The crowd turns as one, and suddenly, she finds herself swept along with a mass of fleeing people. She manages to cling to a wall and heave herself into a doorway.

Her back stings, but other than that, she is unhurt. Slowly, she creeps back up the street. Nothing remains of the parade other than an overturned food stall, its wares trampled beyond recognition. Some discarded flowers stand out against the white ground, their red blooms stark and poignant. It seems no one has lingered, not even the injured.

Making her way back to the horse and cart, she fully expects to find them gone. But Arture's old dray, Traveller, is made of stronger stuff and stands there, large and solid. He nuzzles her hand, and she leans against his massive grey head, lost. What is she to do now?

Her thoughts swirl. Hadders' men have dispersed into the city. Camis has vanished, and she will never get past the guards at the gates without him.

She is so wrapped up in her own worries that she jumps when a small hand touches her arm. The children! They are here.

Looking down, she sees the large brown eyes of a small girl, her face dirty with dust and grime. She is terrified and clutches the hand of an older lad who has a toddler perched on his hip. They look at each other in silence.

More children appear slowly and quietly from around the buildings, and with them are two women, each carrying a young child and holding the hand of another. Perhaps these women will know what to do. They will know how to get out of the city. One of the children begins to cry.

'Try and sooth him, Rowan. Keep him quiet before we are discovered,' says the older of the two women, looking around anxiously. She turns to Nenna and starts to sign.

'I'm Nenna,' Nenna interrupts softly. 'I can still speak. I haven't been mutilated.' There is a spark of the old defiance as she lifts her chin.

The women's eyes widen. 'Right, children. Into the back and into the boxes, quickly,' the older woman says, ushering the children towards the back of the cart.

Some of children have already scrambled on board and one of the older boys helps two smaller children clamber into one of the bigger boxes.

'My name is Jai,' says the woman with the headscarf. 'Zachary told us you would be here, but he said there would be two of you.'

'The person who drove the cart here has . . . has vanished.' It is too complicated to explain what Camis had done. 'And now I'm worried about getting back through the gates.'

'I wouldn't worry about that,' the older woman interjects, climbing up onto the cart. 'The guards will be too busy fighting to stop us.'

Jai climbs up behind and offers Nenna a hand. Nenna looks around. The children are nowhere to be seen, having vanished quickly into the boxes on the back of the cart. She takes Jai's hand and scrambles on board.

The short ride to the gate is uneventful. The road is completely free of people. Nenna glimpses the glow of several fires as they pass side roads. Smoke hangs in the air over the city. Her heart hammers in her chest as the gates come into view, but before they reach them, pandemonium breaks loose.

Men race out of a side street while guards pour out of the gate house. There is shouting, and in an instant, the street is filled with men fighting. Jai expertly hauls the dray to a stop and neatly turns him round. More men join the skirmish. The sound of swords clashing follow them as they escape.

'Not that way then,' says Jai, more to herself than to the others.

Twice more they are turned around as they make their way through the streets, once when there is more fighting, and the second when the way ahead is blocked with falling masonry. Distant booms sound with more explosions. Fleetingly, she thinks of Camis and of her brother, but there is nothing she can do, and she knows they would want her to get the children to safety.

They pass a building on fire, and Jai keeps the horse to the far side of the street, but the old boy is wary and needs no urging. Eventually, Jai pulls Traveller to a stop and handing the reins to Nenna, the two women clamber out. Nenna can hear hurried whispers, and Jai returns, muttering something about 'it being the only way.'

'Where are we going?' Nenna asks.

'To the temple,' Jai states.

'What?' Nenna says incredulously. 'Where the wedding ceremony is? That's madness.'

'If we can sneak the children in the priest entrance, then the Book will hide and protect them until we can find a way to get them out.'

'A book?' Nenna says incredulously.

Jai glances over at her before replying. 'The Book is a person,' she says. 'Taking children to the temple—in fact, taking children anywhere—will cause an uproar.'

'Why?' Nenna asks, genuinely puzzled.

'Nenna, there are no children in Oasis.'

'But where . . . who . . . Don't tell me that you stole these children from Maa Erda too!' Nenna says.

'No, Nenna. These children were born here,' Jai explains. 'They are the children of soldiers and . . . and prim mothers.'

Chapter 34

Camis follows Zachary along the corridor. Gradually, his eyes adjust to the dim light. He can make out the darker shape creeping its way ahead of him towards a thin sliver of light outlining a door which has been left slightly open. The figure stops before the door, flattening against the wall.

'Keep back, Camis,' Zachary whispers. 'My men are keeping some of the more hardened guards occupied.' Hugging the wall, his heart hammering in his chest, Camis can indeed hear fighting. 'This corridor opens into one of the palace's hallways, and we need to avoid getting caught in the fighting in order to get to the temple.'

'The temple?' Camis whispers back.

'Yes. Your uncle is there, about to perform the marriage ceremony.'

'He's a priest?'

'No, not exactly. He is the Book. Keep close.' Zachary pulls the door open wider but doesn't explain any further. The clash of swords and the grunt of men become louder. Zachary peeks for a moment around the door, and then, signalling for Camis to follow, hisses, 'Now, Camis!'

Out in the bright light of the palace, they sprint down a carpeted hallway. Risking a quick look back, Camis sees a huddle of men stabbing, thrusting, and slashing at each other. It's not how he imagined a fight would be. This is messier, untidy, loud. Several bodies are already down, and stains pattern the red carpet with a darker hue.

The smell of bodily fluids—sweat, blood, and shit—reach him. Then they turn a corner, and the sounds and smells of the battling soldiers fades. Zachary slows and straightens up. Taking Camis by the shoulder, he pushes him along.

'Now, if anyone looks, it will appear as if I am escorting you to His Imperial Highness, may The Crystal rot him,' Zachary says, adding the last in a very quiet voice.

They pass through the palace and out into the grounds without meeting anyone else. Out in the palace gardens, several skirmishes can be heard, but none are close or hinder their route to the temple.

The wide doors of the temple are shut and barred, but worse than that, they are heavily guarded by a detachment of mounted royal guards.

'Damnation!' Zachary snaps. 'Round to the priest's entrance, quickly.' And he lets go of Camis, darting away.

'Oi, you!' a voice shouts, and a guard steps out of the shrubbery close to Camis.

Camis freezes. He has no weapons and no knowledge of how to use them if he did.

'Have you seen any of those scum?' the guard asks, moving closer. He is a lean, tough-looking man. Blood smears one hand. A sword is raised in the other.

Camis replies, 'Yes, sir. One has gone around the side of the temple. I was just about to follow.'

'Well, what are you waiting for? You'll be quicker than me. I'll take over guarding here. You get after him. Don't let him get away.'

Camis sprints after Zachary and does not look back. His heart pounds and his knees feel weak. That was lucky.

He skirts the side of the temple. The smooth walls stretch back, disappearing into shrubbery, and he cannot see any sign of Zachary. Maa Erda, where is he?

Camis peers around to the back of the temple. The high white walls stretch up and away in front of him. There is no sign of any soldiers.He looks back, expecting to see the guard watching, but no one is there.

He retraces his steps, searching the grounds, hoping to catch sight of any movement that might tell him where Zachary has gone. He feels a connection with this man, even though he has only just met him. He frowns, wondering at this feeling. A hand closes on his mouth and an arm pulls him backwards.

'Keep quiet,' a voice whispers urgently in his ear.

He is dragged back through an opening, and a door hisses softly as it closes behind him. The hand releases him. Camis turns and finds that Zachary has pulled him into a low-lit chamber with a long corridor extending directly in front of them.

Camis remembers to breathe, trying to calm his heart rate. Hands on his knees, he looks around. The small circular room has pegs on the wall, all filled with white garments, each elaborately decorated with gold trim.

'This is the priests' entrance into the temple,' Zachary explains. 'They use this entrance during public ceremonies, but there haven't been many of those over the last few cycles.'

Camis looks again at the ornate clothing hung around the room. Two of the pegs are empty, but dust webs trail from the others. Crystal powder coats everything.

In one corner, there are rusty-looking swords and carved sticks poking out of a slender sculpted box. Camis crosses to the box and selects one of the ornamental staffs, not trusting himself with a sword. He would probably cut his own foot off.

He holds it out, feeling the strange coolness of the material. A beautifully-carved wyrm winds itself around the staff from one end to the other. It even has the striations of the wyrm's segmented body. The head ends with a gaping mouth, displaying realistic rows of circular teeth. The top of the stick looks as though it is protruding from the creature's mouth.

Zachary nods in approval. Putting his finger to his lips, he gestures for Camis to follow.

A corridor leads upwards, widening, and the ceiling curves. The corridor ends in in a wide-open arch. Camis can hear voices in the chamber beyond. Zachary crosses to the opposite wall, signalling for Camis to remain where he is. Mirroring the other man's movements, Camis creeps to the edge of the archway and peers out.

The vaulted ceiling rises to a huge green dome. In the centre of the cavernous hall is a large circular plinth on which sits, crossed legged, a naked man holding a very large book. Camis can make out strange black shapes swirling and wriggling over the man's body.

Standing below the seated man are several figures. A tall, dark haired man has his back to Camis and holds something that Camis cannot see. In front of the seated man are six guards. They surround another man who is down on his knees.

Two priests stand apart from the rest. One is extremely old and is supported by a younger man who watches everything, a predatory smile ghosting his face. They all look towards the figure on the plinth. They seem to be waiting for something.

'Well, what is your answer?' the tall dark-haired man says.

Camis instantly recognises the voice of His Imperial Highness, the man who wanted Camis executed. A distant boom shakes the floor. His Imperial Highness shifts his feet for balance. Camis can see he is holding a woman. His arm around her neck—a woman with red hair decked in jewels. Camis stiffens. His mother.

'D'Ruja,' Zachary gasps, his hand going to his sword.

But before he can move, a deep calm voice reverberates in their minds. *Why do you need to marry her? You could just take your damn crystal and leave.*

'I will rule legitimately. I have bought witnesses who will confirm it publicly,' D'Ruja says, glancing at the two priests. 'I will have the people on my side. They will cheer as their new king and queen leave on their quest to reclaim their homeland.' D'Ruja's voice echoes around the chamber.'

No one speaks or moves.

'Choose,' His Imperial Highness commands. 'Marry us and I'll free him. If you do not, then Kanta dies.'

Suddenly the world revolves at speed. Everything happens at once, and at the same time, it happens so slowly that the things appear to be under water.

Zachary storms into the chamber, sword raised, rushing towards Camis' mother and D'Ruja.

'No!' Camis shouts as D'Ruja turns and slashes a knife across his mother's neck. She is thrown to one side, all in one fluid movement.

'The palace traitor shows his face at last!' D'Ruja shouts, drawing his sword. He turns and engages Zachary, slashing and thrusting with skill and ease. 'I knew I had a rat in the pack.' His expression is a sneer of contempt. Zachary says nothing but returns the parry with ease.

Camis is immobile. His mother lies on the white marble floor, her blood spilling out around her, the vivid red highlighting the colour of her hair. His mind rages. She had renounced him, publicly disowned him, and he hates her. She is his mother, and he loves her. She'd sent Zachary to free him and . . .

Camis! The deep voice shouts in his head. *Save her.* He looks up at the figure on the plinth, who stares directly at him. *Now or she will die.*

He is galvanised into action. He races towards his mother and presses both his hands to hers, which are clasped tight to her throat, trying to staunch the flow of blood. Her eyes, usually so green and vibrant with life and reassurance, are pale and yellowing. They are wide and full of fear as they latch onto his pleadingly.

Closing his own eyes to shut out the raw emotion, he also shuts out the sight and sounds of the sword fight. He forgets about them and the temple, forgets his anger, and delves down to concentrate on saving her life.

I am so sorry, Camis. His mother says. *I—*

Shhh, he replies. *Let me work.*

It is too late, comes the faint response as her heart stops.

He moves quickly. In his mind, his hands plunge into her chest, reaching for her heart. As he throws out his hands, white lightening zags across the space between them. Her heart begins to beat but it is feeble and weak. He heals the gash in her neck, stopping the flow of blood, and deep within her bones, speeds up her body's natural regeneration of red blood cells. She desperately needs water, but that will have to wait.

Slowly, he draws back, waiting to see if her heart can continue unaided, when suddenly, he is aware of another presence beside him.

Lift her up to me on the dais, and I will continue to heal her, says the same voice that had urged him to save his mother.

Who are you? Camis asks.

I am Myriad, the voice says. *I am your uncle and your mother's twin brother.*

If you can heal, why didn't you just do it? Why did you need me? Camis asks.

Because I needed to help someone else first before he was murdered. And knew you would cope, came the reply. *Please hurry.*

Carefully and gently, Camis scoops his mother up and sets her at the feet of the naked man. The fighting continues unnoticed around them.

A force takes over the beating of his mother's heart. She starts to respond. Fluid from somewhere begins to swell her cells and tissues.

How did you do that? Camis asks his uncle.

I borrowed blood from my own body. You must only use this method in dire emergencies as it will leave you weak and you might not be able to continue healing. Myriad pauses. *Now you must go and fight. You are the only one able to defeat that monster. I cannot fight him. He has tied me to him by the words of the Book. If I raise my hand against him, someone I love dearly will die. You are our only hope.*

But I am not a swordsman, Camis states. *I can't kill . . .*

You have the power, Camis. Use it. I will join you shortly and help you. Go!

Chapter 35

Serin's hands climb to her throat at the same time that her eyes fly open. Nothing is in focus. Her mind scrabbles for something to grasp onto, anything that will tell her what in Maa Erda is going on. She was . . . she was . . . Her legs won't move. Faintly, in the distance, she can hear fighting and the sound of swords clashing. She tries to call out, but it is a whisper.

Lie still, little sister, and I will support you, a voice says in her head.

Myriad! She sends out wildly. *You are here! What is happening? I . . . I was riding . . . I can't remember anything else. I can't see properly. Where are you? What is happening?*

Shh, Serin. Close your eyes and let me work.

She floats away, a single silver spider thread drifting on the wind.

Gradually, with the slowness of honey dripping from the comb, she surfaces back into the world. She is lying in her brother's arms. He looks down at her, his face grim.

Don't move, her brother commands. *Keep still, and he will not notice you. You are with me on the dais.*

How? How did I get here?

I asked Camis to lift you up to me.

All other thoughts speed away at that one word—Camis! Everything floods back. Her shock at seeing him at the parade. The flight through the chaos, explosions, fighting. It had not been at all what she'd been expecting when Zachary had said they would disrupt the proceedings, but she didn't really know what she had been expecting. A few bangs and a bit of smoke maybe, but not this—this carnage. Men fighting and dying in the streets.

Tears spring to her eyes as she remembers again the look on Camis' face, the betrayal when she'd said she didn't know him.

D'Ruja cut my throat! The memory is vivid and clear—the shocking pain. Her hands fly up to her neck.

Shh, Myriad speaks quietly into her mind. *You are healed. But you must listen now. I need you, sister. If you've ever loved me, you will help me now.* There is an urgency and intensity to his words that stills her questing fingers. *I cannot fight him directly, but I can lend my strength to someone who can. I know his tricks and can help to defeat him once and for all. But I need you to hold the Book for me.*

The request is so unexpected and so outrageous that she fumbles to take it all in.

I can't, she says. *The Book does not tolerate women. It will kill me.*

No, it won't. It was one of his lies to keep me in my place. That along with imprisoning Kanta.

But Kanta—he will kill him. She struggles again to rise, but his arms hold her tight.

Kanta is free, Serin. I killed the guard that held the knife. I lent Kanta my strength, and he fought the guards. Two chased after him, and we finished them together. My mind could only go as far as the temple door with him. He knows I will not be following him.

She can see the pain and grief etched on her twin's face. She reaches a hand up to wipe away his tears.

The instant her hand touches his face, she is attacked. The words resume their whirlwind of spite. They dive at her, stabbing and trying to blind her. The roar of the tempest is unbelievable, and she doesn't know whether to cover her eyes or her ears from the onslaught.

Then faintly, as though from a great distance, she hears her brother's voice.

It will be difficult, and the Book will fight us both, but it can be done. I know that now, after you healed me. Quickly, reach out for me. We waste time.

But all this time bound—you will die.

I am dying anyway; you know that. This will be faster, but it will be my choice, and I have a chance at revenge for both of us. I have a way to defeat him.

You have?

Serin, there is no time. He battles now with Camis. I need you to help.

Camis? she says, breaking free and sitting up. She can't see Camis or her uncle, there are men fighting everywhere. She can hear the clash of swords and the thud of hand-to-hand combat. She can hear men swearing and the cries for help from the injured.

Please, Serin, free me, and let me do this. Become the Book. Hold the city and our people in your hands. Help them. Protect them. I can save Camis and rid us once and for all from this tyranny.

But you will die, she says again brokenly.

Yes, he says, *but I will die free.*

She nods her head, and suddenly, she is fighting the words again. She holds up her arms to protect her head and pushes through the spiteful words, towards the centre, towards her brother. The wind whips and howls and pushes her back. But this time, hands reach out and pull her in.

Her brother grows larger and larger, enveloping her. Looming massive and becoming opaque, he sinks into her.

Speak the words sister, never stop.

Then he is gone, and she is left holding the Book.

Words scroll across the page in front of her, and for a moment, she is too stunned to even read them. Mesmerised, her eyes follow the black writing as it scrolls upwards to the top of the page and vanishes.

The word 'column' wavers and melts away as she watches. A loud crash vibrates through the hall, shaking the plinth.

Startled, Serin looks up to finds one of the pillars in the temple disintegrating in front of her. People scream and run. Hurriedly, she looks back at the Book in time to see the word 'wall' reach the top.

Quickly, she stutters the word out as it wavers in front of her. Horrified, she sees it disappear, and she waits for the resulting noise of a wall collapsing. But tiny pinpricks start at her fingers and travel up her hand to her arm, and the word reappears on her skin. A knife-sharp pain follows its path.

She stifles a cry because the next word has materialised on the page, and there is no time to think about anything but keeping the city whole.

*

Chapter 36

The temple is heavily guarded. Men sit on horseback outside the main steps, and Jai is forced to take the horse and cart back a few streets before turning towards the palace grounds.

'You are bringing supplies to the palace by order of His Imperial Highness D'Ruja A'Riman, may The Crystal preserve him,' Jai says. 'At least, that is what you say if you are asked. Exactly that. Now repeat it back to me.'

'I'm bringing supplies to the palace by order of His Imperial Highness, D'Ruja A'Riman, may The Crystal preserve him,' Nenna repeats.

'Hopefully, we can get around to the grounds at the back and carry on to the temple itself.' Jai hands the reins to Nenna.

'Where are you going?' Nenna asks.

'I might be recognised,' Jai replies, 'as I brought material into the palace recently for the princess to pick for her wedding gown.' She slips into the back. 'Just keep the main palace building on your left and then bear towards the back of the temple. Look for a small door, the priest's entrance.'

The palace and grounds are deserted. It is quiet. Too quiet. Nenna guides the horse and cart around to the back of the grand building, trying to look as though she and the horse know where they are going. Once behind the temple she checks there is no one around and halts the cart.

Nenna helps the children and women out of the boxes. The older boy–Rowen they called him– helps the younger ones. He keeps up a quiet constant stream of reassuring remarks, sometimes even making them smile.

'Come on now, don't tell me you're stuck. Oh, no, you've got fat on all that rich food the princess sent over. That's it, out you come. Right, it's no sweets for you for today.' All this was said to a slip of a thing with huge dark eyes with shadows underneath them. But it did the trick.

They are unhindered as they quietly usher the children towards a door. But the silence makes the hairs on the back of Nenna's neck stand up. The other woman with the children checks the priests' door and finds it unlocked. She slips inside, signalling for them to wait. A few moments later, she reappears.

'All clear,' she says and leads them into a small antechamber. Again, she tells them to wait, putting a finger to her lips. As Nenna passes her, she touches Nenna's arm and whispers.

'I'm Onora. Thank you.'

The women leave Nenna in the chamber and climb the narrow passageway that leads up and away from the small room they are in. They keep themselves pressed to the wall, gradually sidling towards the opening at the top.

Nenna looks around. The room is unkempt, and many strange objects litter the floor, all of them incomprehensible to her. There is also a tall narrow box in a corner with ornately carved sticks, some with metal ends, and some rusty swords. A tray of odd-looking lanterns stands neatly next to it. They have sides of the finest gold filigree that Nenna has ever seen.

Rowan crosses to the box of sticks and selects two. They are taller than he is, but as he tosses one to a girl who looks to be about seven, he gives a wide grin.

Watching Rowan heft the stick in both hands, Nenna gets the impression that he knows how to use it. She has a brief image of her brother and his friends play-fighting with similar sticks and thinks of the cuts and bruises they had inflicted on each other.

'Where are they going?' Nenna asks, making to follow them.

Onora touches her arm. 'Stay here with the younger ones. They know what they are doing.' Onora gestures towards the vanishing children. 'They are going to cause chaos and disrupt the ceremony.'

'What?' Nenna cries 'They will be hurt or captured or—'

'They will surprise the soldiers who haven't seen children for so long, and in the confusion, give our men a chance. We might even be able to get the princess away.'

There has been silence above, but now screams and shouts can be heard. Nenna steps around Onora and runs to the opening, stopping abruptly on the threshold.

In front of her, in the centre of the huge domed room, is a large stone dais on which sits the woman that she had seen on horseback at the parade. The woman's red hair is loose now, free of its elaborate curls and gems, it falls about her pale shoulders. Black shapes wriggle over parts of her exposed skin. Her exquisite gown is spread out around her but it is marred by a dark staining. An enormous book sits in her lap, and she appears to be reading from it, mouthing words, while she ignores the havoc all around her.

Children screech and scuttle away from outstretched hands. They slide and trip people, whooping and calling out. Soldiers battle rebels in small groups—some hand to hand, others with swords. Bright yellow missiles fly through the air. One lands at her feet, splattering in a mess of yellow flesh and juice. It gives off a citrusy smell, and she looks down at what appears to be the remains of some sort of fruit.

There are men lying on the floor, clearly injured or dead. Not all of them are wearing the black uniform of the guards. Two of the children have upended one of the massive pots that line the temple hall, a tall, uprooted plant lies discarded on the floor. They roll the earthenware vessel towards a group of fighting men. No one sees its approach, and soldiers and rebels are bowled over in the pot's wake.

Other children have armed themselves with yellow fruit from the trees in the pots and are yelling loudly as they throw them. Handfuls of soil are added to the children's arsenal. Rowan expertly wields the stick in his hands, poking and thumping soldiers in turn. Nenna has lost sight of the young girl with the other stick.

Off to one side, three figures stand facing each other in a small circle. They stand rigid and unmoving. They don't even blink, but somehow, she feels that they are in the epicentre of the battle. She stares at them more closely.

The man in black faces her with an angry sneer. He is the man she saw riding the black stallion at the parade. Another man stands with his back to her, painfully thin and entirely naked. The third man is Camis.

Her heart thumps. Camis is here.

She is about to run to him when Jai catches her arm.

'Don't be a fool,' Jai hisses angrily at her. 'Do not draw His Imperial Majesty's attention to you. With one snap of his fingers, he can stop your heart.'

'But Camis is here,' Nenna says, trying to wriggle free.

'And so is the Book. Whatever they are doing, your interference will not help. They fight in a way that none of us can help with. It is a battle of wills.'

Jai hands Nenna some torn cloth and one of the lanterns. 'Put these around the room and get as much oil as you can onto the cloth. We will set a fire and try to panic them out.'

'But what—'

'Just do it!' Jai says, gliding around one of the temple pillars and away.

Nenna stares at the cloth in her hands. It is madness. They will all choke in the smoke, or worse, burn. She sees it in her mind's eye—panicking men rushing out. The soldiers outside will rush to help—that's if they can control their frightened horses. Pandemonium–A chance for them all to escape.

She steps out into the noise and chaos of the hall after Jai. She tucks an oil-soaked cloth behind a pillar. She slips around the room until she runs out of cloth and oil and returns to the

323

passageway that leads down to the room where the younger children are. Vaguely, she wonders how they will light so many separate areas. She looks back at the total turmoil and sees Jai across the temple, staring across at the woman on the plinth. Jai nods, and the room erupts in flame.

It is exactly the chaos Nenna had envisioned. Soldiers shove and push as they cough and splutter, making for the doors outside. Some of the rebels rush for the exit too, but Jai and Onora are there, directing the ones they can, towards the passageway behind the dais. Smoke billows blackly around the room, obscuring Nenna's view.

There is a loud crash, but she can't see what it is. She holds her breath, peering in vain through the dense smoke, trying to see Jai and Onora as she pulls up the neck of her tunic. The air is dense with smoke and filled with the sound of coughing.

Suddenly, the smoke is gone, and the temple is clear. It is as though the fire has never been. Jai and Onora are unhurt, they race across the space, jumping fallen bodies and skirting around some masonry that has fallen from the roof towards the passageway.

They raise a hand in salute towards the woman on the plinth, ignoring the small group of men who have not moved. And grabbing an arm each, they steer Nenna back down into the priests' room below.

Chapter 37

Camis gradually becomes aware of the devastating scene around him. Zachary's body lies on the floor, his severed head at the feet of his opponent. D'Ruja, his black uniform pristine, is breathing heavily, and his hair is flicked over onto his face. He looks beyond the man on the plinth to where four of his guards litter the floor. There is no sign of the remaining two guards or of the prisoner.

'No matter,' D'Ruja says aloud, addressing Myriad. 'I will still take her. I knew you would not let her die. Your lover will not get far, though, I must admit, I never thought he had it in him.'

D'Ruja waits for a response. 'Nothing to say? Ah, well. I'll leave you to your dying world and take the princess with me.' He looks to where Camis' mother is lying in front of her brother, her eyes closed as though asleep. 'When she awakes, I will tell her that you married us and that I freed your lover in return. She will know no different.'

D'Ruja strides confidently towards Serin as Camis rises to his feet.

'You will not touch my mother,' Camis states, blocking D'Ruja's path with the staff. D'Ruja stops,

'It was you on the parade route,' he hisses.' He abruptly turns away. 'So, the whore had a prim lover. I should have had you both executed. But no problem. I will do it now.' And whirling he blasts out a column of air from his raised hands.

'I will not have sullied goods!' D'Ruja yells, his face twisted in a sneer and as the air hits the ceiling, it dislodges chunks of masonry. Plaster and stone rain down.

Camis stands unhurt and unmoved, the debris sliding off an invisible dome that surrounds him and the plinth. He has no time to think about where the protection has come from as D'Ruja raises his arms towards him, readying another blast of air.

'She was already pregnant with me when she ran away, so you were too late even then,' Camis states coldly.

The air in the temple stills. Dust hangs frozen in the space. Time stops.

'You are mine?' D'Ruja eyes are wide, he lowers his arms, an expression of awe waring with disdain, and it is Camis' turn to be confused.

'No,' Camis stutters. His legs feel weak and threaten to give way. Not this man. His mother could never love someone like him. 'No, I would have known. I am nothing like you.' He glances at the broken figure of Zachary, and an overwhelming sadness fills him.

D'Ruja follows his gaze. 'Him?' he states incredulously. 'A lowly soldier in my pay. Don't be ridiculous. He had no gifts or power. You clearly have.' And he barks a laugh. 'A son! She gave me a son!'

Stop! D'Ruja bellows. The fighting around them stops.

Camis can see men frozen in the act of killing one another. They haven't stepped back and lowered their weapons but have halted exactly where they are. One pair have stabbed each other simultaneously, the blood spraying out in an arc that hangs solid and still in the air.

We will be powerful beyond measure, you and I. D'Ruja's eyes glint blue. *I will teach you everything and more.* He lowers his arm and takes a step towards Camis. Camis backs away, but his foot knocks against the dais.

Come. We don't need any of these, he says, waving his arm to take in the people around them, oblivious to their suffering and pain. *We will take the fittest and strongest, and together, we will conquer Lakhth al-Dubb. We will rule together and be the most powerful men in history.*

So you think to take the boy. Myriad's voice booms out around them.

And what exactly will you do? D'Ruja thunders. *You know the word bond I have. You kill me, and no matter where your slut of a lover is hiding, he will die instantly. And you are forbidden in your vows to touch me.*

Oh, I know that only too well, Myriad says. *I freed Kanta. But I'm not going to touch you.* There is a short silence. *He is.*

D'Ruja glares at Camis, his lip curled in a sneer. *Him? He doesn't even know a fraction of what he is capable of.*

But you intend to teach him. Myriad says. *You intend to use him and his power to rule for as long as you can, to cause untold misery.*

And that is . . .

'ENOUGH!'

Camis' bellows brings more debris fluttering down from the dome above. It falls softly, settling on the human statues around them. 'I will not be used by either of you!'

Now he has their full attention. 'I have no intention of fighting and killing anyone.' He looks at Myriad but catches D'Ruja's smirk of triumph. 'And I am *not* going anywhere with you.'

He turns his full attention to D'Ruja. 'I am not your son. We will leave and go on our way, peacefully. You can have this moon and its soul-destroying crystal. You can conquer anywhere you like, but without me or my mother.'

D' Ruja lifts his fingers dramatically in the air and snaps them. The world jumps into motion. The fighting resumes as though nothing has happened. Camis tries to twist around to face his great uncle, but now he is the one frozen in time. An unseen force is holding him there.

You are mine, and I will take you, D'Ruja says, spinning on his heels and walking to the door.

Camis' feet lift from the floor and he follows obediently behind. He passes a motionless Myriad, and their eyes meet. In that instance, Camis is overwhelmed by a surge of power that floods into every part of him. Suddenly, he has the strength to resist. He stops walking.

D'Ruja is halfway across the chamber before he realises that he is alone, that Camis has stopped following and is standing alongside Myriad. D'Ruja stops midstride and turns back, his eyes open wide in surprise. He glares at Myriad, then glances to his left, towards the dais.

You . . . how did you? It's not—

Possible? Myriad continues for him. *Ah, but as you can see, it is. I am free.* They stand for an age, children flocking around them, adding to the chaos.

An invisible force slams against Camis, taking him by surprise. He is bowled over and over as he spins across the floor, knocking people aside like skittles. He hits the temple wall with a thud, and stars flash across his vision, the staff torn from his hand. Myriad is thrown against him, knocking his remaining breath away. They lie there in a tangle of limbs, bruised and dazed.

Myriad's voice says quietly and calmly, *You can do this Camis. You can save us all.*

But there is no time, because D'Ruja is there, looming over them.

You fool. Now that I have no more use for you, you will die.

The two men confront one another. Slowly, Myriad's face turns blue, but he looks up at his uncle and gives a sad little smile. With a shock, Camis realises that D'Ruja is choking him.

'Stop!' Camis tries to shout, but no sound comes out.

Pushing himself against the wall, he gains his feet. 'Stop! You're killing him!'

But D'Ruja doesn't look away from Myriad, doesn't acknowledge Camis.

Camis reaches out with his mind, pushing against the force that he can feel there. Abruptly, the force snaps, making D'Ruja stumble forward a step. His attention swings to Camis. His face twists in anger.

You insolent pup! How dare you interfere! he rages, sending out a pulse of air towards Camis, but the blow dissipates before it reaches him. Tendrils of vapour are briefly visible, then vanish in the space between them.

D'Ruja raises a hand, sending out waves of energy towards Camis. Each one blows away harmlessly before reaching its target, the only sign of its passing a slight breeze that ruffles Camis' hair.

Snarling, D'Ruja thrusts his hands downwards. Faint sparks shoot from his fingers, and Camis doubles over in agony as every nerve fibre in his body catches fire. The intensity of the pain takes away all coherent thought, and he howls with shock and misery, falling to the floor.

Myriad voice reaches through the throbbing torment. *Camis, think. You can do this. You are a healer.*

How . . . will . . . that . . . help? Camis says, straining through the pain.

Refuse it.

And Camis understands. It is all in his mind. There is nothing burning, stabbing, or cutting him. He thinks of the candle flame and breathes deeply.

Abruptly, the pain ceases, and he regains his feet. Standing straight, he looks intently at D'Ruja.

There is fear in D'Ruja's eyes now. He pushes his power towards Camis who stands his ground and pushes back. D'Ruja's feet slide on the floor, sweeping fallen debris along with him. There is a roaring that increases with the pressure. It makes Camis' ears hurt. A hand gently touches his leg and rests there.

Myriad's distant voice says, *You have my strength. Use it.*

D'Ruja lifts his arms out in front of him, grimacing against the force, and incredulously, Camis feels the force build even higher. Something trickles down each side of his neck. Blood gushes from his nose and ears. There is nothing he can do except hold and push back.

They are equally matched. Power pulses between them. Their eyes are locked in an internal battle. Neither conquering, neither submitting. Colours flash while deep sonic booms shake the temple, bringing down portions of pillars and parts of the dome. Men die all around them, but Camis and D'Ruja are untouched by the falling debris, which slams to the marble floor.

A fire flashes briefly and smoke fills the temple but it is gone as suddenly as it appear. The hand on his leg falls away, and Camis glances down to see Myriad's deep green eyes staring up at him, glazed and sightless. The shock causes him to faulter, and that momentary lack of concentration is all that D'Ruja needs.

He slams a wall of air around Camis, wrapping him tightly. All Camis can do is blink and breathe. He struggles against the invisible bonds. D'Ruja stands, hands braced against his knees, panting. Sweat plasters his dark hair and drips onto the floor. Slowly, he looks up, and smiles at Camis. The smile doesn't reach his eyes. There is no humour in it, no happiness, only the conceit of a power-hungry man used to getting his own way.

D'Ruja stalks from the hall, over dead bodies and through sticky red blood. There is no fighting now, only the dead who litter the ground.

An invisible leash tugs Camis forward, and he finds himself moving across the room. He does not walk but is pulled like a child's kite behind the departing man. They leave the temple together but only one set of bloodstained footsteps smear the steps outside.

Chapter 38

Serin sits with the Book in her lap. It is heavy but comfortable. She holds the life of the city in her hands and cannot afford to look away from its pristine pages. This much she knows, but a second war rages in her head as she fights the urge to look up and engage in the battle going on all around her.

She winces at the pain, and the words falter and stop. Somewhere across the city, she hears a building as it falls and crumbles into dust. She understands now the enormity of her task. It is up to her to keep Oasis standing.

Words appear and glow briefly beneath her fingertips as she runs them across the white page. The words solidify before squirming up and into her fingers, passing from the page and onto her skin. There they wriggle like insects, crawling up her arm, burrowing and stabbing deep into her hand as they writhe. The black words scroll and slice their way under the tissue and up across her back and shoulders.

Plaster, clay, brick, wood, metal, glass, crystal, marble, slate, earth, stone, mortar . . .

On and on the words climb around her body, and she can feel each item harden and stabilise in structures that strengthen all over the city. She closes her mind to the pain. A tiny part of her marvels at the sheer power that flows through her, while at the same time, she is repulsed by the cruelty that has been inflicted on her brother for all this time. She can and will endure—for now.

She knows the instant that her brother dies. A sharp pain lances through her body, causing the words to stutter and stop. The loss of her twin is so tremendous that she is not sure she will survive it. The severing of the bond between them is excruciating, a black hole opening up inside her, cold and empty. She can't breathe. Tears drip down onto the pages of the open Book.

Structures begin to topple and fall into the murky waters of the lake on which Oasis stands. Sounds reach her from far away. Voices call out, shrieking for help, but these are distant. She sits, numb to the agony around her. Her own world is raw and empty.

A huge chunk of the dome above hurtles to the ground, splintering into shards on the marble in front of her.

Bodies lie covered in fallen debris and dust; blood darkens the marble floor. A movement catches her eye. Camis floats unnaturally above the ground. He passes her and floats out through the temple doors, her uncle striding ahead of him. It happens so quickly that she is unable to reach out to him. And even if she could, he believes her an uncaring monster and now it is maybe too late.

All is quiet and still.

She wails, then curses, her hands clenched. Buildings all over the city shake; some crumble and fall. The screams of the dying reach her through the fabric of the Book and pull her back into herself. She cannot leave and follow her son but must stay and preserve the Book or more lives will be lost. But by the Crystal, she will not let him have her son too.

She resumes her reading, a seed of an idea forming.

She will not allow this way of life to continue. Now that she has the Book, she will destroy it all.

How can she warn the people? What if they do not understand that they have to flee the failing city? Carefully, she weaves other words between the ones she is repeating,

Leave. Go. North-east. Shuttles.

Three times she adds the warning, but each time she can feel her hold over the fabric of the city lessen. It is not much, but she hopes that somehow her words have reached everyone. After all is destroyed, she will leave the city. Then she will face her uncle and fight for her son.

Chapter 39

Surrounded by guards, D'Ruja sets a brisk pace. He and Camis ride at a trot through the palace grounds. Camis is mounted on his mother's white mare, which D'Ruja leads behind his black stallion. Briefly, Camis wonders about his mother. Where is she? Was she among the dead in the hall or is she still sitting on the dais with that book? He doesn't thinks she would have sat by and let people die around her.

'Captain, send someone to the palace to order an immediate evacuation. Give the coded word to the palace staff. They will know what to do.

'Yes, sir.'

A horse peels away from the group and canters back towards the palace. There are more explosions in the city. D'Ruja ignores them, riding directly for the north-west gate and out into the blinding white desert.

The ride is long and painful, but Camis is grateful for one thing—the wall of air that binds and surrounds him keeps the vicious stinging sand away from his face, and he is able to breathe and see. They arrive at some sort of camp. A tarp is pulled high above them, covering an enormous black structure. Long huts dot the perimeter of the camps, dwarfed by the black mountain, which Camis realises is one of their ships.

They ride under the protective cover and into the welcome shade, but Camis is left wrapped in air, sitting on the dainty mare, while everyone else dismounts.

'Tell the captain to prepare for take-off,' D'Ruja commands one of the guards. 'And make sure he understands that this is not a test flight.'

Some of the soldiers lead their horses away out of sight, while others tie up their mounts to a picket line and walk briskly to the huts. Commands are shouted and people scurry to obey. The tarp overhead is gradually furled back, letting light and heat reflect blindingly off the ship. Camis looks away. Boxes are hurriedly carried from the huts up the ship's ramp. People scurry in all directions, like ants in a disturbed nest.

The white mare's reins hang loose, but it is obvious that she has been trained not to move when this happens because she stays on the spot. D'Ruja stands halfway up the main ramp to the ship, barking orders. His black stallion stands patiently nearby, a back hoof tucked in rest. D'Ruja keeps glancing back the way they have come, and Camis senses agitation.

A young man in the ship's black uniform approaches D'Ruja and offers him a strange handheld rectangle. He points to its shiny black screen and the two of them peer at it intently. D'Ruja is so engrossed that Camis can feel the bonds that hold him slackening slightly. This could be the chance he needs.

He watches the men on the ramp carefully as they mutter and nod. Squeezing his knees, he finds he is able to turn the mare a little.

A plume of dust in the distance signals more riders coming from the city. A flash of iridescence in the sky catches Camis' eye, but he is unable to turn his head to track it. The riders are much closer now. They are pressing the horses hard.

Suddenly, in a clatter of hooves, wheels, and shouts, carts arrive, bringing dust and sweat with them. Soldiers dismount. Two priests are ushered quickly on board the ship, and men rush to help some women climb down from the back of a wagon. The drays pulling it are unhitched and led away. The women look shaken and pale as they shake out the desert from their head coverings and brush down their outer garments.

One pretty-but-thin-lipped young woman glances towards Camis curiously but forgets him instantly when another elaborately dressed woman takes her arm and steers her towards the ramp.

A *whoomph* vibrates through the air. Over the top of the ship, a huge, snake-like creature flies into view. Iridescent blue-green colours flash on its body, awe-inspiring and terrifying. Pandemonium breaks out. People run, shrieking racing for cover. Horses scream in terror and bolt. Camis' mare quivers and stamps a foot while rolling her eyes at the circling creature.

Swooping lower, it emits an ear-piercing call, and the mare breaks from her stand. Camis is thrown clear, landing on his back. He hits the ground with a jolt, which knocks his breath away. Dazed, he lies there as soldiers try to calm the panicking horses. Men are flung aside as the horses scream and tug at their tethers.

Suddenly, D'Ruja's bonds of air are gone, and Camis rolls onto his side, pushing himself up onto his knees only to dive under a nearby cart as the creature releases another shriek. D'Ruja pulls his black stallion, trying to guide the horse up the ramp and into the dark interior of the ship, but the horse fights him, its eyes rolling in fear and sidestepping. Camis watches the sky. Where has it gone?

He glances upwards, catching sight of the queen wyrm soaring upwards. Part of the canvas above has come unfurled and flaps in the breeze made by the queen's flight. It snaps against her hide as she passes, and she whirls around. Opening her mouth, she spews out a white-hot flame at the offending material. It goes up like dry tinder, igniting instantly, throwing the sky above into a blaze of gold.

This is the last straw for D'Ruja's stallion, who rears up, bringing both his front hooves down on the man who is preventing him from fleeing. D'Ruja crashes to the ground with a howl.

The movement and noise attracts the queen Wyrms attention. With a fury and unbelievable speed, she swoops down. Flames shoot from her mouth, and with a wild primeval cry, she engulfs D'Ruja and the struggling horse in fire. Screaming, the horse breaks free, his body alight with vivid orange and yellow flames. Camis watches in horror as fire streams out behind the galloping horse.

The Wyrm turns to pursues the horse, but something catches her eye, a movement in the desert. Camis is awed at the creature, terrifying in her magnificence. Her body is tattered and pitted, and her wings seem to have more rents and tears than when he last saw her, but she truly is an incredible creature, shining and fierce.

Camis looks back towards the fallen figure of D'Ruja, fully expecting to see a charred mess, but the ramp is empty. Fear grabs the pit of his stomach as he looks wildly around. The man could not have escaped that conflagration, could he? Had someone pulled the body onto the ship? Confused, he does not immediately notice the ramp slowly drawing in and the door closing. A low familiar whine reaches his ears.

Camis scrabbles out from under the cart and races for the nearest hut. He must get to safety. The ship is about to launch.

The whine of the Mastership builds and he throws himself to the desert floor, as the massive ship lifts from the ground. The structure rises up and hovers briefly. The tattered remains of the burning canopy trailing behind it. With a flash of starlight, it vanishes.

The departing ship with its burning kite tail leaves a reverse image on his eyelids that sparkles and flashes, finally fading into three tailing starbursts. He wonders vaguely where he has seen that likeness before.

Chapter 40

Serin focusses in on the south-east sector of the city. There is no one left there. That is where she will begin.

It is easier than she thought to divide her mind. One part of her keeps the litany of words going, keeping some sections of city whole as people flee, while another part concentrates in the south-eastern corner and lets the words slide away.

There is a distant crash, not just of houses and shops collapsing, but of foundations and roads and bridges. The architecture of Oasis fractures and tumbles into the lake below.

A bitter smile tugs at her mouth. Each building lost to the black depths of the lake gives her a grim satisfaction. Revenge for her brother, for Zachary, for her stolen youth. Street by street, she lets go.

A flash high in the sky lights up the dome above her, and her heart freezes. She has taken too long. The Mastership! It has taken off. She'd thought it wasn't ready and that the rebels had successfully disabled what was left. But he has escaped, taken her son and gone.

He always won. It didn't matter what she did to try and hurt him. It didn't matter to him if she destroyed the city and left hundreds homeless. He didn't care; he had gotten what he wanted.

A heavy lethargy overwhelms her. It is over; she has lost. The people are forgotten; the city is forgotten. The Book slides to the floor and closes. The destruction of the city speeds up.

The rest of the buildings splinter and cascade into the water. Total devastation.

It isn't until the palace and temple begin to disintegrate that she realises her mistake. There will be no escape for her now. Not that she cares. All she has loved are gone.

The remainder of the dome crashes to the ground and she automatically covers her head with her arms and leans forward until her head rests on the Book. The destruction is deafening. She waits to die. It is the silence that first makes her aware that she is not dead.

Serin uncoils and looks around. She is kneeling on a tiny piece of the temple dais, the Book in front of her. The light is dim, coming from somewhere above her, and has a strange, thick quality.

She scrambles to her feet and immediately, the ground pitches and rolls, tipping her sideways. Her flailing hands meet an invisible curved wall. She staggers to regain her footing; her arms and legs spread-eagle, and she braces herself against the strange contraption, realising she is inside some kind of bubble.

She takes a deep calming breath and turns her head slowly around. The light grows brighter, and looking up, she sees the white sky come towards her as the bubble rises and breaks the surface.

Everywhere around her is water. It stretches in every direction and extends below her in an unfathomable darkness. She is in the lake, inside a transparent sphere which revolves slowly.

The city gone. The sphere slowly begins to sink.

Chapter 41

A terrified horse is caught by its reins on the outskirts of the camp, and Camis spends time calming the petrified creature. It had tried to flee the fire-breathing monster in the sky but had become entangled. Its eyes roll, the whites flashing as it trembles uncontrollably. After gentle strokes along the horse's neck and sides and quiet soothing words, the horse relaxes.

Mounted, Camis heads back towards the city, passing charred human remains, still smouldering where they lie in the desert. Closer to the city, he comes across more evidence of the queen Wyrms passage—the delicate white mare his mother had ridden is now a blackened ruin, only identifiable by two completely unscathed white front hooves. It had died at full gallop, its head stretched up and back, it's mouth gaping and teeth barred.

In the distance, he can see a long line of people as they stream out through the northeast gate, heading away from Oasis and spreading out across the desert. Some walk while others ride. All hurry towards one of the main shuttle landing sites.

He dismounts and presses his hands to the ground, feeling for the tell-tale vibrations of an imminent Wyrm uprising. But the ground is silent and as he mounts up, he hopes the people fleeing make it to safety.

Pressing the horse hard, he gallops for the lake just as a tall tower in the city collapses, causing a huge spray of water. He urges the stallion onwards. He has friends in the city! Has

Nenna gotten away? And his mother? Is she free now that D'Ruja has gone? Or is she still trapped in the temple?

Arriving at the gate, he finds a few remaining rebels directing people, helping to get everyone to safety. Among them are Nenna and Tiberius. His heart lurches at the sight of them.

He pushes against the press of people who mutter and curse as they step aside for his horse. He reaches his friends and dismounts. Grinning foolishly he stands awkwardly looking at them both, until Nenna breaks the spell and rushes forward to hug him. Tiberius joins them.

'Do you know if the temple was evacuated?' Camis asks.

'I don't know,' Nenna says. 'They are saying that that bastard took all of his soldiers out through the northwest gate. Shortly after, some carts were seen leaving the palace. The horses were driven hard.'

People nearby overhear her remark and cluster around. Camis can hear their quiet murmurings.

'Where has His Imperial Highness gone?'

'What about the princess?'

'What has happened to the Book?'

Another large building falls. Its blue dome tilts at an alarming angle and then slides silently down until it vanishes beneath the black water. A huge bubble of air bursts onto the surface. The buildings closest to the shoreline begin to crumble, sliding into the water. A large hole appears suddenly in the ground, revealing the black water far below.

People scream as water swells towards them. The crowd disperses, surging forward in panic, pushing through the open gates and under the thick arch of the city wall, out into the desert.

Some have never left the city before and stand dazed and frightened until the press of those behind push them forward. Some dither, clearly torn between what might be out in the desert and the failing city. They are strangely silent.

Camis, Tiberius, and Nenna hurry after them a short distance and then turn to watch.

The city is unrecognisable. The colourful buildings are crumbling and vanishing. Chunks of masonry crash to the ground, then the ground drops away, bearing everything with it.

They can see the palace and the dome of the temple untouched, perched safely on a hill as the houses in between vanish.

Then a sound like the crack of a whip reaches them. The distant dome of the temple parts in two at the same time that the palace collapses and vanishes. Camis drops the reins of his horse and starts forward. Both Nenna and Tiberius grab hold of him.

'There is nothing you can do,' Nenna says quietly.

Together, they watch the final destruction of the city until there is nothing left to fall. Then the water settles, lying flat and still, reflecting the endless white sky.

Epilogue

The early spring morning brings with it more than the smell of new growth. Buds swell and the rich dark soil teems with life. It also brings with it a feeling of optimism, of new beginnings—an energy that anything is possible.

Camis looks around from his vantage on the fallen log in the clearing where, all that time ago, he had watched the children of Hill Village learn archery under the Nenna's tutelage.

Nenna is instructing a class, but this one includes adults from Oasis, keen to learn new skills and to contribute to the food store of this sizable town—one that has grown up practically overnight from the tiny village.

Down on the terraces below, hammering indicates the building of yet another home. It won't be long before all those sleeping outside, or even those accommodated in the winter hall, will have their own place to live. It may take a little longer for the other residences to become less crowded, but he feels sure that given time, everyone will have a home.

Camis looks up into the bright cloudless sky. It will be a while yet before the moons rise, but looking up always helps him to focus his thoughts on his mother. Does she sit on a plinth, in the dark waters of what would have been the city centre, her limp fingers floating over the Book? Or had she cast the Book aside once everyone was safely away?

Part of him still wants to race back and try to find her, but if it had been hopeless then, it would be even more hopeless now. He had watched the magnificent city plunge to the depths of the lake. Shops, homes, roads, and bridges had sunk silently into the black water. And finally, he had seen the palace and temple vanish with the hill on which they had sat. There had been nothing he could do.

They had even scoured the area from the viewers on the shuttle. All it showed was a large flat empty lake surrounded by a pristine desert. Even the queen Wyrm had vanished.

Now, back here on Maa Erda, Rowan is resetting the target, dragging it back a distance. Onora sits, sewing in a circle of other women nearby, all of them keeping a close eye on the young children that play happily in the dirt with sticks and stones. It is hard now to distinguish the village children from the ones from Crystal Moon.

Arture has been invaluable in so many ways with Tiberius becoming his right-hand man. Camis understands that it has helped Tiberius to work and keep busy since he too discovered that his family had perished –a neighbour sadly informing him that his grandmother had refused to leave and that the family had stayed with her.

Arture's knowledge of the crystal sickness has helped Martha and Camis to ease the suffering of a few of the former slaves—Camis refuses to call them prims—to a kinder death. He takes a deep breath to supress the rage he feels inside for what D'Ruja so callously inflicted on others. Did he escape? Or did he die in the frenzied attack of the queen?

He wonders about those that had managed to get on board the ship, did they go willingly or were they coerced? Were they trying to escape the carnage in the camp and then found themselves caught up in a flight to Maa Erda knows where?

Camis looks up at Nenna, her hair untidy and wild as she encourages a student to slow their breathing as they sight the target. His own breath catches in his throat, and he looks away quickly, hoping no one has seen the flush rising on his cheeks.

Hadders waves from below as he passes by with a long timber balanced easily on one shoulder, making his way towards one of the unfinished homes.

Camis' thoughts turn back to his mother. What would she want him to do? He isn't sure he can answer that or if he even needs to but he does know two people who will be very glad to see him—Anna and Luk.

Maybe soon he will return to the farm, taking old Misty and the cart with him. As soon as he isn't needed here of course.

And after that? Well, he'd just have to wait and see.

Acknowledgements

Completing this book has been a journey spanning 15 years, a testament to persistence, growth, and the invaluable support I've received along the way.

To Rachel Song at Songbird Editing, thank you for untangling the complexities of my manuscript and shaping it into something I'm proud of. Your expertise was indispensable. (www.songbirdediting.com)

Michelle Diprose, not just a beta reader but a cherished friend and a talented illustrator. The artwork you've contributed is nothing short of stunning. (www.diprose-art.co.uk)

Cameron Ferguson, my son, you've worn many hats: from providing endless IT advice and marketing insights to diligently reading through the most tedious parts of publishing. Your support has been multifaceted and deeply appreciated.

Natasha Ferguson, my daughter-in-law and beta reader, your advice, encouragement, and insights have been a beacon of support. Your contributions have been pivotal.

To Ellie Robinson, my daughter. Thank you for reading countless editions.

Charlie and Amie at Urban Writers Retreat, your space was a sanctuary for creativity, offering the quiet and focus needed to bring my thoughts to paper. (urbanwritersretreat.co.uk)

The Open University, for arming me with the tools necessary for this craft. The knowledge I gained there has been a cornerstone of my writing. (open.ac.uk)

Elizabeth, your early advice and encouragement have been a guiding light from the beginning. Your belief in my work bolstered me through the toughest times.

To my husband, for the unwavering support you've given me over the years. From granting me endless time and space to write each day to joining me on getaways where I could immerse myself in writing, and for enduring my endless tirade of ideas for the book. Your patience and love have made this journey possible.

Lastly, a special thanks to Lochlytic.com, for taking the helm of the marketing campaign and ensuring the world gets to see my work. Your strategic insights and dedication are setting the stage for this book's journey into readers' hands.

This book is not just a product of my imagination but a collective effort of many hearts and minds. To everyone who has walked this path with me: thank you from the bottom of my heart.

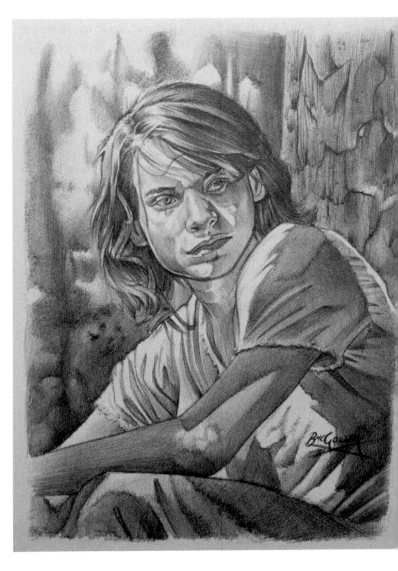

Picture of Camis drawn by Barry McGowen

Printed in Great Britain
by Amazon